WARRIOR GIRL UNEARTHED

ANGELINE BOULLEY

ROCK THE BOAT

For the 108,328 ancestors still held by institutions,

and those working to bring them home

A Rock the Boat Book

First published in Great Britain, Ireland & Australia by Rock the Boat,
an imprint of Oneworld Publications, 2023

Copyright © Angeline Boulley, 2023
Cover Art © Michaela Goade, 2023

The moral right of Angeline Boulley to be identified as the author
of this work has been asserted by her in accordance with the
Copyright, Designs and Patents Act 1988

ISBN 978-0-86154-419-6 (hardback)
ISBN 978-0-86154-420-2 (export paperback)
ISBN 978-0-86154-421-9 (ebook)

Book design by Rich Deas
Printed and bound in Great Britain by Clays Ltd, Elcograf S.p.A.

This book is a work of fiction. Names, characters, businesses, organisations,
places and events are either the product of the author's imagination or are
used fictitiously. Any resemblance to actual persons, living or dead, events,
or locales is entirely coincidental.

Every effort has been made to trace copyright holders for the use of material in this book.
The publisher apologises for any errors or omissions herein and would be grateful if they were
notified of any corrections that should be incorporated in future reprints or editions of this book.

Oneworld Publications
10 Bloomsbury Street
London WC1B 3SR
England

WEEK ONE

[W]hen questioned by an anthropologist on what the Indians called America before the white man came, an Indian said simply, "Ours."

—Vine Deloria, Jr., *Custer Died for Your Sins: An Indian Manifesto*

CHAPTER 1

MONDAY, JUNE 9TH

I speed across Sugar Island in the Jeep I share with my sister. The rising sun escapes the tree line to my left. I adjust the sun visor against the blinding brightness. It's what good drivers are supposed to do: minimize distractions.

Focusing on the road ahead, I watch for cultural-camp signage. Next to me, Pauline makes a production of craning her neck to check the speedometer, shaking her head, and sighing. I take it as a challenge, smoothly shifting into fifth gear while rounding a corner. The tires squeal.

"Remember what Auntie Daunis said," she warns.

"About our birthday gift that came with a bonus scolding?" I say.

"'Happy Sweet Sixteen, my girls.'" Pauline imitates Auntie's slightly deeper voice. "'Enjoy this good pony, but—'"

I interrupt, practically growling, "'But hear me now. I will repossess her and kick your asses if I catch yous being foolish.'"

We laugh in twin harmony.

I don't mention Auntie's next words, directed solely to me: *And that includes speeding.*

"Why are you in such a hurry?" Pauline says. "It's not like *you* have anything going on."

My sister irritates me like nobody else. I glare at her.

"Hold up. You're still mad about last week? Seriously? A week of touring universities was torture for poor Perry? It was supposed to *inspire* you." She drags out the word: *in-spy-yer*.

"It cost me a week of fishing!"

She huffs. "Well, I wish you hadn't come. Then no one would've suffered Elvis Junior's atomic farts."

I for sure weaponized our stinky dog, who gets hella gassy from people food. I hide my smirk while checking out a faded sign announcing that the Sugar Island Ojibwe Tribe's cultural camp is a quarter mile ahead.

"Oh my *God*," Pauline continues, still sensing my annoyance. With an extra syllable and some shade, it sounds like *Gaaw-duh*. "It was just a few schools."

"Nine universities." I repeat the number in Ojibwemowin. "Zhaangaswi!"

She startles at my sharp tone. I feel her eyes on me even without looking over. My voice softens in tandem with slowing down for the coming turn.

"Pauline, it was nine places I'd never get into even if I wanted to go. Which I don't." I tap my brakes while using my left turn blinker, because you never know who's watching and reporting back to Auntie. "I don't want to be anywhere except Sugar Island."

"Never leave Sugar Island?" she asks, in that same surprised and judgy way she uses. "Like, never *ever*?"

"Never ever sounds good to me," I say, making the turn.

"There are other schools you might like, you know. Mackinac State College is my safety—you could apply there."

"Nah, all the statues there are old Zhaaganaash dudes. Non-Natives.

Colonizers. You really wanna study where women and people of color are invisible?"

Ignoring me, Pauline checks for any strands that might have escaped her tightly wound bun of jet-black hair. She pauses a hand at her ear, smoothing the area.

"You look good, Egg," I assure her.

She rolls her eyes at the private nickname, but allows the tiniest smile to break through.

The narrow dirt road is an obstacle course of curves, dips, and bumps that continues for a half mile. It ends in a loop at a dilapidated log building where our tribe used to hold camps for learning stuff, like how to smoke whitefish or make maple syrup.

"Why's the Tribe having the summer interns come here for orientation instead of the bougie new camp in town? Isn't this place condemned?" I ask while pulling up to the entrance.

As usual, my sister knows the answer to everything.

"No Wi-Fi. No decent cell-phone signals." She uses the visor mirror to apply the coral-pink lip gloss that pops against her blemish-free dark complexion. "To immerse us in culture without distractions."

"More like immersed in mosquitoes." I grab the can of bug spray from the center console.

Pauline takes it before reaching for the door handle. She waves to a group of friends dressed like her, in short floral-print rompers and wedge sneakers. They hug as if it's been a year instead of a week since they last saw each other.

My sister offers mosquito repellent and is praised for her smart thinking. She stretches a long, slender brown leg coated in shimmery body lotion for someone to spray with the bug dope.

A loud bang jolts my attention.

Lucas Chippeway stands in front of the Jeep, palm raised over the dark green hood; he follows up with another crisp beat. Before he can launch into a drum solo, I tap the horn and roll down the window.

"Move it along, Luke-Ass," I say.

He breaks into the lopsided grin that makes him a certified hottie to everyone except Pauline and me.

"Woke you up," he says. "Hey, sorry I couldn't give Pauline a ride this morning. Had to stay at Granny's last night and didn't think I'd get back on the island in time."

Lucas nods hello to a trio of girls taking selfies they won't be able to post until later. They giggle before turning their backs to him. He pretends not to notice when they angle their phones to include his mischievous smile and compact, muscular body in the background.

"You regret not getting an internship?" He struts over to my window. "Four hundred a week for ten weeks. That's serious bank."

"Do I regret skipping the interview to go fishing?" I laugh at my own joke before faking stone-cold seriousness. "Guess what, hey? Pauline got assigned to intern with Tribal Council. The *only* high school student to *ever* get placed with them in the history of the Kinomaage Summer Internship Program."

I delight in making fun of my sister, but I'd never do it in front of anyone but Lucas.

"I may have heard. Should I ask her anyway?" He absent-mindedly flicks away a mosquito that dares to land on his bronze skin.

"Please do. Tell her you heard that interns were selected on grades. It's what I told Mom and Pops, so they'd stop asking me about it."

Pauline shouts for Lucas and motions toward the building entrance.

"Gotta go, Pear-Bear. Sorry you ain't me." He flashes his trademark grin.

"Too bad. So sad. Gonna fish with my dog and my dad," I riff to the tune of M.I.A.'s "Bad Girls."

Back on the road, I floor it for the best possible reason: just because. Just because the Jeep is mine while Pauline is at her internship orientation all day. Just because I can already taste the fish I will catch today and fry tonight. Just because I survived last week's college visits, which stole the first precious days of my summer vacation.

I trill a fierce, high-pitched lee-lee to begin the Perry Firekeeper-Birch 2014 Summer of Slack. My loose hair whips around my face like a tornado. I crank the music and sing along with M.I.A.:

"*Live fast, die young. Bad girls do it well.*"

Up ahead, someone crosses the road. I recognize the thin, long-limbed guy dressed in black. Stormy Nodin used to be my uncle Levi's best friend. I tap the brakes and dial down my music.

"Aaniin," I greet him.

He raises his chin in acknowledgment.

"Ando-babaamibizodaa," I offer, though he has never accepted a ride from me.

He declines with a quick hand motion.

I try with another invitation, this time for fish dinner tonight.

"Onaagoshi wiisinidaa. Giigoonh gi-ga-miijimin."

He immediately accepts with a head nod. My best fishing spot better come through because, as skinny as he is, Stormy Nodin has an enormous appetite.

"Baamaapii," I say with a wave.

My tires kick up roadside gravel as I race home.

The fat black dog comes out of nowhere. Not a dog. A bear cub. Dashing across the road.

Sick dread jolts through my body. In the instant it takes for my foot to reach the brake pedal, I am already following my parents' repeated instructions.

Tap. *Slow down.*

Tap. *Don't swerve.*

The cub disappears into the ditch.

Tap. *Where there's one, there's two.* My parents echo in unison.

I blink and the mama bear is there, rushing after her cub.

My heart skips a beat when she halts in my path. I swerve before my parents can repeat themselves. The Jeep shoots across a gravel driveway. I aim for lilac bushes but skid toward a metal gate instead.

I close my eyes as metal grinds against metal and something explodes in my face.

The deployed airbag blocks my view. My heart thumps at triple pace. I take a deep breath. The cross-body seat belt is tight against my chest—uncomfortable but not painful. I can move my arms and legs.

I'm okay.

Grab your phone, begin recording, and get out of the vehicle as quickly as possible, Pops's voice instructs. *Use the three-in-one tool tied to the door handle to cut through both straps of the seat belt. Don't forget to take the emergency cell phone from the center console. Get a safe distance away. Continue recording your surroundings and the vehicle.*

I aim the phone camera at the steam rising from the hood of the Jeep as I back away.

Use the emergency cell phone alert button so that me, Mom, Aunt Daunis, and your sister get a call and text with your location.

I pause before pushing the alert button. My heart rate is back to normal. The radiator is damaged, but I think that's all. This was more like a fender bender than a major accident.

Pops is on his way downstate for something he bought on Craigslist. Pauline is at orientation. Mom is at work. Auntie? No way. I hear her warning again about being foolish.

But I wasn't being reckless. It was a bear. Everything happened so quickly.

I could walk back to Stormy Nodin, but unless prayers in Ojibwemowin will fix a radiator, the traditional healer won't be much help.

I need to get the Jeep off Sugar Island and into a repair shop. Although Pops can fix anything, Auntie wanted Pauline and me to be responsible for the cost of upkeep and repairs. With the birthday and babysitting money in my bank account, I can cover a wrecker.

Jack's Towing has a radio ad with a deep-voiced guy repeating their phone number and saying, *Anytime you call, I'll come for you.* Once when I was in Auntie's car with Granny June, the ad played on the radio. Auntie mentioned wanting to file a complaint. Granny yelled, *The hell you will! Cheap thrills are all I can afford.*

I use the emergency phone to call the number I know because of their radio ad. I keep recording while I wait for Jack. Since I don't need the bulky emergency phone for anything else, I shove it into the back of my jeans. Storing a phone near your butt crack isn't as funny as it might seem. Pops wants us to take every situation seriously. Dark-skinned men, whether they're Anishinaabe or Black—or both, like Pops—do not fuck around with their kids' safety.

I pass the time trying to envision a scenario where Auntie doesn't get mad about the Jeep. Thirty minutes later the wrecker truck barrels down the road, and I have yet to come up with anything. When Jack gets closer, I see a Tribal Police vehicle following the wrecker.

Jack pulls over just beyond the private drive. The cop car stays a few yards behind the accident scene. I recognize the cop getting out of the vehicle and shut off the recording.

Officer Sam Hill is harmless. Everybody calls him What-The, as in *What the Sam Hill?* It's an old-timey saying that I don't understand. But I do get how nicknames can be weird. He used to be the safety officer at the tribal elementary school. What-The heads over.

"Miigwech, Jack." I get to the point, handing over my debit card. "Can you take it to your brother's body shop?" If Jack and Zack are twins, I'll ask for a twin discount.

"He know it's coming?" Jack's voice doesn't sound as deep as it does on the radio ad.

"I'll call from your truck."

What-The chimes in. "How'd it happen, Perry?"

"Bear." I cheese a huge smile. There's no reason to question anything. I wasn't at fault. No need for a ticket. No need to search me. And no need to inform the Tribal Police captain.

Jack hooks the Jeep's tow hitch to the wrecker. Officer What-The leaves with a wave. Still smiling, I climb into Jack's truck for the ride to Zack's Body Shop in town. My ears ring with Pauline's familiar beef about me.

Must be nice to stroll through life with no worries.

My reply always pisses her off.

It sure is.

One look at Auntie Daunis ruins my fried perch feast. She stomps toward the campfire with her huge dark eyes blazing. Her messy brunette topknot adds three inches to her already considerable height. And with the stacked heels on her black ankle boots, she is halfway between six and seven feet. Auntie could be the medicine man's twin, dressed in black jeans and a black Henley. Her slash of red lipstick is pressed in a disapproving glower.

I silently curse whoever snitched. Jack. Zack. Officer What-The. Anyone on the ferry to the mainland. Everyone except Stormy Nodin, because he speaks only to pray.

Conveniently, Mom and Pops go inside the house for more potato salad. Pauline is as mute as Stormy, who's filling up on perch like it's his last meal. Even Elvis Junior goes silent.

Closing my eyes, I brace for impact.

"Were you speeding?"

"It was a bear and her cub—"

"Were you speeding?" she repeats.

"A bit."

"You speed like that with my kid in the car?"

"No."

"Zack says thirty-two hundred in damages," Auntie says.

Pauline looks like she's gonna burst into tears. Screw that. I ain't scared.

"I'll work out something with him," I say evenly.

One of Auntie's eyebrows arches. Now I'm scared.

"I paid Zack. You owe *me*," she says.

Shit. His terms would've been better. Zack said he'd accept an IOU with two years of interest for when I turn eighteen and start getting per cap, the profit-sharing dividends that our tribal citizens receive from the Superior Shores Casino.

I'm tempted to mention that the Jeep's bumper was duct-taped to the frame a long time ago. The metal gate was not its first battle. That good pony has seen some shit.

My sister is a genius, but I am not an idiot. I await Auntie's sentencing.

"The Kinomaage program has one internship spot still open. You start tomorrow at nine a.m. Every paycheck will be turned over to me until your debt is paid in full. You don't drive it until then. Show up at the tribal museum. Your supervisor is Cooper Turtle."

Pauline gasps loudly, but I feel the sharp intake in my own lungs.

And with that, my Summer of Slack goes up in smoke. Just because.

CHAPTER 2

TUESDAY, JUNE 10TH

Pauline and I have a system for who gets to ride shotgun when Mom or Pops drives us someplace. She gets the front seat on the way there; I get it on the ride home. So, when we hitch a ride with Mom to our Kinomaage internship assignments, I'm momentarily surprised when my twin chooses the back seat.

Not one to turn down an unexpected gift, I sit in front and release a huge, maple-flavored burp. Mom made pancakes this morning, which she never does on a weekday. Their actions must be part of an unspoken agreement: *Be nice to Perry because she's working for a goofball*. The realization makes my next burp taste more sour than sweet.

I should be fishing with Pops and Elvis Junior instead of heading into town.

While we wait to board the ferry, I take the bag of pipe tobacco from the center console. I offer a pinch of semaa to both Pauline and Mom before taking twice as much of the aromatic, loose flakes for myself. The semaa is for our offering when we cross the St. Marys River.

The deckhand waves Mom on board. I roll down my window

before she shuts the engine off. The cool breeze carries the smell of fish and engine exhaust.

"Why aren't we taking off," my sister yells over the punches and wings noises coming from her phone.

"St. Marys traffic jam," Mom says, referring to the humongous ship downriver. "And turn down that Floppy Birds game."

"Flappy Bird," Pauline corrects.

I braid my long black hair over one shoulder while we wait for the iron-ore freighter to pass by on its way toward the Soo Locks and, from there, to Lake Superior.

Pops worked on the freighters as a young man. I cannot imagine him working belowdecks in an engine room, because his favorite place to be is in our garden. Or tending a fire for ceremonies. Or on a fishing boat. Anyplace outdoors, really.

Just the thought of working somewhere with stale air and no windows gives me hives.

With a single, long toot of the ferry horn, we head out. Mom chuckles at something in the rearview mirror. I stick my head out the window and look behind at the familiar figure.

Cooper Turtle stands at the back corner of the ferry, gazing upon Sugar Island. His clothing—a navy golf shirt and khaki pants—is the only normal thing about him. One walnut-brown arm is bent in a salute as he poses like an old-timey cigar-store Indian statue bidding baamaapii to the island of our Anishinaabe ancestors.

He's been doing this silent protest for a few years, ever since Tribal Council voted to relocate the Sugar Island Cultural Learning Center— which included the library, genealogy archives, and museum—from the island to downtown Sault Ste. Marie. Lots of tribal citizens were upset, Mom and Auntie included. But Kooky Cooper Turtle is the only one still protesting.

I give thanks to Creator for the river before releasing my semaa out of the window to the water. I tack on an additional prayer. Pauline gives me a sympathetic look before continuing her own prayer. She's probably echoing my plea for help in surviving the summer.

Mom drops us off in front of the Tribal Administration building. The Cultural Learning Center is next door. Her mouth twitches, so I wait for her words of wisdom.

"Well, it'll be interesting," she says before driving away.

Pauline hangs back. She was probably told to keep an eye on me. *Make sure Perry enters the museum.* As if I'd risk skipping work and having Auntie's spies track me down.

"Go on, den," I shout.

With a huff, Pauline yanks open the glass entrance door.

I should be kinder to my sister. The Jeep is half hers. She hasn't bitched about this major inconvenience. Had the tables been turned, I would not have reacted the same way.

There is a good reason why people call her the nice twin.

I sigh before walking next door. The Tribe renovated the building, intending it to be a small indoor shopping mall. Mom said they over-improved the building, and no entrepreneur could afford the rent. It remained empty for a year before Tribal Council decided it would be "forward thinking" to relocate the Cultural Learning Center here. Their rationale was that a downtown location would be convenient for everyone who wanted to learn about our history and culture.

For an instant I imagine Kooky Cooper adjusting the straps on a sandwich board he makes me wear like a sleeveless wooden tunic around town to advertise the tribal museum.

I enter a wide hallway, which runs the length of the building. The cultural resource library is on the left; the museum is on the right. A sign directs museum visitors to check in with the receptionist at the library across the hall.

"Aaniin," I greet the receptionist. "Perry Firekeeper-Birch reporting for work."

The sour-faced lady makes a show of looking at her watch.

"You're early." She says it as if I'm three hours late.

I smile and peer at her name tag. "Won't happen again, Miss Manitou."

The receptionist picks up the phone handset, presses a button, and monotones, "She's here." After a moment, she hangs up without so much as a baamaapii.

"He'll meet you in the museum. Wait at the door until I buzz you in."

"Mino giizhigat," I say, wishing her a good day.

She responds with "Hmph."

"Hey, um . . . Miss Manitou? I need a minute before you unlock the door. I'll be right back." Without waiting for her response, I dash out of the building.

There is a tiny park next to the administration building. I find a cedar bush behind a bench. I whisper a prayer and offer the semaa from my pocket before breaking off two flat sprigs from the bush. Giizhik offers protection and strength. I kick off my sneakers, place the medicine on the insoles, and gently slide my feet back in. Now I'm ready.

"All set," I call out while standing at the museum entrance.

A buzzer goes off, and I hear the tiny click of an electronic lock being disengaged. I've been here for field trips, but never with the lights off. The spooky lobby spans the width of the space. One archway leads visitors to follow a winding U-shaped path through the museum before exiting through another archway at the other end of the lobby. Gift-shop shelving runs the length of the wall between the two arches.

I use the flashlight on my phone to check the admissions desk for any notes my supervisor might have left for me. Seeing none, I start on the path to the exhibits. The first room is round, with seating along the perimeter. In the center of the room is a thick, dark column extending from floor to ceiling. My sneakers interrupt a barely visible red laser light across the threshold. The motion detector activates the first exhibit—our creation story. The domed black ceiling becomes a night sky filled with twinkling pinprick lights. The column is actually an LED cylinder screen, now displaying a realistic-looking campfire surrounded by rocks and with wisps of smoke rising to the sky. A crisp drumbeat reverberates around the space. An Elder's voice speaks first in Ojibwemowin and then in English.

Does Cooper Turtle expect me to walk through all the exhibits?

Rather than continue, I return to the museum entrance. I'd ask Miss Manitou if Cooper mentioned a specific meeting spot, but she doesn't seem the helpful type.

Light from the end of the exhibit spills into the far end of the lobby. Someone must have turned it on a moment ago or I'd have noticed before. I follow the light like a moth.

Since the museum tells our story from past to present, the final section is about how—today—we are a bridge between our ancestors and those still to come. Examples of contemporary art are next to older pieces to show the inspiration from previous generations.

The large room has recessed lights on their dimmest setting. Across the room, a single spotlight shines on a dozen black ash baskets on top of a display case across the room.

I make my way toward them. My breath quickens at the largest basket in the center, directly beneath the spotlight. Something about the shape is familiar. It calls to me.

Nokomis Maria's weaving technique was as unique as her fingerprint. My maternal great-grandmother used flower petals to create vibrant dyes for the thin strips of ash splints. She layered two different colored strips to use as a single accent ribbon twisted into a curl between each weave. The second color peeked from inside each curl.

Trembling, I approach the display case.

Nokomis signed baskets with her name, the year, and a symbol for the month. A maple leaf with a liquid drop symbol, for example, meant Ziisbaakodoke Giizis, the Sugar-Making Moon.

I glance around the room, suddenly creeped out as if I am being watched. There's no sign of Cooper. I reach for the basket, needing to see my great-grandma's signature.

"Do. Not. Touch," says a gravelly voice.

I spin around. My heart races.

"Mr. Turtle?" I call out, looking for Kooky Cooper. There is no reply. I scan for security cameras and speakers. After a moment, I turn back to the display case. Keeping my hands behind my back, I lean closer to inspect the inside of a curl.

Something beneath the basket catches my eye. A hand. Inside the long glass case. Attached to a brown arm. I step back to eyeball the full-length statue inside the case.

It blinks.

"What the fuck!" I shriek.

Cooper Turtle rolls out of the coffin-size display case, its back panel lifted like an old garage door, and lands in a heap behind the case. His laughter is a wheezy *heh-heh-heh-heh* that goes on so long I wonder if he's having an asthma attack. He waves me away when I check on him.

"That was not cool," I say when he finally stands up. He's layered another shirt over his navy one. Black letters on a white T-shirt read: THIS IS A REAL INDIAN.

"I'm sorry, Little Sister." Cooper bends over to catch his breath. He wipes tears of laughter from his eyes. "I couldn't resist. You know why?" His pause is a single beat. "When I was born, my ma got real sick. She didn't have any sisters or cousins nearby. So, my dad gave me to a Zhaaganaash lady to nurse. I fed from her till my mom got better.

Years later, I met my wife's relations at a family reunion, and her aunt said I was the Indian baby she saved from starvation."

I have no words. But Cooper? He's just getting started.

"Everything is connected, Little Sister. The past. The future. The beginning and ending. Answers are there even before the question. You're supposed to go back to where you started. And if you step off the path, you better keep your eyes wide open."

I want a different job.

My first assignment is to clean the outside of every glass case in the museum. Cooper demonstrates on the display case he used for pranking me.

"Start with a clean cloth. Spray the cloth, not the glass." He pulls a microfiber cloth from the pile in a laundry basket and sprays from a bottle of purple glass cleaner. "You want to wipe back and forth on the inside but wipe in a circular motion on the outside. That way if you see a streak, you'll know which side of the glass it's on." He provides a way to remember. "Inside—straight lines like a cage or a jail cell. Outside—swirls like clouds."

Cooper motions to the laundry basket. I grab a cloth and accept the purple spray bottle he hands me. He puckers his lips to point toward the next glass case. I get started, mimicking his swirling motions.

"That's it, Perry-san. Wax on. Wax off." He cracks himself up quoting from the *Karate Kid* movie. His laugh is the same *heh-heh-heh-heh* as before, minus the wheezing.

My new boss leaves me in the large exhibit room. He must reach a light panel somewhere, because a shock of bright light fills the place. There's probably a hundred display cases.

I want—no, I *need*—a different job.

I know the exact instant my lunch break begins. Dropping the cleaning cloth in my hands, I make like a bank robber and flee the building.

"Holaay," Pauline exclaims from the park bench. "That eager for lunch?"

I halt. Eager? Yes. For lunch? Chi gaawiin. Big no.

Pauline rises. After a quick glance toward the building, she rubs a finger behind her ear.

"What's up?" I ask as she looks at the brick wall again.

"Um . . . Tribal Council bought us lunch, and . . ." Her hand remains at her ear.

Why is she getting worked up about lunch?

It dawns on me a second later. She doesn't mean *us* as in her and me. Tribal Council is treating their interns. Pauline feels guilty about not joining me for lunch.

"No worries," I say easily.

"I could sneak a sandwich out to you," she offers.

"Nah. I got something I need to do, hey?" Her brow furrows, so I add, "It's all good, Egg." Her face brightens. "Talk later," I yell while continuing down the sidewalk.

I dodge tourists meandering by the many gift shops across from the Soo Locks. The sunshine feels warm against my neck, but I can't savor it. It doesn't take long to reach one with a HELP WANTED sign in the window. Catching my breath, I check out my reflection in the glass. My single thick braid falls over one shoulder. I swat something dive-bombing my head before practicing a toothy smile. I'm glad Mom made me change my shirt this morning. Wearing a MERCILESS INDIAN SAVAGE T-shirt would not have created the best first impression while job seeking.

Every surface of the store is covered with tchotchkes for tourists.

Mugs, photo frames, and hand towels feature the Mackinac Bridge, freighters, bears, or fish. Oversized cribbage boards are hand-painted with mosquitos and the header OFFICIAL MICHIGAN STATE BIRD.

I stand at the checkout counter for a long minute before the store lady makes eye contact.

"Hi. My name is Perry and I'm interested in working here. I'm available right away." I smile the same way that Pauline looks at her teachers.

"We already hired someone." Her eyes do not match her polite words.

Oh, so it's like that, I say in my head.

Pauline's voice chimes in. *It's not always about skin color.*

"Would you like me to take down the sign from the window?" I offer in a syrupy voice that crystallizes into something gritty between my teeth.

Her cheeks go scarlet. I don't bother waiting for her to stumble over an excuse.

Back on the sidewalk, I take a deep breath and continue walking. The next HELP WANTED sign is in an ice cream shop window. I recognize the employees as some of my former classmates. They would vouch for hiring Pauline, but not me.

Turns out that fighting back when kids call you any number of racial slurs in the school hallway gives you a reputation as someone to avoid. Posing as my well-liked twin is not an option either. We may have started out identical, but, according to Mom and Pops, sixteen years of my living life "full throttle" has left visible distinctions. My left eyebrow is nicked by a scar. At nine, I hid a broken pinkie so well that by the time anyone found out, my fingertip had healed at an odd angle. Basically, my body is a road map of adventures that my more cautious twin has avoided.

I stop by the front office of a nearby motel. It's one of the few that hasn't been torn down and is now considered retro cool. The sign reads NEW OWNERS instead of HELP WANTED, but it's worth a try. I ask the scruffy-looking boy if I can talk to the manager about a job.

"How old are you?" His abnormally deep voice is unexpected. I thought he was younger than me, though it's hard to tell with light brown hair obscuring everything above his shoulders.

I answer, "Sixteen."

"Dude," he says. "They don't hire minors."

"To clean rooms?" I raise my scarred eyebrow.

"Juvenile records don't show up on a background check."

"But I don't have a record."

"Congrats." He claps his hands unenthusiastically.

Well, shit and strike three. I check the time. If I run, I can get a sandwich and make it back to the museum.

I decide to mess with him. "Hold up. *You* passed a background check?"

He laughs, which sounds more like rumbling thunder.

"They don't hire smart-asses either," he says.

I call over my shoulder when I reach the door, "Sure looks that way to me."

Mom pulls up in front of the park bench where I've been since 5:01 p.m. and Pauline only just arrived.

"Ambe." She motions for us before pointing to her watch. "Wewiib."

The ferry leaves the mainland on the quarter hours, so we either hurry to make the 5:15 or drag ass and end up on the 5:45. I intend to be fishing by then.

I take the front seat. Not only is it my normal turn, but it's three feet closer, and I hurt all over from hours of cleaning glass. Reaching for the door handle, every muscle burns.

"Gichiwipizon." Mom reminds us to put on our seat belts while running a yellow light.

Pauline launches into a recap of every super-awesome thing Tribal Council had them do.

"We spent all morning in a talking circle, listening to each Tribal Council member tell stories. We each had to answer questions about ourselves, but they did it like a game show. Oh, and guess what!" she says, without waiting for us to guess. "Four Tribal Council members each get to select an intern to shadow them. Since I'm the only high school student, I probably won't get selected by any of the Executive Council members. I hope I get Wendy Manitou. She travels to Washington, DC, all the time for public hearings. But she'd probably pick one of the prelaw interns. Mom, who do you think will pick me?"

I do my best to tune out the discussion. My plans are to change clothes and grab my backpack, tackle box, and pole. The best spot for yellow perch is the shallow water along the north shore, about a half mile from our property. Plenty of grasshoppers, minnows, and wigglers around for bait. I can fish all evening.

"Earth to Perry," Mom says with a laugh. "I asked how your day went."

"I spent eight hours cleaning glass displays," I grumble, leaving out the job-hunt part.

Mom turns into our half-circle driveway. Elvis Junior, tail wagging, dashes toward the SUV. Pops sits on the front steps next to a small boy enjoying a homemade lemon ice.

"Oh, I forgot," she says. "Daunis is hoping one of yous can play with Waabun. She needed to run an errand and didn't want him in the car for three hours when he could be outside."

Our little cousin is chill and enjoys fishing. But bringing him along changes how much I'm able to relax. Waabun is a five-year-old who is too quick and quiet for his own good. He's taken off before without a sound.

On the other hand, doing a favor for Auntie might help make amends for the Jeep.

"Hey, Waab, race you to the monkey bars," I shout.

In a flash he's halfway to the enormous jungle gym and tree fort spanning several trees at the edge of the front yard. Waabun bypasses the castle-like tree fort and heads to the woods. His single braid of dark brown hair bounces rhythmically against his shoulder blades. Junior, running next to the boy, nudges him back to the yard.

Somewhere in my rez dog's lineage is a sheepdog ancestor.

I didn't think it was possible for my body to feel worse than when I climbed into the SUV. Every muscle tightened during the ride home. Even hobbling over to the castle is an ordeal. But playing with my little cousin helps. He's so quick and unpredictable that I react without thinking about how much each movement will hurt.

It takes an hour of playing to feel somewhat stretched out. After a break for dinner, I grab our fishing poles and make Waabun carry the tackle box down to the water.

There are so many things I love about my cousin. Right now, I appreciate his willingness to bait his own hook. Pauline still gets squeamish and makes me do hers.

"How did you get so good at fishing, Auntie Perry?" Waab asks as the fish I reel in spins like a ballerina. His sparkly light brown eyes are wide with awe.

I also adore his adoration.

"When I was a kwezans, even younger than you, Pops took me and Pauline fishing for the first time. She cried for the worms, even though we offered semaa to say miigwech for their lives. I kissed each worm before I put it on my hook. Pops said that was good thinking."

Waabun gives me his full attention.

"I caught a fish right away. Pops said I had a gift. I could sit still and listen to everything. The water, wind, trees, birds, critters . . . they all speak if you pay attention. They leave clues for you to figure out."

"Does Auntie Pauline listen too?"

"She hears some things, but not everything," I say.

"But she reads more books than you," he points out.

I'm known for saying exactly what's on my mind. But when I'm talking with my little cousin, I choose my words carefully. He's a deep thinker, and I don't want to warp him.

"Waab, books are wonderful. But so is learning directly from Gichi-manidoo. Creator gave us helpers to teach us things even before books were invented. We learned from stories told from person to person. And we learned that we are helpers too. We are connected to every creature, tree, and river. Fishing teaches me that. Every time."

I pick up another worm.

"Gichi miigwech, akii-zagaskway." I kiss the squirmy worm. "You know what I said?"

"Big thank you . . . worm?"

"Yes. Earthworm. *Akii* means 'earth.' *Zagaskway* means 'leech,' a bloodsucker." I have him say each syllable with me. "Those are the stubby worms that clamp onto your toe if you let your feet stay in the water too long."

"Is *bloodsucker* a bad word?" He whispers the word, just in case.

"No," I assure him. "Bloodsuckers are good helpers. Your mama taught me about its medicines. Zagaskway has medicine in his mouth that keeps blood from clotting. Sometimes that's a very helpful talent to share with us. Everything and everybody has gifts to share."

"Is your gift talking to fish?"

I laugh. "Maybe. Or maybe it's listening to them."

Waabun heaves a big sigh. "You're so smart, Auntie."

He's still holding his rod, so I whisper something in his ear instead of squeezing him tight.

"What did that mean?" His alert eyes are the color of a fawn.

"You have my heart, Little Cousin. I am an earthworm wrapped around your little finger."

CHAPTER 3

FRIDAY, JUNE 13TH

Mom drops us off at Chi Mukwa recreation center for the full-day seminar all Kinomaage interns must attend every Friday. In addition to the ice rinks, basketball courts, volley-ball courts, fitness center, and Tim Hortons coffee shop, it also has meeting rooms. I'd rather be anywhere else in Chi Mukwa than a large meeting room with nineteen other interns.

Pauline ditches me for her fellow Tribal Council interns. They wear royal blue polo shirts. I notice a cluster of four interns in red shirts and another four in shamrock green. My sister didn't mention the matching shirts when she said there was a dress code for our Friday seminars—collared shirts and non-jeans pants, shorts, or skorts. So now I resemble a Lands' End catalog model in a striped golf shirt and khaki pants.

I beeline to the refreshments. Then, donut in hand, I sit at a table at the back.

"Pearl Mary Firekeeper-Birch, right?" says a perky Nish kwe wear-ing vintage cat-eye frames. The high ponytail, fancy scarf tied around her neck, and clipboard in her hands complete the cruise-director vibe, which must be intentional.

"Perry," I say, mouth full of powdered-sugar cake donut.

"Pardon?" She pronounces it *par-DOH-n*.

I swallow. "I go by Perry."

"Well, you can write whatever name you want." She places a blank name tag and a red marker next to my half-eaten donut. "Be sure to write your office assignment below your name." Her name tag reads: CLAIRE BARBEAU, INTERNSHIPS & STUDY ABROAD.

People are still trickling in. So far, I recognize about half the interns. I assume the rest are college-age tribal citizens who didn't grow up in the area. They get to live in the dorms at Lake Superior State University for the ten-week summer internship.

"Did you write 'Smart-Ass' on your name tag?" The voice is deep and reminds me of Jack's radio ad. It's the motel guy, except his curtain of light brown hair is slicked back in a hair tie, like for senior pictures or court. Now I can see his blue eyes, which match the polos worn by the Tribal Council interns. Without the shaggy hair in his face, he looks manly. An oversized square jawline deepens his cheek hollows to an extreme. His body is lean in a boyish way. It's as if he's going through puberty from the top down, and everything has stalled below the neck.

"You get fired from that motel?" I say with a scowl.

"Nah," he says with a smile that reveals apple cheeks. "Was there on my lunch break so my mom could run an errand."

He sits next to me and reaches for a Sharpie. His smooth forearm is light bronze. He scribbles on his name tag. Erik Miller . . . and his assignment has something to do with shopping?

"You got the handwriting of a serial killer," I say.

Erik Miller's laugh is all bass and no treble.

Lucas enters the room, sees me, and struts the entire length like a male runway model, Blue Steel and all.

"Scooch over," I tell Erik. I point my lips toward the empty seat on his other side.

Lucas greets me with "Hey, it's the second-best angler on Sugar Island."

"I know you are, but what am I?" I say.

Lucas laughs, taking the zinger in stride. He motions to Erik and raises an eyebrow.

"Luke-Ass," I say, intentionally mispronouncing his name. "This is Erik, who is a smart-ass. His mom works at the Freighters Motel. And, evidently, he's tribal."

"My parents own the motel," Erik clarifies. "My mom and I are tribal members."

I correct him. "Tribal citizens. Members belong to clubs. Citizens belong to nations."

"Tribal citizens," Erik repeats. "I like that."

I continue the introductions. "This is Lucas Chippeway. His Granny June has been paying me a weekly allowance to be his friend ever since we were six years old."

They nod at each other in that bro way before Lucas starts bragging about all these huge fish he supposedly catches whenever I'm not around.

Claire, our cruise director, claps her hands to get everybody's attention.

"Welcome, everyone, to our first Friday seminar," she says. People cheer and clap, which makes her face light up. I'm tempted to lee-lee just to watch her reaction.

Pauline sits with the other royal blue shirts claiming the table at the front of the room. She turns back to me, mouthing, *Be nice.*

Pssshhht. Nice is overrated. I pretend to pick my nose with my middle finger. She rolls her eyes before facing forward.

Claire continues, "As you know, your Kinomaage placement is four days a week at your assigned department. Every Friday you'll spend here with your fellow interns participating in team challenges and learning about our history, government, and programs to gain a broader understanding about our tribe."

Claire begins clapping again, continuing until we join in. She reminds me of my Little League coach, who clapped for each player, even the ones who struck out. Not that I ever struck out; I was great. Coach was mad when I didn't sign up the next year. Mom and Pops have a rule about not quitting a team once you make a commitment.

Wait. If I get hired somewhere else, will Mom and Pops be okay with me substituting one job for another? After all, my commitment is only to pay back Auntie for the Jeep repairs.

"Okay, let's go around and share what we did this week," Claire says.

Pauline's hand rises so quickly that I have flashbacks to middle school, the last time we had classes together. My twin spent all of grades six through eight waving frantically for every teacher to call on her.

When the Kinomaage coordinator picks my sister, I lee-lee. Every head jerks my way.

"Oh my," Claire exclaims.

Meanwhile, Pauline rises to tell everybody about: The Best Week of Her Life.

"Aaniin. Pauline Firekeeper-Birch indizhnikaaz. Waabizhish indoo-dem. Ziisabaaka Minising indonjiba. Hello. I'm Pauline Firekeeper-Birch. Marten Clan. From Sugar Island. I attend Sault High School, where I'll be a junior in the fall. I'm part of the Tribal Council team, and the best part of the week was getting to know each council member. Our elected leaders really care about all of us."

I tune out subsequent introductions and play tic-tac-toe with Lucas. I don't look up until Erik stands for his introduction.

"Hey. I'm Erik Miller from Escalante. It's downstate in the middle of nowhere. My parents recently bought the Freighters Motel." He clears his throat, which makes his voice drop even lower. "I'm going to Mackinac State College this fall."

Seriously? I thought he was still in high school. Thankfully, Erik correctly pronounces Mackinac. It ends with the *ac*, but that gets pronounced like *aw*. *Mackinaw*, not *Mackinack*.

After a few ums and aahs, he remembers what else he was supposed to talk about.

"Oh right, I'm assigned to shipping and receiving at the Superior Shores. Uh . . . the most interesting thing I did this week? I dunno. I helped unload a bunch of mini-fridges?"

I smile. Erik's week sounds a lot like mine. I'm debating which highlight to share—Tuesday's glass-display-case cleaning, Wednesday's wood-surface-polishing extravaganza, or Thursday's double feature of vacuuming every carpet in the museum and sweeping the scary basement that Cooper calls "the archives."

Obviously, I'll keep quiet about my lunchtime efforts to score a better job.

I barely pay attention to Lucas's introduction until he mentions fish.

"I'm working for Tribal Fisheries and Wildlife Management, which means I earn zhooniyaa while fishing, tracking, and trapping. I refuel the boats, so my highlight was taking each boat for a spin. It was sweeeeeeeet!"

I'm so jealous, I could kick him. If I'd known I'd be forced into an internship, I would've fought Lucas for that Fisheries spot.

Still unsure what to share, I take my time rising to address the room.

"Aaniin. Perry Firekeeper-Birch indizhnikaaz. Waabizhish indoodem. Ziisabaaka Minising indonjiba. Ni-wiisagendam giizhiishiig." Lucas snorts next to me. Pauline giggles and rolls her eyes. I glance around to see if anyone else caught on. Two of the local interns are smirking. "Hi. I'm Perry Firekeeper-Birch. Marten Clan. From Sugar Island." I don't translate my last sentence.

A bead of sweat takes its time going from my neck to the waist of my khaki pants. Is the AC even on? Okay, school and highlight of the week.

"I'm going to be a junior at Malcolm." I recognize flickers of judgment from a few interns who think the alternative high school is for bad kids.

"I'm working at the tribal museum with Cooper Turtle." A few people whisper to their teammates. I can imagine what they're saying about my supervisor.

I pause, considering whether I should share a highlight that would play into everyone's narrative about Kooky Cooper. Yesterday, for example, when I finished sweeping the basement storage room, my supervisor entered and closed the door to be alone in the archives. A few moments later I caught the sound of a hand drum and a song too muffled to translate.

"My highlight was giving guided tours to museum visitors." The lie flows like sweet sap from a sugar maple tree. I sit quickly, not bothering to gauge any reactions.

"Hey." Erik nudges Lucas. "What was the thing she said that made you laugh?"

Lucas chuckles. "It's an old Indian trick to see who knows the language." He flashes a proud grin my way. "She told everyone, 'It hurts when I pee.'"

After we finish with our highlights, Claire has us sit with our teams. She groups me, Lucas, and Erik with a girl named Shense Jackson. All four of us have solo placements.

Shense is a year ahead of me at Malcolm, but we might be at the same credit level. She missed most of last year because of extreme morning sickness that lasted her entire pregnancy.

Claire makes a few announcements.

"I said this during orientation, but it bears repeating," she says. "You may get transferred to a different team for any number of reasons. It happens every summer."

Next, Claire announces that we are to come up with team names. She makes her way to our group first. She offers a suggestion: "Team Lone Wolves."

I groan, and pretend I banged my knee. I take action before she offers another name.

"Team Misfit Toys," I say. "You know? *Rudolph the Red-Nosed Reindeer*? The Christmas show where Santa sends all the toys to that island?"

Claire frowns. "That implies a group less worthy than the others."

"The water pistol that shoots jelly and the train with square wheels!" Lucas shouts.

"Charlie-in-the-Box," Shense says. Her heart-shaped mouth looks like a lipstick ad.

"That's right," I say, trying to remember the other toys. "Wasn't there a bird that swam?"

"Yeah, yeah, yeah." Lucas practically does a happy dance.

"Hey, Smart—" I catch myself. "Erik. You good with Team Misfit Toys?"

"Sure," he says.

"Then it's settled," I tell Claire. "Team Misfit Toys. One of a kind. Janky, but in a good way."

Our cruise director's smile falters as she walks away with a bit less pep in her step.

Erik turns to our fourth member. "How do you pronounce your name?"

"*Shense* rhymes with *Chauncey*," she says, probably wishing for a dollar every time someone asks her that.

Shense's name tag lists her placement in the surveillance office at the Superior Shores Casino and Resort. Her dad is the head of surveillance. There are hiring policies against nepotism, but it's possible her dad requested an exemption since she's an intern rather than a permanent employee. Good for Shense. I'd work with my Pops in a heartbeat if I could.

Claire requests our attention at the front of the meeting room.

"Each week your team will compete in challenges to earn points. I'll keep track of all points and update the count at the end of each seminar."

She pauses to build suspense. I'm not feeling it, but others seem excited.

"Each team will also plan and conduct a community service project sometime over our ten-week program. During the final Friday seminar, there will be team presentations about each project, which will be independently evaluated. Your project score, combined with the weekly challenge points, will determine the winning team." Claire peers over the glasses at the tip of her nose. "The winning team will receive a bonus of four thousand dollars . . . for each team member."

"Holy shit, that's a one hundred percent bonus," Lucas declares loudly. Everyone laughs at his outburst.

"Lu-CASH," I tell him.

"You know it."

We silently plan how to spend our bonuses. I'd have enough for a jon boat. Something small enough to get into places around the island that Pops's boat can't get into.

After a bathroom break, we reconvene for the first team challenge.

Claire explains. "First up is a *Jeopardy!*-style game where every category has something to do with our tribe: tribal history, language, cultural teachings, and Sugar Island trivia. You will select one teammate to represent you."

I could win this for Team Misfit Toys.

A member of Team Tribal Council tells the other two about Pauline: she's from Sugar Island, top in her class, speaks Ojibwe language, and knows many of our cultural teachings. I don't like the way one guy, a preppy prelaw student, takes a step back to assess my sister like she's a side of beef.

"Our language is called Anishinaabemowin," she says. "Or Ojibwemowin."

Someone says, "See? That's why she should be our representative."

I notice Pauline turn away from Preppy Guy to smooth the hair behind her ear.

My twin's anxiety has levels, like military defense readiness. As the DEFCON level number decreases, Pauline's anxiety rises.

DEFCON 5 = No visible signs of distress.

DEFCON 4 = Repeatedly tucking her hair behind her left ear.

DEFCON 3 = Rubbing the tip of her pointer finger into a groove behind her left ear.

DEFCON 2 = Using her fingernail to scratch along the groove.

DEFCON 1 = Pulling out individual strands of hair until there is a dime-sized bald patch behind her left ear.

I stand in front of Erik and say, "I choose you, Pikachu."

"Seriously?" Erik's eyes bug out. "I literally know nothing about the Tribe."

"I sense the Force is strong in this untested Jedi," I tell Lucas with a wink.

"Test him we will." Lucas does a decent Yoda impression.

"Shouldn't we at least try to score a few points," Shense asks.

"I say we enjoy Erik in the hot seat. Like hazing, but in a good way," Lucas says.

"Let's tank this so everyone assumes we're Team Participation Ribbon," I say. "Then we can shake them up when they least expect it. I like messing with people."

"This is true," Lucas adds.

Erik's grimace slowly cracks into a smile.

"I volunteer as tribute," says our sacrificial lamb.

Claire has pizzas and salad brought in. Apparently, if we have a working lunch during our Friday seminar, we can end our workday an hour early. Our working-lunch assignment is to brainstorm ideas for our community service project.

Instead of offering a suggestion, Lucas asks what Pauline and I are doing tonight.

"Full-moon ceremony," I say. "Auntie's giving Granny June a ride to our place."

"Ah," he says. "How 'bout you, Erik?"

"Working at the motel," Erik says with a shrug.

When Lucas doesn't ask Shense, she volunteers the info.

"I'm driving my baby to St. Ignace for her weekend visit at her dad's." She gives us a wry smile revealing a canine tooth that juts forward.

Claire reminds everyone this is a working lunch for brainstorming ideas, not idle chatter.

"I vote for whatever Perry wants." Shense excuses herself to pump breast milk.

Winning a four-thousand-dollar bonus is tempting, but I still want to quit the Kinomaage internship if I find a different job. Maybe I should take the back seat on brainstorming ideas for the project.

"I got nothing," I say, getting up to throw away my paper plate.

I wander over to the nursing lounge next to the restrooms. Knocking on the door, I enter and ask Shense if I can get her anything.

"Yeah. I grabbed two slices, but I want more." She jiggles the handheld device clamped onto her breast. "My breastfeeding appetite is the exact opposite of my pregnancy appetite."

"Be right back," I say.

"Miigwech. Veggie if they have any, hey?" Before I close the door behind me, she adds, "No pepperoni—even the grease makes me puke still."

I return three minutes later with an entire veggie pizza. Shense bursts into tears. Happy tears, she assures me while reaching for a slice.

"Popping out a binoojii completely fucks up your hormones." Shense fiddles with the breast pump to switch to her other nipple. She winces when the motorized humming resumes.

"Wonder what project they're coming up with," she says.

I focus on each topping of the veggie pizza.

"Shense, you know anywhere that's hiring?" I feel her gaze but don't look up.

"That bad, huh?"

"Just want another option," I say.

Kooky Cooper isn't awful. He's not mean or creepy. Just an oddball. The tasks I'm doing are more tedious than horrible. But if I've got to work, I want it to be somewhere I choose.

Shense lists a few fast-food places. I am mid-shrug when I decide to be honest.

"Last time I was in one, some asshole shouted the N-word at a Black girl working the drive-through window. That wasn't the worst part. I mean, I've been called so many horrible names, and each one is like another wave trying to knock me down. But it was the fact that no one said anything, not even the manager." I shake my head. "It's like when waves crash against rocks and rebound back into the lake. Waves come at me every which way. It's the ones you never see coming that pull you under."

"Wow. That is completely fucked up," she says.

"I wouldn't last long in a place like that, Shense."

"You could get your aunt's police-captain boyfriend to track down license plates and hunt down anyone who'd shout shit at you."

"Daunis is just friends with TJ Kewadin," I clarify.

She laughs. "Yeah. I was 'just friends' with someone, and now I'm squeezing milk from my boob to feed his kid."

At the end of the day, we watch a video recording from our second challenge of the day. No one knew what the afternoon challenge was until Claire led one team at a time to the enormous wooden playscape area. Specifically, to the lengthy stretch of monkey bars.

"Each team was given the same goal: to get at least one team member across the monkey bars by touching as few bars as possible," Claire says.

The safety net—a wide, flat rubber runner bridging the platforms on either end—had been removed. This allowed for an eight-foot drop between the monkey bars and the sand below.

"You also received the same instructions. A team could pick one or more persons to represent the team, but the decision needed to be unanimous. Every rung touched would be counted. The challenge was also timed from start to finish. The number of minutes would be multiplied by the number of rungs. The team with the lowest score would win."

Team Tribal Council is up first. We see Pauline tell them she has plenty of practice with our jungle gym at home. Preppy Guy says she did a great job with the first challenge, but someone else should get a chance to participate. In the end, Preppy Guy touches five rungs.

Team TCB (Taking Care of Business) quickly selected the intern who was on the gymnastics team at Michigan State. He used only three rungs but slipped before reaching the dismount platform. He needed another turn to finish the challenge, which doubled their points.

Team Golden Girls, four female interns assigned to the Nokomis-Mishomis Elder Center, did well with a long-limbed girl who spanned the distance using four rungs.

Team Shrek-reation, the interns from the recreation program, also completed the challenge in four rungs but took twice as long for all team members to agree on the participant.

"We won, right?" one of the Golden Girls asks.

"There's one more team," Claire says, resuming the video.

The screen shows our quick huddle. The video captures Lucas's rousing speech.

"Me and Perry trained our whole lives for this. I'm talking years of playing Castle with Pauline and Auntie Daunis. We are magical flying squirrels, and this is our moment."

Erik and Shense cheer us on.

"We've seen Team Misfit Toys do this all day," Claire says. "They discuss strategy and make a decision everyone supports. Now, it didn't quite pay off during the *Jeopardy!* challenge."

Erik waves to the room; his deep laugh comes easily.

Claire continues, "But keep watching."

Lucas stands at the launch platform. He winks at the camera

before leaping forward to catch a rung about one-quarter of the total distance. Then he hooks his legs over the same rung to hang by his knees upside down. He becomes a trapeze artist, swinging back and forth, while I step onto the platform. He counts down, and I leap when he calls out for me. We perfected this catch years ago. Lucas is considered short, and I am average height, but with our arms linked, we are a long, mighty force. We swing back and forth once to build momentum for my legs to hook a rung. I do the reverse of Lucas, switching from my knee hang to a hand hang. A few more swings, then I take a deep breath before launching myself toward the other platform. I stick the landing, arch my back, and raise my arms like a gymnast completing her dismount.

In the meeting room every pair of eyes is on me. Surprise becomes reassessment.

"They touched two rungs. Teamwork. Trust. Perfection," Claire says.

Shense leans over to whisper in my ear.

"You might not want the option anymore, magical flying squirrel, but I texted my cousin after lunch, and he just got back to me. He's a commercial fisherman licensed by the Tribe. If you want to join his crew, he'll hire you."

I smile so hard that my cheeks hurt.

"He said to take a few days to think about it," Shense adds, "because if you love fishing, working on a fish boat will change all that. Let him know next week, hey?"

There's nothing to think about. I have a new job. On a fish boat.

Now all I need to do is tell Mom and Pops, Auntie Daunis, Team Misfit Toys, and Cooper Turtle. That's all.

WEEK TWO

You have significantly more deceased Native people in boxes on your campus than the number of live Native students that you allow to attend your institution.

—Shannon O'Loughlin, chief executive of the Association on American Indian Affairs, in a letter to Lawrence S. Bacow, president of Harvard University, February 18, 2021

CHAPTER 4
MONDAY, JUNE 16TH

I show up for work on Monday feeling more dread than excitement. Telling Cooper shouldn't be a big deal. I rehearsed my speech all weekend. *Another opportunity came along. Nothing personal. Working on a fish boat fits better with my life plans. Today will be my last day at the tribal museum.* But when I see my supervisor, my mind goes blank.

"We got an important meeting today in St. Ignace," he says.

Telling Cooper I quit on the way back will be better than ditching him now. I follow him to the parking lot, where his canary-yellow El Camino sticks out exactly as you'd expect from a vehicle that looks like a vintage lowrider mated with a pickup truck.

"We're taking that? I thought the antique-car show wasn't until the end of the month."

He laughs. "Beautiful day like today? She's perfect for a drive."

"'She'? I thought Old Yeller was a boy's name," I say, sitting in the passenger seat.

"This here is Sunny. Miss Sunshine Days." He turns the key in the ignition switch, and she coughs before starting. "What you think about that," he says, full of pride.

"Sunny sounds like a four-pack-a-day smoker."

I get sleepy on the drive. Listening to Johnny Cash does that to me. It reminds me of trips that Pauline, Auntie Daunis, Uncle Levi, and I would take with Mom and Pops. Berry picking. Car bingo. Camping. Powwows.

We usually picked wild blueberries near Paradise, but one time Mom and Pops took us to a berry farm. Uncle decided he and I should challenge Auntie and Pauline to see which pair could pick more pounds of blueberries. We were supposed to pick only from certain rows of bushes the owner designated. Uncle had me be the lookout while he sneaked over to the bushes loaded with more blueberries. We won easily. The losers had to help Mom and Pops with canning and freezing while Uncle let me watch him play *Jedi Outcast* on the Xbox he kept at our place. Uncle Levi said I was his favorite twin and was way cooler than Pauline.

Cooper jostles me awake in a parking lot at Mackinac State College.

"You talk in your sleep," he says.

Shit. I hope I didn't quit during the forty-five-minute drive. I wait for him to tell me what I said, but he remains silent while retrieving something from behind his seat.

Two portfolios, both saddle-brown leather. One is weathered: full of scratches, its edges rubbed smooth. The other is brand-new and has my initials, PMFB, engraved on the brass tag in the bottom corner.

"Miigwech," I say, mentally kicking myself for not quitting by phone over the weekend.

Leather portfolios in hand, we approach the student union, a reddish sandstone building with a bell tower. It is a mini version of the grand, historic buildings from Pauline's university tours. He shares the giizhik from his pocket, dividing it so we both have a tiny sprig for each shoe.

Cooper leads me to a meeting room with a square table covered with white tablecloths and vases of white lilacs. I count six seats on all four sides. It isn't until I sit down next to Cooper that I notice the white place card with my name in fancy black script.

Introductions are made, but there is no way I can remember twenty-two names. I can't read everyone's place cards, only the few nearby. I forget about writing things on the lined pad in my new portfolio. Then it's our turn to speak. I don't recognize the faces turned in my direction any more than I do the names on the place cards.

Cooper introduces himself in Ojibwemowin before providing the translation. He is Crane Clan from Sugar Island. His Spirit name is Seven Crane Man, although he leaves that part out of his English translation.

When it's my turn, I keep my introduction brief. Name, clan, homeland. No sharing my Spirit name or any hidden messages. I provide the translation and quickly sit back down. My face takes more than a few minutes to cool down.

I try to pay attention to the person speaking, but it sounds like another language. NAGPRA, MACPRA, and a host of acronyms I don't understand. I glance at the wall clock above the portraits of important people, who are nearly all male and white. Cooper taps my portfolio. I'm about to mean-mug him when I follow his fingertip. He points to documents inside the half flap opposite the pad of paper. I pull the items from the portfolio to inspect.

The first sheet of paper has a list of acronyms and what the letters mean. NAGPRA means the Native American Graves Protection and Repatriation Act. MACPRA stands for the Michigan Anishinaabek Cultural Preservation and Repatriation Alliance. The list covers the entire page.

I look over the next piece of paper, which is a list of everyone at the meeting. Even my name is included: *Pearl Mary "Perry" Firekeeper-Birch, student, Sugar Island Ojibwe Tribe.*

The last item looks like a stapled report, but on closer inspection it is a copy of the NAGPRA law. Since I don't know what's going on, I read the first section: "Definitions."

The meeting pauses for lunch served by catering staff. They offer a choice of steak, chicken, or fish to each person. I pick chicken because no one can prepare fish as good as Pops. I place the cloth napkin on my lap and drink ice water from a crystal goblet. This lunch is almost as fancy as when Auntie Daunis's mom got married a few years ago.

"Young lady, what school do you attend?" asks the elegant older woman to my left. Her pretty silver hair is cut in a precise bob. Something about her feels vaguely familiar.

"Malcolm," I answer after swallowing a forkful of chicken and rice pilaf.

"Oh, I'm not familiar with the historically Black colleges," she says, turning away.

She reminds me of Auntie's prissy Zhaaganaash grandmother, GrandMary.

"Is she for real?" I mumble to Cooper.

"They're all for real, Perry-san."

The meeting continues after lunch. I'm able to finish reading the law.

Basically, every institution—except the Smithsonian, for some reason—that has a Native American Collection and receives federal funds since the Act was passed in 1990, is supposed to prepare an inventory of everything in their collection. Indian tribes and Native

Hawaiian organizations are notified about the inventories so they can request the return of human remains and items they believe to be culturally affiliated with their tribe, village, or group.

The meeting concludes an hour later. I have no idea what, if anything, was accomplished. I follow Cooper so we can hit the road, but he walks with everybody else to the college museum across the quad. A third of the group fills an elevator, and another group fills a second one. Cooper takes me aside while we wait for the next elevator with the stragglers. He digs in his sport coat pocket and retrieves a small perfume bottle. As he uncaps it, the scent of giizhik reaches my nostrils. Cooper demonstrates applying the roller-ball applicator to each side of his temples. He then offers the cedar oil to me.

"So, you read all about NAGPRA," he says, more a fact than a question.

"Yeah. Seems straightforward. Inventory the collection and notify the tribes. Then the tribes request the items and the university or whoever returns the stuff back to the tribes." I finish applying cedar oil to my temples the way my boss did and hand the bottle back. I'm not exactly sure why we are protecting ourselves, but I do know that Cooper Turtle wouldn't mess around with our medicines without a good reason.

"The stuff?" He raises an eyebrow.

"Well, I meant the funerary objects, sacred objects, and items of cultural patrimony," I say, feeling proud at having remembered these terms.

"And the human remains," he says, motioning for me to enter the elevator first.

I'm surprised when we reach the basement. I figured we would tour the exhibits on the main floor and second level. The door ahead is labeled ARCHIVES.

"What year was NAGPRA passed?" Cooper continues his pop quiz.

"1990," I answer, again pleased with myself.

"Do you remember how long museums are given to complete their inventories of human remains and associated funerary objects?" he asks.

This answer I am not as sure about. "Three years?"

"Five," he corrects. "But if the institution makes a good-faith effort to carry out an inventory, they can request an extension. The law was passed in 1990, and now it's 2014. That's twenty-four years for public museums and universities to inventory their collections, notify tribes, and process their requests for the return of human remains and . . ." He pauses to use air quotes. "'Stuff.'"

I feel embarrassed for having used such a casual word in my summary of NAGPRA.

"Now ask me how many ancestors this museum has agreed to return to our tribe."

He doesn't wait for me to respond. Not that I was going to. Cooper's eyes are flickering with something grievous and combustible.

"The answer is none, Perry. Not a single ancestor has been returned." With that, he leads me into a storage room with the other tour participants.

The museum staff distributes paper booties and thin white gloves. Dr. Fenton, the dismissive lady from lunch, pulls out a long, flat drawer for us to peer inside. I expect to see maps or drawings. Instead, cardboard boxes are labeled with catalog numbers and descriptions. The first one reads: CRANIA.

Crania? As in, cranium? The same name as the board game that I refuse to play against Pauline because she goes straight to DEFCON 2 with her first incorrect answer. I think it means . . . brains. I step back, horrified. Seeing Cooper across the room, I rush to his side.

"Cooper, I don't want to be here."

"Is it your Moontime?" He sounds alarmed. "I'm sorry I didn't ask sooner."

"No. It's not that." I whisper, "Are they storing brains? Is that what crania means?"

"Crania is plural for cranium, which means the part of the skull that covers the brain," Cooper says.

Plural skulls.

"How many of our ancestors are here?" I don't bother to whisper.

Neither does Cooper. "The inventory is not complete, but there are thirteen from Sugar Island and four from Neebish Island. There is also one ancestor whose origins have not been ascertained. Before we go, I'd like you to meet her. That's all I ask of you today. But it's up to you."

My supervisor looks intense; this request means something important to him. I'm going to disappoint him when I quit later today.

"Just one?" I ask. Cooper nods vigorously.

He leads me to a guy in a suit and bow tie who looks like the fussy Monopoly dude except he's younger and his hair is red instead of white. His slacks have razor-sharp creases; his vest has an actual pocket-watch chain draped from a buttonhole into a front pocket. There is a second chain that may actually lead to a monocle tucked into a higher pocket. All that's missing is his top hat and cane. Cooper shakes his hand and calls him Dr. Leer-wah.

"Mr. Turtle, it's good to see you again. Back to see my girl?"

Cooper's jaw clenches an instant before replying. "Yes, please. But first I'd like to introduce my intern, Perry Firekeeper-Birch."

"What a pleasure to meet you, Miss Birch." He holds out a white-gloved hand.

"It's Firekeeper-Birch, but you can call me Perry," I say as my gloved hand meets his.

Leer-wah takes a metal box from a nearby shelf. He sets it on a large stainless steel table. The box is three feet in length and half as wide and deep, with a hinged lid. He stretches the end of his faculty ID badge lanyard to use a key on the padlocked hasp of the box. Before continuing, he digs into his breast pocket for the monocle, which turns out to be a pair of half-moon reading glasses. Once they're perched on the tip of his nose, he lifts the lid of the box. Inside is a large bundle wrapped in tissue paper. Leer-wah unwraps the bundle carefully . . . reverently, even.

"Breathe," Cooper instructs me.

I do so, immediately realizing I've been holding my breath to the point of light-headedness. I take in unfamiliar scents. Auntie would probably know. Her sense of smell is like a superpower. Plus, she knows a lot about chemicals and stuff.

Bones. A skull, or rather, a cranium. Long, sturdy leg bones alongside fragments of slender ones that might be from an arm. A thick, curved section that I realize is part of the spine. There are smaller, tissue-wrapped packets. I glimpse a few of the labels: TEETH and LEFT HAND and AFO.

This was a person.

I've seen and heard the term *human remains* at least a hundred times today. But it registers differently now. The remains of a human being who lived and breathed.

"Perry, it's my honor to introduce you to Warrior Girl," Leer-wah says proudly. "Now, remains are generally disarticulated, but we made an exception for her."

"Dis-ar-tic-u-la-ted?" I pronounce each syllable of the unfamiliar word.

Cooper answers before Leer-wah can. "The bones are separated and stored by body parts, not by individual." His voice is calm, but his eyes sear through me like a laser.

There are drawers of crania and others of leg bones. I look down at my bent pinkie and wonder if there is a drawer of pinkie bones. And how many are janky like mine?

I force myself to focus on what Leer-wah is saying.

"She was in her early to mid-teens—post-puberty, but her hips indicate that she had never been pregnant or carried a child beyond the first trimester. And see this?" He points to a gnarled line along her thigh bone. "She sustained a major injury from a knife even larger than her own AFO. We know it was a knife because animal claws would have left parallel lines."

"*AFO* means 'associated funerary object,'" Cooper says, reading my mind. "Her knife was a significant possession to her if she was intentionally buried with it."

When the tip of Leer-wah's white glove touches the bone at the mark, I fight the urge to smack his hand away. He continues speaking in a voice like a teacher conducting class.

"This is called knitting. It's a pattern the bone makes when repairing itself. This tells us she didn't die from this injury. But these marks on her rib cage?" He points to a vertical gash involving two ribs. "There is no knitting. She died from this wound."

Her knife is an eight-inch flint blade that must have been lashed to a deer-antler handle. I reach for it without thinking.

"Dr. Leer-wah, may my intern hold the blade?" Cooper asks.

My gloved hands are open before the *yes* reaches my ears.

The museum guy slides the flint blade into the notched handle before handing it to me. Resting in my palm, the flint is heavier than I thought. *Substantial* would be the right word. I wrap my fingers around the handle. It's a good weapon. It fits me.

I'm filled with an urge to steal. To run as fast as I can with the treasure.

I turn the knife handle before gently placing it on Leer-wah's open palm.

I don't want to steal the knife. It belongs to the Warrior Girl.

I want to steal *her*.

After we've toured the archives, Dr. Fenton invites us to her office. Cooper quickly accepts, not even checking with me. I have had enough of this place and these people.

We cross the small campus. I follow Cooper like an afterthought. His voice sounds different—younger somehow? Eager. That's it. He's eager to see something in her office.

Adding to my bad mood, a black fly bites the back of my upper arm. Tiny fucker. A few summer students cut through the quad, heading to late afternoon classes. A marching band plays the theme to *Star Wars*. Okay, that's kind of cool. Another black fly gets me, this time on my neck, like a one-fanged vampire.

We approach a row of large, historic homes on the edge of campus. Each one is painted white; the only difference is the pastel color of its shutters. The "sorority row" vibe grows stronger with the identical lawn signs identifying each department or program housed inside.

Just like that, I'm reliving Pauline's college tour and her nonstop yammering:

I would put up with community bathrooms, Mom, if it meant I could get a single room.

Pops, that interdisciplinary program would mean I wouldn't have to choose between environmental science and economics.

They even have a Native American Studies program. C'mon, Perry. We could test out of the world-languages requirement if they let us speak Ojibwemowin.

The last house is massive, with a fancy round tower and pale turquoise shutters. The sign reads HUMANITIES AND SOCIAL SCIENCES. Bypassing the front porch and an accessibility ramp, we take a narrow, cracked sidewalk to the back. Dr. Fenton continues toward an overgrown hedge of lilac bushes. The sidewalk gives way to flagstones nearly covered by moss.

The small square house must have started as a garage or, considering its age, a carriage house. Half the faded turquoise shutters are missing. One dangles, tired and ready to let go. An engraved sign on the front door announces: OFFICE OF RAQUEL FENTON, PHD, PROFESSOR OF ANTHROPOLOGY.

Raquel? It's a flashy name that doesn't match her GrandMary vibe. Maybe I should've given more than a passing glance of the list of meeting attendees earlier. It had included everyone's full names and a bunch of other stuff.

The only reason I watch GrandRaquel enter her four-digit code on the electronic keypad for the front door is to make sure it's not something ironic, like 1492. Her code is boring: 0011.

Offices reveal clues about their occupants. The principal at the tribal school had inspirational quotes from Indigenous leaders. Malcolm's principal has a gigantic beanbag chair that you can plop onto if she's in the office with the door open. Mom's corner office at the Tribal Health Center doesn't have any plants or personal belongings, except for one framed photo on her desk. Despite having been the Tribal Health director for thirteen years, she believes a day will come when she upsets one Tribal Council member too many and gets shit-canned. She tells her staff: *Never get cozy. Make the tough decisions. Be prepared to leave with your head held high.*

According to her office, Raquel is an unorganized hoarder whose office pets are the cozy dust bunnies napping everywhere. Suddenly she isn't GrandRaquel anymore. My little six-year-old mind can still remember how fancy-schmancy GrandMary's house was . . . and this is not that. I stand beside Cooper in the middle of what might be a living room. File folders, loose papers, and shoeboxes are stacked floor to ceiling. Assorted coffee mugs rest on outcroppings of books. Her desk appears to be a dining room table covered in a patchwork of books and papers and . . . what the hell?

She has a ceremonial medicine bag made from an otter pelt. It's spread across her desk like a fur scarf with loom-beaded patches on its paws and tail.

I barely hear Raquel offer to get bottled water from the fridge and Cooper accept. As soon as she heads to the kitchen, Cooper growls into my ear.

"Not. A. Single. Word."

She returns with bottled water. Cooper thanks her for both of us. I chug the ice-cold biish.

"I'd love to see anything you'd care to show us." He gestures around the room.

"Well, there's this big guy." She points at the otter bag. "What can you tell me?"

Her tone irritates me. I picture her dressing the otter in baby clothes and bonnets.

I don't want Cooper to tell her anything, but he does.

"Otter is part of our creation story, and otter medicine bags are part of our ceremonies. Do you know this one's provenance?"

"One of our history professors passed away last spring," Raquel says. "The cleaning crew discovered some boxes in his office closet and even more boxes in the attic." She motions for us to follow her. As we do, she continues speaking. "They came across these boxes marked with his name. They opened one, saw items that looked old and odd, and brought the lot to me."

Raquel grins and gestures like a game-show host, revealing a hallway of rickety metal shelving units packed to capacity with storage bins, cardboard boxes, and—*Jesus, take the wheel*—several fruit boxes. It seems ridiculous that a box originally for shipping bananas might be filled now with bones or cultural items. More boxes are stacked on the floor, practically blocking the hallway. She must have to squeeze sideways to reach the kitchen and bathroom at the other end.

"His boxes are on the floor. I still haven't finished a proper inventory of my own items."

Her items? She doesn't own them.

"As I mentioned in the meeting, I need more time to finish the inventory," she says.

More time? I'm about to get in her face when I catch Cooper mean-mugging me. There is no misinterpreting his clenched jaw and furrowed brow.

"Cooper, you know NAGPRA didn't include appropriations for institutions to complete the inventories. I'm responsible for the museum's collection. You know I do my best, but I cannot be more specific in describing the items in the inventory without the time and resources to properly catalog them." She motions to the boxes on the floor. "And, as you can see, we get an overwhelming number of additional items."

She hands a box from the floor to Cooper, telling him to give it to me.

"*Give* it? As in take back to Sugar Island?" I blurt.

"No, dear. Wouldn't that be an unorthodox repatriation?"

She is the only one who laughs.

"Let's see what's in these boxes. It will be like Christmas." Her giggle turns childlike.

The box is very light. I use my nails to pick at the packing tape when an odd feeling comes over me. As if I were tuning Pops's old radio and the static just became a crystal-clear signal. I glance around for a source.

Cooper and Raquel are each opening a box but don't seem to feel anything odd.

"If you need help completing the inventory," my supervisor begins, "I'd be happy to gather our volunteer committee for—"

She interrupts. "That's kind of you. But I need a highly skilled assistant."

I fight the urge to throw the box at her smug, highly skilled head.

Instead I open the box to find four baskets woven from black ash and accents of braided wiingashk. I pick one basket and hold it to my nose. Maybe I'm only imagining the faintest whiff of sweetgrass, because how could the soothing scent linger for decades? As I tip the basket to check for a signature, a soft rattle calls to me like a lullaby.

Something is inside.

I look up. Their backs are to me as they look through the contents of one box together. I turn my back as well, and gently pry the snug basket lid from the base.

The basket is filled with flat, almond-shaped seeds. Some type of squash.

I tilt the base until a dozen or so seeds slide into my palm. My heart races from the thrill that I might be holding heirloom seeds from a variety that hasn't been planted in decades. Maybe these were handed down over several generations. Or even ancient.

If the basket was stored somewhere cool, dark, and dry . . . the seeds might be viable.

"Dr. Fenton," Cooper begins. "The Sugar Island Ojibwe Tribe accepts funding requests twice a year from local governments and nonprofit organizations. They recently voted to expand the eligibility beyond Chippewa County to include Mackinac County. I would be happy to help you submit a request on behalf of the college for a collections assistant."

"What a wonderful idea," she exclaims. "But, Cooper, why limit ourselves to just one collections assistant? We could request an entire team. We'd complete the inventory and conduct our tribal consultation sessions. We would model a process that could be presented at academic conferences. We could become the premiere institution for cultural anthropology."

Raquel's ambition fills the room like one of Elvis Junior's atomic farts.

I've heard wiindigoo stories my whole life. A wiindigoo is a greedy cannibal that grows larger and more powerful with each person it consumes. This is the first time I've heard one be born.

With my back still turned, I gaze upon the ivory seeds cupped in my palm. They look like eye openings. Staring back at me.

"Might be better to start with a modest request," Cooper reasons.

"Nonsense," she declares grandly. "Let us aim for the stars."

I slide the seeds into my pants pocket. They might be the only items that get repatriated from Raquel the Hoarder's house in my lifetime.

Cooper leaves the radio off for the drive back north. I stay awake. My hand rests on my thigh, covering the small mound of seeds in my pocket.

I am still quitting. I'll tell Cooper when he drops me off at home. Just announce it, turn, and walk away. No reason given; no looking back.

I have a job lined up on a fishing boat. Hard work demanding my entire focus, leaving me too exhausted to think about our ancestors in the basement archives at Mackinac State College.

It's early evening when Cooper drives onto the ferry and shuts off the engine. A plastic bag of whole-leaf tobacco fills one side of the drink holder riding the transmission hump. He takes one leaf before getting out of the El Camino. Miss Sunshine Days. I do the same.

Cooper holds his pose. He's rooted to the same spot. It's the back corner when he leaves the island and the front corner for the journey home. He always faces Sugar Island.

I make my semaa offering to the river before standing beside him. The sun is at our backs, casting Ziisabaaka Minising in salmon light.

"You gonna give me your resignation or your word?" he asks.

I blink my surprise before staring at his profile.

"Perry, your resignation or your word to help me get her back."

He breaks his gaze upon Sugar Island to look at me.

"Ogichidaakwezans. The Warrior Girl. Because she is ours and we are hers."

I open my mouth to quit. But what comes out is this:

"Cooper Turtle, you have my word."

CHAPTER 5

TUESDAY, JUNE 17TH

The following morning, Pauline and I practically skip into work. Chief Manitou surprised everyone by selecting her as his shadow. Meanwhile, I'm ready to repatriate the Warrior Girl.

"Mino gizhep, Miss Manitou," I say brightly as I pass the receptionist's desk.

"They don't pay extra for punching in early," she calls out.

I reach the employee break room and slide my time card into the punch clock. Today the *ka-chunk* sounds less irritating. I am thirteen minutes early.

Next to the time clock, one flyer stands out among the mosaic of documents on the bulletin board. Urgent red letters shout, *HAVE YOU SEEN ME?* The color image below the header shows a Nish kwe named Darby O'Malley, whose aquamarine eyes seem too vivid to be real. It's easier to believe in colored contacts or wonky printer ink. Darby is twenty-five and works at the Superior Shores Casino. She is smiling in the photo.

I look away, wanting to focus on my exciting workday. My lunch container goes into the fridge. As I exit the break room, I swear that I can feel Darby's eyes on my back.

Cooper's office is at the end of a hallway. I try to imagine the activities he might assign to me now that I made a commitment to help bring the Warrior Girl back home.

He sits at his desk, facing the doorway. His button-down shirt is red, the same as my T-shirt. If he's wearing black jeans, I'll take it as a doubly strong sign that we are on the same wavelength.

"Teach me, Obi-Wan," I announce.

He looks up from his newspaper and cup of coffee.

"Perry-san," he greets me pleasantly.

"I've been thinking . . . ," I start.

"Uh-oh." He laughs.

"No more Perry-san *Karate Kid* references. We are Repatriation Jedi. You are the Jedi ogimaa and I'm your Padawan."

"*Star Wars*, hey?" Cooper rubs his chin thoughtfully.

"Yes," I say.

He nods before frowning.

"Perry-Padawan, I owe you an apology."

"What for?"

"I put you into a situation yesterday without preparing you for the potential trauma you might have experienced. It was irresponsible of me to not have your well-being as my primary consideration. I am sorry, and I will do better moving forward."

It hadn't entered my mind until Cooper spoke. I suppose it was a lot to toss me into. And, now that I think about it, seeing our ancestors and explaining that human remains are disarticulated to be stored as parts . . . it was a lot.

"Next time, can we smudge before and after we are around the ancestors?" I ask.

"Absolutely," Cooper promises.

When my Jedi leader rises, I note the black dress slacks. A close-enough match to my black jeans. He goes to the floor-to-ceiling book-shelves spanning an entire wall of his office. There's even a wooden ladder attached to a rail at the top shelf. I doubt one person could read every book, much less remember everything they read. I check for dust bunnies, but the wood shelves practically sparkle. Taking a good look around, I realize every inch of Cooper's office is spotlessly clean and super organized. It's the exact opposite of Raquel's hoarder house office.

I am still marveling at Cooper's office when he hands me a book: *Grave Injustice: The American Indian Repatriation Movement and NAGPRA* by Kathleen S. Fine-Dare.

"What the . . ." I stop myself before swearing in front of my Jedi ogimaa.

I don't hate reading. But a person could read about fishing . . . or they could *go* fishing. Pauline has, in fact, sat in the boat and read a book about gillnetting while I checked our nets.

"Okay, Perry-Padawan, read this book, and let's discuss when you finish."

I check Cooper's face for any sign that he is pranking me.

"Seriously?" I say, hoping my gobsmacked reaction is supposed to be part of the joke. "I told you yesterday that I'm all in. Let's go get the Warrior Girl."

He shrugs. "You need to walk before you can run."

I flip through a few pages. Tiny print and too few photos. I wait for his *heh-heh* laugh.

Instead he says, "There's nine weeks left in your internship. You need to immerse yourself in NAGPRA. What led up to the law? What was it intended to accomplish?" When I don't reply, he continues. "Sit in the library and read, or at your desk, or outside at a picnic table. Doesn't matter where. Just be ready to talk about it on Thursday afternoon."

"That's in two and a half days," I sputter. Then: "Wait . . . I have a desk?"

Cooper shows me a broom closet that has a constant hum from the mechanical room next door. My office has a chair and a desk with a vintage, behemoth computer on top.

"What's the computer for?" I ask.

"You have two tasks this week. Read the book, and go online for an eBay account."

"For real, eBay?" I echo.

"Yeah. The online auction site."

"I know what eBay is. But why?"

"Perry, if you want to be a Repatriation Jedi, you need to learn about auctions of Indigenous antiquities. Because NAGPRA applies only to public institutions in the United States. Not to private collections or international institutions." He points with his lips toward the book in my hands. "On Thursday afternoon, we will talk about the book. I also want you to show me five Anishinaabe items either currently for sale or recently auctioned online."

"Wait . . . that's three tasks," I point out.

Now Cooper laughs. I take it as my cue to leave.

"Baamaa, Wiidookaagewikwezans," he says.

Later, Helper Girl.

Deciding to read in the sunshine, I walk to the Soo Locks Park. I sit on a concrete bench at the large circular fountain. The constant splatter helps me tune out noisy tourists.

Grave Injustice begins with a NAGPRA success story. In 1999, after eight years of negotiations, Jemez Pueblo repatriated almost two thousand Pecos ancestors and their sacred items from Harvard University's Peabody Museum. An archaeologist had excavated these human beings and their belongings in the early 1900s for academic research. More than seventy years later, they made the return trip home in a semitruck. Their descendants had to create a new ceremony for reburial because the community had never experienced the need to return ancestors to the earth.

I stare at random tourists and wonder how they would react to their ancestors being stolen for research. I'm guessing they would see it as sacrilege. So why were my relatives fair game?

Changing benches to follow the sun like a cat, I keep reading. The first chapter goes on forever. It's about Manifest Destiny, the belief in a divine right to conquer America. It was how they justified forcing people off their ancestral lands, only to make way for plantations later on. Committing atrocities and calling it the will of a supreme entity wasn't just an America thing. Holy wars were fought for control over sacred sites. Every war, holy or not, is a battle for control over land and other resources. The winners were due the spoils of war, including gold and silver, people enslaved and trafficked, and the cultural and religious relics of those considered less than human.

Lucas's Granny June always says: *They came for our land, women, timber, water, fish, game, spirituality, and children. Anything we value, the Zhaaganaash claim for themselves.*

I wonder how much more can be taken? What is left for us to lose?

The concrete is warm against my backside while a cool breeze keeps me from overheating in my black jeans. I lie back, stretching the length of the bench. The continuous patter from the fountain is like a steady rainfall. I rest my head on the book.

Auntie told Pauline and me that she kept schoolbooks beneath her pillow in case osmosis worked with written words. She was the valedictorian of her graduating class at Sault High, so maybe she was onto something. It seemed more Pauline's thing than mine. But right now I wouldn't mind absorbing every word of *Grave Injustice* into my brain. Just so I could know everything without having to read it. Or to feel it.

Cold water from the fountain shocks me awake. The wind shifted, spraying me as the center spurt went off course. I pull my phone from the front pocket of my dark jeans.

Three hours! I wasted the entire morning. I didn't even finish the first chapter.

Back at the office, I eat lunch while beginning task two. When the old computer takes forever to boot, I decide to sign up for eBay on my laptop tonight as a swap for the nap.

Pushing the computer to the back of the desk, I create a small surface and open *Grave Injustice*. I read to the constant hum of the mechanical system on the other side of the wall.

From the instant we get into Mom's SUV for the ride home, Pauline talks nonstop. Each sentence is *Chief Manitou* this and *Chief Manitou* that. I ignore her until she taps my shoulder.

"Did you know Chief Manitou was just three years older than us when he first got elected? He's been on Council either as a regular member or the chief for twenty-nine years. Just think, for Auntie's whole life, he's been on Tribal Council. Can you believe it?"

Just to piss her off, I say, "Sounds like three decades of grifting to me."

She doesn't catch Mom's smirk, but I do.

"You're so negative," Pauline says in her most snippy tone.

I let her stew until we're on the ferry. Then I reach back with a pinch of semaa for her offering. The rain is warm and gentle, like a cleansing. I exit the car and lean over the railing. My prayer starts with my Spirit name and other identifiers that place me in this world and the next one. Tossing the semaa downriver, I wonder if any flakes will reach Neebish Island.

Maybe the Warrior Girl is from there. Does it matter? Neebish Island is so close to the southern end of Sugar Island. Plenty of Elders talk about crossing the ice bridge that sometimes formed between here and there. It was how they visited friends and relatives back in the day.

I end my prayer by thanking the Warrior Girl and saying that she is not forgotten.

"Miigwech, Ogichidaakwezans. Mikwendaagozi."

At the car, I start to tell Mom I'll walk home, but she interrupts before I can finish.

"Gaawiin! You're not ending up on a flyer. A wiindigoo is hunting Nish kwewag."

"What if Pauline jogs with me?" I plead. "C'mon, Mom. I been reading all day."

My sister looks up and nods enthusiastically. She is my secret weapon. Mom might refuse my solo requests, but the instant I bring Pauline on board, my ask gains credibility.

"What if we keep you on speakerphone?" Pauline offers without consulting me.

Mom says, "How about if yous jog ahead and I'll follow behind a quarter mile?"

But I'm not done negotiating.

"Done! Since you're following, you don't need to call. Miigwech, Mom," I say.

If you state your terms as a conclusion, the other party focuses on the acceptance and not the terms. Especially if you end on a positive note. Pops says when I put my mind to it, I can out-negotiate anybody. Mom says I'd make a great hostage negotiator.

Pshhhht. I'd rather captain my own fish boat.

Pauline and I jog the causeway before heading north on Westshore Drive as it follows the curve of the island. I make us alternate between jogging and walking. Auntie always invites us to run with her, but I never do. I like doing what I want: walk, jog, walk, sprint, whatever.

"You know, we'd get home faster if you ran consistently," Pauline huffs.

"Sometimes it's about the journey." I imitate Granny June's wise Elder voice.

"Fine," she snips. "If we ever get chased by a wiindigoo, I'll out-run you."

I hit back with, "Well, I'd trip you and then it wouldn't matter how fast you were."

Pauline halts, wide-eyed. "You'd really do that to me?" She bursts into tears.

"Oh, Egg," I say, pulling her into a tight hug. "You know that if a wiindigoo comes for us, we stop and grab a handful of earth to put in our mouths so we can face it together."

With that, I hold my twin's hand, and we two-step jog the rest of the way home.

After dinner, Elvis Junior follows me to my bedroom. I sit on the bed with my laptop. He's not supposed to be on our beds because he likes rolling around in animal shit. Since he smells okay, I let him lie next to me.

My laptop starts quickly, and I'm on eBay an instant later. I make an account for one Elvis Birch, Jr. Task two is done.

I begin task three by typing *Ojibwe beaded*, which prompts *Cultures & Ethnicities* as a category. I click on the suggestion and swear loudly enough for Junior to pop up.

Dozens of items—vests, bandolier bags, and belts—are listed. Many are beaded in the familiar Anishinaabe floral style. An *Antique Vintage Native American Beaded Vest Ojibwe Cree Metis* is listed for $2,750.00 or best offer. Twenty-one people are "watching" the listing. I zoom in on the pictures. It isn't a full vest, but rather two mirrored front panels edged in pale tan hide. The beadwork is a beautiful example of Anishinaabe floral art—a scrolled vine on one side of the vest, mirrored on each vest half, vibrant flowers and berries against a background of white beads. Some of the tiny glass beads are missing. The edging is worn. Loose threads are visible. The description states, *Early 1900s*.

This was someone's vest they wore to special events. Maybe even to ceremonies.

The seller answered standard questions about the item.

Condition: Used. Well, duh.

Seller Notes: Vintage, Very Good Condition for Age. Some bead loss and fraying. You'd have loss and fraying if you were over one hundred years old too, I think.

Handmade: Yes. Again, duh.

Country/Region of Manufacture: United States.

Culture: Native American / Ojibwe. Elsewhere in the description, the seller states they believe it to be Ojibwe but could possibly be Cree-Metis.

Provenance: Ownership History Not Available.

Cooper used that word in GrandRaquel's office. I look up *provenance*, which means "origin or source." Merriam-Webster says it's also known as "history of ownership."

How might a true history of the vest read? I wonder.

Provenance: This exquisite vest was created for the Migizi Clan ogimaa when he traveled with other Eagle Clan leaders representing their Anishinaabe bands. His daughter drew the design that she, her mother, aunties, and grandmothers took turns beading. They kissed him when he left for a gathering. He never returned, having been killed in a town near the gathering.

From there, the vest was sold to a wealthy woman who thought Indians were beautiful people, more intelligent than society believed. On her deathbed, she willed it to her granddaughter. But the granddaughter had dated an Indian guy once, and he wasn't as great as all the stories her grandmother had told her growing up. He didn't ride a horse or play a flute. He worked in a factory and had good days and bad days, same as any other guy. She sold the vest to a collector but didn't want her grandmother's name connected in case any relatives took her to task for selling it. (Side note: With the vest money, she traveled to Woodstock and saw Santana, Janis Joplin, and the Who perform. Drenched and hungover, she left before Jimi Hendrix took the stage, but would go on to tell her grandchildren his performance changed her life.)

The collector's family lore included a grandma with high cheekbones who was an Indian princess. When he died, his widow held a garage sale a month later to get rid of all his "junk." The vest sold to a savvy buyer who hid it in a box of clothing and offered her a hundred bucks for the lot. When Dances With Wolves *came out, the savvy buyer sold the vest for ten times what he'd paid. The most recent buyer eventually listed it on eBay after his 23andMe ancestry results showed no connection to Indigenous populations.*

Shit, maybe Pauline was right. I am a negative person.

CHAPTER 6

THURSDAY, JUNE 19TH

I wake earlier than usual. Pops is already in the pole barn with Elvis Junior. I slip into my rubber boots and walk across grass slippery from dew.

"Mino gizhep, Pops." Petting my dog, I add, "Mino gizhep, Junior."

"Mino gizhep, Indaanis."

Pops takes care of our garden with such devotion and enthusiasm. He's like a kid on Christmas morning each day. The bulletin board above his garden workshop table has various charts, a colorful hardiness-zone map, and a poster-sized diagram of our garden layout.

I pause in front of the calendar. Today is the start of day three for the thirteen repatriated squash seeds, which are in biodegradable starter pots in a tray beneath the grow lights. I told Pops the special seeds were a gift from an Elder, which is sort of truthful. Thankfully, he didn't probe me with more questions like Mom would.

"Hey, Pops, it's Grandma Cake's birthday." I never met her, but the few memories Pops has of his mother all involve her baking sweet treats. "Did she have a favorite cake of her own?"

"She passed when I was four." Pops sets a box of canning jars down on the main worktable. "I don't remember a lot from then—a birthday cake, splashing in mud puddles, her laughter. Maybe some other faint memories that come to me whenever a cake is baking."

Grandma Cake, whose real name was Pauline, grew up in Lansing, Michigan. She met Grandpa Birch when he worked on the assembly line for General Motors. After she died in childbirth with their next baby, Grandpa took Pops back to his rez near Marquette. Photographs of Grandma Cake show a beautiful Black woman with a familiar nose and lips. Her golden-brown coloring is the same as mine, which is a few shades lighter than Pops's. My skin color announces my Blackness, but it's the part of my family that I know the least about.

"I'm going to make a cake for after dinner tonight," I announce.

"Mmm. Sounds good." He pauses his inspection of the glass jars. "Molasses. I think I remember something with molasses."

As soon as I clock in, I head directly to Cooper's office.

"I'm ready to talk about my tasks anytime you're available," I say.

"Eager Padawan." He aims his lips toward the chair on the other side of his desk.

I unfold the pages I printed in our home office. Five Ojibwe antiquities for sale on eBay. I start with the vest.

"Do you think it's authentic?" Cooper asks.

I nod. "The beads are glass and not plastic. The edging looks like deer hide, the way it's worn down. But I'd want to feel it to know for sure." I hesitate before continuing, but Cooper might be the one person who would understand. "It seems weird to buy something without seeing it in person. I'd want Stormy Nodin or another traditional healer to pray over it."

Cooper stares at it but doesn't speak for a solid two minutes.

Finally, he gestures toward *Grave Injustice*.

"Tell me one thing you remember from the book," he says.

Since I expected to show him all five auction items, I scramble to collect my thoughts.

"It was cool when those college students in the 1970s applied for a federal grant to excavate a pioneer cemetery. Just to show how messed up it is. How one person's grave robber is another person's archaeologist."

Cooper and I alternate between discussing the eBay items and talking about what I recall from the book. When I get mad about things I read, he doesn't tell me not to swear.

"What really pisses me off is the part where Hopi carved figurines, sacred items, were sold to a collector who ended up destroying them to avoid getting caught. The authorities knew who did it, but no one ever got charged." Remembering more than I thought, I keep talking. "And another situation where an art dealer sold three masks he knew had been stolen from the Hopis. He only got fined a piddly amount. The buyers donated the masks to a museum instead of returning them to their tribe."

The fourth item I show him is a black ash basket and matching lid with thin braids of sweetgrass woven into the design. None of the photos included in the listing showed the underside of the basket, which is where the artist would have left their unique marking. I tell Cooper about my great-grandmother Maria's way of signing her baskets.

"What would she draw for January, the Spirit Moon?" he asks.

"Manidoo Giizis was a horizon with wispy lines for the northern lights."

Talking about my namesake makes me think about lineal descendants and NAGPRA.

"So, if I was related to the Warrior Girl, I could make a claim for her and her knife? I could get her back? Because the NAGPRA law says human remains and their associated funerary objects can be returned . . ." I try to remember the exact wording. "Upon the request of their known lineal descendants."

"The archaeologist at Mackinac State College says her bones are a thousand years old. He claims it's from before we Anishinaabeg were in the region. So he's designated her as culturally unidentifiable and, therefore, unavailable to be repatriated."

"That Leer-wah guy?" I yell.

"Yes," Cooper says. "You read the NAGPRA law about how institutions were given five years to complete their inventory and identify all human remains and cultural materials, so tribes could request to repatriate the ancestors and items that are culturally affiliated, right?"

"Yeah," I say sullenly. "Raquel the Hoarder says everything is culturally unidentifiable until she can take the time to determine whether it's ours or another tribe's."

"Dr. Fenton," Cooper corrects me, "is delaying the identification process, which slows down our request to bring our ancestors home. But Dr. Leer-wah is outright denying that we even have a claim to the Warrior Girl."

I start swearing up a storm. Cooper holds up his hand for me to pause.

"His rationale is that without more research, the college might return her to the 'wrong' tribe. And that, as new technologies are developed, he can learn more about her." He softens his voice. "Perry, I share your feelings. We can talk about this more. But, for now, how about you tell me about your fifth eBay item?"

My final item is a cradleboard. I try not to cry like when I found the listing online and began imagining its provenance. The Warrior Girl was once a binoojii held in her mother's arms, maybe even wrapped in a cradleboard like this one. Auntie had a beautiful cradleboard made for Waabun, beaded with a design that had flames, clan symbols, blueberries, and strawberries. It wasn't for everyday use, only for special occasions. It takes all my effort to speak.

"Cooper, how do you do this work when your heart feels so heavy?"

When Mom picks us up after work, I ask if we have molasses and lard at home.

"What in the world do you need lard for?" she says.

"It's Grandma Cake's birthday," I say, clicking my seat belt into place. "I found a recipe online for molasses tea cakes. It's something she might have made for Pops."

I expect her to go off on a rant about cooking with lard. This usually leads to a history lesson about government-issued commodity foods and the Zhaaganaash colonization of our Anishinaabe digestive systems and food insecurity during or after chattel slavery and how that's why Pops has diabetes. When Mom makes fry bread, it's her gluten-free, almond-milk version that is fried in coconut oil instead of lard.

Nobody asks for fry bread at our house.

Instead of going directly to the ferry launch, Mom stops at a grocery store and hands me a five-spot.

"I suppose your dad having one treat on this special occasion would be okay," she says.

I let Pauline help me with the molasses tea cakes, which means I make her stir the mixture into dough when my arm muscles have flashbacks to

Cooper's cleaning assignments. After she finishes, I have her roll out the dough so I can use the round cookie cutter to make the biscuit-like tea cakes.

The instant Pops comes in from the garden, the aroma of molasses makes his eyes water. He seems overcome with sadness, and for two seconds I wonder if the tea cakes were a good idea. Then it's as if five hundred wonderful memories wash over him all at once. He wipes his tears away and crosses the room to squeeze me in the best hug.

"Gizaagi'in, Indaanis," Pops says, kissing my forehead.

During dinner, Mom has each of us share about our day. I tell about the five auction items on eBay and the five most memorable items from the *Grave Injustice* book. I don't mean to Pauline the conversation, but Mom and Pops keep asking questions.

When we eat the molasses tea cakes, Pops tells us everything he remembers about Grandma Cake. His face lights up with each memory, photos from albums that are still in Marquette. My favorite is when he talks about her big laugh. One time, little Pops was on her lap when she was laughing and hugging him.

"I felt her laugh go through me, and I was part of her," he says.

Mom reaches over to stroke his cheek, and he holds her hand to his face.

CHAPTER 7

FRIDAY, JUNE 20TH

Our Friday seminar is canceled so the Kinomaage interns can help look for Darby O'Malley. She was last seen eight nights ago at a bar on Sugar Island with her women's hockey league teammates. When their designated driver reneged on staying sober, Darby decided to walk to an old boyfriend's hunting camp instead of ride with someone who had been drinking. The ex's trail camera didn't show anyone at the property either before or after she should have arrived. Tribal Police set up a search command center at the Nokomis-Mishomis Elder Center on the island. The dining room has poster boards displaying a map of the search area, a timeline of events, and assorted photos of Darby showing that her eyes are, indeed, aquamarine.

All interns arrive wearing jeans, long-sleeved shirts, wide-brimmed hats, and hiking boots, despite the June heat. We are part of the foot search in the woods, where the mosquitoes and black flies are ruthless. Tribal Police already searched the roads and culverts between the bar and the hunting camp. Now the theory is that

Darby may have attempted a shortcut through the woods and run into trouble—perhaps falling somewhere or encountering a bear.

Each team is paired with a tribal cop. Team Misfit Toys—along with our honorary member, Elvis Junior—is joined by Officer What-The Sam Hill. We carpool to the hunting camp where Darby was headed. Our assignment is to hike from the camp to the bar.

What-The has a plastic storage bag with an unwashed T-shirt of Darby's for Elvis Junior to sniff every so often. My dog understands the assignment, bypassing a rotting deer and bear scat that he would otherwise have rolled in. Junior runs ahead, sniffing the ground and peeing a few drops to mark his territory, before returning to Lucas's side.

Using my old-timey compass, I lead our team as we navigate the trails around the hunting camp. I draw on the map, sketching various landmarks.

"How'd you learn all this stuff?" asks Erik.

"My parents taught me to track," I say, pointing out coyote scat in the middle of a trail.

"Me too," Lucas chimes in. "They taught me, too."

"Plus, I go collecting medicines with my auntie."

"What if your family didn't have those skills?" Erik wonders.

I answer. "The old cultural camp used to have weekend workshops where you could learn to smoke fish, tan hides, or tap maple trees and boil the sap into syrup, depending on the time of year. They even had a winter survival camp for building shelters and learning how to conserve your body heat. Stuff like that."

"That's the place we had orientation," Lucas reminds Erik.

"Yeah. So, is there a new cultural camp?" Erik asks.

"Yeah," I answer. "On the mainland. Behind the powwow grounds. But it feels different—like, tamer." Lucas nods his head in agreement.

"Why would they do your orientation there?" What-The says. "I heard Council's gonna tear down the old cultural camp this fall."

"No cell signal. Interns couldn't be on their phones," I say.

"Did the missing woman come from a family like yours?" Erik wonders.

"Don't know," I say. "She was from a different tribal community."

"Darby moved here to play hockey at Lake State," What-The answers. "I don't think she graduated. Works at the casino. Hooks up with guys *and* girls." He sounds scandalized.

"Holaay! Does every missing Nish kwe have her sex life investigated?" I ask.

"S—s—sorry," What-The stammers. "I didn't mean it like that." He flushes pink.

"Speaking of hooking up," Shense says, "I gotta pump. This hike is releasing my milk."

What-The's blush turns fuchsia against his barely tan skin.

Shense sits on a log and pulls a battery-operated breast pump from her backpack.

"Ah, sweet relief," she says after the pump begins to hum. Her smile is wide enough to reveal her rebellious tooth that goes its own way.

"Hiking makes the milk flow?" I ask.

"Yeah. That, and when the baby cries. And when Claire Barbeau's voice gets squeaky."

When Shense is done pumping, I announce that break time is over.

"I'm the one in charge, hey?" What-The says.

"Of course you are," I say.

At the end of the day, we gather back at the Elder Center. No one found any sign of Darby O'Malley in the woods. Some of the college interns make plans to meet for drinks. When Lucas gets a call to pick up his little sister, Lola, in town, Erik offers to drive Pauline, Junior, and me home. I accept just as my sister exits the bathroom. Her eyes are red from crying.

"Erik's giving us a ride," I say, opening the car door to offer her the front seat.

Pauline takes the back seat instead, sitting behind Erik and staring out the window.

"You want to come over tomorrow?" Erik asks. His giant Adam's apple bobs as he gulps.

"And what? Clean rooms?" I scratch Junior's back while he sits on my lap.

"No," Erik says with a laugh. "I'll be done by two at the latest. We could go somewhere."

I glance at Pauline. Although her left side is hidden from view, she brings each pulled strand of hair to inspect the root before flicking it away. We are at DEFCON 1.

"I'll let you know," I say when he pulls into our driveway.

Pauline ignores Junior and rushes toward the house. I catch up with her.

"I don't want to talk about it," she says before I can ask anything.

"Please, Egg?" I watch for any softening of her face or stride.

She halts and turns to me. Her glare is unbridled fury.

"Aunt Daunis is an interfering bitch."

I'm shocked. We do not talk that way about Auntie.

"If you must know what happened," she says through gritted teeth, "get my weed gummies and meet me in the clubhouse." She makes a beeline for the tree fort.

Junior doesn't know who to follow. I point my lips toward Pauline. He trails after her.

I dash into her bedroom and retrieve the plastic bag of edibles from a hollowed-out copy of *Great Expectations*. My sister self-medicates her anxiety with weed candy. Since she also has anxiety about getting caught with it, I'm the one who buys for her and carries it around.

Not hearing Pops anywhere in the house, I find him in the garden, harvesting the last of the asparagus. I shout for him and wave.

"Your mom's working late, so she'll grab some pizzas on the way home," he yells back.

I jog across the yard. Junior waits at the bottom of the ladder to the tree fort.

"Skoden," I say, which he understands as *Let's go, then*.

He jumps so I can hold him on one hip like a toddler. With my free arm, I climb the ladder to our clubhouse. Pauline has already grabbed an old blanket from the watertight storage bin. I set down Junior to sniff the perimeter of the clubhouse.

"Here." I toss her the weed candy.

She quickly chews two gummy lumps before offering me one, knowing I always decline.

"You want?" We go through our usual routine. When I shake my head, she says, "Of course, *you* don't need any help relaxing."

"You worry enough for both of us." I cut to the chase. "What's got you so worked up?"

Pauline accompanied the chief to all his meetings this week. "He was impressed with my background research for the meeting yesterday morning with one of the trustees from Mackinac State College about turning it into a tribal college."

"Holaay, the Tribe wants to take over the college?"

"The trustee, Grant Edwards, brought the idea to the chief," Pauline clarifies. "Anyways, since it was lunchtime, Chief Manitou got burgers at the west side drive-in. He parked alongside the river so we could watch the freighters heading into the locks. Because there is *nothing wrong* with doing that."

"So, what happened with Auntie?" I ask.

"She parks next to us, waves, and comes over all full of smiles. Says hi. Asks how I like working for Chief Manitou. Blah, blah, blah." Revisiting anger makes my sister's voice rise. "Then she asks him about his car. Perry, since when is it a crime to own a Mercedes-Benz? She drives a fancy Range Rover, so I didn't know what her beef was. Then she brags how her car can fit so much stuff, especially in the back. And how good it is off-road." She rises to pace around the tree house. "You know what she was doing, don't you?" she practically spits.

I do, but Pauline continues as if I don't.

"She was hinting that he'd get blanket-partied if he did any-thing inappropriate with me. She may as well have come right out and said"—here my sister imitates Auntie—"'I will roll you up in a blanket, throw you in my spacious trunk, and drive you somewhere remote on the island so me and my friends can kick the shit out of you.'"

We've both heard whispers about blanket parties, but this is the first time one of us is talking about it as something that could happen for real.

"Everything was normal for the rest of the day, so I didn't think anything more about what she said." Pauline sniffles. "I should've known she wouldn't let it go."

She plunks down next to me. Her head rests in her hands.

"Chief Manitou picked *me*. Not for any dirty perv reason, like Auntie thinks, but because I'm the smartest and I work harder than anyone. I am the best intern." Pauline is sobbing now. "At least, I *was* the best. Claire met with me today and said I was being reassigned effective immediately because the Tribal Police Department needs help with the missing-person stuff. Meddling Auntie interfered with my job just like she made you work for that fucking weirdo at the museum. Pulling strings like we're her puppets."

I put my arm around Pauline while she cries. Junior rests his head on her lap and makes a sympathy whine. We sit like that until we hear Mom's car turn in to the driveway. When we climb down the ladder, I slow my pace behind my sister.

Here's the thing: Pauline isn't wrong. Auntie did exert her power over us. But that doesn't mean Auntie was wrong. I know my sister cannot fathom Chief Manitou doing anything sketchy with her. But if Auntie got a pervy vibe from the chief and Pauline being in a car together, then maybe she was right to strike fear into the guy.

Something bad happened to Auntie when we were little. Her best friend, Lily, who was Lucas's older sister, died. But no one talks about it to us. The high school hockey coach was involved. Uncle Levi went to jail. Stormy, too, for a little while. It was about drugs, but there's probably more to the story. There always is.

CHAPTER 8

SATURDAY, JUNE 21ST

The Warrior Girl stands next to me in the pole barn. We look at the seeds in their starter pots beneath the grow lights. She's taller than me, and leaner in a way that comes from a hard life where food is not guaranteed. Her buckskin coverings are plain and practical. She sizes me up. Her eyes pause at my tumble of hair—jet black like hers, but thicker, curlier. How would she describe it? Has she ever seen someone with skin like mine? I look down at my sleep shorts and T-shirt. My clothing isn't what holds her attention; it's my curves and softness. My road map of injuries pales in comparison to hers. I show her my crooked pinkie, hoping to impress her. She scoffs. Her eyes linger on my forehead—no, on my eyebrow nicked from a broken branch that would've skewered my eyeball if I'd been an inch or two taller when it happened. I wish the scar had a more interesting story, like a battle wound, instead of playing Castle with Pauline and Lucas. She stares at it. Her hand reaches for it. The instant she is about to touch it, Elvis Junior barks. She's gone before he reaches me.

Pops makes a huge breakfast for day one of the asparagus-canning weekend. Our large garden provides for us year-round, thanks to canning and freezing the fruits and vegetables we harvest. Sugar Island has a shorter growing season than downstate, but Pops enhances our garden with indoor starters, grow lights, and hoop houses.

I'm working on my second helping of homemade biscuits and sausage gravy when Pauline kicks me beneath the table. She mouths, *You promised.*

I'm supposed to find out if Auntie is coming over. It's my sister's turn to help Mom and Pops with canning asparagus. But if Auntie—who Pauline has decided to shun for the rest of the summer—is joining them, then I'll swap turns with my twin. Pauline will do my laundry also, in exchange for swapping with her.

"Hey, Mom. Is Auntie coming over to help?"

Pauline grimaces at my directness. She would've danced around the question all morning.

"No. Daunis and TJ are taking the boys to the water park in Mount Pleasant," Mom says.

"Separate hotel rooms?" I ask, thinking about Shense's *just friends* comment last week.

"Wouldn't know. None of my business," Mom says pointedly.

"Well, she never talks about Waab's dad," I say, sneaking half a biscuit to Junior. "And she does spend a lot of time with TJ and his kid." I had always assumed it was because Waab and Teevo are close in age.

Mom shrugs. "If you want to know, ask her. It's her story to tell."

My sister rolls her eyes before leaving the table.

"What's up with her?" Mom says, watching Pauline go upstairs.

"It's her story to tell." I mimic the shrug as well.

Pops's mouth twitches in a hint of a smile before he speaks.

"Why don't you keep that mooch inside with you?" Pops gives Junior some head scritches. "It's still raining hard, and we don't need a wet dog shaking himself around us."

Keeping him inside is no easy task. My dog loves rolling in the mud even more than rolling around in animal shit. Trapped in my bedroom, he whines for the nice twin to rescue him.

I retrieve the book Cooper assigned for next week: *Repatriation Reader: Who Owns American Indian Remains?* It's edited by Devon A. Mihesuah. She's Choctaw, an enrolled citizen.

My heart swells with pride—that an Indigenous woman edited a book about NAGPRA. She got to call the shots, picking other experts who shared her desire to talk about bringing our cultural artifacts back where they belong. I don't know her, but I'm proud of her. Ignoring Junior's sporadic whining, I eagerly dive in.

I read for a few hours, pausing only to grab an umbrella and take Junior outside to do his business. He's ticked off that I put the leash on him. I know his tactics—look for any opportunity and make a run for freedom. Pauline falls for his shenanigans, but I don't.

When I take him out for his third zhiishiig of the day, a text comes through, buzzing in my back pocket as I pull Junior away from a waterlogged animal carcass. Between the umbrella and the leash, I don't have a third hand to grab my phone. I tether Junior's leash to my rubber boot and check my text messages.

> ERIK: Finished cleaning early. You doing anything?
> ME: Hanging out with my dog in the rain.
> ERIK: Want to come over?
> ME: No wheels.

When Mom and Pops found out I had been speeding before the accident, they grounded me from driving until Auntie is repaid in full. Pauline is allowed to drive Pops's truck, because she wasn't at fault. But me? Ten weeks of no driving. That mama bear truly fucked up my summer.

> ERIK: I could get you. Go to movie theater? I haven't seen the
> new X-Men yet. Or How to Train Your Dragon 2.
> ME: I saw X-Men DOFP with Lucas but wouldn't mind

WHUMP.

I'm flat on my back. The leash is wrapped around my ankles. Elvis Junior jumps on me with muddy paws and a trickster grin.

"Why you little . . ." I halt mid-scold to finish my text to Erik.

> ME: Hey. Whatever we do, I gotta bring my dog. He's too clever
> to be left alone.

By the time Erik arrives, I've given Junior a bath and cleaned myself up as well. I greet him on the front porch, holding tightly to Junior's leash.

"I can't get over how cool your tree fort is," Erik says, turning to look at it. He brushes his loose curls away from his face. "Is that what your dad does for a living? Build things?"

"Nah, he used to be an engineer on a freighter. But he had to take a medical retirement because of his diabetes. So he stays home and takes care of us." I point my lips toward the pole barn. "My parents and Pauline are canning asparagus all weekend. Our garden's behind the garage." I lead Erik inside the house.

"You remember me, good boy?" Erik scratches behind Junior's ears. When we reach the great room, Erik stops in place. "Whoa. Check out that view. You're that close to Canada?"

"Yeah." I motion toward the staircase. "My parents' room is upstairs, and me and my sister's bedrooms are down here." He follows me downstairs.

"Whoa," he says again.

The family room has a rowing machine, treadmill, and home gym with another waterfront view beyond the walk-out patio beneath the expansive great-room deck above.

"Yeah. My parents have been on a fitness kick ever since Pops's diabetes started giving him problems. We all work out to keep Pops on track."

There isn't much to see in my bedroom except for the huge bulletin board filled with photos of my fishing escapades over the years. Lucas's crooked grin is in a bunch, even when he and I were little and didn't have a full mouth of teeth between us.

"You been friends with Lucas a long time," Erik comments.

"Yeah. He moved here, like, ten years ago. He had an older sister named Lily who was best friends with my auntie. Lily died, and that's when Auntie Daunis became Lucas's auntie too." I sit at my desk and open my laptop. "Hey, I gotta check out this one auction on eBay. It's kind of for work." Erik watches over my shoulder as I log into eBay. "There's a birchbark basket, and the auction ends at one."

"Did you bid on it?"

"No, but I wanna see how much it sells for." I explain: "My boss wants me to learn how easy it is for our art and even sacred objects to get sold. I'm supposed to let him know if I come across stuff the Tribe should know about. In case they should bid on it, I guess."

"You could just set up an alert and get notified of anything," Erik says.

"What, like on eBay? I haven't quite figured out all the account settings and whatnot."

"Yeah. You could also set up a Google alert," he says.

"Cool," I say, rising from my desk chair for him to sit down. "Show me."

"What do you want to keep an eye on?" Erik sits. "I need keywords, descriptors."

He types as quickly as I speak: *Ojibwe* with an *e*, *Ojibwa* with an *a*, *Ojibway* with an *ay*, *Chippewa*, *Anishinaabe*, *birchbark*, *black ash basket*, *quill box*, *bandolier bag*, *drum*, and *cradleboard*.

"I'm setting up different alerts. Some with the category as a screening factor, but a few with broader search parameters in case the seller listing the item doesn't quite know what they've got and lists it more generically."

"Holaay," I say. "You got skills."

Erik's cheeks redden as he continues typing.

"You're all set on eBay. I'm setting up a Gmail account for your Google alert notifications. Here," he says, moving over. "It's asking for your primary email address as a security backup."

I enter my information. He looks away while I type, which makes me laugh.

"What's so funny?" he asks.

"You giving me privacy. I'm sure you could hack into my accounts easy-peasy."

Now it's Erik's turn to cheese a grin. The room fills with the clacking sounds of words being typed at warp speed. After finishing his task, Erik goes back to the tab with the eBay auction item I was watching.

"Sold for a hundred and seventy-five dollars," he says. "Don't know if the buyer overpaid or got a deal."

I peer at the screen. The birchbark basket is the size of a small wastebasket. The artist carved delicate maple leaf shapes into the pale bark. The cutouts reveal a layer beneath that's the dark orange underside of the birchbark facing out.

"They got a steal," I say quietly.

Erik goes back to the laptop, giving me privacy to wipe away angry tears. After a discreet minute, his posture snaps to attention.

"Perry. Look at this." He points to the screen. "The seller is from St. Ignace. That's, what, less than an hour away? His name is Frank Lockhart. He has other items listed on eBay. And a business called Teepees-n-Trinkets." He quickly finds the address on Google Maps. His voice goes as high as I've ever heard. "They're open today until seven p.m."

"Road trip," I announce.

Junior, who's been napping on my bed, perks up at the words. He's all in.

My family is taking a lunch break when Erik and I go upstairs. Pauline empties a heaping ladleful of wild rice and hominy soup from the slow cooker into her bowl. She uses her soup spoon to dig for more chunks of buffalo meat. Erik's Adam's apple bobs as he salivates.

"Let's eat something before we hit the road," I say, nudging him toward my family. "Hey, everyone, this is Erik. He's part of the summer internship program, and his parents bought the Freighters Motel across from the Locks." I raise an eyebrow as Pops inspects my new friend. "Erik, this is my dad, Art Birch."

"Nice to meet you, sir," Erik says, holding out his hand.

Pops raises an eyebrow at the deep bass of Erik's voice and shakes hands a bit too long.

Seated at the dining table, Pauline giggles between spoonfuls of soup.

"I'm Teddie Firekeeper, Perry's mom. It's nice to meet you, Erik . . ." She waits for him to provide a last name.

I roll my eyes while preparing two bowls of soup. Mom does internet searches on every boy who dates Pauline. I didn't realize she would treat my intern friend the same way.

"Miller. Erik Miller. We moved from Escalante at the end of the school year."

I motion for Erik to sit next to Pauline.

"What are yous doing this afternoon?" my nosy sister asks.

Erik addresses my parents. "If it's all right with you both, we'd like to take Elvis Junior for a ride." He gulps nervously even before his first spoonful of soup.

Wait. They're all acting like he's *my* boyfriend.

"We're going to St. Ignace to check out a Native art store. It's research for work," I say.

"The good store or the tourist trap?" Mom asks.

"I don't know. Maybe both?"

Pops's silence must make Erik nervous, because soup dribbles off his trembling spoon.

After we rinse our bowls and put them in the dishwasher, Erik thanks my parents for lunch and reiterates his *Pleased to meet you* statements. While he heads to his truck, I attach the leash to Junior's collar. Pauline joins me in the mudroom, handing me a blanket.

Ugghh. Not her too.

"Why you giving me a snag rag?"

Pauline laughs. "Holaay. It's for Elvis Junior so he won't shed all over Erik's back seat. But feel free to use it for . . . whatever. On your date." She winks while I fight the urge to twist her bun of black hair like a doorknob.

The rain has let up. At least Junior is acting normal. He's happy to go for a ride and sniff the air. To him it's just an ordinary ride in a truck.

Because this is not a date. Right?

"This is not a date, right?" I say, once we're on the ferry. Erik avoids looking at me, but I see the way his cheeks turn red.

"Do you want it to be?"

Pauline would mull over her answer, practicing it in her head, and only after considering how much she's willing to risk would she reply. My twin would then agonize over her decision, convinced she chose unwisely. That ain't me.

"I don't know if I like you without the rest of Team Misfit Toys."

Erik whips his head my way to gauge whether I'm being sarcastic or serious.

"You don't pull any punches, do you," he says.

"What does that even mean? I punch plenty."

"That you don't hold anything back, figuratively speaking, with your verbal punches."

"I'm a punch-first-and-the-rest-will-fall-in-line type of person," I say unapologetically.

"Perry Pulls-No-Punches." Erik's deep voice sounds amused.

"Pissed-off Perry Punches Plenty," I say. My dog adds a half-hearted howl from the back seat. "Elvis Junior agrees with me." While we both laugh, I consider that if this does turn out to be our first date, it's going really well.

I give directions for Erik to take back roads to St. Ignace instead of the highway.

"Plus, it's always good to have an escape route," I add. "You have any in Escalante?"

"Yeah," he says slowly. His expression is guarded.

"I was just joking. You really had an escape route in a town in the middle of nowhere?"

He shrugs. "Yeah. Made some enemies."

"Turn right," I say. "Enemies how?"

"I got kicked out of school. Got my GED. Laid low till we moved here."

Before I can ask the first of many questions swirling in my mind, a robust fart comes from the back seat. The smell hits my nose a nanosecond before Erik yelps.

"Did he eat a skunk?" Erik rolls down his window. He alternates between gulping air and laughing. "I think I swallowed some of it. My eyes are watering."

"Don't blame my dog for your gas," I tease. "You might want to pull over so I can take him for a dump and dash."

We stand next to each other while my dog takes care of business on the side of the road. I close my eyes in the afternoon light, letting the heat soak into my body. Even if I won't get my usual fishing tan this summer, it's nice to remember how the sun shows its love for my bronze skin.

"You know the mascot for Escalante school district is the Eskimo?" Erik asks.

My jaw drops. "I didn't know. That's so . . . fucked up."

"Well, I hacked into my school's website." He glances at his black Converse sneakers. When he looks up, his blue eyes sparkle. "Everywhere it named the mascot, I added the words *a racially insensitive nickname and image*."

I'm impressed. "You got expelled for stating facts?"

"Officially expelled for unauthorized access to school property. I got charged with computer use in an attempt to defraud, and interference with an educational institution. My parents settled with the school district, who didn't want news about the incident to go viral."

"Erik, you're a bona fide hacker," I say while leading Junior back inside the car.

"I'm a white hat," he clarifies. "I put my infiltration skills to work for the greater good."

"Are black hats the bad hackers?" I click my seat belt. "Don't you think those terms are racist? White, good; black, bad?"

Erik pauses, key in hand. His thoughts tell a story—surprise, denial, embarrassment, consideration, realization.

"I never thought of it before, Perry. But, now that I have, I want to be . . . mindful."

I like Erik. The way he took in a new idea and spoke with care . . . it's appealing.

"You have got to be kidding me," Erik says, as we approach Teepees-n-Trinkets.

A literal teepee—a twenty-feet-tall painted structure—is between the parking lot and the road. Next to it, there are life-size paintings of cartoon "Indians" with faces cut out so tourists can stand behind and peer through the oval openings for a photo opportunity.

"More like Stereotypes and Souvenirs," I comment.

Erik snorts a laugh. His round cheeks go red. I poke one side with my finger.

"So pretty," I tease. "Like ripe crab apples."

"You really have no filter, do you?" Erik says, still blushing.

I wrap Junior's leash to a shady tree next to the car before we enter the store.

"If there's a cigar-store Indian in this place, you owe me an ice cream cone," I say.

He holds the door open. "How do I know you didn't scope out the place ahead of time?"

"Pshhht. My parents would never bring us here."

Erik points to items he finds especially ridiculous: headdresses with brightly colored feathers, a bow-and-arrow set with the structural integrity of a toothpick, and a feathered mandala depicting a busty Native woman in a buckskin bikini.

Our fingers touch when we both reach for a purple glitter dream catcher. Neither of us pulls back. His slender fingertips are soft.

"You'd be a good pickpocket," I say, further evidence that I have no filter.

Erik throws his head back and laughs. I feel it, deep and warm, in my own lungs.

We pass a cigar-store Indian on our way toward the back of the store. The carved statue is as tall as Erik. Its painted colors have faded.

"You owe me ice cream," I say.

"That's fair." He pats the wooden shoulder. It's a compassionate gesture, as if to apologize for the idiotic things people have done while posing next to the statue.

We pause at the tall, square display cabinets that bracket the doorway to the museum room. A thick layer of dust adds an antique patina to the items inside. Each glass shelf has a folded index card stating: NOT FOR SALE.

"Look at this, Erik. They've got a ceremonial pipe," I say. "Holaay. It's not supposed to be assembled outside of ceremony." I squat to see what they've got on the lower shelves.

Erik lists the contents of the shelf below the pipe. "I see a basket shaped like a strawberry, and a bunch of arrowheads." The last thing he says sounds far away. I can feel my chest tighten.

Erik pats my shoulder like he did to the cigar-store Indian.

"Hey, Perry, what's the matter?"

I sit with my knees pulled up to my chest, forcing myself to expand the shallow breaths into slower, deeper, calming ones. My hands are cupped over my mouth. I can't take my eyes away from the woven basket no bigger than a coffee cup. Three rows of the black ash splints are twisted to form curls around the basket. I feel for his arm when he sits next to me.

"I think that's my great-grandma's basket." My muffled voice is barely audible.

Since it's on the next to the lowest shelf, I lie down to view the bottom of the basket.

It's hers. Maria Paquette, 1940. She drew a raspberry. My great-grandmother finished the basket in July. Miskomini Giizis is the Raspberry Moon.

"Do you want to see if you can hold it?" Erik asks.

"No," I say sharply. "The more they know, the more valuable it becomes."

I rise quickly, not wanting to draw any attention to myself. Having been followed around stores too often in my life, I scan for security cameras and any lingering gazes of the workers. One dark dome is mounted above the checkout counter. There isn't anything in the corners of the room. The windows have no unusual hardware or wires. It's a dinky, unsophisticated store.

Would I take the basket if I could? Absolutely! It should be with my family.

Erik and I tour the "museum," which consists of a skewed history of the area. Jesuit priests saving us pagan heathens. Pshhht. As if they wouldn't have starved without our help. I mean, truly, who saved who?

We approach a row of moccasins at eye level behind glass. Toddler size at one end, two pairs of adult moccasins at the other end, and a variety of sizes in between. A family's deer-hide moccasins on display.

"Whoa," Erik comments. "Every age. Every size."

I know why Mom and Pops never brought us here. A sign says the moccasins belong to an entire family who died together, were buried somewhere local, and were excavated in 1976. The family was AN INDIAN BRAVE AND HIS INDIAN MAIDEN AND THEIR CHILDREN. There's no mention of their remains.

I tell Erik, "These moccasins were taken off of ancestors in their graves."

He looks horror-struck. I take deep breaths before continuing.

"If they had been discovered today, there'd be a protocol for how to take care of their bones and associated funerary objects." More breaths. *Calm yourself, Perry.* "These were found in the 1970s. Before NAGPRA. That's the law for returning ancestors and their belongings to the tribe." I think about the eBay listings. "It's open season on anything found before 1990." I look around the dusty museum, which is the same size as my bedroom. "Private collections like this are only covered by the law for what they collect after 1990, Erik. That's why the owner can list these things on eBay."

There is so much crammed into the space. I could spend an entire day cataloging this inventory. Instead, everything in my body screams to get the hell out of here. Before they put me in a glass case marked INDIAN MAIDEN, CIRCA 2014. Because what's the difference between one set of Indian bones and another? Just years on a label, really.

"I've got to get out of here," I say, voice shaking from rage, horror, and panic.

On my way out of the room, three little boys circle me. They whoop and holler on toy horses. For an instant I'm transported into a bad Western. Wait . . . are there any *good* Westerns? Why do these wannabe cowboys assume they're the heroes?

One boy plows into me. It must have been on purpose, because how could he not see me? He bounces off my unyielding body and into the display case. The glass tower tilts in slow motion. Contents shift sideways as it falls. Glass shatters upon impact.

The boy lands in its destruction. He cries. His outstretched palm is bleeding.

"Hey, it's okay. It's a small cut. You'll be okay," I say, squatting down to comfort him. His eyes are big and green. Tears make his lashes stick together. Maybe someday he'll woo the world with them eyes. But right now he's a pissant hellion, creating havoc in a store after his ma's told him a dozen times to settle down.

My great-grandmother's basket is next to him.

Then it's in the pocket of my hoodie as I help the boy rise.

I leave the store with Erik as the boy's mom demands to speak with the manager.

I pick Mackinac Island Fudge. Erik gets mint chocolate chip. The ice cream place even has dog-friendly frozen treats. Junior is delighted.

My breathing has returned to normal. Erik watches me. I wonder if he is considering me as girlfriend material. Pauline is the one who dates, who has a rotation of guys begging to take her out. No one's ever really caught my eye for long, and not just because of Mom's constant reminders that everyone from Sugar Island is related.

The warmth on my arm closest to Erik's is new but not unwelcome. I imagine the type of angst that Pauline channels and apply it to Erik. *Is this a date? I like her, but do I* like *like her? Do I want to take things to the next level?*

Does Erik think I'm pretty? Pops says my eyes sparkle like the north sky on a clear night.

Pauline says boys are scared of me. Good, I say. Weeds out the weak. Who wants that?

"Did you take the basket," Erik asks without inflection. He already knows.

"Yes." I am many things, but I am not a liar.

"How could you?" He is upset.

"Because it was right there," I say, retrieving it from my hoodie pocket. She finished it during Miskomini Giizis. The Raspberry Moon is a time for big changes. Flowers and fruit emerge past thorns in preparation for the upcoming harvest.

Erik stares at me. His eyes have gone dark. All shadows. No light.

"You put me at risk," he says. He pushes his green ice cream aside. "I'm on probation. If I'm pulled over for so much as a parking ticket before I turn nineteen, the school can bring up the original charges. My parents would need to mortgage the motel for attorney fees." He looks at me. "Did you even think about the consequences if you got caught?"

"No," I say.

"What about me? Your accomplice?"

I tell the truth. "I didn't think about anything except getting that basket."

"Perry." My name leaves him in a whoosh. Not as an endearment, but as disappointment.

My hands ball into fists. Rage builds, gaining steam with each breath. Junior stands, suddenly alert next to me.

"You know what? Screw you," I say.

His head whips back like I've smacked him.

"How many baskets and moccasins are in dinky museums like that one? Or in someone's house? Grave robbers and private collectors owning our ancestors and the objects they were buried with." I point toward Mackinac State College on the hill. "Or in a cardboard box in a professor's dusty office? Someone who will *never* give them back." I refuse to cry. I won't look at Erik. I return the basket to my pocket. "I could not leave her basket behind."

My ice cream melts into thick white soup with tiny cubes of brownie dodging my spoon.

"I guess we should go home," I say finally.

"Yeah," Erik says flatly. "I guess we should."

WEEK THREE

Our ancestors' bodies and funerary objects have been written on with markers and pens, handled, and studied by professors, researchers, and students for far too long. Their bodies, laid out in cardboard boxes, on metal shelves, is your university's shameful reminder of the disrespect for human dignity . . . We ask, would you want your grandmothers and grandfathers to be treated in this way?

—Joseph Sowmick and Shannon Martin, "Remarks from Saginaw Chippewa Indian Tribe to the University of Michigan Board of Regents," March 20, 2008

CHAPTER 9

THURSDAY, JUNE 26TH

The next week flies by. I don't text Erik. He doesn't text me. Pauline tries fishing for information, but there isn't anything to say. It wasn't a date. It was nothing.

I arrive early to work on Thursday morning. Cooper and I have been preparing all week for a visit by the board of trustees and repatriation team from Mackinac State College. According to my Jedi ogimaa, their previous college president had a background in anthropology and viewed NAGPRA as 'putting politics ahead of science.' The tribe's request to repatriate the thirteen ancestors was ignored for the entire length of his presidency. Apparently, with a new college president, they want to show they can play nice and will "work with us" in the return of our sacred items and ancestors. The fact that the tribe will now entertain funding requests from Mackinac County, making the college eligible to receive grants from us, is just a coincidence.

But first Cooper wants to discuss my weekly reading assignment: *Repatriation Reader.*

"Well, what did you think of the twelve categories of viewpoints Dr. Mihesuah describes in the introduction?" he begins.

"Eleven viewpoints too many," I say.

He chuckles. It's not his asthma-wheezing *heh-heh-heh*, but I'll take what I can get.

"Seriously," I continue. "Stealing our bones is wrong. Always was, always will be. The only point of view that matters is the one by those of us who want our ancestors back."

"I don't disagree with you." He rubs his chin. "But knowledge is power, especially during negotiations. We need to know their perspective and be fluent in their language."

"I'm a fan of five-fingered negotiations," I say, imitating a punch.

Cooper's smile doesn't reach his eyes.

"You'd never be part of another reclamation, Perry," he admonishes. "You'd set back any efforts to bring our ancestors home. Every action has an equal and opposite reaction."

His last sentence makes me think about Erik. Did I realize that getting my great-grandma's basket back would cost me my friendship, or whatever, with Erik?

"What if it cost them?" I ask Cooper.

"Who dem?" he asks in his rez accent.

"The grave robbers and wannabe Indiana Joneses. The scientists and museum people. What if it cost them something? One of their ancestors for each one of ours?"

He thinks about it for longer than I expect him to.

"What would we gain by that?" he finally says.

"It would be an equal and opposite reaction." My voice rises. "The knowledge they claim is so important . . . would it be worth giving up their own great-great-grandparents' bones?"

"Is there any justification for using bones as currency?"

"No," I say sullenly. "But they took from us, and all it cost them was tuition."

His patience frustrates me. I'd rather he yell or tell me I'm a goof-ball. Instead he continues to rub his nonexistent chin hairs.

"Remember Dr. Fenton?" he finally says.

"Raquel the Hoarder?"

At least that gets a *heh-heh-heh* out of Cooper.

"Dr. Fenton wants to sit next to you at lunch today," he says.

"Why?" I say, wrinkling my nose as if Elvis Junior did a nasty boogid.

Cooper shrugs. "Maybe she's gathering information about us for negotiations."

This brings up something that has bothered me since the hoarder house.

"Cooper, why did you tell Dr. Fenton about the otter medicine bag?"

"It's in *The Mishomis Book*, by Eddie Benton-Banai," he says with another shrug. "Any basic literature review or Google search would find it. It didn't cost us anything to part with the information, but it fostered the spirit of negotiation."

"I suppose," I say, unconvinced. "But, speaking of books, can you give me the list of everything you want me to read this summer? I want to buy my own copies to write in them."

Cooper shudders. "You write in books?"

"Pshhht. How else am I supposed to make notes about the readings?"

"Maybe a notebook or, perhaps, a leather portfolio?" He smiles. "Now, what do you say about forging a connection with Dr. Fenton?"

"Well, boss, I'm on the clock, so I'll do whatever you assign."

He regards me. "Why not do the right thing for the right reason?"

"Does it matter, if the outcome is the same?" I ask.

"I think so, Perry-Padawan," he says. "I think intention matters."

After we arrange the library tables into a large circle, I go outside to offer semaa and collect giizhik for our shoes. Back inside, I hand two flat sprigs of cedar to Cooper.

"Ah, miigwech, Wiidookaagewikwezans," he says.

I like that nickname, Helper Girl, even more than Perry-Padawan.

Next I check on the meal preparations before our guests arrive. Part of my duties earlier this week included recruiting community volunteers to cook food for the event. The Paquette sisters' fry bread is in a tinfoil-covered warming pan. Other volunteers have dropped off slow cookers of chili and a half dozen varieties of soup. Miss Manitou complains about the extension cords. She calls the casino to bring an extra-long floor mat or else someone will trip and sue us.

I see a familiar tiny figure near the food table.

"Aaniin, Granny June," I say to Lucas's great-grandmother.

As soon as Miss Manitou's back is turned, Granny June motions for me to move her cast-iron pot to the end of the food table. I don't need to lift the lid to know it's her baked beans, cooked down to a dark, molasses-sweetened paste, with hidden jewels of salt pork.

"You put the best food last." She attempts a whisper. "That way only the smart ones who kept room on their plates will get any."

"Like a reward." I laugh.

"Bizaan ayaan," she scolds, flapping her twiggy fingers for me to hush.

I have just enough time to change my clothes and shoes. My ribbon skirt is a soft brown floral print with the bottom third wrapped in inch-wide satin ribbons in shades of blush pink, light brown, and ivory. The silky brown top matches my skin. Pauline offered her shimmery-gold ballerina flats, but I opt for my shiny black Doc Martens. I do add pale pink lip gloss and the delicate gold necklace Auntie lent me when she talked me out of wearing my MERCILESS INDIAN SAVAGE T-shirt.

"But it's a quote from the Declaration of Independence," I told her. "It's a conversation starter."

"That's a longer conversation than lunch and a tour," Auntie said.

Cooper reminds everyone—including Tribal Council and their three remaining interns—that our goal is to welcome our guests and foster opportunities for the Tribe and Mack State to work together. I don't hear anything else he says because Erik arrives from the casino with the floor mat to cover the spaghetti network of extension cords behind the food table. He's bent over with his back to me, so he doesn't see me staring.

"Dr. Fenton, it's nice to see you again," I say when our guests arrive by casino shuttle bus, grateful for this distraction. My handshake is firm but not combative, just like Pauline made me practice.

Dr. Fenton and her colleagues rubberneck the tribal library like curious owls. I don't get it; this place has been open to the public for four years. Maybe it's like when Mom yells for us to come to dinner and says, "Did yous need an engraved invitation?" I guess they did.

I invite Dr. Fenton to sit next to me. Another professor joins us, sitting on my other side. It's the redheaded Monopoly guy who showed us the Warrior Girl. Dr. Leer-wah. He looks just as stuffy as before, wearing a suit even though it's eighty degrees today.

The event agenda, which I typed and had printed on special paper, begins with a welcome by Chief Manitou. He does his usual greeting, starting by introducing himself in the language, followed by a few brief sentences thanking the Mackinac State College governing trustees and academic leaders for coming.

An Elder says a prayer in Ojibwemowin, blessing the food and the hands that prepared it.

Cooper speaks next, introducing himself before addressing our guests from the college.

"When we gather for a meal, we invite our Elders to prepare their plates first. We honor their sacrifices, for all they've endured and what they carry for us in their memories—their conscious memories shared as stories and those blood memories that flow through them to the next generation. I'd also like to invite my intern, Perry Firekeeper-Birch, to fix a plate for our ancestors and those who have left our community, whether by choice or not. We keep a place for them at our table so their spirits might be nourished and know they are not forgotten. Aho."

I lead Granny June to the table, where Erik is still adjusting the floor mat. He doesn't glance up. I go about filling my plate with a small spoonful of each dish.

"Who's that boy who keeps staring at you?" Granny June asks loudly, though I'm right next to her. "The one who doesn't know how to straighten a rug?" Erik makes a hasty exit.

"Just a boy," I say.

"Hmm. I knew a boy like that once. Maybe twice," she says.

Granny wants Leer-wah's seat next to me. He seems good-natured, shifting over without a fuss. He introduces himself, making his fancy name sound even more posh.

"Hello. I'm Doctor Leer-wah, associate professor of archaeology at Mackinac State College. I grew up—"

"I'm June Chippeway," Granny interrupts. "And the way I remember it, Elders didn't eat first." She says it like a scolding. "They let the binoojins go first, and those kwewag who were pregnant or nursing binoojins. Our Elders would've starved so them new ones could eat."

After lunch and the requisite bathroom or smoking break, Cooper addresses the attendees, welcoming everyone and kicking off the introductions. He gives a shout-out to "Miss Manitou, with the beautiful penmanship, who will provide place cards for each person." She made them ahead of time with a list of attendees Cooper provided.

After the Leer-wah guy introduces himself, Miss Manitou sets down a name card that reads *Dr. H. LeRoy*.

I turn my suppressed laugh at the pretentious pronunciation of an ordinary last name into a coughing fit. I don't hear anything else until "Leer-wah" asks if I'm okay. His hazel eyes are full of concern. I feel ashamed for laughing. Then I realize it's my turn for introductions.

I introduce myself in the language and provide the translation. Then I add what I've practiced all week at Cooper's suggestion.

"Since this meeting is about ancestors, I wanted to share about some of mine. I come from Theodora Firekeeper, who was the daughter of Pearl Paquette, who was the daughter of Maria Norman, who was the daughter of Sophie Williams, who was the daughter of Louise John, who was the daughter of Katherine Waakaayaabide, who was the daughter of Netamop Ogidaaki, the one they call Gichi Nokomis Giizis, or Great-Grandmother Moon. Through her, I am related to nearly every Ojibwe person on Ziisabaaka Minising, because Netamop had thirteen daughters—who we refer to as the Thirteen Grandmothers—who all married into different families on Sugar Island. My tribe teaches us to think seven generations ahead when we make decisions. Netamop would have thought about me. I am her seventh generation, and she was someone else's seventh generation. Our Anishinaabe teachings are not abstract concepts or folklore. My ancestors had names, and they lived through good times and bad times. They dreamed of me. And I dream of them. Aho."

As soon as I shut my mouth, I begin shivering and sweating at the same time. I was calm while speaking. But now all the nervous energy is catching up to me. I give speeches in front of groups all the time for school, and usually it's cake. What's up with me now? Is it because today is technically part of the repatriation negotiations process? Is this how Pauline feels every day? Is it why she eats weed gummies like candy?

Dr. Fenton introduces herself. She names every university she attended, who she studied under, her scholarly publications, and the research fellowships she has received. She is the only person who includes her credentials.

Did *I* unsettle *her*? My ancestors connect me to this work. Maybe Dr. Fenton felt the need to demonstrate her connections, the ones tied to prestigious Ivy League schools.

After all the meeting attendees introduce themselves, Cooper is supposed to provide an overview of NAGPRA and the roles of institutions like Mack State, and tribes like ours. Instead Chief Manitou motions for his cousin Rocky to join him at the front of the room. Rocky is dressed in his hoop dancer regalia and immediately launches into an exhibition dance.

What. The. Fuck.

Cooper looks like a deer in the middle of the road, frozen in fear. Dr. Fenton is gazing at Rocky Manitou, who could be a cover-art model for romance novels about Indian braves and Zhaaganaash women. Pshht.

I decide to "check" on the food, which gives me cover to text my sister for help.

ME: Chief hijacked MSC event. Brought Rocky to dance.
PAULINE: Rocky's kind of cute.
ME: 😳 He's a dude with kids on every rez.
PAULINE: His own Gathering of Nations 😂

ME: How can we end this?

PAULINE: idk throw a sacrificial virgin at him?

ME: I ain't throwing myself at nobody.

PAULINE: Did you know Auntie and TJ text back and forth all damn day? Are they fuck buddies?

ME: This isn't why I texted.

PAULINE: Chief Manitou should have kept me as his intern.

ME: Pauline. For realz.

PAULINE: Seize control as soon as Rocky finishes his first dance. Chief Manitou won't interrupt a speaker but if he takes the 🎤 first, you're fucked.

ME: 🙇

I grab a tribal-library tote bag from the cabinet by Miss Manitou's desk. At the food table where volunteers are cleaning quietly, I wrap the leftover fry bread in tinfoil and fill the tote bag. My stomach rumbles; I barely got to touch Granny June's baked beans on my plate before this day went off the rails.

The instant Rocky Manitou finishes, I am at his side. Our guests clap, and I do a game-show host flourish toward him.

"Miigwech, Cousin," I say. "We are so proud of you. On behalf of the library and museum, I am honored to gift you with this token of our appreciation." I look directly at Cooper, who nods. "My boss has asked that I have our guests from Mackinac State College join me across the hallway at our museum. I am being evaluated on my museum-tour skills, so please help me earn a gold star."

I have no idea what else Chief Manitou hoped to do, but I have retaken control of the airplane and am bringing it in for a safe landing.

Our tribal subchief, Tom Webster, stops to shake my hand. Where

Chief Manitou is a showman who wears designer suits and carved onyx medallions larger than a hockey puck, our tribe's second-in-command has an understated, quiet confidence.

"You are one to watch, Little Cousin." He grins.

I lead my group to the museum and into the first exhibit. I override the laser sensor at my feet, so the creation story won't begin until everyone is seated. Once I've pressed the correct button to launch the multimedia presentation, I take my seat next to Dr. Fenton. The drumbeat gets everyone's attention. The domed ceiling appears to be filled with stars, while the digital campfire fills the cylindrical screen.

During the Great Flood, Muskrat sacrifices himself to swim deep enough to grasp a tiny handful of earth that his companions find after his body resurfaces. Many people tend to get emotional at this part. I glance over at Dr. Fenton, who is dry-eyed at Muskrat's noble death. The only sniffle I hear is from Leer-wah on my opposite side. He continues to be affected when Muskrat's friends, including Otter, place the dirt on Turtle's back, where it takes root and new plants spring to life. Turtle's back expands to form our continent as the narrator explains why, what some call North America, we call Turtle Island.

When we move on to the next exhibit, Leer-wah squeezes himself between me and Dr. Fenton. He asks more questions than anyone else. "Question" is a generous label when it's more like a mini lecture ending with *Don't you agree?* I imagine his own classroom lectures are monologues that his captive audience of students are forced to endure. Sheesh. Wearing a nice suit that says he's part of the academics but with a forced "coolness" factor from his single gold earring, unshaved stubble, and red hair long enough to be pulled back with a leather tie.

Since Cooper was unable to give the presentation he worked on all week, I want to incorporate what he planned on sharing into my tour.

"Mr. Turtle, is it true that these items were part of the first repatriation you were part of?"

"Ah yes," Cooper says, without missing a beat. "It was a successful partnership with Central Michigan University that still continues today."

Staying close to Dr. Fenton is a harder task than I'd have imagined. She observes everything quietly and doesn't want to engage with me. If only she was more like Dr. Leer-wah, who asks a ton of questions: *What can you tell us about these star charts? What about these plants? And the rounded top of the wigwam—does that signify Mother Earth's womb?*

Remembering Cooper's lesson about only giving information that doesn't cost us anything, I stick to the descriptor tags—which I know by heart from having cleaned, polished, and vacuumed every inch of the exhibits.

"Is thirteen a special number in Ojibwe culture?" Leer-wah asks.

Telling them about the Thirteen Grandmothers was to show how connected our family ties are on Sugar Island. I didn't mean to open a portal into cultural teachings.

"No," I say. "I mean, there are thirteen moons in a year and thirteen plates on Mishiike's—I mean Turtle's—back. But the number of daughters Netamop had was a coincidence."

Leer-wah tilts his head as if considering my answer. I'm not sure he buys it.

We arrive at the final exhibit: contemporary Ojibwe storytelling through art, celebrating the connections past, present, and future. Dr. Fenton has done little more than peer at object labels next to display items.

Maybe a story about my family would help her connect to this museum?

I lead the tour group to the glass display case with my great-grandmother's basket. I gather two pairs of white cotton gloves from a nearby drawer and hand one set to Dr. Fenton.

Nokomis Maria's basket feels light enough to defy gravity as I take it from the case. I hold out the basket to Dr. Fenton. She hesitates before taking it.

"In 1942, my grandmother Pearl was a newborn who became ill. It scared my great-grandmother Maria so much that she wrapped my grandmother to her chest before dressing to walk to the nearest neighbor on Sugar Island. Her neighbor was Zhaaganaash, which is what we call non-Native people. The neighbor agreed to give them a ride, in exchange for a basket. My great-grandmother agreed and had to get the basket before they crossed the river."

I look around the room. I have everyone's attention except for Dr. Fenton's. Her eyes are fixed on the basket. She runs a finger lightly along the twisted band of black ash that was once dyed purple or brown but now is somewhere between the two colors.

"At the hospital, the neighbor said that if my great-grandmother wanted a ride home, it would cost two baskets. And the neighbor wanted to choose for herself which baskets."

Someone in the tour group shakes their head. Another one mutters, "Shame on her."

"My Nokomis Pearl had diphtheria. She survived. I mean . . ." I stumble over my words. "If she hadn't, I wouldn't be here. When I see this basket"—I motion toward Dr. Fenton, who can't meet my eyes—"I wonder if it's one of those three baskets. And I'm thankful it's part of our collection now."

At the end of the day, Cooper and I say goodbye to our guests. He's had the opportunity to speak with each person throughout the afternoon. I did my best to stick to Dr. Fenton, although I don't think she changed her opinion of us.

After the shuttle bus departs, Dr. Leer-wah enters the facility. He drove his own vehicle, he explains. I assume he wants to continue a conversation with Cooper, so I give a polite wave and turn to go.

"Please, Perry, I'd like you to stay for this," Leer-wah says. I fight the urge to check my phone for the time. Instead, I smile blankly. He continues. "Dr. Fenton has been appointed to a task force committee at the college, which means I will take over as the lead negotiator on the repatriation team."

Cooper stands slightly taller at this news. Maybe he wishes he'd had me shadow Dr. Leer-wah instead of Raquel the Hoarder? Maybe I should've paid more attention to Leer-wah's questions that weren't actual questions?

"Your intern was a fantastic tour guide," he tells Cooper. Then, he addresses me. "How long is your internship?"

"Ten weeks total," I say. "Seven weeks left."

"Any chance to continue beyond that?" he asks. We both look to Cooper, who plays it cool.

"Possibly. Why do you ask?" My boss keeps his gaze on Mack State's lead negotiator.

"Well, Cooper, I was impressed and hoped Perry might stay on as part of the negotiation team." Leer-wah offers a warm smile. "I was hoping to set a target date—perhaps one year from today—for repatriating the thirteen sets of human remains culturally affiliated with Sugar Island." He holds up a hand. "I can't guarantee anything, but now that I am the lead negotiator, I am eager to demonstrate a success-ful repatriation."

Holaay.

Leer-wah laughs. I must have exclaimed out loud.

But . . . stay on a year? I made a commitment to bring the Warrior Girl home, not thinking through how that might play out. Maybe I have a gift for hostage negotiations, after all. I mean, isn't Mack State holding our ancestors hostage?

Cooper has a solid poker face. He rubs his chin, as if mulling over the idea.

"Let's talk tomorrow. Sound good?" he checks with Leer-wah. They nod and mention the possibility of going to lunch together.

I wait for Leer-wah to leave a second time, watching him walk toward the downtown parking garage, before I do a celebratory leap with a side kick of my Docs.

"So, what's next, boss?" I say, cheesing a huge grin. "You need me to tackle world peace next?"

"I come back tomorrow to keep fighting the good fight; you come back on Monday." He tries to maintain his poker face, but I can see the excitement in his eyes.

"You can't get me out of the intern seminar?" I whine.

"A Padawan must learn from many teachers." He clears his throat, and when he continues, his eyes are dancing, but his voice is serious. "Gni-ta na-kii, Wiidookaagewikwezans."

It's maybe the best compliment I've ever received.

He continues, now back to his normal tone: "We identify tribal citizens who might want to get involved with the repatriations, help-ing to prepare for when we finally bring our ancestors home. I will follow up on the lunch invitation tomorrow. We wait and see if the college's governing board adds an action item to their next meeting agenda. Ideally, we want them to make a commitment specific to the thirteen ancestors."

"Along with a list of the hoops they want us to jump through?" I add.

He nods. "Speaking of hoops, you got us back on track after Rocky's exhibition."

We do identical eye rolls.

"Why would Chief Manitou do that?" I ask. "I mean, we sent the schedule to the entire Tribal Council. Why hijack the meeting? And with Rocky?"

"I don't know. Tribal Council doesn't let us in on the 'big picture' until they're ready."

"Well, I just hope the rest of them museum people noticed that our archives were cleaner and better organized than theirs," I say. "I mean, how can Dr. Fenton look down her nose at us when her office is such a train wreck? Seriously, I could've taken all the seeds from that basket instead of just a few. She won't finish her inventory for another decade at least."

It's later than I thought, because Mom's SUV pulls into the spot left by the shuttle.

"Just a sec. Gotta grab my stuff," I say before heading back inside the building.

Mom asks Cooper about the visitors from Mack State. I wish I could overhear all the good things he is telling her about how today went.

His earlier praise echoes all the way back to the ferry. *You are a good worker, Helper Girl.*

CHAPTER 10

FRIDAY, JUNE 27TH

I'm thankful when my sister sits next to me at the Friday seminar, which moves Erik an additional seat away. The only issue is that Pauline is in one of her moods, because she still wants to be on Team Tribal Council.

"Staring at them won't change the situation," I tell her. She ignores me for Lucas.

I turn to Shense. "How's life, Teen Mom?"

"My baby's shit is even stinkier than before," she says. "How is that possible when she is a hundred percent breastfed and my diet hasn't changed?"

Claire starts off with, "Who wants to tell me about their week?"

Ordinarily, Pauline would be waving her paw in the air to be called upon. Instead my sister whispers something to Lucas that makes him laugh.

I nudge Shense. "Tell them about your baby's shit." She snickers.

All three people from Team Tribal Council collectively rave about the amazing things they did this week. Pauline begins tucking her hair behind her ear. Here we go. DEFCON 4. Before Claire can ask them any follow-up questions, I raise my hand.

"Perry. You have something to say?" Claire says, sounding surprised but delighted.

"The tribal museum hosted the board of trustees and some professors from Mackinac State College. I gave a tour," I say.

"Wow, Perry, you must be getting really good at giving tours," Claire says.

I remember my lie from the first seminar. Two weeks later, I am giving tours for real.

After our weekly updates, the guest speaker presentations begin. The first one today is Cooper's wife. I recognize Mrs. Turtle from Malcolm High School. Her silver hair always looks pretty. It's short and stylish and has a shimmery lavender glow.

The way Mrs. Turtle goes on and on about Malcolm, you'd think it was a posh private academy instead of the alternative high school. Her recruitment efforts are wasted on the Kinomaage interns already in college. She's preaching to the choir with Shense and me. With Pauline aiming for class valedictorian and Lucas playing every sport offered at Sault High, Mrs. Turtle is pitching to six interns, at best. She should've taken them to Dairy Queen instead.

"We cap our enrollment at eighty students. This allows our teachers to give each student the attention they need," she says. "We have classes four days a week, with Fridays reserved for independent research or work-study programs."

I hope Mrs. Turtle doesn't call on me to speak about my experience at Malcolm. My "independent research" involves me sleeping in on Fridays and spending the rest of the day helping Pops. We have a special permit for subsistence and ceremonial hunting and fishing on tribal and state land. If someone is doing a naming feast and wants to serve traditional foods like venison, smoked whitefish, or turkey, we can provide the wild game or fish for the event. There are a few Elders who like to eat rabbit stew or other traditional dishes. I just need to keep a journal and make a presentation each term. It's an easy A. I am all for that.

"At Malcolm, we can help students recover credits and graduate on time," Mrs. Turtle says. "We even have a few students who use the credit-recovery option as an accelerated program to graduate ahead of time. Our purpose is to help each student meet their goals, and support the unique ways that people learn."

Someone in front of us whispers a joke about alternative schools. Shense and I kick his seat at the same time. He turns around.

"Malcolm says to go fuck yourself," Shense says.

"Holaay! Where'd you learn to stand up for yourself?" I whisper to my friend.

"At Malcolm," she says without missing a beat.

Claire brings up next week's seminar.

"As you know, next Friday is the Tribe's annual Fourth of July picnic. Kinomaage interns receive double pay for working the picnic." Lucas is among those who cheer enthusiastically about the extra eighty bucks. "We help Elders get their food and drinks throughout the day. We alert the staff at the first-aid tent if any Elders get overheated or have any other medical emergency."

Claire continues. "We will also seek out Elders who want to tell stories that we can record for future generations. I'm passing around a box of voice-activated mini recorders. Take one and pass the box along."

After giving brief instructions on how to operate the devices, she talks about consent. "We ask if they want to tell a story. We ask if we can record it. If they say yes to both, then you gift them tobacco. Why don't we give the tobacco tie before we ask?"

I expect Pauline to raise her hand, but Lucas does instead.

"Because they might feel like they don't have a choice once they accept semaa."

A large basket of tobacco ties is passed around. We each take a handful of the tiny fabric bundles, each filled with loose-leaf pipe semaa and tied with thin ribbon.

"If they consent, that's when you will turn the device on. State the date and time, your name and spelling, and the Elder's full name and spelling. Then ask both questions again—if they want to talk and if we can record it—so their consent is part of the record.

"We'll have a traditional healer, a behavioral health counselor, and Elder Services caseworkers at the picnic. If at any time your Elder becomes upset during your interview, please ask if they want to end the interview and if they'd like to speak with a healer or counselor."

Someone in the audience raises a hand. "What do they talk about? Do we ask a question to get them started or what?"

"Great question," Claire says. "Your team can focus on a specific topic, such as growing up on Sugar Island. But, usually, Elders who want to talk need very little prompting."

Lucas mumbles something about his granny. Pauline giggles.

"So, who's looking forward to interviewing our incredible Elders?" Claire says hopefully.

She really considered everything: obtaining consent from Elders, using semaa in a good way, and having resources available for Elders if they become overwhelmed. I'm impressed.

When I raise my hand, Claire takes a deep breath before calling on me. She acts as if she's expecting a wisecrack.

"I'm all in, Claire."

After another guest speaker, Claire announces that our team challenge this week will take place at the new escape-room business downtown. There are five rooms they've adapted to be the same level of difficulty. Each team will draw a room assignment from a hat and start at the same time. After escaping, we are to get sandwiches at the Tribal Council conference room and come back to Chi Mukwa to discuss ideas for our final challenge.

"At least we get out of here for a while," I tell Pauline.

She continues looking at her old team. I nudge her.

"C'mon. You get to be a Misfit Toy," I say enthusiastically.

"I don't think you're selling it, Pear-Bear," Lucas says. He puts his arm around Pauline. "With you on our team, we are gonna clean up." This makes her stop frowning.

"Yeah, Pauline," Shense adds. "Let's escape fast and eat all the sandwiches."

"Sounds like a plan." Erik's deep voice startles me. I forgot about him.

He's been in the sun. His skin is darker, and his hair is lighter. His blue eyes are more vivid than before. Not that he's looking at me. "Malcolm says go fuck yourself," I mumble.

Team Misfit Toys escapes so quickly that we arrive at the Tribal Council meeting room before the food. Pauline greets the executive secretary, who mentions that Chief Manitou is in St. Ignace for the day. I hope the update helps my sister relax, because watching her repeatedly scratch behind her ear is annoying. Her anxiety makes me wish I had packed an extra emergency weed gummy for myself.

I only brought one for her today, and she needed it after the weekly updates.

I think I got a slacker brain because Pauline's is always going full throttle. I could try for better grades, but then I'd probably be gobbling down weed gummies along with my sister. She says they help her sleep because her brain won't shut off. If anxiety is the price to pay for being the Smart Twin, then I'm fine with being Team Participation Ribbon.

Subchief Webster joins us while we wait for the lunch delivery.

"Wow. That must've been a fast escape," he says.

"Shense picks locks," Lucas reveals.

"Don't tell our secrets," I say, shoving my best friend. I am only half kidding.

"Pauline figured out anything that required figuring out," Lucas says. "Perry barked orders at us." I shrug and he continues. "I pretended to listen. Erik found a loophole in the rules. And Shense picked the lock because the instructions said we could use anything in the room. She found a paper clip and a McDonald's gift card in the garbage to jimmy the lock."

When the secretary comes in with the lunch, she looks upset. Pauline goes to hug her, and the woman breaks down. Pauline holds her while the distraught secretary mumbles something into her shirt.

"I'm so sorry to hear that," my sister says. "We can set up the lunch." She turns to the subchief. "Mr. Webster, the Tribal Police found a body they think is Darby O'Malley."

Subchief Webster tells the secretary to take the rest of the day off.

"They played hockey together," he explains. "She was with Darby the night she went missing." The subchief leaves the meeting room.

We eat quietly. Only Shense has much of an appetite.

Team Tribal Council arrives, as rowdy as we must have been a half hour ago.

"Wait," their ringleader says. "You guys beat us?" The other two teammates laugh.

Pauline contacts Claire to get permission to go back to Tribal Police, since they will need her help. We offer to go with, but Claire asks our team to return to Chi Mukwa.

I ride back with Shense. She looks in the rearview mirror at Erik's car.

"That flamed out quick."

"Pshhht. No flame. No spark," I say.

"Huh." She looks in the mirror again. "Bad kisser?"

"No. That's not what—he's not—" I catch Shense's know-it-all smile. "We went somewhere together, and I did something, and he got mad."

"Mean mad or disappointed mad or annoyed mad or—"

"Holaay. How many types of mad do you know?" I ask.

"Don't avoid answering or I'll get mean mad," she says.

Shense makes me laugh. She's someone who is funny without trying to be.

"Okay, okay," I say. "We went to some store in St. Ignace so I could look at their stupid little museum full of"—I make air quotes—"'Injun' things. A bratty kid knocked over one of the display cases, and I took a basket that I recognized as my great-grandma's. Erik got upset." I relive the moment when he said my name like a gut punch. "He was . . . disappointed that I did something . . . reckless."

"Was it that Teepees-n-Trinkets place?"

I nod and look at Erik's car in the side mirror.

"Did you look around for a security camera at least?" she asks.

"Yeah. Force of habit from having store security on my ass all the time."

"Good," she says, eyes still on the road. "Most small businesses go overboard with a system they slack on after a few months. Or they do nothing except put fake security-alert stickers in their windows."

"Holaay. The daughter of the casino surveillance director." I laugh. "How's that saying go? The apple didn't fall far from the tree."

She laughs too. "Shit, if my dad wanted me to be quiet, he'd toss me an old lock and a bobby pin. It used to keep me occupied until I got too good at it."

"Will you teach me?"

She pulls into the parking lot at Chi Mukwa. "Sure. The trick is to figure out how to do it with your eyes shut. You hear better and get a feel for the lock's innards that way."

We spend the afternoon in our designated breakout room, talking about ideas for our final challenge. I try texting Pauline with updates until she replies that it's too hectic at work.

"We should do a project that gets us into the community and out of this tiny room." Lucas paces around the card table. "That's it," he declares. "If that Claire lady asks, tell her I'm visiting my Granny June about our final project."

"Take me with you," I plead.

"Don't be ditching us, Perry," Shense says.

A few minutes later, Shense does exactly that, telling Erik and me that she's gotta pump breast milk. She leaves me with a wink and an obvious tilt of her head toward Erik.

I text Auntie to see if she's heard any updates about the body that was found. She doesn't respond immediately.

"So, um . . . the museum tour went well?" Erik asks.

"Yeah. We have a good chance to get thirteen ancestors returned."

"That's . . . that's cool."

"Yeah."

"You looked really pretty. Dressed up like that." He coughs. "I mean—"

We are interrupted by the ringleader from Team Tribal Council bursting into our room.

"You're still in first place." He sounds pissed off.

"Cool," I say flatly.

"Team Shrek-reation is still in the second escape room. They can't escape." The ringleader laughs, joined by the other two interns.

I don't laugh. Neither does Erik.

"Do you have a final project figured out yet?"

"Why?" I say. "Do you need a better idea to replace yours?"

The ringleader stares at me a beat too long before joining the laughter with his group. Everyone leaves. His voice trails behind as the door closes.

"Probably waiting for the next missing person so they can organize that search."

What. The. Fuck. I am through the door and at the ringleader's side in an instant.

"You think we should wait for the next missing Nish kwe?" I shout. He's taller than me, so I glare up at him. "For our team project?"

The ringleader instantly backpedals. "I didn't say anything like that. I'm sure you misunderstood." He looks around for support.

I keep my eyes locked on his.

"Because anyone who would speak that way about our missing women would be a complete piece of shit, right?" My voice is low and steady.

"Again, I apologize if you misunderstood anything," the ringleader says.

"Perry Firekeeper-Birch?" It's Claire's voice coming from behind me.

He walks away, but I remain frozen in place staring at his back. Waiting for him to—

Yep. There it is. That one last look he can't help himself from taking. I stand tall, proud, strong, defiant. This is the image that asshole will remember when he thinks about challenging me ever again.

This is not my first showdown. It's not just about the one currently underway; you've got to neutralize any future threats from the current asshole and the bystander assholes.

"Perry Firekeeper-Birch," Claire repeats. "I need to meet with you in my office."

Shense was right about her voice's slightly screechy quality.

I follow Claire to her office overlooking the volleyball courts. She leaves me sitting in front of her desk. I look around to make sure she's left. I am alone and shaking. Now that the incident is over, every quake and quiver I didn't feel before makes my legs and arms feel like jiggly Jell-O. It could be eighty degrees in this office. My teeth chatter like it's January.

Why am I in trouble? I didn't hit the guy.

I focus on something, anything, to pass the time.

Claire has a framed photo on her desk. One of those square Polaroid photos with the white border and thick white bottom edge, where she's written *Mom, Frank Lockhart, Me—May 1993*. The blue ink is fading along with the photo. I can barely make out a young Claire, an older white man, and an Ojibwe woman between them who holds their gazes. A freighter is in the background of the photo. Pops would know which one just by the faint image.

Wait, that name sounds familiar. Frank Lockhart. Where have I—

The door opens behind me. I turn to see Cooper. He moves stiffly to sit behind Claire's desk. His eyes are puffy and bloodshot. Did they confirm it's Darby O'Malley's body?

He speaks before I do.

"How many seeds did you take from the basket in Dr. Fenton's office?"

Auntie calls this odd feeling déjà vu. *Already seen*. In Ojibwemowin, it is inaabandan. *See it like in a dream*. Except that when it happened before, Erik was the one with sad eyes.

"I took thirteen and left a few dozen," I say.

Cooper blows out a breath of air. When I meet his eyes, I know he isn't nimamiskojaab over Darby O'Malley. He cried all night because of what I did.

I look down at the shaking fingers on my lap.

"I have to let you go." His voice cracks. "I can't work with someone I don't trust."

With that, he rises and goes to the door. I listen for it to open, but the sound doesn't happen. I won't look up from my lap. I don't want to turn around and see the way he must be looking at me. Or maybe he's frozen in place because time is standing still for everyone except me.

"Nimaanendam," I say quietly.

"I know, Pearl Mary. I am sorry too."

I sit there, unsure of what happens next. In the movies, when a person gets fired, they slink away with a box of their personal belongings. Mom has prepared for it, knows with unwavering certainty that she will walk away with her head held high.

I am not righteous or defiant. I am ashamed.

Claire makes a show of coughing loudly while entering the office. She sits down and slides a box of tissues to the edge of her desk. I don't need them. I've already gone into myself. My face is a blank mask. I breathe calmly. Even my shoulders are relaxed.

It must be nice not to have any worries.

"It happens," Claire says with a sigh. "Sometimes a supervisor and intern have different communication styles or incompatible personalities. Sometimes it's just a bad fit."

It wasn't any of those things, I want to tell her.

She continues. "I'll email a notice of availability to see if any of the supervisors in the Kinomaage program could use another intern. They might want to contact you directly. Is that okay?" She reads off my phone number.

I nod.

"Perry, you aren't the first intern to have an unsuccessful match. Every summer there are different reassignments for any number of reasons. No one will know why. Those details are between you and your former supervisor unless you or he alleges there was misconduct. He hasn't done that. Is there any inappropriate behavior you experienced that you want to report?"

"No," I say quickly. "Cooper is a good boss."

Claire's brow furrows, wanting details but taking her cue from me.

I ask, "Will you pull someone from another team and reassign them to the museum?"

"No," she says, firmly. "Cooper Turtle rarely accepts an intern. I was surprised when he requested you."

"I think my aunt Daunis recommended me," I tell Claire.

"That might be, Perry. But Cooper requires a reference from a traditional healer."

"A healer recommended me?" Now it's my voice that has a bit of a screech to it.

Claire types into her laptop. She peers closer at the screen.

"Yes. There's a note that Cooper received a verbal recommendation from an S. Nodin."

Stormy Nodin gave a verbal recommendation for me?

I've never heard Stormy Nodin speak a word except as part of a prayer in the language. But he spoke to Cooper and vouched for me? My lunch sours even more in my stomach.

"I'm really sorry it didn't work out," she says kindly.

There is nothing else to say. "Yeah. Me too."

CHAPTER 11
SATURDAY, JUNE 28TH

I wake up tired. My eyes sting as if I cried all night. From what I can remember, my fitful sleep included versions of me getting fired over and over. In one dream, Erik sat at the front desk of the motel; his long curls covered his eyes. Instead of a job, I asked if I could be his girlfriend. He told me, *I can't be with someone I don't trust, Pearl Mary.*

I leave a note on the dining table for my parents: *Gone fishing with Jr. on the dock.* It's the only thing that will make me feel better. Junior races me down the path to the boathouse and our small sandy beach. He stays by my side as I cast my line at the sunrise to the right.

Mom and Pops will be so disappointed in me when they find out I was fired. I try to envision a scenario where they understand why I had to take the seeds. Maybe the best thing is to keep the news from them until I have another job. Claire said she'd alert other supervisors that a Kinomaage intern was available. There are still eight weeks left in the program, after all.

Holaay. I didn't even last three whole weeks. True, it was a week longer than Pauline's stint with Tribal Council, but she got transferred because the chief was a guilty perv. I got sacked for being an untrustworthy thief.

While walking back to the house a few hours later, I detour to the workshop. It's been twelve days since I took the squash seeds. They should've germinated by now, but since they were stored for decades, it could be a few more days. Unless . . .

What if I got fired for stealing seeds that were too far gone to ever germinate?

Sheesh. My fishing high wore off quickly. I'm back to feeling tired and sad as I reach the workshop. I turn on the grow lights and—there it is!

A tiny sprig emerging from the soil.

"Aaniin. Gwe taan ka mi! Aab ji taan en na kii yin!" The encouragements come from me like a song. My heart, feeling a little less empty, thumps to the rhythm. Junior adds his voice as I repeat myself twelve times, serenading each starter pot.

Hello. Way to go! Keep up the good work!

Pops slides an omelet onto my plate. The onions, peppers, and mushrooms are sautéed to perfection. Next to me, Pauline chomps on the raw veggies folded inside her omelet like a taco.

"Daunis is coming over with Waabun," Mom says. "Perry, maybe you could take him to catch dinner? She says he wants to kiss earthworms and fish with you." She laughs as she sits down at the table in front of the vase of white lilacs that Pops must have cut this morning. She inhales their scent with her eyes closed and a serene smile.

"Absolutely," I say enthusiastically. More fishing, more fun.

It isn't until Pauline stomps over to the kitchen sink with her half-eaten breakfast that I remember she is still shunning Auntie.

Pops comes to the table with Mom's omelet. My parents kiss a beat longer than a normal good-morning kiss. It's an ordinary Saturday morning that feels . . . extraordinary.

I watch them, hoping to lock in the memory. Maybe you can help which memories get preserved. Like storing seeds in a cool, dark, and dry place to keep them alive.

Maybe someday I'll think back on the awful college-tour week, and it won't be about Pauline being eager to ditch us. Maybe all I will remember is how we sang along with our Helen Roy music CDs. Patsy Cline, Johnny Cash, and Elvis songs with Ojibwemowin lyrics.

Maybe someday I'll remember when I was sixteen, and it won't be about getting fired or having the first boy I liked dump me before we even got started. Instead I'll only remember fishing off the dock with my dog, and my dad cooking omelets to order. And my parents kissing just because the lilacs were in bloom.

After breakfast, I help Pops with the weeding. Junior keeps us company from outside the chicken-wire fence surrounding the garden. The sun feels good on my skin. I wear a swimsuit—a one-shoulder top and boy shorts—so I can run through the sprinkler if I get too sweaty. Pops moves the sprinkler from inside the fence to outside so Junior can play. We laugh when Junior tries to chomp down on the water. I join my dog, leaping across the swirling spray.

Junior does his warning bark to let us know someone's car is in the drive. His next bark is his playful one. I come around the pole barn to find Erik's car. A second later I see Erik throw a stick that Junior brought to him.

Yesterday, Erik waited for my meeting with Claire to finish. Shense did too. They knew something had happened. Both offered to give me a ride home. I went with Shense.

Here he is, wanting details and to rub my nose in the consequences of my reckless actions. I try to brace myself with an excuse but come up blank.

Instead, Erik walks to the front porch where Pauline is waiting for him.

After weeding, I decide to sweep Pops's workshop. Avoiding the house is no problem because the pole barn has a bathroom. There is a refrigerator stocked with water and sugar-free beverages, except for orange juice in case Pops's sugar feels low. I find some venison jerky in a cabinet. We make our own, so it has less salt than other kinds and is okay for Junior to have. Leaning against the workshop countertop, I chew on a piece while Junior sits at my feet.

"Mizhakiinoodin," I say. When I say it a second time, I add a swirl of my hand to show what I mean: *tornado*. He spins himself around as if he's chasing his tail.

"Gi maa mii kwen min," I say, voice full of pride. I toss him a bit of jerky.

He looks away to assess something but turns back to me for more Ojibwemowin lessons. My dog's need for treats overrules his momentary curiosity.

"Gagiibaajishimo," I command. When he doesn't respond, I repeat myself and dance in a silly way.

This time he stands on his hind legs to do his goofy dance. That earns him more jerky.

"Gi maa mii kwen min," I say, because I am proud of my dog for learning the language. He is a kinesthetic learner like me.

I test him on a few more words until we're interrupted by Waabun dashing into the pole barn. My little cousin hugs my legs. Junior wants in too. A minute later, Auntie strolls in.

"Who was that?" she says, looking over her shoulder.

Erik's car heads out of the driveway.

I shrug. "Pauline's friend."

Auntie says nothing, just watches the group hug. Waab breaks away first, shouting for Elvis Junior to race him to the tree fort. My dog catches up and does his sheepdog thing—nudging Waab back into an imaginary corral.

"Ingozisens. Gego ozaam waasa izhaaken." Auntie instructs her son not to go too far.

"Haaw, Nimaamaa." *Okay, Mom.*

Auntie and I walk to the picnic table near the tree fort. She sits on the table and makes room for me to sit on the bench with my back to her. Usually, it's Pauline who plunks herself in front of Auntie to get her hair braided. I never like sitting still for that long. Plus, my hair is slightly coarser than my sister's. I need product for a decent braid whereas it's optional for her.

"She still mad at me?" Auntie asks. I know she means Pauline.

"Yeah." I turn to look up at Auntie, larger than life. "Did you get her transferred?"

"No." She sighs.

"Can you massage my brain?" I haven't asked Auntie to do this in years. When I was eight, I thought massaging my scalp might help my brain work better than Pauline's.

Auntie removes my hair tie and undoes the thick braid.

"I just put the fear in Chief Manitou not to mess with her. Then TJ requested an intern to work on the missing and murdered Indigenous persons database and the chief decided to cut bait. Literally." I hear the smirk in her voice.

"Auntie, if you got a bad vibe about the chief, then you were right to shake him up."

She goes silent again. Her fingers press and rake my scalp in the way I love. We watch Waab and Junior playing their usual games.

"There's a look that some men give a young girl," she says. "He sees her as something to claim." Auntie's fingers pause. "I didn't see the way he looked at your sister. But I did see his guilty expression when I parked next to them."

"But I rode in a car with Cooper to St. Ignace," I point out.

"Did he ever behave inappropriately? Or have you ever gotten a vibe that he was anything other than a museum professional mentoring you?"

I think back to the way Cooper listened whenever I spoke. He was attentive, respectful, and way more patient than I'd ever be if the situation was reversed.

"No," I say.

"Okay, then. That's great," she says while gathering my hair into a low ponytail. "Always listen to your body, like the prickles on the back of your neck. Our survival instincts have been developed over millennia to alert us to things that are . . . hinky." She taps the back of my neck, making her fingers dance lightly. "And no matter who, no matter when—pay attention to your body when it goes into alert mode."

"And then fight, right, Auntie? If it's fight or flight, you stand and fight."

"Depends on the circumstances," she says.

That surprises me. I thought she was a fighter. It's the one attribute I thought I had more in common with Auntie than my twin did.

"I was raped the day after my nineteenth birthday," she says calmly. I spin to look at her, but she gently turns me back around and glides gentle fingers along my shoulders. "I couldn't fight him off. So I got myself out of that room. Not physically, but I shut down the parts of myself that I could. I went numb." She kisses the top of my head. "Fight or flight. There's more than one way to flee a bad situation."

I move to sit next to her and put an arm around her.

"Did the guy go to jail for what he did?" When she shakes her head, I whisper, "Did you blanket-party him?"

We watch Waabun playing for a while before she says yes. I look at her, but she continues staring forward. Her features are slightly larger versions of Mom's. She looks like the photographs of Levi Firekeeper, Sr., her dad who died when she was a little girl.

"Did it help you? Getting him back for what he did?" I ask.

"I thought it would, but it didn't. Not when I still see him around town."

"He lives in the Sault?" Waabun and Junior look over at us.

"I didn't help at your museum event because I knew he'd be there," she says quietly. "I trust you, Perry. With this information." She takes a deep breath and speaks on the exhale. "His name is Grant Edwards. He's on the board of trustees for the college. The bald guy in the designer suits. Zhaaganaash."

There is more than one bald Zhaaganaash dude on the board, so Auntie's description doesn't narrow anything down. But I vaguely remember his name from Pauline. Something about the college and the tribe. But how can he be on the board of trustees if he did something that bad?

"How could he get away with it?"

"He made sure to commit the crime on tribal land, because the federal government wouldn't bother prosecuting the case." She adds, "He used to be a defense attorney."

I watch her son playing. My heart feels heavy. It's the part of me that wishes I had joined Waab and Junior instead of sitting with Auntie.

I pause in the doorway to Pauline's bedroom.

"So, why was Erik here?"

She doesn't bother looking away from her laptop. "He helped me with the database."

"That's all?" I ask.

"Yeah . . . ," Pauline says slowly. She glances up. "Why?"

"I thought he came over to gloat about me getting shitcanned."

"You're obtuse." She resumes whatever she is doing on her laptop.

"What's that mean?" I say.

"Look it up."

Gaah! I hate when Little Miss Vocabulary does that.

Waab can barely keep his eyes open at the dinner table. Between playing with Elvis Junior at the tree fort and then the walk to and from my best fishing spot, he is one tired little guy. Pops counts the number of times Waab's head jerks upward instead of landing on his plate.

We watch Waab pick up a strand of spaghetti and kiss it.

"Oh, my boy," Auntie says with a laugh. "What are you doing?"

Between extremely slow blinks, he says, "Fishing with Auntie Perry."

Everyone laughs, even Pauline, who has been silent throughout dinner.

Auntie lifts him into her arms, and he's fast asleep before they reach the front door. Mom kisses Auntie before pecking multiple kisses on Waab's squishy cheek.

After a bubble bath, I smell like cherry-blossom lotion and my nutty leave-in conditioner. I put on a clean T-shirt and pajama shorts. Junior is also freshly washed, so I let him jump onto my bed with me. While waiting for my laptop to power up, I take a closer look at the sheet of paper I found earlier on my desk. Pauline must have printed it out.

It is from an auction site in . . . France? The words are in English.

Auction: 8 JULY 2014
Estimated Value: 12000–15000 EUR
Lot 6—Important Ojibwa Turtle Shell Ceremonial
    Shaker
Ojibwa, Great Lakes, United States
Circa early 19th century
Snapping turtle, gourd seeds, sinew stitching, deer
    hide wrap
L. 36 cm
Provenance:
—(Oral history): Obtained by American soldier near
    Fort Brady, Sault Sainte Marie, Territory of Michigan,
    United States

—Collection: Yves Alarie, Paris, France
—Sale: Cadieux Auction House, Art of the Indians of
   North America Collection, Yves Alarie, 26 March
   2002, Paris, lot 13
—Private collection, acquired at the sale above
Shakers were used by medicine men during holy
   ceremonies. This shaker, dating from the early 19th
   century, is a remarkable testimony to the ancient
   practices of the cultures of the Native American
   Indians of the Great Lakes region.

This item should be returned to wherever it came from. If we could bid on it and have Cooper, Stormy, and others take a closer look for any identifiers, then we'd know what to do.

I find an app that converts euros to U.S. dollars, plug in the estimated value, and . . . the auction house estimates the "important" item will sell for $16,000 to $21,000.

I can't access my per cap savings. I've been receiving a share of our tribe's casino profits my entire life. My parents put everything into long-term, low-risk government bonds that we can't touch, or invested in stuff like silver and gold that is stored somewhere, "just in case." If I asked them to help me, it might bring up working for Cooper—which I don't want to tell them about until I can play it off as a simple transfer.

Auntie Daunis has money. I could ask for a loan. I already owe her for the Jeep repairs, but this is different. She would understand the significance of the shaker.

Junior's ears perk up. He's off the bed and at the window in an instant. A low growl forms in his chest.

"Hey, it's okay," I say. Heaving a sigh, I pull him away from the window and draw the curtains. "Just Pauline getting her freak on."

It isn't until Junior goes back to his napping spot on my leg that I think about who my sister might be meeting. She doesn't take her phone because our parents can track us on our devices. She has a burner phone for her secret hookups. I text her.

> ME: Who you meeting for a sneaky snag?
> PAULINE: I don't want to tell you.

My stomach turns to lead. Is she hooking up with Erik?

> ME: Not cool. You need to be safe. #wiindigoo
> PAULINE: Still not telling.
> ME: Seriously. #mmiw stands for Missing and Murdered
> Indigenous Women. You're an IW at risk of getting M+M. Duh!
> PAULINE: Not telling, but someone we both know and like.
> ME: Tell Erik I said whassup fucker!
> PAULINE: OBTUSE

I google the damn word.

> ob-tuse
> 1. annoyingly insensitive or slow to understand.
>   Similar: stupid, dull, slow, unintelligent, half-
>   baked, crass, dopey, dumbass
>   Opposite: clever, astute, shrewd, bright
> 2. an angle more than 90° and less than 180°

I get up to open my bedroom door. Let's see how obtuse Mom and Pops are when Elvis Junior alerts them to Pauline's post-shenanigan reentry around three a.m. Then she'll know that I'm the clever one. My hand is on the doorknob.

She would retaliate by telling them about Cooper firing me. I'd end up getting into bigger trouble for getting fired *and* for keeping it from them. My sister knows that if she can deflect their anger and disappointment toward me, then her punishment will be less than if they focus everything on her. She is shrewd, I'll give her that.

The door remains shut. I go back to bed. Still seething, I give in to my need for the last word.

ME: Well, I for sure don't like Chief Manitou.

I roll over to cuddle Elvis Junior. If I don't read her response, then I win.

WEEK FOUR

The baskets that I'm fortunate enough to have from my mother, I still feel close to her because I'm surrounded with her life yet. This basket still has her spirit and the original tree spirit, and now they're both in the basket together, combined to give life. The tree still lives.

—Sydney Martin (Match-E-Be-Nash-She-Wish Band of Pottawatomi), interviewed in the film *Black Ash Basketry: A Story of Cultural Resilience*

CHAPTER 12

MONDAY, JUNE 30TH

Mom drops off Pauline at the Tribal Police department before bringing me downtown. I make my way, like I always do, toward the Cultural Learning Center entrance. Keeping an eye on Mom's SUV, I pretend to check something on my phone. Once she turns at the stoplight and can no longer see me in her rearview mirror, I walk the few steps to the Tribal Administration building. My new workplace.

Subchief Tom Webster welcomes me with a huge, cheesy grin.

"Perry Firekeeper-Birch, my new intern, welcome!" He introduces me to the two receptionists behind the counter before walking through the lobby to the back entrance where the time clock is. If I squint, I can imagine the building's department-store origins. The space sat empty for a decade before our tribe bought and renovated it, giving it a new purpose.

I was purposeless for less than a weekend.

Yesterday, I had my waders on for fly-fishing at Baie de Wasai. The yellow pike were latching onto everything. Pops had dropped me off with strict instructions to stay around the Zhaaganaash old-timers who fish along the St. Marys River near the Catholic church. They're always telling fish stories: "Remember that one time . . ." Sometimes they ask me for a story. I usually make something up right on the spot.

I wasn't even an hour into my fishing when a runabout passed by and doubled back. The old-timers get upset whenever a boat crowds into "their" space. I looked up to see who was gonna get scolded by the guys. It was the tribal subchief, the one who had been kind to the devastated executive secretary.

"What's up, Aanike-Ogimaa?" I called out, using the Ojibwe words for subchief. I hoped he knew Ojibwemowin. Not all elected leaders do; some couldn't even name the Seven Grandfathers from that basic teaching about living our good way of life.

"Perry Firekeeper-Birch!" His voice boomed the forty feet between his boat and the shore. "You want to work for me as my intern?"

"Sure," I said without missing a beat. Then I cast my line, and it was a beauty.

Tom Webster's laugh was easy and contagious. Even the old-timers cracked up.

"All right. See you Monday morning." He drove off, leaving waves of laughter that washed ashore in his wake.

My new boss leads me to the elevator. Next to it is an open stairwell.

"Coast or cardio?" he asks. Tribal Council's offices are on the third floor.

"I never back down from a challenge," I say, taking the stairs.

The subchief is a few years older than Auntie. He keeps pace with me but grabs a stitch in his side as he catches his breath at the top.

"Subchief Webster, let me know if you see a bright light at the end of a dark tunnel. My mom's a nurse and I know CPR."

His quick chuckling is lighter than Cooper's asthmatic *heh-heh-heh*.

"You can call me Web, hey? And what would you like me to call you?"

"Perry. Miigwech for asking."

"Just want to get it right," he says, stepping into the conference room. He coughs. Three interns glance up from the large wood table inlaid with our maple-leaf tribal logo.

"Hey, everyone, this is Perry Firekeeper-Birch," Web says. "Since Chief Manitou poached my intern"—he cheeses another grin—"I poached the wonderful Perry. Introduce yourselves and get her up to speed on your projects." To me, he says, "Let's talk in an hour."

Two interns resume working on their laptops. But the ringleader guy has yet to finish his once-over. I'm tempted to glare at him, but he looks away.

I sit in one of the several remaining seats and wait for introductions that don't come.

Maybe the Kinomaage program shouldn't pit teams against each other. It sets us up to be adversaries. Our tribe has enough of those already.

"I'm Perry," I say. "You worked with my twin sister Pauline for a hot minute."

They give first names. Nothing more. The ringleader's name is Flynn. He tries to play cool like he doesn't remember me calling him out on Friday. But he twitches when I go to take a sip of water. Doesn't surprise me, the jerk.

Tribal Council members trickle past. Each has an office off the conference area. The offices have sliding glass doors that can go from clear to foggy. I wander around the conference area, checking out the desks that appear empty and the framed photographs of previous Tribal Council members.

After the hour has passed, I knock on Web's door. The glass in the door changes to clear. He motions for me to enter. The sliding door is surprisingly heavy. Two of the interns begin talking about the agenda for this week's Tribal Council meeting. Their voices are silenced the instant I slide the door closed behind me. I crack the door open and hear the continuation of their conversation.

"Soundproof office," I say, closing the door again. "Cool."

"That's not all." Web presses a button on his desk phone. The interns' voices sound through the speakerphone.

"I know, right? How do we know she won't sabotage our team challenges?" Flynn says.

"Do they know you can hear them?" I ask, all wide-eyed.

Web shakes his head and grins. "Just mine and the chief's office."

"Hold up. You shared this with me in my first—no, second hour as your intern?" I glance around his office. "Can I be honest?" He nods, so I dive right in. "I don't see myself getting anything out of this internship as part of Team Tribal Council. I'm Rudolph and they . . ." I point my lips toward the conference area. "They don't want me joining in any reindeer games."

Web's smile crinkles the corners of his eyes. Maybe he's older than I first thought.

"At Malcolm, I get to do subsistence and ceremonial hunting and fishing as independent study. Can I do an independent-study internship and not deal with the other reindeer?"

"Tell you what," Web begins. "Pitch your ideas to me and I'll support what I can. You'll still need to attend Tribal Council workshops and official meetings. You probably know the drill from your mom, but I'll say it anyway. Workshops are Wednesdays from ten a.m. to two p.m. We preview agenda items to ensure we've got what we need for the official meeting, from four to seven p.m., when we vote on resolutions that become tribal law."

"Got it," I say. "And I already have an idea for my independent study." I sit in the chair in front of his desk. "I found an auction site that's got a turtle-shell shaker for sale. I think it was used in ceremonies. It shouldn't be out there." I take a deep breath to get rid of the quiver in my voice. "Do you think I could research it? And maybe ask Tribal Council to buy it?"

"When is the auction?"

"A week from tomorrow?" I say, bracing myself for a letdown.

Web pays particular attention to his dress shirt before answering.

"Could you put something together by Wednesday afternoon?"

"The day after tomorrow? Holaay. You sure don't mess around," I say.

"I admire warriors," he says with such intensity it's like a spell. "Those who are willing to do what others can't or won't do for the community." He smiles. "Any questions?"

"I get hazard pay for sitting through council meetings, right?"

Web laughs. "We're going to be a great team, Ogichidaakwezans."

I beam at the name. Warrior Girl.

After dinner, I ask Pauline to drive me to Stormy Nodin's place. She doesn't want to but owes me for keeping her sneaky snag secret. Junior wants to come along for the ride.

I bring a large envelope filled with printed copies of my online research about snapping-turtle shakers or rattles. There wasn't much, but I downloaded what I did find into a file on my laptop before printing two copies of everything. Tribal Council's hella high-tech printer even has photograph paper for the color copies of the turtle-shaker images. I hope Stormy will be able to help me, because I am not ready to face Cooper anytime soon.

Nishnaabs from remote areas say they live in the bush. It usually means living off the land in a good way—hunting, fishing, and gathering, taking only what you need. Sugar Island was like that until the last hundred years or so.

Stormy Nodin is probably as close to a bush Nishnaab as you can get around here now. He lives on the east side of the island, in a simple cabin overlooking Lake George. I've only been here twice before, both times with Auntie.

Stormy smiles and waves when Pauline stops along the two-track path to his place. She stays in the car with the windows rolled down, reading a book. Junior greets him first. I hand him a hearty helping of fried walleye, asparagus, and potato salad. He offers for me to join him. Since I already ate, I nibble on a spear of asparagus just to be polite.

He was Uncle Levi's best friend. I loved tagging along with them, two smart-asses always goofing off and getting into mischief. Stormy seems so different now—silent and solitary.

When Uncle Levi got in trouble, Stormy wouldn't speak to the federal investigators. Not one word. Not even his own name when the judge asked him. He ended up serving two years for "contempt of court." Stormy came back to Sugar Island and bought this property with his per capita payments that had built up while he was incarcerated. Uncle Levi got banished for five years because he was convicted of a felony drug crime, and the Tribe passed a banishment referendum a while ago. But Stormy's wasn't a drug crime.

Stormy gives Junior the last bites of fish and looks at me expectantly. I offer semaa to him, along with the printout of the auction listing and enlarged color photos of the shaker.

"Ekinoomaagaazad ndaaw," I say, introducing myself as a student.

It's the best way to let Stormy know why I am here. I'm not sure if he will pray or talk. I still have a hard time believing he gave a verbal recommendation of me to Cooper.

He speaks in Ojibwemowin, beginning with a story about how Mishiike gifts us with a teaching about the lunar year. Thirteen large plates on his back, one for each moon. The perimeter of his shell has twenty-eight sections, one for each night in a lunar cycle. Mishiike reminds us of activities we do to survive.

Stormy asks me to visit tomorrow night, after he has prayed about the shaker.

"Gichi miigwech, Nisayenh," I say.

His eyes brighten at "older brother." In an instant, he's the Stormy I remember.

"Nigwaiinomaa Levi." It bursts forth, Uncle's absence overwhelming me. I miss him so much.

"Gii-ishkwaa bimaadizi niizhoodenh," he says, rising and turning to go.

What does that even mean? *My twin has passed away*. Uncle Levi is still alive.

CHAPTER 13

WEDNESDAY, JULY 2ND

Two bad things happen just before my presentation to Tribal Council this afternoon.

First, a Tribal Council member announces that Tribal Police have confirmed that the body found last Friday is Darby O'Malley's. Chief Manitou pauses the workshop for a fifteen-minute break that turns into an hour. Enough time to regret not taking the edible Pauline offered this morning.

Second, I make the mistake of looking around the meeting room just as a bald-headed Zhaaganaash guy in a well-cut suit walks in. I instantly recognize him as one of the Mack State trustees and somehow know with absolute certainty it's Grant Edwards.

What. The. Fuck. Why is he here?

He's a rapist. He raped Auntie Daunis when she was three years older than I am now. She is strong. An athlete. A hockey player on the boys' varsity team in high school. Auntie runs five miles every morning. She does Krav Maga now.

But he overpowered her, and he got away with it.

When I address Tribal Council, my voice shakes. Anger masquerades as nerves. I click through slides I made during lunch. *Focus, Ogichidaakwezans. Focus.*

"The way I learned it, turtle shakers like this were used in our medicine ceremonies as part of the shake lodge." This morning Stormy said it was okay to mention the shake lodge, but not to provide any details about that ceremony. I continue.

"Its provenance traces back to 1820, when the Treaty of Bwaating was signed." The Tribal Council members should know this already but, according to Mom, assumptions make asses of you and me. "That's the treaty signed by clan leaders from Sugar Island and both sides of the St. Marys River agreeing to move Nishnaabs further downriver to make room for the Soo Locks after the original navigation lock on the Canadian side was destroyed in the War of 1812." I pause to let the history lesson sink in. "We know the shaker comes from this area because of the etchings on the plastron—or underbelly—of the snapping turtle." I forward to the next slide, a close-up of the faint carving. "This is a diagram of how the clan leaders would sit inside the ceremonial lodge. The symbols for the clan leaders have been rubbed down, but a few are still legible. These three markings are the same as the signatures from the Treaty of Bwaating, which our leaders signed." I show my final slide, which is a side-by-side comparison of the markings.

"Why don't we just file a claim to repatriate it, since it's ours?" Web asks, just as we had planned.

"Because NAGPRA—the Native American Graves Protection and Repatriation Act—applies only to museums and institutions that accept federal funding. It doesn't include private collections or museums outside the United States. That's why this snapping-turtle shaker, which belongs to a private collector, can be auctioned from a French auction house."

Web nods attentively at each point I make. He's puffed up like a proud parent watching his kid in a spelling bee. But . . . he's the only one paying attention. The others look bored.

Why can't they be more like Web?

I get to the asking-for-zhooniyaa part.

"The auction takes place next week, on Tuesday. In order to bid, we need to set up a bidder profile and method of payment tied to a bank account. It would only take about fifteen minutes." I don't mention that I've done everything so far except for adding the banking info.

"In closing, I am asking for approval to bid on this item, which should be back with us on Sugar Island instead of in someone's private collection out in the world."

Someone in the audience claps. A few council members look uncomfortable. Web's crinkly-eyed smile is the only positive expression coming from Tribal Council.

My heart sinks to the bottom of my feet, resting atop the sprigs of giizhik in my shoes.

"Miss Firekeeper-Birch," Chief Manitou begins. "Miigwech for the well-done presentation. It is evident you care deeply about our ancestors and our ceremonial items. Our next step would be to take a formal vote at tonight's meeting." He pauses before turning to his right. "I thank Subchief Webster for sponsoring the resolution."

I know the chief is going to turn down my request. Is it because Auntie Daunis threatened to blanket-party him if he messed with Pauline?

He continues. "I'm tabling your request for a future meeting. Our focus right now is on acquiring a private collection that's being donated to the Tribe. Our interns are organizing an event to celebrate the announcement and could use your help. We requested your recent transfer from the tribal museum specifically for this project."

What the actual hell? I look to Web for confirmation.

"I support Perry's request and want it on tonight's agenda for an official vote," Web says.

The other leaders look pissed. Mom says they don't like going on record as voting against something cultural.

"Our first order of business at tonight's meeting is to approve the agenda," the chief says. "You can request to add it then. If it doesn't pass the motion to revise the agenda, then it's officially tabled. Understood?"

Web raises his hands in mock surrender. We both know it doesn't have any support.

Web finds me when Tribal Council takes a smoke break.

"I am really sorry," he says. "I didn't realize the private donation meant they weren't going to consider acquiring any other important items."

"You mean you thought Tribal Council could chew gum and walk at the same time?"

Web laughs. "Fair point. Spot-on." His expression changes. "Listen, you did a fantastic job. I'm extremely impressed with what you pulled together in two days' time."

"Miigwech," I say. "But what's this about a private collection being donated? The other reindeer haven't mentioned anything."

"There's a guy named Frank Lockhart who—"

"Lockhart?" My voice attracts the attention of passersby.

"Yeah. You know him?" Web's eyebrow raises.

"He owns Teepees-n-Trinkets, that dinky museum in St. Ignace. Sells the finest Indian art made in China."

"That's him. He also owns the southern tip of Sugar Island. Been in his family ever since they got it from our families." Web pauses. "The other interns haven't mentioned anything?"

"They trickle out for secret meetings in the stairwell."

Web shakes his head at their pettiness.

"The formal announcement will be made a week from Friday. At Mack State, per Lockhart's wishes."

"That's weird. Why wouldn't he do it here?" I motion around the resort.

He shrugs. "Lockhart's a . . . quirky man. Kind of grouchy and particular."

"In my village, we call that an asshole."

Web's quick laugh ends in a snort that makes us both giggle.

"You are way funnier than my previous intern," he says.

A thought comes to me. "Why would you request me but then let me do independent study instead of helping with the Lockhart announcement?"

He tilts his head as if seeing me for the first time.

"In my village, we call that being astute." Web continues, "The announcement is just for show. We've got three interns who can event-plan. Your part comes after the announcement, when we nail down specifics on the transfer of the collection. We're going to need you to run interference with Cooper Turtle. He can be a bit . . ."

"Quirky," I offer. The hallway lights flicker, signaling the break is over.

"Yeah. Let's go with that," he says with a grin. "You work well with him." He motions for me to lead the way. "Back to the meeting we go, Ogichidaakwezans."

After the evening meeting concludes, Web has me request permission from a parent to let him drive me home. Since I texted Mom earlier about needing to attend the Tribal Council meeting, it provided a lead in to now inform her that I got transferred to work with Subchief Tom Webster. And to get permission in writing via text for Web to provide transportation home. I'm guessing that Chief Manitou didn't have Pauline get permission to be in his car. Thank goodness I work for the non-skeevy guy.

When I arrive home, Mom warms up dinner leftovers. She serves me at the kitchen island where Pauline eats a bowl of ice cream.

"So, you got transferred to Tribal Council?" Mom asks.

I glance at my sister for clues about what Mom knows about my situation. Pauline texts someone on her phone. Maybe her sneaky snag from Saturday night? I strain my neck but can't get the correct angle.

"Holaay," Pauline says. "Creeper peep much?" She makes a big deal of turning her phone away from me.

Mom is still waiting for an answer.

"Yeah. Subchief Webster requested me. I'll be helping with the donation of cultural items the Tribe will be getting from Mr. Lockhart."

"It doesn't seem fair to Cooper Turtle. Tribal Council had four interns and he only had one." Mom shakes her head.

Pauline chimes in. "Claire Barbeau said interns could be transferred at any time because that's what happens in"—she makes a one-handed air quote—"'the real world.'"

Okay. Sometimes my twin comes through for me.

A thought dances across my mind. Claire Barbeau and Mr. Lockhart. He was in the old photo on her desk at Chi Mukwa. Mr. Lockhart and Claire, with her mom sitting between them. Are they related? Web said Lockhart was grouchy. Maybe Claire could give me tips for getting along with him. But if they aren't close, she might not be any help.

Mom's voice interrupts my thoughts. "Perry, are you listening?"

"Huh?"

"I said that your dad and I volunteered for the new Repatriations Committee. Cooper wants people to travel to other communities and learn how they prepare ancestors for reburial."

"Oh," I say. It feels like I'm juggling too many ideas at once.

Mom continues. "Auntie Daunis agreed to stay here when Pops and I travel next Friday."

"Like a babysitter?" Pauline screeches indignantly.

"Like a trusted relative of two sixteen-year-old girls who live in a community where Nish kwewag go missing," Mom replies. She turns to me. "We were excited to support your work."

I smile in response, hoping it hides the worry in my face. I wonder if Cooper will tell Mom and Pops about firing me.

CHAPTER 14

FRIDAY, JULY 4TH

Instead of our usual Friday seminar, we are working at the Tribe's Fourth of July picnic. Lucas swings by to get us for the ride to the mainland. Pauline reaches his car first but takes the back seat. I don't remember doing anything to warrant this kindness.

"Why are you being nice?" I ask. Lucas laughs.

"Oh my gawd, Perry. You're so suspicious," Pauline says.

We reach the powwow grounds, where the Superior Shores crew has set up a huge tent that reminds me of Auntie's mom's wedding to the Mack State men's hockey coach a few years ago. Except these round dining tables are covered in red-checkered tablecloths and have red, white, and blue carnation centerpieces instead of elegant white linens and white roses.

Beyond the dining tent, huge grills are set up, and three smokers fill the air with applewood and brisket. The Tribe goes all out for the community picnic. There will be a parade downtown this evening, followed by a huge fireworks extravaganza that the Tribe cosponsors with the City of Sault Ste. Marie. But the picnic is just for tribal citizens and registered guests, mostly family members who aren't enrolled citizens.

There used to be different colored wristbands for guests, until a council member said their unenrolled grandchildren were made to feel like freeloaders. Granny June says we just gotta wait until there's enough council members with unenrolled relatives, and then Tribal Council will vote to lower the blood-quantum requirement. Pops says only three things still have pedigrees: dogs, horses, and Indians. His tribe avoids all that by using lineal descendancy, which still involves a family tree but without any colonizer blood-quantum nonsense.

I spy Team Tribal Council's royal blue polo shirts and reluctantly join them. Pauline gave me her polo after bitching for the millionth time about getting transferred. My new team seems surprised to see me wearing it. I only did so because I knew they weren't expecting it. Sometimes—no, always—it's good to ruffle snobby feathers.

"Hi, team," I say, because Perry Firekeeper-Birch owns any space she occupies.

Only one says hi back. She's a prelaw undergrad named Ellen.

"I had an idea for our Elder interviews," I say.

"We already decided to ask for stories about past Tribal Councils," Flynn replies.

Of course they already decided something. Across the tent, Shense approaches Pauline and Lucas. Her baby is wrapped across her chest.

"Sounds great," I say, already checked out. "Catch yous later."

I approach Shense. All I can see of her baby is a full head of dark hair sticking up like the wispy tufts of afterfeathers.

"This is Washkeh, short for Washkiyaanimad." Shense introduces her daughter by sliding the wrap just below the baby's plump cheek. One eye opens—a brown eye so dark that I can't tell where the iris stops and the pupil begins.

"Aaniin, Washkiyaanimad," I say. "The wind that changes directions."

The baby blinks once before hiding her face between Shense's breasts.

"That's really beautiful," Erik says beside me. "The name, I mean. And the baby."

"What about Shense's boobs?" I add. Lucas and Shense crack up. Erik's face goes red. I remember touching him during our not-a-date. Teasing about cheeks like ripe crab apples.

"Oh my gawd, Perry." Pauline parrots herself from earlier.

"What? I thought Shense's breasts deserved praise." I remember my other purpose for hanging around Team Misfit Toys. "What topic are yous gonna ask the Elders about?"

They look from one to the other. Even Pauline, who I had assumed would bring printouts of conversation starters and interview checklists.

I get to my point. "Because I thought we could ask Elders to talk about black ash baskets. Like, what were their earliest memories about family members making baskets? Who in their family made them? Did they have any distinctive weaving techniques? And did they sign their baskets with a name and a date, or their Spirit name, or some other identifier?"

Shense says, "Oooh. Those are good questions."

"Sounds like our topic is decided," Lucas says to Pauline. "All good?"

She nods before commenting, "'We'? Since when did you rejoin Team Misfit Toys?"

"Pleeeaaassseee?" I beg while cheesing a toothy smile.

"Once you're a Misfit, you're always a Misfit," Erik says. "Welcome back."

His words feel good, a reminder of when our friendship was germinating.

It's great that we get paid double to work at the picnic. Last year, Pauline and I did it for free. We refilled pitchers of ice water until I dumped one on Pauline and got yelled at by Auntie. I wonder how many interns would have shown up if it hadn't been a work assignment. My sister's whiny *Oh my gawd, Perry* rings in my ears. *You're so negative.*

I stop at a table of Elders to refill coffee cups. Granny sits next to her best friend, Minnie.

"You got any whiskey for our coffee?" one Elder asks.

"'No alcohol. No dogs. No politics,'" Granny quotes from the sign at the entrance to the tent. "No fun," she adds.

"Nobody twisted your arm to show up, June," Minnie snipes.

"If they twisted your arm, it would snap like a twig." Granny turns to me, "Speaking of twisted, do you got any Twisted Tea? Minnie can't handle the hard stuff."

"The hell I can't!" Minnie yells. "I don't know why I'm sitting with you after what you did this morning." She gets up and leaves abruptly.

"Why are yous fighting today?" I ask.

Granny shoos me away. "She didn't text this morning, so I called Tribal Police. They showed up while she was still entertaining an overnight guest."

"Holaay. All that fuss for not texting back?"

"We text to let each other know we made it through another night." Granny shrugs. "She didn't text back this morning. How was I to know she was up to shenanigans in the bedroom? Or that her grandson would be the officer making the wellness check?"

Claire is next to me as soon as I sit down with my own plate of food after all the Elders have been served.

"I wanted to check in and see how your week went with Team Tribal Council," she says.

"It's good," I say finally. "Web—I mean Subchief Webster—is a good supervisor."

"How wonderful," Claire exclaims. "And your new teammates?"

"Like I said, I enjoy working for Web." I shovel a forkful of potato salad into my mouth.

"I see," she says. "Teamwork is an important part of the Kinomaage program."

"I was a great team member with the Misfit Toys," I comment. I say nothing about unofficially rejoining my former team earlier at the picnic.

"Yes, I could see that," Claire says. "It's too bad you couldn't work with Team Tribal Council during the week but be part of Team Misfit Toys on Fridays."

I pretend as if she just gave me the best idea. "Claire, that would be a great learning experience for me, to work with two teams."

"Hmm," Claire considers. "Perhaps you could prepare a report comparing and contrasting the two teams?"

Here is where my negotiating skills come in. I want to be back on Team Misfit Toys, but I don't want to spend time doing anything extra like a report.

"Miigwech, Claire. I'll work out the specifics with Web . . . I mean Subchief Webster."

"Well, you know him far better than I do," Claire says.

Shense was right about Claire's voice being on the squeaky side at times. A weird feeling tickles the back of my neck. Maybe I'm forgetting something? Something about Claire, perhaps?

"Oh," I say, suddenly remembering. "When I was in your office last Friday for the, um, meeting with Cooper Turtle . . . I saw a picture on your desk. I wasn't being nosy but . . ." I pause because I am totally being nosy. "Are you related to Mr. Lockhart?"

She blinks her surprise.

"Frank Lockhart was my stepfather for a short while." Claire looks uncomfortable.

"Oh. Okay." Why did I think asking her about Lockhart would be a good idea? I backpedal. "Just curious, because he's donating his private collection of cultural items to the Tribe. I'm helping Web—um, I wanted to know anything about Lockhart—um, Mr. Lockhart."

The more I ramble, the more Claire picks at her cuticles. I scan for anyone who might get me out of this awkward situation. Erik and Pauline talk and laugh together.

My sister and I haven't been in a situation where we liked the same person. Her "type" is all over the place, whereas I really haven't been attracted to anyone.

I jump a little when Claire starts talking.

"He owns over five hundred acres of property on the south end. I lived in his home for two years." Her voice sounds clipped. Like when Pauline is being pissy, and when I ask what's wrong, she says *Nothing* when she really means *Something I don't care to discuss with you.*

"Well, um, miigwech for telling me." I look around. Anywhere except at Claire.

"Enjoy your lunch, Perry," she says, rising and disappearing into the crowd.

After we finish eating, the other Misfits and I interview Elders about black ash baskets. I am surprised to learn that not every story is uplifting. My great-grandmother wasn't the only Nish person who had a Zhaaganaash seek an unfair deal on baskets.

Minnie tells me about a Zhaaganaash lady who brought over a pot of iigw when Minnie's grandmother was sick. She expected the ill woman to sign over a portion of their land in exchange for the soup but settled for a basket.

Half the Elders remember parents and grandparents making black ash baskets, and the other half don't remember because they were taken away and placed in boarding schools.

I've known about the boarding schools since I was a kid. Whether the school was government-run or church-run, the stripping away of Ojibwe culture was the same. Haircuts, uniforms, military-style dormitories, and marching everywhere like soldiers instead of children. Beaten for speaking Ojibwemowin or for doing anything considered "Indian." Unable to return home unless parents received permission from the school administrators or the priests. Parents had to pay for the roundtrip transportation and were threatened with loss of future visits if the children were delayed in their return.

I never thought about the connection between baskets and boarding schools. But listening to story after story today, I realize it's obvious. Children weren't home to learn basket making, beadwork, wood carving, and porcupine-quill art from their families. Or to gain subsistence skills like fishing, hunting, and trapping. The activities our families relied upon for survival and to make a living—these traditional Anishinaabe ways of being and expressing our culture through art and storytelling—were not passed on as they had been for previous generations.

I say a silent prayer of thanks for my parents teaching Pauline and me. They taught Lucas alongside us as well. I never thought about how important the cultural camps are for citizens like Erik who wouldn't have any other way of learning these ways.

I take a break from interviewing Elders to walk away from the tent. Eyes closed, I raise my face to the sunshine. The warmth feels like a caress. The noise from the tent fades. I stay there, smiling and breathing deeply.

"Pear-Bear and Erik," Lucas shouts, interrupting my solitude.

Except I wasn't alone. When I open my eyes, Erik is nearby. I wonder how long he's been here?

"I thought stories about baskets would be nice and fluffy," Lucas says. "Some of these Elders got up in my feelings." He lifts his chin. "What about yous?"

"Same," Erik and I say in unison.

"I haven't seen Auntie yet. Have you?" Lucas asks me.

"No. Why? You need an ass-kicking or something?" Sometimes I crack myself up.

"Yeah," Lucas says. "You wanna try instead, Pear-Bear?" He stands in front of me and raises his palms. He flexes his biceps and smiles expectantly. We've played Palm Push for years. He waits for me to accept the challenge.

"Oh, all right," I say, mirroring his pose and starting off with a lackluster push.

Our palms meet a dozen times; we both keep our forearms limp. Finally, I put some muscle into my push. Lucas laughs. A few pushes later, the muscle connecting his neck to his shoulder tightens. He doesn't know it's his tell. When Lucas pushes next, he puts his weight behind it. I know the perfect moment to push him off balance. I strike quickly. Down Lucas goes, falling onto his ass.

"Aw, man," he says, getting up. "Now you're showing off in front of Erik."

I protest. We do handstands next; Lucas has the bigger muscles, but I'm more agile. Plus, holding a handstand is about balance, not strength. Same as with Palm Push. Lucas thinks he has the advantage because of his arm muscles. But I own that game because I watch my opponent. The moment they make their move, it provides a half second of vulnerability.

I even bested TJ Kewadin once, and that guy is a mountain.

When Lucas gets tired of losing to me, he tells Erik to show us what he can do. I'm surprised when Erik holds a fairly decent handstand. His untucked golf shirt falls to his neck. His armpit hair is dark and his abs are more defined than I expected. Lucas adds a distraction by pulling Erik's hair tie off. It makes Erik laugh and fall backward. Erik sits up; loose curls cover most of his face. He is still laughing. When he gathers his hair back into the hair tie and both arms are raised, there is a moment when our eyes meet. He blushes. His cheeks seem redder than I remembered. He looks away first, and then it's my turn to feel flushed.

It's the only time I feel a pang of regret for taking the basket from Teepees-n-Trinkets. But I can't undo it, and in all honesty I know I'd do the same thing if given another chance.

Lucas helps Erik to his feet before running off to find Pauline.

"That was a good break," I tell Erik.

I motion toward the tent, but he keeps his feet planted as he faces me.

"Perry," he says.

Hearing my name in his deep voice makes me feel tingly.

"That afternoon at the teepee store," he continues. "I get it now. When the Elders talked about baskets they remembered . . . It wasn't just about a basket. They're talking about more than that. I know seeing your great-grandmother's basket brought up a lot of emotions for you. I'm just starting to learn what it means. But I understand why you did it."

I stare into his bright blue eyes. Neither of us looks away.

"Miigwech," I say softly.

We walk back to the tent. It was a really good break.

When Cooper's wife leaves the table to talk with Shense, I take advantage of the opportunity to speak privately with my former boss.

"My parents volunteered for the Repatriations Committee?" It's not exactly a question, but I don't know how to talk with Cooper anymore. "Will you tell them about . . ." I can't even say the words.

"That's for you to share. Or not," he says.

"I, um, found out Tribal Council was going to request my transfer anyway because of Frank Lockhart's donation. Did you know about that?" I look down at my hands.

Cooper replies, "I didn't know about the donation or the transfer."

I want to say that it seems so wrong for our tribal leaders to keep their museum director out of the loop when they're getting a major donation of cultural items to be displayed in our museum or returned to the earth. That's what I should tell him.

Instead I blurt, "But if I hadn't screwed up and I was still your intern, would you have fought to keep me?"

He shrugs. "Council wants; Council gets."

I didn't think it was possible to feel worse than when I heard the sad basket stories.

Auntie enters the tent. She sees Lucas and gives him a hug. Auntie! I can ask her for a loan. The auction is Tuesday. She speaks French—she could register on the site and do the bidding. It makes perfect sense.

"Auntie, I have a favor to ask," I say, breathless after sprinting to her side.

"Not now, Perry." She turns away.

"But it's important."

She turns toward me in slow motion. Auntie is solid muscle stretched taller than any woman I know. But right now, her scowl is the most intimidating thing about her.

"What," she says impatiently.

"You seem in a hurry, Auntie." I shift uneasily. "We can do this another time."

"Perry," she says, now impatient *and* annoyed.

I steel myself. "There's a ceremonial shaker—a snapping-turtle-shell shaker—for sale through an auction house in France." I sound like the end of a drug commercial where they word-vomit all the side effects. "I did my research and talked with Stormy. It's from Sugar Island and has been missing for over a hundred and fifty years. The estimate is between sixteen and twenty-one thousand dollars. The auction is online on Tuesday. Please lend me the zhooniyaa and help me get it back."

She heaves a heavy sigh. My legs shake as if I sprinted a mile instead of forty feet.

"I can't." She looks away, unable to say it to my face. "My friend Robin-bah . . . her mom just died." Auntie's voice catches.

Robin-bah. Adding the 'bah' means Robin is no longer in this world either.

"Her dad is a mess. I need to help him. For my friend. My old teammate." Auntie walks away with her head down.

My eyes sting with tears held back. The snapping-turtle shaker isn't coming home.

The Warrior Girl stands with me in the sunshine. I show her the trays of my plants, which I suspect are pumpkin plants.

"I have to toughen them up," I say. "See the dark green leaves with jagged edges? Those are their true leaves, not their sprout leaves. I need to build up their tolerance to withstand long days of sunshine. They need to become hardened. It's the only way to survive."

She raises an eyebrow. A smirk plays at her lips.

Me—the tenderest of true leaves—instructing her about survival.

WEEK FIVE

There is a strong convergence between the "end of the Indian wars" in 1890 and . . . the development of the tourist and ethnic arts market . . . It was not just pottery and "curios" that collectors were after, but Indian skulls, bones, scalps, and sometimes whole heads and bodies. Many of the remains of the Cheyenne men, women, and children slaughtered at the Colorado Sand Creek massacre of 1864 were sent to the Army Medical Museum . . . Other remains from this massacre, such as scalps and women's pubic hair, were strung across the stage of the Denver Opera House.

—Kathleen S. Fine-Dare, *Grave Injustice: The American Indian Repatriation Movement and NAGPRA*

CHAPTER 15
MONDAY, JULY 7TH

I stomp into Web's office on Monday morning. He looks up from his espresso cup and motions for me to sit. I close the sliding door behind me.

"What's on your mind, Ogichidaakwezans?"

"Just another crappy Monday morning. You heard about the woman from Whitefish Reserve? A tribe even smaller than ours, but still big enough to have women go missing." I stay angry; it feels better than being meek and scared. "So, Web, ask me how it feels to be an endangered species."

He sets down the dainty cup. "I'm co-sponsoring a resolution to fund two new positions at the Tribal Police Department. One full-time and one part-time spot. They'll focus on the MMIW database and working with other tribal communities to create a statewide missing and murdered Indigenous women database. If your sister wants to continue working on this issue, the part-time spot would be ideal for her." Web leans forward. "I know it isn't a complete solution, but it would be a decent start, hey?"

"Yeah. It's something," I say, unconvinced.

"What else is on your mind?" Web asks.

"It was hella dirty to keep the Lockhart deal from Cooper Turtle," I say. "I know he's an odd duck, but in the three weeks I worked for him, Cooper always did what was best for our ancestors and their belongings."

I look over his shoulder at a framed diploma. I didn't know Web had a degree in business management from the University of Michigan. *Focus, Perry. Focus.*

"It was disrespectful to Cooper."

Web checks his shirt for lint or cat hair. It's the way he buys a few seconds to think about what he wants to say.

"Fair point. I will talk with him and own up to the decision," he says.

I know it's not a competition between Kinomaage supervisors, but I admire Web's ability to take action. It makes me feel disloyal to Cooper.

"And about the donation?" I begin. "Lockhart sells fake Native stuff at Teepees-n-Trinkets in St. Ignace, hey? But he also displays funerary objects—items that were buried with ancestors, or on them, like moccasins. He's got sacred objects on display too; I saw a ceremonial pipe fully assembled." He grimaces. "You get it, Web. Lockhart shouldn't own it, and he for sure shouldn't be displaying it like that."

"Yes, it's an extensive collection." He nods his head in agreement. "We are incredibly fortunate that he reached out with an offer to donate it to the Tribe."

"Do you think the Tribe will get everything he's got?" I say.

He chuckles. "Perry, why don't you tell me why you don't think we will get everything?"

I stand and begin pacing Web's office.

"I think he's got illegal items. Did you know he has an entire family's moccasins on display in St. Ignace? With a label about the items coming from the graves of 'an Indian brave' and 'his maiden' and their children. But what happened to the ancestors' remains if he's showing off their mocs? I think he's a grave robber. And if any items were collected after 1990, they're illegal for him to own." I stop in front of Web's desk. "He owns a shit-ton of property on Sugar Island. I think the graves he's robbing are in his backyard. They're our relatives."

"What would you do, Ogichidaakwezans?" Web asks. "If anything was possible and you could get away with it, how far would you go to bring our items home?"

I go silent. Not to mull over the question, but because my answer scares me.

I admire warriors—those who are willing to do what others can't or won't do for the community. Web's voice is so clear in my head, he may as well have said it aloud just now.

Finally, I answer, "I would do whatever it takes to reclaim every ancestor and object."

While Team Tribal Council works on final details for Friday's big event, I wear noise-canceling headphones to listen to the recordings of Elders telling their basket stories. The voice-to-text transcription software doesn't recognize Ojibwemowin, so I listen and correct any errors.

After finishing one interview, I get up to stretch, use the restroom, and refill my water bottle. I return to the conference room, get comfortable, and reach for the headphones.

"Hey, Perry?" It's Ellen, the only one who has been somewhat nice to me. "Do you want to wear your regalia to the Lockhart event on Friday?"

I ask why. The two interns look to the ringleader.

"Thought it might be nice to have someone dressed to represent Ojibwe culture," Flynn says.

"Nah," I say. "That feels like just for show."

"We thought it was a way to include you," Ellen adds.

I mull it over. "I'll wear a ribbon skirt, because that's a way of dressing up for special events. But I'm not doing feathers and braids."

"That sounds really nice, Perry," Ellen says. "Ah, my partner has a ribbon vest they said I could borrow. Do you think I could wear it with pants and a dressy top?"

I'm about to make a crack about not being a fashionista, but I decide to answer sincerely. After all, when Lockhart makes the formal announcement, it will be a special evening.

"Sure," I tell her. Ellen's face lights up, and I'm glad I wasn't an asshole.

Not quite ready to dive back into the basket stories, I decide to research Frank Lockhart on my work laptop. It doesn't seem right that as Cooper's intern, I had an ancient computer, and as a council intern, I scored a new MacBook Air.

I do a Google News search for Frank Lockhart and quickly discover there was a race car driver in the 1920s with the same name who was killed in a two-hundred-mile-per-hour crash. I add *Sugar Island* to the search. A laundry list of articles, mostly business headlines from local newspapers, appears. I add another term to the search: *wife*.

A wedding announcement from 1991, CARON BARBEAU WEDS FRANK LOCKHART, shows a beautiful and very young woman next to an older guy. The bride has pale skin and dark hair and eyes, just like Auntie. I scan for interesting details. They honeymooned in Paris. Her daughter, Claire Barbeau, served as flower girl. The article doesn't list anyone's ages, which, given this particular couple, seems like the most interesting aspect.

The next article, LOCAL WOMAN REPORTED MISSING, is from 1993. A friend of Caron Lockhart's reported her missing, and Caron's sister indicated that Caron had left her husband after an argument. It was not unusual for Caron to take weekend trips by herself. Nor was it unusual for Caron to leave her daughter behind, since her sister and brother-in-law worked for the Lockharts and lived on the property with a child of their own. But an absence going on two weeks, at the time of the article, was alarming.

Another headline, POSTCARD RECEIVED FROM MISSING WOMAN, appeared two months later. Connie Leroy, the sister of Caron Lockhart, received a postcard postmarked in Barcelona indicating the missing woman was fine and was not ready to return home. Caron Lockhart thanked her sister for looking after her daughter Claire, age eight. The sister confirmed the handwriting was that of Caron Lockhart.

Holaay. I can understand why Claire seemed uncomfortable talking to me about Frank Lockhart at the Fourth of July picnic. It must have brought up painful emotions. I can't imagine having your mom leave you behind. What does that do to an eight-year-old kid?

I round out my stellar day staring at the auction listing for the turtle-shell shaker. The auction is tomorrow. I don't think I can bear seeing the word *SOLD* across the listing, along with the winning bid. I block the website and delete my browser history. I drag the file with my presentation slides into the trash icon. I'll do the same thing tonight on my laptop at home.

Sometimes you need to protect your heart from the pain.

CHAPTER 16

THURSDAY, JULY 1OTH

On Thursday morning, I am alone in the conference room. The other Team Tribal Council interns are running errands ahead of tomorrow's big event at Mack State. Although I don't need to use the headphones—since no one is around to complain—I find it harder to concentrate without them. I anticipated taking all day transcribing the Elders' black ash basket stories, but I'm pleasantly surprised to finish two hours into the workday.

The stories make me want to go next door to see all the black ash baskets on display. It's like each one is a survival story. Maybe I'll independent-study the rest of the day in the museum. Just because I'm no longer Cooper's intern, it doesn't mean I'm banned from the place.

Miss Manitou glances up from her game of solitaire when I enter the library.

"Aaniin. I'd like to tour the museum and spend time with the black ash baskets," I say.

"I'll buzz you in," she says. "And when are you going to clean out your mailbox?"

I never used my mailbox. Each staff member has a cubby with

their name on it, for any incoming mail or interoffice documents. I never paid attention to mine, because Cooper told me anything I needed to know. Besides, no one ever sent me anything.

My leather portfolio is wedged diagonally in the cubby that still bears my name. As I retrieve it, a sheet of paper slides to the floor. I recognize Cooper's perfect penmanship: *A Reading List for Repatriation Jedi Padawans*. Ten books are listed in alphabetical order by author's last name.

He must have prepared the list before he fired me. I tuck it inside the portfolio. My fingertips caress the smooth leather cover. The engraved brass nameplate is cool to the touch. I hug the portfolio to my chest as I turn to leave.

The *Have You Seen Me* flyer on the bulletin board isn't Darby's. It's the latest missing woman I told Web about, the one from a nearby tribe. Her personal details differ but the flyer is the same. Our Tribal Police Department created a form, gave it a file name, and saved it on a shared drive for easy access. They needed a form to standardize the info because creeps keep taking us.

I spy Darby's flyer crumpled in the trash bin. I retrieve it and smooth the wrinkles as best I can. Darby's aquamarine eyes sear into mine, as if to say, *Can you believe this shit? I never thought it would happen to me.*

Miss Manitou buzzes me into the museum. Cooper's voice carries from the first exhibit. I cross the lobby toward the final exhibit room. I just want to be alone with the baskets.

"Perry," Cooper calls out.

I reluctantly turn to see Cooper and Dr. Fenton. She smiles pleasantly.

"Hello, Dr. Fenton. Aaniin, Cooper. Just here to do research for Subchief Webster."

Dr. Fenton speaks. "I'm here for the day to prepare the funding request with Cooper's assistance. After all, those boxes won't inventory themselves." She giggles lightly.

They'll never get inventoried if we wait for you to do it, I think.

"Dr. Fenton," I begin. Cooper makes eye contact and a slight shake of his head. I take it he doesn't want me to engage with the anthropologist.

Screw it. Cooper Turtle isn't my supervisor anymore.

"My mom is the Tribal Health director. She's made hundreds of funding requests to Tribal Council over the years. She always says they like small projects that can be scaled up instead of large projects that get defunded for overpromising and underdelivering."

Dr. Fenton giggles again. "Is Perry your mini-me? She sounds exactly like you, Cooper." She turns to me. "Small dreams equals limited results."

If I stick around, I'll say everything Cooper is afraid I'll say.

"Nice to see you again, Dr. Fenton." I give a small wave and retreat.

In the final exhibit room, I stand in front of my great-grandmother's basket for a while. When I turn around and scan the room, it's as if I still have the headphones on. Elders' voices, fresh and familiar, tell me what they can remember. Which family members were good at finding the best trees, and the ones who took turns pounding the fallen black ash logs to loosen the rings. Which flowers made the best dyes for the accent strips.

Some Elders spoke about baskets as if they existed only in dreams; a few were scared to speak of them at all. The priests, nuns, and government folks at the boarding schools were not satisfied in beating children's bodies; they sought to beat Anishinaabe memories into oblivion.

How many dusty stories are inside the boxes in Dr. Fenton's office?

Maybe if our Elders could see and hold the baskets, the stories would breathe again.

What would you do, Ogichidaakwezans, if anything was possible?

What if I looked through the boxes and found baskets signed with familiar surnames?

How far would you go to bring our items home?

For a start, I would go to St. Ignace.

While Dr. Fenton is wasting Cooper's time today, I could go to her office. But how could I make it happen? I need a car and a plan.

First, a car. I can plan en route. Auntie has an old pickup truck. She keeps the key above the visor. If I can get to her place, I'll take it as a sign to keep going.

I call Lucas. "What you doing?" I ask.

"What you want," he says, a smile in his voice.

I laugh. "Just a ride somewhere."

"Sounds sketch. Just running back and forth between Fisheries and Culture Camp 2.0 with supplies for next week's Young Environmentalists Camp. Is it somewhere I can drop you off along the way?"

"Yeah. You're the best, Lucas. I'll be in the parking lot behind Admin."

I've got a ride to Auntie's. She's working today at Traditional Medicine. Waab is at his Grandma Grace's house.

Taking a cue from Pauline's stealth sneaky snagging, I decide to leave my phone behind. The women's restroom off the main hallway is rarely used. Silencing the ringtone, I slide the phone above the cabinet of cleaning supplies.

Minutes later, I climb into Lucas's truck and tell him to take the back way to the ferry.

"Hi to you too," he says.

"Drop me off at Auntie's place, hey? And don't mention it to anyone."

"Intrigue."

"I need to borrow her truck to run an errand. I've done it before and so has Pauline."

"Sneaky sisters," Lucas says, looking especially amused.

I reach for my phone to check the time and remember that I left it behind on purpose. I glance at the dashboard clock. "Pick me back up in four hours, hey?"

"Super sneaky and bossy."

It takes all of ten minutes to reach Auntie's house downriver from the ferry launch. Just before I get out of the truck, his STUDENT RECY-CLING CLUB T-shirt catches my eye.

"One more thing," I tell Lucas, already shucking my polo shirt. "Switch shirts with me and give me your ball cap."

"Geez, Pear-Bear. Leave something to the imagination." The sight of me in my sports bra makes him move quicker. His T-shirt is on me four seconds later.

"See you at four p.m. sharp," I say with a tip of his ball cap.

I take a back route to St. Ignace. No need to pass someone on the highway who would recognize me or Auntie's truck. I park in the residential neighborhood a block from campus and cut through the woods to the carriage house. I remember Dr. Fenton's entry code and punch it in.

Her office seems even messier than before. I find a stack of folded brown-paper grocery bags that would be good for hauling baskets, a discarded pair of white gloves, a box cutter, and packing tape. Starting with the box nearest to the kitchen, I move quickly to open it, peer at the contents inside, and retape. I repeat the process until I lose count of how many boxes I've searched.

When I open a box with baskets, my heart leaps into my throat.

I admire warriors who are willing to do what others can't or won't do for the community.

I check the bottom of each basket for a signature. Some are difficult to read, but the ones I can make out aren't names I remember from transcribing the tapes. On the fifth box, my breath catches. Kingfisher is one of those old family names from Sugar Island.

The round gathering basket fills the brown paper grocery bag.

Six boxes later, another familiar surname. An Elder who said their grandfather had a basket where he stored a folded certificate, signed by U.S. President Ulysses S. Grant, deeming the grandfather to be "competent," which meant he spoke English and therefore was eligible to receive tracts of land during the Dawes Act. The basket is empty, but the signature on the bottom has the same last name. It nests inside the first basket.

I freeze at the four electronic beeps followed by the front door opening. Someone is here. I cannot see him, but he's in the front room.

"I'm here," he says.

Do I fight back or make a run for it?

"No." He stretches the word like rubbery goop. How can he read my mind?

Footsteps. A metal drawer opens, then closes. Papers rustle.

"Raquel, I can't find anything in here."

My sigh of relief is a slow, silent exhale. Whoever it is, he's talking to Dr. Fenton on his cell phone. Looking for a document she must need for the proposal.

What if she needs him to check for something in the hallway? Or the kitchen?

Reluctantly leaving the bag, I take one soft step toward the bathroom. Then another.

"Darlin', this isn't a wild goose chase, is it?" The voice is a deep purr.

Holy wah. Raquel has a sneaky snag.

Another step and I'm in the tiny bathroom. The door is probably squeaky. Hiding in the small shower stall might be a better—

Of course she has boxes stacked to the ceiling.

I squeeze into the narrow gap between the boxes and the shower curtain, careful not to disturb the rusty shower hooks. If I stand on the raised threshold, my sneakers won't be visible beneath the curtain. Leaning just so, I can see the hallway reflected in the bathroom mirror.

Why can't Raquel's snag find whatever the hell she wants him to find? Oh right. Because she is a hoarder raising a colony of dust bunnies.

"Now you think it's in the kitchen?" He's halfway down the hall in an instant.

I glimpse the bald head and nearly scream. My heart jumps forward as my head thunks the box behind me. I cover my mouth with my hand to muffle any other noises I might make.

It's Grant Edwards. The guy who hurt Auntie.

He shuffles papers in the kitchen, uttering an occasional "uh-huh" and "not there."

The box behind my head rattled, I realize in delayed awareness. Maybe it's the lack of oxygen because I've been holding my breath. I look behind to see a cereal box in front of a square cardboard box. As I turn forward again, I register what was on the masking tape label.

TEETH.

Just then, Grant Edwards says, "Is this it?" His voice fades as the swirls on the shower curtain seem to come alive with animated movement. "Great. Now you owe me, darlin'." His laugh is smooth. "I told you, Raquel, you scratch my back and I'll scratch whatever you want . . . You want me to email it?" A longer pause. "Okay. I'm on my way. Bye, darlin'."

A beat later, he calls her the vilest name someone can call a woman.

His voice is no longer silky. It's unguarded, raw, and ugly. I assume he ended the call before spewing such filth.

A zipper. Fabric rustling. The tap of toilet lid against tank. Urine streams into the bowl.

I lean sideways, as far from the mirror as I can. Which is when my foot begins to slip from the shower. I brace myself, one hand against the wall of boxes and the other pressed to the shower enclosure not a foot away from the towel rack.

He's going to find me. He will attack me. Or he will blackmail me. Grant Edwards will turn my being here into something that benefits him.

Instead he zips his pants and flushes the toilet. The moment—when he should see my hand and whip back the shower curtain—passes by. His footsteps leave the bathroom and continue down the hallway, through the front room. The door opens and closes.

I've never been so relieved that someone didn't wash their hands. What a nasty, filthy pajog. I still wait another fifteen minutes, at least, to make sure he isn't hiding anywhere.

Once my breathing and heart rate have returned to normal, I step from the shower. I look back at the cereal box and read the entire label: TEETH—S. STATE STREET EXCAVATION, 1956.

I won't look inside. I absolutely will not look inside. I won't—

When I open the box, it's full of teeth. Dr. Raquel Fenton has a cereal box full of teeth.

She is an anthropologist who studies Indigenous cultures.

These teeth did not come from any Zhaaganaash cemetery.

For the next hour, I halt at every noise, real or imagined. Between frozen moments, I move quickly to explore as many boxes as possible in my allotted window of time. There is no time to examine the porcupine-quill boxes or the hand-carved spiles for tapping maple trees.

When I come across a basket with a familiar surname, a thrill zings through my body.

I resist temptation to take other items, though I swear they are calling out to me. Daga wiiji'ishin. Niwanishin. *Please help me. I am lost.*

I stick with my original plan to reclaim only those baskets signed with Sugar Island family names I recognize. If I try to take anything else, I will not stop.

I sing to those I am leaving behind.

Niminjinawez. *I am sorry.*

Nindaatagaadendam. *I am overwhelmed by the task.*

Crying, I take two brown paper bags and disappear into the woods.

CHAPTER 17

FRIDAY, JULY 11TH

eam Tribal Council has me alphabetizing the name badges on the sign-in table.

"So, why didn't Council set this up at the Superior Shores?" I ask Ellen, who might be double-checking my grasp of the alphabet.

"Mr. Lockhart requested it take place at the college," she says, matter-of-fact.

"Yeah, but what's Mack State got to do with the donation?" I press.

Flynn chimes in. "Chief Manitou is developing a proposal to make it a tribal college."

Pauline had mentioned something about that the day she got reassigned.

"It's a great idea, actually," Flynn continues. "The Tribe can get federal funding as a tribally controlled college. We'd be the only tribal college with men's and women's hockey teams. We could recruit Native players from all over the country and Canada. You play?"

"Shinny," I reply, lining up the last of the name tags. I glance up to see Flynn with a confused expression. "Pickup games. Backyard ice rinks."

"Well, if you're any good, you should try out once it's a tribal college team," he offers.

"I am good. I play shinny whenever I want. And if I was into teams, I'd be on a team."

"Yeah. I can see that," Flynn says. I'm not sure if it's an insult or a compliment.

"What do you mean by that?" I try but am not good at keeping my voice light.

"You don't seem like a team player." He shrugs. "Just an observation."

"Maybe I bonded to one team and that's it."

"You bonded with Subchief Webster pretty quickly," Flynn points out.

"Dude, I bond when I'm valued." I walk away with the last word.

The other interns arrive at four p.m. Erik and Shense seem deep in conversation. Pauline brings the ribbon skirt I forgot and a sweatshirt because the air conditioner is on full blast.

"I don't know why council interns had to show up so early," I tell her, donning the plain black sweatshirt. "We had everything set up by noon. Glad I brought a book."

Pauline does a double take. "I've never, ever heard you say that."

I shrug. "I read."

"Which book?" she asks, being all nosy.

"*Skull Wars*." When Pauline's eyes bug out, I add, "It's about the fight to claim the ancestor the Umatilla Tribe calls the Ancient One and anthropologists call the Kennewick Man."

My sister still looks bewildered. "Why don't you put this level of effort into school?"

"Because I don't give a shit about school," I say.

She smooths the hair behind her ear.

"Of all the things you worry about, you don't have to worry about me," I say, taking my ribbon skirt to the nearest bathroom to change. Pauline even slipped my tube of lip gloss into the skirt pocket. The pale pink glows against my sun-kissed skin. I like the way my full lips look smushy and irresistible.

The invited guests begin arriving at five thirty p.m. The Tribe provided two chartered buses to bring tribal citizens to the event. I stand between Lucas and Erik, waiting for the Elders to get off the bus.

"You look beautiful," Erik says. "I mean, you always do . . . I mean, today is extra special." His deep voice bumbles his words.

He has no idea how cute it sounds.

Granny June and Minnie are the first ones off the bus. Lucas and I escort them into the banquet room, stopping to pick up their name badges. Once they're seated, we pour cups of coffee for them before retracing our steps to escort more Elders.

"Granny and Minnie made up, hey?" I say with a smile.

"For now," Lucas says. "But the day ain't over yet." We laugh.

"Miss Firekeeper-Birch," a smooth, deep voice says.

Turning around, I see Chief Manitou and . . . Grant Edwards. It feels like the one time Pauline sucker punched me. I step back as a chill runs up my spine. I look around for Auntie but see Dr. Fenton instead. I wave as if Raquel is my dearest friend.

"Pardon." I sound all fancy, like Claire Barbeau, as I make a hasty exit. My heartbeat calms only slightly—from triple time to double time. What if she knows I took four baskets?

A colleague reaches her just as I do. It's the guy with the posh-sounding last name.

"Dr. Leer-wah," I say.

"Aaniin," he says in unsteady Ojibwemowin. "My, what a beautiful ribbon skirt."

I glance down at the fabric—tiny white polka dots against a black background. A rainbow of colors circles the lower half of the skirt; long ribbons extend from the side seams, fluttering when someone walks past. Black patent-leather Doc Marten platform boots reflect the chandelier lights.

"You're sitting with me, right? And Dr. Fenton?"

Each table has one intern in the mix of people from the Tribe and the college. If Grant Edwards is at our table, I will threaten Flynn with bodily harm to switch with me.

Chief Manitou steps onto the stage, making his way to the podium. He speaks into the microphone, asking people to find their seats so the event may begin.

An old man is at the doorway, familiar in a way I can't place. Chief Manitou approaches the man and shakes his hand. It's Frank Lockhart.

Scanning for Claire, I find her off to the side of the room. Her smile seems especially wide. Excited? It's more likely a grimace. She keeps her former stepfather in her sights, glancing his way too often for it to be random or casual.

Pauline walks past Claire, pulling my attention to how beautiful my sister looks in her peach floral ribbon skirt and ivory top. She's wearing her gold flats, and her hair is in a bun. She walks up to Chief Manitou, who is still next to Mr. Lockhart, when Grant Edwards joins them.

I cross the room, never losing sight of Pauline. She smiles at the men. Shakes her head, saying no to something. The room seems to lengthen as my steps quicken.

From behind, I grasp her arm and pull her back toward me. She resists, ready to ask what the hell I'm doing. My lips are at her ear.

"The bald guy is a wiindigoo."

Pauline looks horrified. She lets me hold her hand as we escape.

"Grant Edwards is a bad man who hurt Auntie when she was nineteen," I say, slowing as we approach her assigned table—the one with Granny June and Minnie.

"How come you know, and I don't?" She sounds hurt.

"Don't make it about that," I say sharply. "Auntie told me when you were shunning her. It's why she was on high alert when you were in that car." I glare at Grant Edwards and hope his smirk is a trick of the lighting. "Did he say anything to you?"

"I told Chief Manitou that I missed working for him. He introduced me to the two guys. Mr. Edwards asked if I was in college and if I played hockey. It was just polite conversation."

Granny tugs at Pauline to sit down as Chief Manitou introduces his cousin Rocky. I saw the printed agenda; there was no mention of an exhibition hoop dance. Yet here we are. Again. There's nothing to do except join my assigned table of museum people, along with Cooper and Web.

People turn their attention away from Rocky, focusing instead on an older Native man stumbling into the banquet room. He's a red-eyed mess in a black suit with his tie undone and white shirt untucked. Between crying and incoherent babbling, he manages to say something about someone who destroyed his world. He bumps into a table, sending a crystal water glass to the hardwood floors. When the man startles at the delicate shattering sound, he sways as if it wouldn't take much effort for him to splinter into shards as well.

As if that weren't enough drama, Auntie rushes in and goes directly to the upset man. She speaks to him, holding his attention. He seems to deflate, suddenly small and broken. Her hand on his arm, she leads him like how I dragged Pauline away from Grant Edwards. Except Auntie's touch looks gentle. She isn't paying attention to anyone else, only this disheveled man. They reach the door and continue into the hallway.

With nothing more to see, heads reluctantly turn to the front of the room. Rocky holds his final pose, suddenly aware that someone else stole the show. He hurriedly exits the stage, mumbling something to his cousin on the way out.

Chief Manitou begins his introduction as if nothing happened. I take the opportunity to escape with minimal attention through the nearest side door. My platform Doc Martens slow me down as I attempt to run after Auntie. I reach them at the main entrance to the student union.

I halt, surprised by the sight of them hugging. Auntie's soothing *I know, I know* is the same comfort she provided when cleaning and bandaging my many childhood injuries.

"He took everything from me," the man says flatly. Even the life in his voice is gone.

"I'm calling a ride for you right now." Auntie then speaks into her phone, offering a hundred-dollar cash tip on top of the round-trip fare from St. Ignace to the Sault. Once her phone is back in her pocket, Auntie turns to the bereft man. "Tell me what Mrs. Bailey would have done to help you."

The man, who must be Mr. Bailey, sheepishly admits he didn't get like this often. "But she would make me take a cold shower and a long nap."

"That sounds like a good plan," Auntie tells him. "She and Robin-bah loved you and would want you to have clear eyes and a strong heart full of love."

He cries softly into my aunt's embrace.

They continue a quiet back-and-forth until the taxi arrives. She helps Mr. Bailey into the back seat and gives a wad of cash to the driver. Watching the car leave, Auntie hugs herself.

When she turns around, I stand in front of her. She gasps. "You startled me." Auntie's brow furrows. In the next instant her stance changes. She is instantly alert, poised to attack and protect. "What's the matter?"

"I wanted to let you know he's here. Grant Edwards." I hate the flicker of fear that crosses her face before she can smooth it away. "He talked to Pauline, trying to be friendly." Auntie's face hardens. "He asked about college and if she plays hockey—"

"He *what*?" She is livid.

"Grant Edwards asked Pauline if she plays hockey," I repeat.

Auntie's ivory complexion reddens as her fury grows.

"Why is that—" I begin before she interrupts.

"He preys on young women who play hockey. He gets off on overpowering us," her voice shakes with rage.

"I got her away from him," I say, hoping to calm Auntie because she is hella scary right now.

"You did good, Nindoozhimikwe."

I breathe a sigh of relief. Not only does Auntie's voice seem calmer, but her calling me "niece" in the language makes me beam. Technically we are first cousins, but Daunis has always been Auntie to me and Pauline.

She continues. "Now go back to the event. It's a very good moment for the Tribe and our ancestors. You need to be there."

Back inside, I sit at my assigned table at the front of the room.

"You missed the welcoming prayer and all the introductions," Web says.

I want to ask him why the college is involved with the donation, but since we are sitting next to a few professors, I keep my mouth shut for once.

Chief Manitou introduces Frank Lockhart as "a Sugar Island man born and raised, a successful businessman, and an avid collector of Ojibwe art and artifacts."

You mean grave robber, I say under my breath. Across from me, Cooper's jaw is clenched.

Mr. Lockhart takes careful steps to the stage. I don't need to watch him shake hands with Chief Manitou or get another look at Cooper's barely veiled distress.

My side view includes Grant Edwards at the next table, and Auntie standing near the door to a service hallway. She glares at the back of Grant Edwards's head.

"Thank you, Chief Manitou, for the kind introduction. Thank you, also, to the Sugar Island Tribal Council and to Mackinac State College for cohosting this event. I especially want to thank board of trustees member Grant Edwards for inspiring tonight's announcement." Lockhart's smile is all teeth, and borderline scary.

The wiindigoo relishes the applause. He licks his lips for more. I cannot look away.

Mr. Lockhart continues. "So, without further ado, I am formally announcing the donation of my 'treasures'—my entire collection of Ojibwe art and relics—to . . . Mackinac State College."

I register the shock on Grant Edwards's face even before it hits me a moment later.

What the fuck just happened?

"Weweni izhichigen," Cooper says harshly.

I must have said it out loud because he just told me to behave.

"Maanaadan," I reply. *It's bad. It's really, really bad.* Web nods along with me as I spew my outrage in the language. "Aanikoobijiganag gaa-jigaazo." *They hide our ancestors.*

"Bizaan ayaan." Cooper scolds me to be quiet.

"Gaawiin!" I refuse and instead point a finger at Dr. Fenton. "Wiiyagasenhkwe! Ziindabi mazina'igani-onaagan wazison." *She is a hoarder! She sits in a nest of cardboard boxes.*

I look away from the table in time to see Frank Lockhart flee the stage and exit the banquet room through the same doorway where Auntie was a moment ago. Grant Edwards follows Lockhart. I rise and chase after the wiindigoo, ignoring Cooper. He can deal with the college people.

When I open the door, Auntie's voice blasts through me.

"—near them, I will end you!"

I am between Grant Edwards and my aunt before I know what I'm doing.

"Get the fuck away from her!" I shout.

"Perry, go back to the event," she orders.

Grant Edwards flees into the next room over.

I hold Auntie's trembling hands. We remain silent, listening to the argument next door.

"I waited ten years for this." I recognize Frank Lockhart's voice.

"Just to spite me? And for what, a woman?" Grant Edwards's voice conveys shock.

"I loved her!" Lockhart bellows.

"And she loved your money. If you weren't going to marry her, the least I could do was show her a good time." Grant Edwards's laughter follows Lockhart into the service hallway.

Ignoring us, Lockhart walks down the hallway instead of returning to the banquet room.

"Auntie, please go sit with Pauline and Granny June." It's all I can think to say. I've never seen Auntie look so pale, like on the verge of fainting.

I follow Lockhart. The service hallway intersects with the main hallway of the student union. People mill about, and I can't see which direction Lockhart went. I turn left. The reserved parking lot is on that side. Lockhart must have planned to drop his bombshell, get his revenge on Grant Edwards, and get out. He probably has no interest in sticking around beyond his moment of glory.

I nearly plow into Flynn in the main hallway. A last-second swerve has me ricocheting off Leer-wah instead. I ignore the archaeologist's question if I'm okay. The exit sign at the end of the hallway leads to a single flight of stairs to an outside door.

The change in temperature is immediate, like crawling into a sweat lodge.

He's nearly to his vehicle when I catch up.

"Mr. Lockhart, why did you change your mind?" My voice quivers, and tears I didn't expect are streaming down my face. "Please. It means so much to bring our ancestors' belongings back home. The college will delay us for decades."

He turns to me. We are the same height. His expression softens the tiniest amount at the sight of me before his face becomes impassive.

"My decision had nothing to do with the Tribe," he says.

"But it should have. You called them your treasures. If you love them, returning them—"

He cuts me off. "My decision is final."

I step away so he won't clip me with his side mirror when he backs out of his parking space. Lockhart drives away quickly. He never looks back.

What can I do except go back inside the building? Dripping with sweat, I wipe my forehead with my sleeve. Everything is blurry in the crowded main hallway. I wipe my forehead again, but nothing improves.

Crying into my sweatshirt sleeve, I feel my way into the small meeting room where Lockhart and Grant Edwards argued. The door automatically shuts behind me. The black cotton sleeve is soaked with tears and snot. I decide more snot will not matter. Just before I blow my nose into my sleeve, I step backward and trip over something behind me.

I land on my butt and continue backward in a near complete somersault. As I roll onto my stomach and try to rise, my hands slip on the hardwood floor. My chin hits the floor and I see stars for a few heartbeats. When my vision clears, two pale blue eyes stare through me. The bald head is turned to the side. Grant Edwards lies on his stomach, just like me. The blood must be coming from underneath him. It's warm and pools around us both.

I blink, not comprehending. Then a door at the back corner of the room clicks shut and everything catches up to me.

Grant Edwards is dead. He'll never touch Pauline.

Auntie will never again tremble at the sight of him.

Someone enters the meeting room and shrieks. I raise my head, and Flynn screams a second time when he realizes it's just the one dead body and me. He flees the scene.

I'm alone again. I rest my cheek on the floor and stare at Grant Edwards. I take comfort in his blank eyes. It's not like he can do anything to me.

Flynn returns with people. Cooper squats next to me. A campus police officer orders him not to touch me, but for once my old boss doesn't follow the rules. He slides his arms beneath me. I try to tell him to lift with his legs and not his back, but the words stay caught in my throat.

"Are you hurt?" he asks, still holding me. I shake my head.

"Did you see what happened?" Web asks. I repeat my movement.

Erik bursts into the room. His gasp is thick and guttural. The campus police guy orders him to leave. Erik complies because he is, after all, still on probation.

Cooper asks for my phone as he sets me down on a table. I reach into my sweatshirt pocket. I unlock my device and tap the saved badge marked EMERGENCY in the Messages app.

   ME: I tripped over a dead body.

I hit send before showing Cooper the message. His eyes bug out when he sees it. He gently takes my phone and makes a call. He addresses Pops as Mr. Birch instead of Art. One more look at the body, and I can't hear anything else.

I sit in a room at the State Police Post in St. Ignace. Web and Cooper are outside the room. Cooper has my phone so he can keep Mom, Pops, Pauline, and Auntie updated via the group text. My parents flew to Albuquerque this morning with two other people from the Repatriation Committee and can't get back until tomorrow.

The detective is kind; she offers water or pop. I shake my head. She says my parents authorized a relative, Daunis Fontaine, to collect me. She explains that my aunt was driving home but turned around when she received the emergency text and will be here any minute.

I haven't spoken since the parking-lot encounter with Frank Lockhart. I understand Stormy Nodin better now. If you stay silent, you can't say the wrong thing. Like when I let it slip about taking the seeds. When I told Erik that I didn't care about the consequences for him at Teepees-n-Trinkets. When I didn't change Frank Lockhart's mind.

I know the exact moment Auntie arrives at the State Police Post. It's like the air becomes electric. She bursts into the room where I sit at a table. Her eyes are red from crying.

I want her to be happy. Grant Edwards is dead.

Auntie wraps me in a bear hug. Her voice is the faintest whisper in my ear.

"Don't tell them anything."

CHAPTER 18

SATURDAY, JULY 12TH

*T*he Warrior Girl watches me from across the parking lot as Lockhart's car speeds away. She stays next to me as I return to the
student union. I sob into the arm of my sweatshirt and enter the
small meeting room. When I trip over Grant Edwards's body, the Warrior Girl squats in front of us. She turns him onto his back. Her deer-
antler handle juts from his stomach. She retrieves it. The flint blade is
covered in blood. She walks away, not the way we entered, but toward
the door at the back of the room. It's the door that leads to the service
hallway, the same door both Grant Edwards and Frank Lockhart used. I
sit up and watch her leave. Her steps are silent. The only thing I hear is
the click of the door behind her.

I wake up snuggled between my parents. Elvis Junior alerted me
to their arrival early this morning. They crawled into bed with me. I
cried and told them about Frank Lockhart's horrible announcement
and how I tripped over Grant Edwards's body.

I fell asleep before getting to the part about Auntie bursting into
the holding room at the State Police Post.

Junior follows when I scooch myself off the foot of the bed and head upstairs. He's been at my feet ever since Auntie and I returned from St. Ignace. He even followed me into the shower last night when I washed off Grant Edwards's blood.

I start a pot of coffee, and by the time it's done brewing, I've visited the bathroom and let Junior outside.

Pauline enters the kitchen, yawning and stretching her arms overhead.

"Mom and Pops got home?" she says, staring at their luggage next to the kitchen island.

"Yeah. This morning," I say. "They chartered a flight to Detroit and drove a rental car. Auntie went home but will be back tonight for the full-moon ceremony."

"Holaay. You're talking now? You went all zombie last night." She hands me a mug.

"Yeah. That was weird," I admit. "I couldn't talk until Mom and Pops were holding me."

Pauline comes around the island to hug me.

I continue. "I went inside myself like a turtle shell where nothing could touch me."

"Oh, Egg." She never uses our special nickname from when I first told her that we started out as the same egg. "I got a ride back with Lucas after Erik said he'd find you. I accidentally shut my phone off and didn't find out until later what happened." Her voice softens. "I'm sorry. I wish I'd been there."

"I'm glad you weren't." Mug of coffee in hand, I walk to the mudroom and slip my bare feet into rubber boots. "Come with," I call to Pauline. "I gotta check on my seeds."

Junior runs ahead as we walk to the garden. I leave him outside the gate.

"The detective wants to talk to me with Mom and Pops there too. But . . ." I trail off, remembering the ride back from St. Ignace. "Auntie told me not to tell them anything." I squat to check on the nine small plants that I transferred to a corner of the garden once their true leaves came in and I hardened them to direct sunlight. "She was acting weird last night."

"Well, so were you," Pauline points out.

"I had a good reason to go all zombie," I say, looking up at her. "But Auntie was a mess. She had to pull over and puke her guts out. When she got back in the SUV, she was laughing." Then I say the bad thought I've had since last night. "I think Auntie was involved somehow."

"You think she did it?" Her voice squeaks.

"Sheesh, Pauline." I give her leg a shove. "I only said she might have been involved."

"Well, she did threaten to end the guy. She said it loud enough for a lot of people to hear, even with all the commotion going on." My sister squats next to me and touches a scrawny leaf. Not all of the plants are thriving.

"I told Auntie that Grant Edwards asked you about hockey," I say. "It really freaked her out. She threatened him right after that."

My twin states the obvious. "That's motive."

We mull over the possibility of Auntie's involvement. I speak first.

"I'm the closest thing to an eyewitness. You work for the police captain. We should look for evidence and find out who killed the guy."

Pauline says what I don't want to consider.

"What if the evidence proves it *was* Auntie?"

WEEK SIX

Do we have to be dead and dug up from
the ground to be worthy of respect?

—José Ignacio Rivera (Apache/Nahuatl)

CHAPTER 19

MONDAY, JULY 14TH

Intern Ellen is surprised when I show up for work on Monday morning.

"Flynn's taking a few days off," she says. "He's too distraught from Friday."

Tim, the fourth Team Tribal Council intern, smirks. "Guess Flynn's not as tough as you."

"Don't be like that," I tell him. "You don't know how you'd react in that situation."

"What are you going to work on if we aren't getting the Lockhart donation?" Ellen asks.

"I need to figure out how to help Mack State inventory the donation quickly so we can begin the repatriation process and get our items back." I grab my portfolio from the desk drawer I've been keeping my work stuff in.

After I returned Auntie's truck last Thursday, I had Lucas drop me off at work so I could get my phone and portfolio from next door. There weren't any Tribal Council members around and the Team Tribal Council interns were running errands for the Lockhart event.

With the conference room to myself, I found an unlocked file cabinet perfect for storing the two brown paper bags with the reclaimed baskets. Just until I can return them to their rightful owners.

I open the portfolio and write a goal statement on the pad of paper, like Pauline always does. *The Sugar Island Ojibwe Tribe will take action to help Mackinac State College inventory the Lockhart Collection.*

My heart hurts just writing the words. The Tribe should be preparing to receive Lockhart's private collection directly, instead of going through an institution that has dragged its heels since 1990.

Resigned to the situation, I try to think of a first step to write down. Instead of an action step to move us forward, though, I replay the awful moment when Frank Lockhart screwed us over. My angry words to Dr. Fenton come flooding back. Even in Ojibwemowin, it was obvious I wasn't saying kind things about her.

I really fucked up.

As soon as Web arrives, I follow him into his office and shut the door behind me.

"How are you?" he asks solemnly.

"I'm okay, Web. My parents are back from New Mexico. We did a full-moon ceremony on Saturday night, and my dad did a sweat with me last night. He's checking on me at lunch."

"Good, good," he says. "Have you spoken with the detective?"

"My parents let her know that I won't be speaking with the police."

"Really?" Web is either surprised or impressed. Maybe both.

"Can I just get back to work? I want to do something, to make a difference."

"But we aren't getting the donation now," he points out.

"Yeah, but we could help the college with Lockhart's collection. The anthropology professor is working on a request to Tribal Council for research assistants. It's a big ask, but they need the extra help for sure now." I think out loud. "There's an archaeologist named Leer-wah who did a big one-eighty and reversed his views against repatriating to us. He was able to get the board of trustees to set an actual date to return thirteen ancestors next summer. We could work on getting his support to inventory the new items as quickly as possible."

"You continue to impress me," Web says. "You *are* Ogichidaak-wezans. Warriors might lose a battle, but they keep their eyes on what truly matters—the final result."

"Miigwech, Web. So can I keep working for you on the Lockhart Collection?"

"You wouldn't want to return to the tribal museum to do this?"

Cooper won't take me back after firing me, but I keep that fact to myself.

"I want to be wherever the decisions about funding get made," I say with determination.

"Now you're being strategic as well as tenacious." Web's smile deepens the crinkles at his eyes. "You are exactly who I want to work with."

I go next door to talk with Cooper.

"We see you just as much as when you worked here," Miss Manitou says dryly.

"Miigwech for noticing." My tone is as sweet as maple-sugar candy.

Cooper comes from his office when Miss Manitou calls him. He directs me toward the reading chairs in the library, in front of the storefront windows.

It stings, being kept in the public area instead of his office.

"How are you?" he begins.

"I'm fine. My parents made it home Saturday morning. We did a full-moon ceremony on Saturday night and a sweat lodge on Sunday. It was exactly what I needed." I pause to watch someone walk past on the sidewalk. "Miigwech for helping me Friday night."

Cooper doesn't say anything, which feels like another sting.

"I am sorry for my outburst in front of Dr. Fenton." I pause to take a deep breath. "Did I harm the relationship?" I force myself to look at him.

"Yes, you harmed the relationship," he says. "Dr. Fenton didn't need to know the language to get the message loud and clear. I blamed your immaturity and impatience, which wasn't a lie."

I look back down at my hands in my lap.

"Did I ruin everything for the thirteen ancestors?"

"I've spoken with every member of Mack State's Repatriations Committee and the board of trustees." He pauses. "Well, except for, ah, Grant Edwards." He falls silent again.

The quiet is too much for me. I look up to find Cooper staring at me. It takes all my willpower to maintain eye contact when I'd rather slink outside and run away.

"Perry, you are extremely lucky the archaeology professor remains an ally in favor of repatriating the thirteen ancestors."

He means Leer-wah. I nod my gratitude.

"Since he will be coordinating the repatriation process, Dr. Fenton will take the lead on the donation," Cooper says. "You jeopardized future repatriation requests, both from the Lockhart Collection and the Warrior Girl."

I sit in my shame. When I realize he has nothing more to say to me, I finally speak.

"I know this doesn't make up for my outburst, but Subchief Webster is willing to support Dr. Fenton's funding request. He knows the next step is to complete the inventory of backlogged items and the Lockhart items. Which means getting her the help she needs."

I hold my breath waiting for Cooper's reaction. Eventually I give up and breathe.

"It's up to your supervisor as to the role you take," he says finally. "But I don't think you should have any public-facing responsibilities."

Public-facing?

"Do you mean not speaking to anyone from the college?" I try to keep my voice from cracking. These stings to my heart are, after all, my own doing.

"Yes. We all need to remember that you are sixteen years old, with limited training."

I don't know how to respond. Then I remember the role that Web wants me to take on.

"The subchief wants me to be a go-between between you and Tribal Council." I consider how best to say something awkward. "If that's not gonna work for you, then I need to let Web—uh, Mr. Webster know." Left unspoken is the fact that if I cannot serve as go-between, I may as well quit the internship.

"Why do you think they want a go-between?" he asks.

"I don't want to answer for them," I say.

"Maybe you are learning about communications after all," Cooper says coolly. "They don't like working directly with me because I follow protocols and I don't take shortcuts."

"Maybe they want to get things done quickly?" I suggest. It's the politest way to say the thing about Cooper that frustrates me.

"Perry, do you understand that working within the process, following the rules, following the laws, that it matters?" He stands. "It's not just about winning; it's about how you conduct yourself and represent your community."

I feel a flash of irritation. If Cooper feels that way, then why does he pose on the ferry like a cigar-store Indian? What does that foolishness represent?

I stand as well because I think he's given me his answer.

"Miigwech for speaking with me," I say, turning to go.

"Yes, I will accept you as the go-between. On one condition," he adds. "That you consider the means and not just the ends."

"Nin-gagwe-nitaa." *I am trying to learn.*

At the end of the day, I clock out and sit on the park bench to wait for Mom to swing by. I replay Cooper's words. *Consider the means and not just the ends.* What does that even mean? Shortcuts are a good thing. Rules are important, I guess. But at what cost?

"Perry," says a deep, familiar voice. Erik stands in front of me. He's smiling. "Can I give you a ride home?"

"I'm waiting for my mom, but I could call her before she gets here." I look at the time on my phone. She's due any minute.

One quick phone call later, I get into Erik's car. He asks if I'm good with the music. It's Keith Urban. A song about being in a car. I nod.

He asks if I want to get dinner. I do.

We go to the drive-in next to the ferry launch. Once we get our food, he parks at the edge of the paved lot. We eat our cheeseburgers and watch the ferry go back and forth.

"I want to ask you something," Erik says.

"Sure," I say. "But first, can you take your hair tie out?"

He blushes. Those crab-apple cheeks do something to me. He tugs at the hair tie and runs both hands through his hair. He pushes some of the curls away from his eyes.

"Now you can ask me anything." I sound calmer than my heartbeat would indicate.

"Could we try again? Spending time together?"

I lean over and push a section of curls aside. When I kiss his cheek, the crab-apple is firm and ripe. It's exactly how kissing a smile should feel.

CHAPTER 20

WEDNESDAY, JULY 16TH

The Tribal Council workshop at the Superior Shores is packed with citizens demanding action on the rising number of missing and murdered Anishinaabe kwewag. Another woman, Razz Williams, was reported missing on Sunday. She is a distant cousin to me and niece to a council member. When an adjoining room is opened to accommodate the overflow, the Team Tribal Council interns help set up the space with additional seating.

"It's good to see you, Flynn," I say as we haul stacked chairs.

He shoots me a suspicious look, searching my face for snark. I have none.

"It was a horrible thing to walk in on. You should take any time you need to deal."

"But you were back on Monday," he says, placing the chairs side by side.

"That doesn't mean anything. Shock affects people differently. I couldn't speak for, like, ten hours. And it wasn't until after I did a sweat that I really felt like myself."

"A sweat lodge? That helped?" He shivers. "I see it when I sleep. That moment when I walked in that room, and you lifted your head. Each time I dream it, your smile is bigger."

I was smiling?

"I think I was relieved that someone found me." The lie forms quickly. I'm not about to admit to Flynn that I was happy that Grant Edwards couldn't hurt Auntie or anyone else ever again.

"My dad is coming by to make sure I eat lunch," I say. "You could ask him about joining the next time he offers a men's sweat lodge, if you want."

Flynn looks at me, considering the offer. "Thank you," he says quietly.

Pauline walks past. She and Erik are on hand to help Police Captain TJ Kewadin talk about the missing-persons database. She anxiously rubs behind her left ear. It's a DEFCON 3 situation and they haven't even started their presentation yet.

I take my seat with the other Team Tribal Council interns. We sit at a narrow table directly behind the council members, who are seated at a long table at the front of the room. If Web needs anything, he will turn around and wave me over.

Since a workshop isn't an actual meeting, the board does things by verbal consensus instead of documented votes. Web proposes to rearrange the workshop agenda to discuss the missing women. All of the council members say yea before Chief Manitou can ask for consensus.

Pauline, Erik, TJ Kewadin, and a Nish kwe I don't recognize move to sit at the lone table in front of Tribal Council. My sister puts the laptop in front of her and Erik. I can feel her anxiety like hives on my own skin.

The woman speaks first. She is the executive director for a nonprofit organization, Uniting Three Fires Against Violence. She provides an overview about the epidemic of missing and murdered Indigenous women, girls, and two-spirit individuals. Instead of referring to it as MMIW, she makes a point of using MMIWG2S to include *all* those who face disproportionate rates of violence.

Most of what she says is familiar to me, like about red dresses symbolizing the MMIWG2S movement and being used in awareness activities. She mentions something that sounds like Vah-wah. It's the Violence Against Women Act that Congress passed last year.

"Under the Major Crimes Act, the federal government—not the state, and not the tribe—has jurisdiction over felonies committed on tribal land where the victim or the perpetrator is Native American," she says. It's the reason why the tribe couldn't prosecute Grant Edwards for raping Auntie, I remember.

The Three Fires lady explains that VAWA was reauthorized last year, and it included a provision for tribes to detain or prosecute non-Natives who harm their wives or domestic partners on tribal land.

"That sucks," I mutter. The law wouldn't have helped Auntie.

Flynn whispers, "Isn't that law a good thing?"

"Yeah, but it doesn't include violence by random creeps," I explain.

I'm not the only person upset, because a council member asks about violence against Indigenous women, girls, and two-spirit people by someone who isn't a spouse or partner.

"That is still up to the federal government to investigate and prosecute. There aren't enough resources to adequately do this for over five hundred federally recognized Indian tribes. Without consequences, we see perpetrators become predators. They prey on Indigenous women because the odds of being caught and convicted are slim to none."

"What can we do about it?" Web asks.

TJ speaks up. "We are trying to improve the data on missing and murdered Indigenous people. We look for ways to communicate and share information with other tribes." He motions for Pauline to bring up the slideshow about the database. "With the help of our Kinomaage program interns, Pauline Firekeeper-Birch and Erik Miller, we've created a database with a variety of data points to look for similarities between cases of missing and murdered people. We started with six victims from this year, and as we can, we'll add those from 2013 and earlier."

The screen shows a spreadsheet, with each column listing a victim's name. Each row lists different details, such as date reported missing, date last seen, last confirmed location, whether the victim had a cell phone on them when they went missing, what activities the victim had been doing just prior to going missing, and on and on.

"Why aren't we doing more for Razz?" someone in the audience shouts. I can't see who, but the irate man sounds older. "She's enrolled, and—no offense—but not every missing person is one of ours. Their tribes should be looking for them."

A few people nod along, but others boo and hiss their disapproval.

"We are keeping data on every missing Indigenous person in the county. It's our historical territory and our recognized tribal service area," TJ speaks with such authority that no one dares say anything in opposition. "We want other tribes to do the same for our citizens."

"There was a full moon on Saturday when my niece went missing. Can that be added as a data point?" one of the Tribal Council members asks TJ.

Erik whispers to TJ, who says, "Yes. We can cross-reference with lunar cycles."

People offer other ideas for data points. Some seem far-fetched, like which clan a person claims. Someone else points out that not everyone knows their clan.

Another person says that some of the women whose bodies were found had played hockey.

"That includes Darby-bah," someone says.

"Razz doesn't play hockey," her auntie on Tribal Council says.

TJ wraps up the presentation, promising to return with another update.

Web says, "I'd like us to direct our Human Resources department to develop job descriptions for two positions, one full-time and one part-time, to help Tribal Police with the database and communicate with other tribal communities. Once we have the information about compensation, we will expect Captain Kewadin to submit a request for funding the positions."

The other council members speak in favor.

"I am thankful for the support," TJ says. "I ask that the directive to HR include the expectation that they seek input from law enforcement and IT when drafting the job descriptions. Ideally, I'd like the full-time position to have law-enforcement experience in addition to computer skills. The person in the position will be communicating with law-enforcement officers from other jurisdictions. Prior experience goes a long way."

"As long as this input doesn't slow the process," Web says.

"My intention is to get it right, not slow it down, Subchief Webster. Again, miigwech for your support." TJ leads Pauline and Erik to the hallway outside the meeting room.

Cooper is a lonely sight when it's his turn to talk to Tribal Council. I wish I was at his side. He explains why losing the Lockhart donation is a devastating blow.

"Instead of receiving the objects directly, we will need to go through the repatriation process with Mackinac State College. It will take years, if not decades, to jump through all their hoops to get the objects returned."

"I don't want anything to do with Frank Lockhart," Chief Manitou says harshly. "He set us up to be surprised and humiliated. And at an event we paid for!"

"I can understand that," Cooper says. "I was upset as well. But the objects still come from Sugar Island; they deserve to be brought back home."

"So, we go to the college and say, what? Give us our items? And then they get to dictate the terms?" Chief Manitou is not backing down.

Cooper speaks calmly. "My purpose today is to reiterate the importance of the Lockhart Collection and encourage us all to remain committed to the repatriations process."

"I agree with Mr. Turtle," Web says. "I think we should take quick action—"

"I'm not requesting action right now," Cooper interrupts.

"But this matter is important, and time is of the essence." Web's willingness to dive right in is my favorite thing about him.

"Again, I appreciate your support, Subchief Webster, but there are steps to follow."

I almost groan at Cooper's by-the-book response.

"Why wait?" Web says. "I'm prepared to draft a resolution to fund research assistants for Mackinac State College to complete the inventory of Mr. Lockhart's collection."

Cooper tries to explain that the funding request isn't ready yet, but he's interrupted.

"You want to give a pile of money to the college, again, for something that should be on their dime?" Chief Manitou is practically shouting. "I don't support any such nonsense."

Cooper looks horrified by the disaster unfolding in front of him.

"I want to go on the record with a request to fund a solution," Web says.

"I am invoking my authority as tribal chief to table this matter indefinitely."

No. This is the worst thing that could happen. I want to shout, but the words stay in my throat. Chief Manitou is ruining everything with his bruised ego.

The college isn't our only obstacle. Now we are our own roadblock.

During the lunch break, I eat the soup and sandwich Pops brings me. It takes everything for me not to cry and ask him to take me home. I manage to introduce Pops to Flynn, leaving out the part of how my fellow intern had been such an ass. Instead, I share that Flynn was the person who found me with the dead body and might want to participate in a sweat lodge.

After Pops leaves, I approach Web.

"Um, Web, do I still work for you?"

"I like your directness, Perry," he says.

"I like that you tried to help Cooper," I say in return.

"I wish I'd been able to do what you wanted." Web looks sad. "I am even more sorry that I can't keep you on. Chief Manitou is adamant. Tomorrow is your last day with Tribal Council."

"Oh." I feel the echo of Pauline's childhood sucker punch once again.

"There's an opening at the Shores. Shipping and receiving, I think," he says.

Erik's spot.

"Can't we do an independent-study project?" I don't like how whiny I sound. "I have an idea for one about black ash baskets."

I don't hear Web's reply because all I can think about are the four baskets in the filing cabinet. I need to get each basket to its new home. Maybe I can get Lucas to take me to the post office on Friday. I could mail a box to each Elder with a typed anonymous note.

"Perry," he says, pulling me out of my thoughts, "I asked if you could text your mom or dad to get their permission for me to give you a ride home after the council meeting."

I nod and ignore the lump in my throat. It's the second time I've started to care about a work project. Twice now, I've gotten thrown away. I wish I'd taken the job on that fishing boat.

"I'll find a way for you to come back," Web promises. "You're still Ogichidaakwezans."

The Warrior Girl stands beside me in the garden. It's sunny and breezy. I squat down to inspect the pumpkin plants; their vines have flourished. Soon they will be in the flowering stage. My thoughts manifest into flowers. The male flowers are supposed to appear before the female flowers. These flowers burst open now as if on my command. Honeybees suddenly swirl around us. We watch the bees go about their pollinating work. If they're successful, a baby pumpkin will grow on the female flower. It happens as if in a time-lapse video—the green bulb forming and expanding into a clearly recognizable pumpkin.

I look up at the Warrior Girl. She isn't watching the baby pumpkins; she is observing me. Contemplating. She stares off into the distance, and when her gaze returns, it's unwavering. She extends her hand, which is holding the flint knife. She's holding the blade and offers me the deer-antler handle.

I reach but something catches my eye. I pause. Beyond her, Erik waves to me before attempting a handstand. He falls and laughs.

She returns the knife to the leather holder at her hip and stares off into the distance again.

CHAPTER 21

FRIDAY, JULY 18TH

Arriving at the Friday seminar, I ignore the whispers and stares of the other interns. I'm the girl who tripped over a dead body. I focus on Shense pointing to the empty seat beside her.

"What's new, niijiikwe?" I ask.

"I've been pumping extra all week," Shense says. "The baby has her first weeklong visit with her dad. I gotta drive down to St. Ignace after work. You wanna come?"

My plan was to ask Lucas for a ride home today so I could mail the reclaimed baskets to their families. The printed letters and address labels are in my backpack.

"Sure, but can we run an errand on the way?"

"Sure, niijiikwe." She stretches *girlfriend* in her funny-without-even-trying way.

When Claire asks for any intern updates, I raise my hand like Pauline on pop-quiz day.

"If yous haven't heard, I start my third assignment on Monday at shipping and receiving at the Shores. Today is the end of week six, so there's still time for even more assignments, hey."

I raise my hands in a double V for victory before I sit down. If the others think I'd fall apart over my latest reassignment, no way. I only freak out about dead bodies I stumble upon.

Claire gives the first presentation today, about the study-abroad program jointly sponsored by the Tribe, Lake State, and Mack State. I barely pay attention to her slides. What if Chief Manitou shuts down every partnership project with Mack State? What if he squashes the study-abroad program and the Kinomaage program all because of Frank Lockhart?

Lockhart never thought about the consequences of his decision. He just wanted to get back at trustee Grant Edwards. Something to do with a woman they both wanted.

She couldn't have been Caron Barbeau because the woman Grant Edwards had referenced was someone that Frank Lockhart hadn't married. Besides, Caron left the area twenty years ago and Lockhart mentioned waiting ten years to get back at his rival. So, who was she?

There is another aspect to figure out. Why would Lockhart changing his donation from the Sugar Island Ojibwe Tribe, giving it instead to Mackinac State College, be a way to get back at his rival?

Grant Edwards was the trustee that Pauline said had met with Chief Manitou about Mack State becoming a tribal college. Flynn mentioned it was the trustee who had the idea. Why would a trustee want their state college to become a tribal college? Wouldn't Grant Edwards and the other trustees be replaced by people the Tribe selected to serve on the board instead? What possible benefit could there be to, essentially, proposing an idea that would likely result in losing your prestigious post as a college trustee?

But how would Frank Lockhart know that changing the donation from the Tribe to Mack State would be a way of shutting down his rival? Could Lockhart know Chief Manitou would be so upset about a public humiliation that the relationship between the Tribe and the college could crash and burn?

The slides show groups of college students in front of the usual landmarks: the Eiffel Tower, the Leaning Tower of Pisa, some big church, and a castle. I only half pay attention, until I see Dr. Fenton in one photo and Leer-wah in another. When Chief Manitou appears in a photo, I nudge Shense.

"I'm so mad at that asshole," I whisper.

"I thought you liked your last boss," she says.

"Who?"

"The subchief."

"I didn't see Web in any photos," I say. "I meant the chief."

"Well, I saw 'Web' in one," Shense says, nudging me at my boss's nickname.

"I recognized some museum peeps from the college, including my least favorite anthropologist." I roll my eyes. "Claire's not selling me on the study-abroad program."

I rejoin Team Misfit Toys officially, not just as a wannabe.

"What did yous pick for a final project?" I say.

"Nothing. We were waiting on you." Lucas cheeses a huge, crooked grin.

"We should investigate Grant Edwards's murder," Pauline says. She takes in Shense's raised eyebrows. "Hear me out. We use our voice recorders to interview every intern today about what they heard and saw last Friday."

"I didn't bring my recorder," I say.

"Claire had extras," Pauline says, handing me one. "Everybody pair up. I'll go solo."

Shense and I say, "Niijiikwe," at the same time.

"If we're pairing up, why do we each need a recorder?" Erik asks.

Of course my sister has an answer. "Redundancy. If one recorder is poorly positioned or malfunctions, you'll have a backup."

"What about you, Lone Wolf?" I ask her.

"I don't mess up," Pauline says.

My twin's confidence is either on overload or it's nonexistent. There's no in-between.

It turns out that nearly everyone heard Daunis Fontaine threaten to "end" Grant Edwards. Definitely not good for Auntie. None of our interviews reveal any bombshells. Hopefully, Erik and Lucas had better luck. And Pauline.

While Shense takes a break to pump breast milk, Lucas challenges me to beat him at hand walking. I win, which prompts Lucas to say it's best out of three. He keeps going with best out of seven, then eleven. Finally, my arms are rubber, and he wins one.

"Last one was winner takes all," he declares, jumping up and down like a fool. "Pauline, did you see that? I beat Pear-Bear. I'm the champ."

"All right, chump, hand over your recorder." She collects from Lucas, Erik, and me.

Shense waits for me when I dash into Tribal Admin and retrieve the baskets from the file cabinet. Then, I get cash from an ATM, and have her wait again at the post office. I have my labels ready, with Chi Mukwa as the return address. I also have four sheets of paper printed with the same message:

This basket found its way back to you.
May it bring only good memories.

I assemble the boxes and use newspapers to pack each basket carefully. I pay cash and throw away the receipt on my way back to the car.

From there we stop by Shense's house, where her dad has the baby ready to go. He must be heading into work soon because he's wearing a suit and tie, with his name badge on a beaded lanyard around his neck. I don't know him well, but I smile at the way he kisses his granddaughter's forehead before heading back inside. I carry Washkeh's diaper bag while her mama puts her in the car.

I coo at the sweet binoojii, making silly faces while Shense pulls out back onto the road. Washkeh's wide dark eyes observe, but she never cracks a smile. I still feel her cool gaze after I twist back around in my seat. Sheesh. Tough audience.

On the drive to St. Ignace, Shense wants to interview me about what I saw and heard at the Lockhart event, because she still has her recorder.

"Not with Washkeh in the back seat," I say.

"Why not? She's three months old and doesn't understand words." Shense is amused.

"You know how when you're around a ceremonial fire and you gotta feed it with good thoughts and prayers? No gossip or politics being carried on the smoke to Gichimanidoo?"

My friend nods her head.

"I think it's like that for babies, too. I don't want to speak about that night around her."

She mulls over my words for a few miles.

"I like that. I never thought about words that way."

We spend the rest of the drive listening to a playlist I have of

Jingle Dress dance songs. So Washkeh can hear what good medicine sounds like.

I'm surprised when Shense pulls up to the State Police Post instead of a house. I was here a week ago, but it feels like yesterday. She looks just as surprised at the expression on my face.

"I'm so sorry, Perry. I didn't think about this being a bad spot for you. It's just that we're working on custody issues, and it's better if we meet here instead of his mom's house."

"It makes sense. I'm fine," I assure her.

A few minutes later, Shense returns with an empty car seat that she clicks into its base.

"We bought the same car seat for the baby so when we transfer her back and forth, she can stay asleep, and the other person takes the empty car seat," Shense explains.

"That's a good system. It puts the needs of the baby ahead of everything else," I say.

"It's my first time leaving her for a whole week."

Shense watches her baby's dad drive out of the parking lot. She doesn't make any move to start the car. Our windows are down. The evening air is beginning to cool.

I sit with her until she is done crying.

Shense drives through St. Ignace on the business spur. We start laughing at the same time when we see Teepees-n-Trinkets up ahead.

"Pull in, hey?" I say. "I need to ask you a favor."

She does, parking in front of the teepee.

I point with my lips toward the building. "Would you check out their security system? I'll wait in the car."

"You planning something, niijiikwe?"

"No. But Lockhart did our Tribe dirty. Changing his donation so the college gets everything. Maybe I just want to know how easy or hard it would be to reclaim something." I picture the ceremonial pipe and the family of moccasins. "If he's donating his entire collection to Mack State, it includes things they shouldn't have."

When she's halfway out the car, I call her name. She pauses.

"There's a ceremonial pipe in a glass display case at the entrance to the museum room at the back of the store. And a family of moccasins displayed in the museum room." I speak quickly, sounding kind of desperate. "Would you pray with them? Tell them we haven't forgotten them?"

"I got ya, niijiikwe," she says.

While I wait for Shense, I think about the four baskets on their way home. I wish I had taken everything I could from Dr. Fenton's office. A shiver runs through me when I remember the close call with Grant Edwards stopping by to help "Raquel." What did he want from her? And what was she getting from him? That whole "You scratch my back and I'll scratch yours" arrangement seems skeevy. He sounded like a lover when he was on the phone with her. Maybe they were snagging. Gaaah. The ugliness of his true feelings meant he was using her affections for his own purpose.

Lockhart had enjoyed telling Grant that the plan to donate his "treasures" to the Tribe was a fake-out, done to spite Grant Edwards and get back at him over a woman.

Was the woman Dr. Fenton? Is Raquel snagging left and right? I don't want to think about it.

Gaaah. Shense needs to hurry up and save me from my imagination.

The first thing Shense says, once she is back in the car, is that the pipe and moccasin family are there, and she prayed with them. Next she confirms that Teepees-n-Trinkets has a substandard security system. The doors are connected to an alarm, but the windows aren't. There are no lasers or cameras except for one above the cash register that I saw in the store myself.

"It's almost like he wants a break-in," she concludes.

"Shense, Lockhart called the items in his collection his 'treasures.' Why would he have such a shitty system if he supposedly loved the items?"

She reminds me that many business owners protect their assets with an exaggerated security system that they slack on over time, and some put security stickers on windows as a fake-out but don't actually connect to anything. Lockhart has some protection, but it's not adequate.

"Maybe he overinflated the value of his inventory for insurance purposes?" Shense guesses. "If there was a break-in, he'd collect a large payment on items that probably weren't even there. He'd want to keep his most valuable possessions in his home, which is probably very well secured. I can ask my dad about that sort of thing."

I insist on paying for the ferry crossing because Shense insists on bringing me all the way home instead of having Mom or Pops meet me at the ferry launch.

"Miigwech for coming with me tonight, Perry. I thought I was prepared, but leaving Washkiyaanimad gutted me."

"You're a good mom," I say. "Washkeh is a lucky binoojii. Don't forget to text me when you get home, hey?"

I know something is wrong the instant I enter the mudroom. It's too quiet, not the usual Friday evening noises like a movie on Netflix or the sound of dice in the Yahtzee cup. There should be a popcorn smell in the air. Pops makes it in a cast iron saucepan on the stovetop.

I find my parents on the sofa, embracing each other. Pauline rushes over to hug me. She's crying and her hand is practically glued to her left ear.

"What's going on?" I ask, afraid already of the answer.

Pops answers. "It's Daunis. She was arrested for the murder of Grant Edwards."

CHAPTER 22

SATURDAY, JULY 19TH

TJ Kewadin stops by in the morning with Waabun, who is going to stay with us for the weekend. Daunis's mom, Grace, is taking care of the legal details with their lawyers.

When TJ heads to his truck, my twin and I follow. Auntie told us TJ has to get his shirts custom-made because his shoulders are so broad, and his biceps are like Christmas hams.

"We have something for you," Pauline begins, unable to contain her gold-star enthusiasm. "It's about the Lockhart event. We interviewed all the Kinomaage interns and came up with a minute-by-minute timeline and transcript. I re-created the seating chart with attendee names. If you notice, I color-coded the seats to show who heard Auntie make the threat and who didn't."

I jump in so TJ won't think I was a total slacker.

"This part that branches off," I say, pointing to the diagram, "is when I followed Frank Lockhart from the service hallway to the main hallway. I lost sight of him in the crowd of people. I wrote down all the names I recalled; those are labeled in red. I cross-checked with those people to find out who they remembered in the hallway. Those names are in blue."

TJ listens attentively, so I keep going. "I figured Lockhart was headed to his car, and it was most likely in the reserved parking lot over here." I slide my finger to the side of the student union. "That's when I had this conversation with him." I point to my portion of the transcript. "I came back inside the building, and I stepped into the smaller room to, um, pull myself together. I was really upset and had my arm covering my face. I wiped my eyes and took a step backward. That's when I tripped over Grant Edwards's dead body."

Looking up, I notice the stubble on his chin. It's only then that I take in all of TJ's appearance. He's always . . . tidy. Not just his police uniform, but the way he carries himself—confident without being cocky, friendly but proper. Even when he's joined Pops and me hunting, I swear he irons his flannel shirts.

But today? His uniform is pristine, as usual, but it looks as if he got ready with his eyes shut. His shaving was hit or miss. There's a spot of dried toothpaste in the corner of his mouth.

I expect TJ to thank us. Instead he looks less than grateful.

"But you didn't tell any of this to the state police," he says pointedly.

"Well, no. I wasn't exactly talking."

"She went temporarily zombie," my sister chimes in.

"But when the detective wanted you to return with your parents . . ." TJ sounds upset.

"My parents didn't want me to talk to the detective. Plus, Auntie said—" I stop short.

TJ steps forward, suddenly alert. "What did she say?"

He towers over me, and his expression is one I've never seen. He's stone-cold serious.

"Can you back up, TJ? You're hella intimidating right now," I say, raising my palms as if I'm about to challenge the police captain to a Palm Push duel.

Pauline's jaw drops, like she can't believe I said what I just said.

TJ takes a step back. He breathes deeply and exhales slowly, in a Zen sort of way. Pauline looks back and forth like she's watching a tennis match.

"I'm sorry, Perry," he says. "Would you please let me know what she said?"

"Auntie held me at the police station and whispered, 'Don't tell them anything.'"

"I wish your statement had been taken right away. Now that she's been charged with a crime, your statement isn't as . . . impactful." He sighs heavily. "You aren't responsible for your parents' decision. I do understand people being reluctant to talk to law enforcement, especially Nishnaabs." He attempts a smile that doesn't reach the dried white toothpaste. "You both did great work. It's just that the crime took place on state land, so the investigation isn't within our jurisdiction. And with my, ah, friendship with your aunt, I'm too close to the case."

"I'm really sorry," I say.

"No. I apologize again for getting so worked up. It's exactly why I can't be an impartial investigator." He walks toward his truck.

"It's okay," I say to his back. "The whole thing is bizarro. I didn't talk for, what, ten hours? I almost joined Auntie when she pulled over to throw up on the highway."

"She did?" TJ spins around. He has that police-investigator vibe going again.

I nod. "When she got back in her SUV, she was laughing and crying."

He looks through me, not with dead eyes like Grant Edwards but like someone only paying attention to the stuff running through his mind.

"Miigwech, Perry. You too, Pauline." TJ is in his truck a heartbeat later and racing off.

My sister waits until the truck is on the road to shout, "I pulled an all-nighter on this!"

That evening, we watch the news on television to see if they have anything about Auntie's arrest. She is the top local story. The Mackinac County prosecutor says everyone must be held accountable for their actions, even those who come from wealth and privilege. They show photographs of Auntie and her Zhaaganaash grandparents. Even one shot of the dorm at Lake State that is named after her grandfather.

That prosecutor is a pajog! He's making it sound like Auntie is a rich bitch who goes around stabbing people just for kicks.

We keep the television on, in case there's anything else about Auntie. Mom tells Junior to get off the sofa. I roll off the sofa as well and lie down on the area rug next to him.

"She can't keep us apart," I whisper. Junior licks my nose.

There is a story on the national news about a Black man who died "at the hands of a police officer." I wonder why the newscaster avoids saying the word murder. A bystander recorded what happened. The news shows clips of protests across the country: so many different people marching and shouting and crying, people who are angry and sick and tired of this happening again and again. I sit up suddenly, overcome with tears that won't stop.

When Mom rises and heads into the kitchen, Pauline and I beeline to the sofa. We sit on either side of Pops. He puts an arm around each of us and hugs us close.

Pops is safe in our house. In the garden. His workshop. On Ziisabaaka Minising. I'm safe. My family is together.

I want us to stay here on Sugar Island forever.

WEEK SEVEN

Many institutions have interpreted the definition of "cultural affiliation" so narrowly that they've been able to dismiss tribes' connections to ancestors and keep remains and funerary objects . . . When the federal repatriation law passed in 1990, the Congressional Budget Office estimated it would take 10 years to repatriate all covered objects and remains to Native American tribes. Today, many tribal historic preservation officers and NAGPRA professionals characterize that estimate as laughable.

—Logan Jaffe et al., "The Repatriation Project: America's Biggest Museums Fail to Return Native American Human Remains," ProPublica, January 11, 2023

CHAPTER 23

MONDAY, JULY 21ST

It's my first day at my new assignment at the Superior Shores shipping and receiving department. My new supervisor is an older Nishnaab named Bucky Nodin, a relative of Stormy Nodin's, for sure. I've known Bucky my entire life as Buck Naked, so it takes a lot of effort to call him Mr. Nodin.

My first task is to go to the Shores deli to get a maple latte, a bran muffin, and the local newspaper for my boss. When I return, Mr. Nodin sips his drink and smiles broadly.

"Best five minutes of my day," he says before taking another sip.

I decide to take advantage of his good mood.

"Um, Mr. Nodin, can I take the afternoon off and make up the hours later this week? My aunt Daunis is being arraigned on murder charges."

"Holaay," Mr. Nodin says. "That's as good a reason to miss work as I ever heard." He lowers his voice in a conspiratorial whisper. "Did she do it? Kill that bad man?"

"I can't say." I mimic his whisper. "In case I get called as a witness."

"Ah, right. I get it," he says. "You know . . . if you worked for a Zhaaganaash business, they would frown at you taking time off on your first day. But us Nishnaabs gotta stick together, hey?" He pronounces it like *Neesh-nobs*.

"I agree. Miigwech, Mr. Nodin."

"Call me Uncle Bucky, Little Cousin."

"Miigwech, Uncle Bucky."

He proceeds to work me like a combination farm mule and carrier pigeon, hauling boxes and running all over the resort to fetch purchase orders for him. Holaay. Is this how Erik spent his workdays? My golf shirt clings to my sweaty back and I have flashbacks to my first week, when Cooper made me clean and vacuum.

The good thing about running my ass off is that the morning flies past. Before I know it, Mom is waiting for me in front of the conference center. Pauline is already riding shotgun. Waab's booster seat is gone, so he must be staying home with Pops. Not that I thought we'd bring him along. Mom drives to the county courthouse in St. Ignace and parks next to TJ's pickup truck. We sit in the back of the courtroom just in time to see Auntie brought in and seated next to her attorney.

I understand very little about what is going on. The county prosecutor says stuff about the charges. He boosts his volume theatrically when saying that Auntie was overheard threatening the "decedent" and that a search warrant at her home turned up a shirt with the victim's blood on it.

"Mom," I say excitedly. "She had blood on her clothes because she hugged me, and I had that guy's blood on me."

"Hush. Her attorney knows."

When it comes time for Auntie's attorney to speak, a Nish kwe next to me stands up.

"I killed Grant Edwards," she says, like something out of a courtroom drama.

Someone gasps, an instant before the room is filled with chatter. Everyone turns to look at her, including me. There is something familiar about her eyebrows and the shape of her cheekbones. She faintly resembles Miss Manitou at the tribal library.

The judge bangs his hammer and shouts for order in the court.

Auntie says, "Macy, no. Don't do this."

Before the lady can say anything else, another Nish kwe stands.

"I killed Grant Edwards. He raped me at a house party on the rez when I goalied for Beer League. He said since I was Native and it was tribal housing, he couldn't get arrested."

Someone lee-lees. The high-pitched trill bounces off every surface.

"Order. Order," the judge yells.

Another Nish kwe stands.

"Your honor, I killed Grant Edwards. He tried messing with me at a wedding reception at the Superior Shores when I played hockey for Lake State."

More lee-lees fill the courtroom. Everybody stands. I climb onto a chair to keep an eye on Auntie. My lee-lee is strong, showing support for all these Nish kwewag who dealt with that wiindigoo. Pauline and Mom join me. All three of us raise a hand as if we're lifting a feather to Gichimanidoo. The judge's hammer is constant as a drumbeat.

"Bailiff, I want this courtroom cleared," the judge says. "I will not have these proceedings turned into a mockery."

An officer motions people toward the door, but it's a slow crowd not at all eager to go. That's when Mr. Bailey shouts from the row behind us.

"I stabbed Grant Edwards in the stomach with my pocketknife."

Auntie tries to turn around, but an officer with the court pushes her through a door.

Mr. Bailey keeps talking. "He got my daughter Robin-bah hooked on painkillers after a hockey injury. He took advantage of her. She died ten years ago, and my wife was never the same. He took everything from me."

Mr. Bailey tries to stand on a chair like me. He's unsteady until TJ holds his hand. "Daunis sent me home in a cab, but I convinced the driver to bring me back. The taxi company will have a record of it. I followed Grant Edwards into a meeting room at the student union. I—"

TJ practically carries him off the chair. Auntie's attorney tries to reach Mr. Bailey.

Mom ushers Pauline and me to the car. We pester her with questions.

"I don't know what happens next. Or why the prosecutor pursued such a weak case."

"But how can we just leave her behind? Why aren't we sticking around?" I ask.

"She knows we were there. She heard our lee-lees. Her mom is there. Her attorney, too. We'll hear what happens, but if I can get you both back to work, that's what I'll do."

"But, Mom," I protest. "Buck Naked said I could take all the time I needed."

"Your new supervisor is Bucky Nodin?" Mom shakes her head. "I should've done what Dan Jackson did and requested a nepotism waiver so I could hire you myself."

"Yeah, like *that* would've worked out," Pauline mumbles my exact thoughts.

Later that evening, Auntie comes by to pick up Waabun. My little cousin thinks his mama was on a work trip. He climbs onto her lap and gives smoochy kisses before dashing after Junior.

"They arrested Mr. Bailey," Auntie says quietly.

"He really stabbed that guy with a pocketknife?" Pauline asks.

Auntie nods. "Fingerprints were smudged, but there were photographs in an album showing him receive the pocketknife as a birthday gift. Mr. Bailey paid the cabdriver to bring him back to the student union. His story checks out."

"So why'd they go after you?" I ask.

"The prosecutor is someone I graduated high school with. Ryan Cheneaux. Tribal Council voted on our enrollment applications the same month. I got in and he didn't." She shrugs.

"Holaay, he held a grudge for that long?" Pauline comments.

"Ten years," Auntie says.

Ten whole years? Sheesh. Wait a minute . . .

"Auntie, do you know if Frank Lockhart and Grant Edwards ever, um, dated the same lady?" I sit up, eager for a missing piece to the puzzle of their rivalry. "Like, um, ten years ago?"

I hate that she shivers involuntarily and wraps her arms around herself.

"Yes. Everyone thought Frank Lockhart got remarried but, apparently, he hadn't because he is still married to his first wife, the one who left him." She relaxes a bit and even manages a smile. "I saw her on the Booster Bus when your uncle Levi played for the Superiors. Everyone called her Sassy, but her actual name was Susan Hopkins."

Disappointment feels like a water balloon popping over my head. I was hoping she was someone I knew, a person whose identity would make sense somehow.

Auntie pauses. "Why do you want to know about her?"

"When we overheard them yelling, right after Lockhart made the announcement about his collection going to the college. It was all for revenge," I say, still stunned that our ancestors were used for settling a petty vendetta.

Auntie nods before yawning. She stretches her arms overhead and sighs.

"I just want to go home and snuggle my boy."

We watch Waab hang from the kitchen island and flip his legs over his head.

"Once he wears himself out," she adds.

"Auntie, did you know those women were gonna show up like that?" I ask.

She shakes her head and stifles another yawn.

"What about the first Nish kwe? You weren't happy about it," I say.

"Macy Manitou played on the boys' varsity team with me at Soo High. After Grant Edwards raped me, I warned her about him. As far as I know, he never got to her."

"But all the others. He never got caught?" Pauline can't hide her disgust.

Mom speaks up. "We thought we put the fear in him."

"A blanket party?" Pauline's eyes bug out.

Auntie nods again. "If we did scare him, it didn't stick."

"The wiindigoo got greedier?" I say.

"He became more strategic," Auntie says. "I think he started targeting Nish kwewag who weren't from here or didn't have families who would come after him."

I've been wondering why Grant Edwards was so keen on Mack State becoming a tribal college. Why would he pitch an idea that would probably result in him being replaced as a trustee? What benefit would he gain?

"Mack State is a hockey powerhouse," I say. "Grant Edwards wanted it to become a tribal college. Isn't that right, Pauline?" My sister nods. "They would need to recruit Native students to enroll at the tribal college and play for their teams. It would mean bringing in Nish hockey girls from all over the country."

Pauline finishes my thought. "Those Nish kwewag wouldn't have aunties nearby to blanket-party his ass."

Perpetrators who don't face consequences become predators. The woman from Uniting Three Fires said something to that effect. The predators know all the loopholes in the law, like how Auntie said Grant Edwards raped her on tribal land.

"Auntie, if Mack State became a tribal college, wouldn't that also make it tribal land?" My question makes her large eyes widen with realization.

"The Tribe would put the land into trust; they would add it to their holdings," Auntie says. Her voice quickens. "Violent crimes committed on tribal land against Nish kwewag would fall under federal jurisdiction. The VAWA amendment extends tribal jurisdiction only for domestic violence committed by a non-Native partner."

"I think Grant Edwards knew he could get away with anything on tribal land," I say.

"But he's gone now," Pauline says. "We don't have to be afraid of him anymore, right?" She looks from Auntie to Mom, and back at me.

Auntie rises and calls for Waab. She lifts him onto her hip. When she finally answers my sister, Auntie's voice sounds all worn out.

"He's not the only wiindigoo out there."

CHAPTER 24

FRIDAY, JULY 25TH

At the Friday seminar, Claire begins with her usual request for intern updates. I wave my hand. She scans the room twice before calling on me. All heads turn my way.

"Just wanted to say that I'm still with shipping and receiving," I announce, before high-fiving Lucas and Erik.

When my palm connects with Erik's, I flash to the dream I had about him last night. I blush as it comes back to me. He took off his shirt, and his hair tumbled around his face. He raised his arms to pull the loose curls into a hair tie. When he brought his arms down, I was in front of him, and he held me against his bare chest. His skin was smooth and warm.

I glance around the room, suddenly flushed. Okay, it was a nice dream. I focus my attention on Shense. She looks upset. Mad or sad, or something.

I nudge her. "Everything okay?"

"No," she huffs. "Washkeh's dad brought her back last night. He gave her formula all week instead of the breast milk I packed for her. She's feeding from me but had cramps all night long."

"That sucks. I'm sorry."

At the front of the room, Claire looks pointedly at Team Misfit Toys.

"There is still a team or two who haven't told me their final project. I need to know today," Claire says. "The team presentations take place in three weeks' time."

Team Misfit Toys groans in unison.

Claire introduces the executive director of Uniting Three Fires Against Violence. Team Tribal Council already heard her talk when she joined TJ, Pauline, and Erik for the MMIW database presentation. Today's training is on "professional boundaries and ethics."

I thought they worked on violence stuff. Looking out the window, I think about everything I'd rather be doing on a Friday in July. Checking nets on the river. Weeding the garden. Playing with Waab and Junior in the tree fort. Reading the next book on Cooper's list. Taking Granny June for a ride in the recently repaired Jeep. Fishing with the old-timers at Baie de Wasai and swapping stories.

Before long, I'm remembering how good it felt when Dream Erik held me. Then I replay the Fourth of July picnic, when he held that handstand and his shirt gathered around his chest. I think about his lean stomach and the way his muscles strained to hold the pose. The warm squish of his crab-apple cheek on my lip, even if it was just for a second.

Pauline stiffens beside me. I follow her widened eyes to the skit that I haven't been following. The woman from UTFAV is pretending to be a supervisor of a male subordinate, played by a very awkward Officer What-The, dressed in street clothes. I missed whatever happened up to this point.

"You're doing such a great job," she tells What-The. "Why don't you go home early today as a reward for getting the Smith project finished ahead of schedule?"

What-The thanks her and leaves. He returns a minute later.

"Good morning, Director," he says. Evidently, it's the next day.

"Good morning to you," she says. They blather on about work stuff. Then she teases him about clocking out early yesterday and mentions human resources wanting supervisors to crack down on time thieves. Before What-The can say anything, she adds, "Don't worry, your secret is safe with me."

"Let's talk about how someone with more power in the workplace might try grooming a subordinate for inappropriate activity," the executive director says.

"Does it always have to be sexual?" someone asks.

The discussion continues until Claire announces break time.

Pauline grabs my arm and leads me to a quiet place in the mezzanine.

"I think that's what Chief Manitou was doing." She looks around to make sure no one can overhear. "Grooming me."

"Really?"

She nods. "He was all professional that first week when we were getting to know the council members. But after he picked me, he made everything casual. Maybe too casual." Pauline avoids my eyes. "Whenever we were in his office, he'd make the sliding doors opaque so no one could look in. And, you know . . . his office is soundproof when the door is closed." She looks at me expectantly.

"Web's office is soundproof too," I tell her. "But he always kept the doors see-through."

"Chief Manitou would say the same tired joke each time he made the sliding doors opaque." She makes her voice gruff. "'Whatever happens in the chief's office stays in the chief's office. Ha-ha-ha.'"

"That's not just tired, it's skeevy," I say.

"I laughed the first time, but not the next time or the one after that," Pauline explains. "Then he asked if I had a sense of humor."

"Did you say, 'I do when shit is actually funny'?"

"No way." Pauline looks appalled at the thought of saying such a thing to a supervisor. "I wanted him to like working with me, so I laughed the next time. It worked, because he started letting me take longer breaks than the other interns." She blushes. "He said I was special."

"You are special," I tell her.

"That's fine coming from you, but from my supervisor? After three days of working side by side?" She rubs behind her ear. "There's something else I haven't told you. When we got lunch that time, I joked how my loyalty is to the other drive-in because it's next to the ferry launch. Chief Manitou made a point of watching me eat my cheeseburger and joking about loyalty tests."

"That's *hella* skeevy," I say. I'm once again grateful to have been transferred to Web, and now Uncle Bucky.

"It's definitely icky. But at the time, all I thought about was wanting to impress him." She hesitates before continuing. "I think he should've modeled appropriate boundaries, like the training lady said, out of respect for me and for himself and his leadership position."

Pauline doesn't respond when I ask if she's going to apologize to Auntie for shunning her.

After lunch, each team heads to their designated small meeting room. I toss my backpack in the corner before taking a seat next to Shense. Erik sits across from me. He winks when no one is looking.

"I really want to win. Or at least beat Team Tribal Council," Pauline says. "And I know Perry wants the bonus zhooniyaa." She glances my way. "So you have something in your bank account since you just paid Auntie for the Jeep repairs, right?"

I nod, hoping it's her lead-up to a great idea for our final project.

"My idea is to build on what we started at the Fourth of July picnic." Pauline stands as if making a classroom presentation. "Our project will be about black ash baskets. We'll call it Project Bigiiwen Enji Zaagigooyin. It means 'Come Home Where You Are Loved.'"

Sometimes Pauline and I experience "twin brain," like finishing each other's sentences or having a visceral reaction to something the other is experiencing. I remember asking Web if I could do an independent study project about black ash baskets.

My sister points with her lips at me. "Perry transcribed the interviews we did with the Elders." She digs into the backpack in front of her. "Here are your recorders so we can do more interviews."

Erik reaches for a recorder at the same time as me. We look at each other and smile. His vibrant blue eyes can read my mind, I'm sure of it.

I touch every part of my recorder with forced intensity, so Erik won't see last night's dream play out across my face. Then I toss the device on top of my backpack in the corner.

Pauline explains that we can show how important the baskets are to our Elders.

"We can highlight a few Elders' stories, see if they will let us video-record them. Add photos. Show different basket-weaving techniques, different styles. Then we challenge tribal citizens to look for baskets at garage sales and auctions so we can bring lost baskets back home."

My sister looks around the room, suddenly anxious.

"So, um, what do yous think?"

The other three Misfits and I look at one another. I see my own emotions reflected on their faces: awe, excitement, pride, reverence.

My lee-lee ricochets around the room. Lucas, Erik, and Shense clap. Pauline beams.

On the surface it seems like a simple idea, but each basket has a story. When we learn the stories, we see the baskets in a different light. Maybe our project will bring more baskets home and heal hearts. It could revive basket making for the next generation.

"I'll go get Claire," I say, rising and hugging Pauline. "We've got a winning idea."

At the end of the day, Erik and I hold hands as we leave Chi Mukwa. Halfway across the parking lot, I remember my backpack. I kiss his cheek before dashing back into the building.

I burst into our breakout room and immediately trip over something. My heart skips as a high-pitched shriek fills the small room. I land on top of someone, who pushes me away. I roll over and scoot myself into a corner. I feel nauseous. Cold and sweaty at the same time.

Claire's surprised shout gives way to laughter.

"Oh my, Perry. You gave me a fright. I dropped my favorite pen. I thought you left."

My heart needs another minute to go back to normal. It was nothing, a completely different situation from lying next to a dead body.

"I did," I say, rising quickly. "But I forgot my backpack." As I grab it, my voice recorder falls to the floor. I shove the device into my pants pocket.

"I meant to ask how everything is working out in your new assignment." She stands between me and the door.

"It's fine. Bucky Nodin is a good guy," I say, eager to get back to Erik.

She steps aside. "I don't mean to keep you. Just dreading dinner with my 'stepfather.'" Claire makes air quotes around the word.

I snap to attention. She means Frank Lockhart.

"Frank Lockhart?" What I wouldn't give to cross paths with that jerk right now.

Claire nods. "He always reaches out before a trip. He's off to Europe, several countries." There's a sadness in her eyes—the way she looks off in the distance and sees memories.

Something nags at me about the photo on Claire's desk. Lockhart's gaze was fixated on her mom, who was smiling at young Claire. The joy on her mom's face looked genuine. Caron Barbeau loved her child. Loving moms don't leave their children. Not willingly, at least.

I have many questions, but no reason to ask about such a sensitive matter.

"When's your stepdad leaving?" It's the only thing I can think to say.

"After dinner. He likes driving downstate the night before a big trip. Stays at the airport hotel. Then he's off to Frankfurt." She sounds bitter, maybe even envious.

"Have you ever traveled with him?"

She scoffs at my question. "No. We barely speak. I don't know why he insists on meeting me before each international trip. I never do the same when I go anywhere."

"Like with the study-abroad program?" I offer.

"Yes. And personal trips. My cousin Hugo lived in France for a while. I visited quite often. I saw more of him then than I do now, and he lives less than an hour away." Claire smiles at something over my shoulder. "My stepfather's shorter trips are three weeks. Longer trips, maybe six weeks?"

"Have a good dinner," I say, turning to go. I walk away quickly, eager to spend time with Erik.

Web appears at the top of the stairs, gym duffel in hand.

"Wassup, Web? Miss me already?" I say lightly, even though getting dumped still stings.

"Has Cooper Turtle talked with you?" he asks.

"No. Why? You both get seller's remorse?" Sometimes I crack myself up.

Web doesn't seem amused. He motions to follow him to a far corner of the mezzanine.

"The college issued a memo to Tribal Council about the Lockhart Collection. Cooper was copied on it. They toured a storage unit in St. Ignace next to his Teepees-n-Trinkets store. Based on what Frank Lockhart told them, he acquired the contents from another private collector, and the records were destroyed during a water leak at the storage property. They're claiming there is no proof the objects are connected to Sugar Island. I think they used the term 'culturally unidentifiable'?"

"What the——" Those shifty Mack State assholes. And that liar Frank Lockhart.

"How does that work, Perry? If they have no records of where anything came from, how do we make a claim for it?" Web's voice rises.

I pace while attempting to remember everything I've read or learned from Cooper.

"Cooper says museums use that label 'culturally unidentifiable' as a catchall if they don't have the resources to do a proper inventory. He says they also use it even after tribes provide evidence, because then, the museum can still hold on to the funerary belongings." I halt in front of Web. "Lockhart owns the south end of Sugar Island. Does he honestly expect us to believe that he didn't dig up his property for buried treasures?"

"All I know," he says, hands raised in mock surrender. "Nothing was labeled."

"What did Cooper say about the memo?"

"I haven't spoken with him," Web says.

Will Cooper continue accepting every delay in repatriating our ancestors? Or is this the moment he second-guesses his belief in the law, the process, the rules?

Cooper Turtle's by-the-book approach assumes a fair playing field. But there isn't one.

"Web, they're using every tactic to deny and delay us. Cooper said museums sometimes send notice of a public meeting and think it meets the tribal-consultation requirement in the law. And even if they do a formal consultation, institutions aren't required to follow the tribe's input."

I think about my reading list. What I've learned about the mindset of some researchers.

"They disregard our oral history as folklore."

I remember that Leer-wah guy showing me the Warrior Girl.

"Their archaeologist thinks any ancestor from more than a thousand years ago can't be claimed by any 'modern-day' tribe. But he goes around like, 'This here is *my* girl.'"

Dr. Fenton's office comes to mind.

"They don't think we can take proper care of human remains and sacred objects. But they have our ancestors in fruit boxes, Web. Actual banana boxes. They're okay with storing teeth in a fucking cereal box, but not with turning our relatives over to us."

I'm so furious, I want to go back to Dr. Fenton's office and take everything.

And then what? Cooper asks in his infuriatingly calm manner. I turn around. Of course Cooper isn't here. Just Web, giving me a curious look.

"Remember when you thought Frank Lockhart had illegal items in his collection?" Web's voice is nearly a whisper even though we're alone. "The Mack State people didn't mention any ancestral remains in the warehouse."

"Lockhart has ancestors stored somewhere else," I say excitedly. "You believe it too."

Web glances beyond me, making sure that no one is nearby.

"I do, Ogichidaakwezans." His smile reaches the crinkles at his eyes. "What did you call it when you get to hunt and fish on school days? 'Independent study'?" He nods as he continues: "Lots of great fishing spots on the south end of the island." He draws out the words like Pauline does for emphasis. "Secret locations. Hidden but ready to be discovered. As a fellow fisher, I'd enjoy hearing your stories. Always good to know where the best fish are hiding."

Web walks away, pausing to chat with Officer What-The at the top of the stairs.

Lockhart is going overseas tomorrow. He will be gone through the internship and, possibly, even into early September. Why is he making the trip now? His collection of legal items is being donated . . . but what about the illegal items? Ancestors he dug up on his property, objects he acquired after NAGPRA went into effect. Foreign museums aren't required to repatriate anything.

An idea takes root.

If anything was possible and you could get away with it, how far would you go?

I practically dance out of Chi Mukwa and across the parking lot to Erik's car. The windows are down and he's listening to music.

"Sorry for taking as long as I did," I say, getting in the car.

When Erik smiles, I feel a strange mix of feelings—tenderness and a wave of sadness.

"No worries," Erik says. "I went inside to check on you. It looked like an important conversation with the subchief, so I came back out to wait."

It *was* an important conversation. It's only now that I realize how important.

By the time we board the ferry, the wave of sadness is a tsunami.

I memorize Erik's profile. He removed his hair tie while waiting for my conversation with Web to finish. The breeze ruffles his hair. His top lip is thinner than his bottom lip. The hollow beneath his cheek seems deeper today. His nose has a bump on the bridge of it. I don't know how old he was when he broke his nose. Or how it happened.

There is so much we don't know about each other. I should've jumped in with both feet instead of taking it slow.

He stays for dinner. We play with Junior afterward. Erik confesses having watched me the day he came over to help Pauline with the database. When I was teaching my dog Ojibwemowin. The words for *dancing* and *tornado*.

We kiss by the monkey bars at the tree fort. I run my fingers through his hair, trying to memorize the wavy curls, their texture and color. His hair is already a lighter shade, and it's not even August. By the time Erik starts college, he might be blond. Sun-kissed.

He holds me close, the way he did in the first dream I had about him.

"Perry Pulls-No-Punches," he says. "Tell me what you've been avoiding all evening."

My breath catches. "I'm going to do something that you can't be part of."

We cling to each other for a long time. He kisses me one last time—slowly, tenderly—like the way you do when you want to commit something to memory. Then he drives away.

Tonight, when I dream about the Warrior Girl, I'll accept her knife.

CHAPTER 25
SUNDAY, JULY 27TH

After breakfast on Sunday morning, Mom and Pauline go shopping in Petoskey. My plan is to wait for Pops to run his errands so I can borrow Lucas's truck to explore Lockhart's property. But first Pops and I tend to the garden.

I goof off with Junior in the front yard while Pops takes a shower. He waves when he gets in his truck and drives off. We stay in the front yard, in case Pops forgets something and backtracks. I practice Ojibwemowin with my dog while waiting to hear the ferry horn twice.

Junior halts, ears perked. A minute later, Shense's car turns into the driveway. He growls. In addition to sheepdog and bloodhound, somewhere in his DNA is a fierce guard dog. He doesn't reveal that ancestor often, but we are home alone so it makes sense.

"Onizhishin." I tell him it's fine. To Shense, I say, "Wassup, nii-jiikwe?"

"Just wanted to take Washkeh for a drive. She's being fussy."

I think about Lucas's truck down the road. Maybe going for a ride with Shense would be a better option. At least I wouldn't need to worry about driving past Pops or someone who knows I'm grounded from driving this summer.

"Do you want company? I've been wanting to check out Frank Lockhart's property on the south end of the island," I say. "Hypothetical reconnaissance."

"Sure," she says without missing a beat. "Sounds great. Bring your dog, too, hey?"

I put Junior on his leash and have him sniff Shense and the baby. His tail wags like Washkeh is his baby girl. I still make him sit up front with me.

We take a scenic route across the island. I direct her to take a side road so we can park and not have any traffic.

Shense puts her binoojii in the baby-wrap thing across her chest. Again, Washkeh peeps a huge dark eye at me before turning toward the softness of her mom's breast.

I put my binoculars around my neck before letting Junior off his leash. If we get caught trespassing, my excuse is that I'm bird-watching and chasing after a naughty dog.

"What do you know about the property?" Shense asks.

"The way I heard it, all this land belonged to the Nodin family. They sold bits and pieces during hard times. My mom said that used to happen a lot." I track Junior, whistling for him when he gets too far ahead of us. He runs back, tail wagging. I continue talking. "At some point, Frank Lockhart's father started collecting ten-acre parcels like . . . like baseball cards, I guess. Now all of this belongs to him." Mindful of Washkeh, I keep my thoughts about Frank Lockhart to myself.

Junior runs ahead to a cluster of simple tar-paper houses in varying stages of disintegration. Roofs collapsed under the weight of heavy snowfalls. Single-pane windows used for target practice at some point. These rustic homes were occupied by generations of Nodins.

"My mom said that after the Tribe built the casino and tribal citizens had good jobs and started getting per capita payments, families like the Nodins tried buying back their land. By then, Frank Lockhart had built a large home and wasn't interested in selling."

My dog is fascinated by one of the shacks that's barely standing. I imagine a family of raccoons or squirrels claiming the place. Since Junior loves rolling in dead-animal carcasses even more than rolling around in animal shit, I call for him. He ignores me, sniffing around weathered wood planks and twisted window frames with shards of glass like broken teeth.

I make my way toward him. He sniffs with the intensity of a bloodhound. The ground is soft in places. A wood plank shifts like a seesaw.

"Maanaadan," I yell to my dog before repeating myself in English. "It's bad."

Finally I clip the leash to Junior's collar and pull him away from the ruins.

"I think I might do that thing at Malcolm," Shense says, sidestepping a fallen log.

"What thing?" I can't imagine that Malcolm has a "thing."

"That thing Mrs. Turtle talked about—earning credits on an accelerated schedule. I could graduate on time. Start college on time. Keep living with my dad. Focus on baby and school."

We follow an overgrown trail. Junior tugs his leash, wanting us to reverse course.

"What do you want to study?" I ask.

"Don't laugh," she says. "I was thinking about electrical engineering."

"Why would I laugh?" Junior marks yet another tree.

She shrugs. "I'm guessing I'd be the only teen mom in my classes."

"My mom said she was a better student after she had me and Pauline. Being a mom helped her focus on getting things done," I say.

"You could do the accelerated thing with me, Perry. Finish your junior and senior year in half the time. Go to college with me." She sounds excited.

"I'll think about it," I say without conviction.

"We could carpool to Mack State with Erik," she says, "if you don't mind a third wheel."

"I broke up with Erik on Friday night. My hypothetical reconnaissance isn't hypothetical. He can't be involved," I say. "You either. I mean, I know you're walking around Frank Lockhart's property with me, but that's as far as you go. I gotta be a lone wolf on this."

"So, you're done with him forever?" She wipes sweat from her forehead.

"I don't know what's gonna happen. If I get caught, it would be bad. Chi maanaadan."

When we cross the road, Shense points out the main power line.

"Any decent security system needs juice," she adds. "You need to take out the power to disable the system."

"That's all?" I laugh. Washkeh's dark hair has grown since the last time I saw her. It's thicker and sticks up taller. The more I think about it, I shouldn't have brought my friend here. "Seriously, Shense, I'll figure out how to do this on my own."

She ignores me, taking the lead. Junior follows her and pulls me along. By the time I realize we're tracking the power line, the outbuildings are visible. Shense halts at the edge of the woods. She points at the binoculars around my neck.

"There's a structure next to the barn," she says, after I've handed the binoculars over.

I squint. "The silo?"

"No, it looks like a fence around a carport. It's got a roof but no walls." She hands over the binoculars for me to find it. "See? That's where the generator is located. When there's a power outage, his generator kicks on."

"How long can a generator last?" I ask.

"A day or two? Depends on the size." She nudges me. "My dad got himself a drone for his birthday. I could borrow it and get video."

"Shense, I'm serious about this being a lone-wolf operation."

"But if it's so important, you should have help. Lucas might have access to a drone at work. He and Pauline could work together on mapping the property." She rocks the baby, who has started fussing. "Good excuse for them to spend time together. Then we can try to search all the buildings somehow."

"What do you mean about Lucas and Pauline?"

Shense doesn't answer. Instead she gives me a funny look.

"He's like our brother," I say.

"I must have gotten it wrong. Probably imagined it because Washkeh's dad and I were friends." Shense coos to the baby. "I'm gonna need to feed her soon."

We retreat through the woods until reaching a fallen tree. Shense sits on the trunk and adjusts her bra so Washkeh can feed. She hums to her binoojii. I sit next to them. Junior tugs at the leash. He didn't listen too well earlier by the crumpled shacks, so I'm not taking any chances.

There, in the peacefulness of the woods, I imagine pulling off a heist. Dressed in black. Slinking around trees in the dark, as uncatchable as a shadow. Boxes of ancestors are stored somewhere nearby.

Once I find them, I'll sing to them like Shense does to Washkeh, her voice full of love and comfort.

Amii izhi nibaan. *Go to sleep now.*

Gego gotaajiken. *Do not be afraid.*

Gizaagi'in. *I love you.*

WEEK EIGHT

After an FBI investigation determined that Donald Miller may have knowingly or unknowingly improperly collected artifacts, archaeologists and other experts joined authorities to begin parsing through the collection—which includes Native American items, and objects from at least nine other countries including China, Russia, Italy and Greece—and identifying which artifacts, if any, must be repatriated.

—Noah Rayman, "FBI Raids Home of Real Life Indiana Jones,"
Time, April 3, 2014

I have never seen a collection like this in my entire life except at some of the largest museums.

—Larry Zimmerman, professor [emeritus] of museum studies at Indiana University-Purdue University Indianapolis, interviewed in "FBI Raids Indiana Man's Private Collection Of Historical Artifacts," *All Things Considered*, NPR, April 6, 2014

CHAPTER 26

THURSDAY, JULY 31ST

When I get Uncle Bucky's coffee, bran muffin, and daily newspaper on Thursday morning, the headline makes me gag.

DATE ANNOUNCED FOR LOCKHART COLLECTION DONATION

I force myself to read every word. The reporter quotes Lockhart praising Mackinac State College as the perfect location to house his "treasures." The article identifies the day the official transfer will take place: October 13.

Lockhart is turning over our ancestors' belongings on Columbus Day.

Columbus Day?

It's beyond irony. The explorer who got lost and discovered a "new world" full of resources: Indigenous peoples he could enslave to work in gold mines and on plantations. "Indians" to be trafficked, just another resource to be extracted from the land.

Lake Superior State University did a red-dress exhibit last spring to bring awareness to the MMIW epidemic. Mom and Auntie had me and Pauline come to campus with red dresses we no longer wore. The Native American Center hung the dresses on hangers from trees around campus. Someone had posted a sign: MMIW BEGAN IN 1492.

I take out my anger on the cardboard boxes Bucky wants me to tear down and haul to the garbage and recycling area. I'm a sweaty mess in a foul mood by lunchtime. When I take my break, I return to the casino deli for a sandwich and an apple. It's supposed to storm later, so I take advantage of the sunshine and eat my lunch outside. As soon as I bite into my apple, I decide to borrow Lucas's truck tonight and repatriate the ceremonial pipe from Teepees-n-Trinkets. I spend the rest of my workday planning out every detail.

When I turned thirteen, Auntie bought me a black wet suit for diving. I went through a phase where I liked being in the water more than on land. The wet suit provided insulation so I could snorkel and explore the river without risking hypothermia. Pauline called it my ninja suit.

It's perfect for tonight.

More than once, I've been out at night with friends and someone says, "Oh, Perry, I didn't see you." It's this weird thing that never seems to happen to anyone lighter-skinned than me or Pauline. The memory comes back as I think about how to make myself invisible, to blend into the night, on purpose.

My preparations include alerting Lucas that I need to borrow his truck. I tell Pauline she needs to keep Elvis Junior in her room.

"What if I had plans?" she challenges.

Remembering what Shense hinted at last Sunday, I debate whether to say something about Lucas. It's still too weird to think about the possibility of him being her sneaky snag.

"Do you?" I volley back. I feel a twinge of satisfaction when Pauline backs down.

As soon as my parents go to bed, I change into my ninja suit. It was a bit snug the last time I wore it. I try to recall if I've added any pounds or inches—which could ruin my plan—but my growth spurt was primarily during my middle school years. I strip down to the one-piece swimsuit beneath my pajamas. Sucking in my gut to make it concave, I pull the back zipper while exhaling. It's the opposite of a snake shedding its skin. Then I slip on my water shoes, grateful that my feet haven't grown.

Like last time, I leave my iPhone behind. But I do take the emergency phone, cash, and a black nylon backpack with black leather gloves and a few tools.

Distant flashes of lightning and low rumbles of thunder accompany me as I climb out of my bedroom window. I scamper to the road and then jog the short distance to Lucas's yard. He's left his truck at the end of the driveway for me. The keys are above the visor.

Lucas has been our best buddy since we were six years old. Shense must be wrong about Pauline and Lucas. That's all there is to it. Shense sees every male-female friendship as Friends With Benefits. I'm friends with lots of guys and have never been tempted to lose my pants.

There are a dozen cars filled with rowdy people ahead of me on the ferry. The deckhand doesn't collect fares on this leg of the trip, so he chats with the rowdies. I go unnoticed.

I park Lucas's truck down the road from Auntie's place. I help myself to her old pickup truck that can travel stealthily like a ninja. From there, I take back roads to St. Ignace, listening to music so I won't think about Lucas and my sister. A Keith Urban song begins. It's the one that was playing when Erik asked if we could try again. I thought it was a happy song, but I must have been projecting my mood that evening. Actually, it's a sad song about a girl who breaks a guy's heart.

What if the girl was just as brokenhearted as the guy?

A block away from Teepees-n-Trinkets, there's a run-down apartment building with a parking lot. Auntie's truck blends in. Still, I pick a parking spot behind a dumpster that someone has filled with twin mattresses, packed upright like McDonald's hash browns.

I pull the wet-suit hood over my black swim cap and add a black ski mask to be extra stealth. The temperature dropped during the hour-long drive. I won't overheat in my ninja outfit.

Remembering what Shense told me about the security system, I pick a window at the back of the store. The exterior lighting is a broken sconce holding a bird nest. It's a vinyl window, which means it most likely hasn't been painted shut. The sash lock has a fifty-fifty chance of being unlocked. If not, I brought a glass cutter from a hardware store.

I hold my breath while pressing gloved fingertips upward on the lower sash. It takes four tries until the window budges. I work my fingers beneath the bottom edge to lift the sash.

Sticking my head through the window, I quickly scan the shop. There is a red glow inside the building, coming from the EXIT sign above the front door. I am just outside the museum room. A clothing rack blocks my view of the display case with the ceremonial pipe.

"Just climb in, take the pipe, and leave," I say out loud.

I almost forgot to make an offering. I dig in my backpack and take out the tobacco tie I added this evening. I say a prayer and release the semaa in front of the open window.

I toss my backpack inside before climbing headfirst through the window. I end up doing a somersault, which makes me feel like a ninja. Except ninjas don't have racing heartbeats. They probably slow their heart rate and breathing. I try to do the same.

As I tiptoe past the rack of clothing, I can't help feeling excited to the point of giddiness. I'll leave the pipe with Stormy; he'll know what to do with it. If I don't tell him where I got it, he won't be an accessory to anything. Everything will be—

The display case is empty.

For a solid minute, I stare at the space where the pipe used to rest. What? How? Why?

Someone moved it . . . maybe to the museum room. It's three steps away.

Car headlights shine through the windows at the front of the store. I drop to the floor. Lying on my stomach brings an image of Grant Edwards's pale blue eyes staring through me. I push the memory away so I can focus on what is happening now. Is it a cop car? Was Shense wrong about there not being window alarms?

I try to ninja myself backward, toward the open window. If someone is going to enter the shop, I need to get myself outside.

The headlights move sideways.

I lift my head enough to see the car using the parking lot to turn around and leave. It wasn't anything. Just a coincidence: someone making a U-turn.

I return my cheek to the floor and wait for my breathing to return to normal. I'll leave the way I came. Empty-handed but a clean getaway.

Except when I rise, I remember the family of moccasins in the museum room. Maybe I can repatriate those. Or maybe the ceremonial pipe is there. The store people could have moved everything after the boy knocked down the case with my great-grandmother's basket.

I follow the wall, ninja-like, to the entrance to the museum room.

"Just tiptoe in, look for the pipe, take it and the moccasins, and leave."

Before I move, I realize the museum room is darker than the main shop area. The red glow doesn't reach it. I have a small flashlight in my backpack, beneath the window.

A few heartbeats later, I'm back with the flashlight. I step into the room and turn it on.

The entire room is empty.

I'm too late.

The storm hits as soon as I reach the Sault. The lightning and thunder match my anger toward Frank Lockhart for using my tribe and our ancestors as pawns in a pissing contest with Grant Edwards. And toward the college for declaring everything in Lockhart's collection to be "culturally unidentifiable." And at Dr. Fenton keeping teeth in a cereal box and an otter medicine bag splayed across her desk like a pet. And at me . . . for not taking action sooner.

I remember to fuel up before returning Auntie's ninja pickup truck and heading back to the island. It's Thursday night, technically Friday morning. There are plenty of vehicles trying to make last call at the bar on the island. I pay my fare in cash and wear the black trucker hat from my backpack. I keep my head down and don't engage with anyone.

Driving along the causeway, I think about Lockhart's property. About how Web and I both think Frank Lockhart has ancestors stored there. And how he's overseas right now, making arrangements to sell human remains and sacred items to the highest bidder. I picture the family of moccasins and the ceremonial pipe. If I had only acted sooner.

Instead of turning left toward the north end of Sugar Island, I head south.

Warriors are willing to do what others can't or won't do for their community.

The rain is coming down hard enough that I'll be invisible on Lockhart's security camera.

I park the truck down the same side road Shense used on Sunday. I keep the black trucker hat on. The black leather gloves go back on before I slide my arms into the backpack loops.

I start with Lockhart's boathouse. The roof provides cover for a wraparound deck spanning three sides of the structure, which is partially on the water. One of the windows is open, so I peek inside. He has three boats under one roof: two on lifts and the third in the water behind a garage door that opens to the lake. I rule out the boathouse as a place to store anything beyond the obvious.

Next I head to the barn. It is odd to have farm buildings on land that has more sand and rock than soil. Finding the barn's purpose seems a good starting point. Oversized garage doors take up considerable space on one side of the structure. There is a single door on the east side of the barn that has an entry-door keypad that locks upon punching in the code. Shense told me that people don't always set the lock each time they leave the building. I grip the handle, expecting it to open.

It doesn't.

I find a window to peek inside. Each time lightning flashes through the square windows on the upper section of the barn, I glimpse more of the interior. There are four vintage cars inside. A hydraulic hoist for working on vehicles. One wall is filled with tool cabinets and a workbench. It's a fancier version of my dad's workshop in our pole barn. Unless there is a secret basement, this isn't where Lockhart stores anything other than car stuff. Just to be sure, I run around the building looking for storm-cellar doors or anything suggesting there is an underground level to the barn. Finding nothing, I turn around to look at other structures.

There is a small home with a garage. It must be the one Claire's aunt, uncle, and cousin lived in. I hesitate to check it out, not wanting to see where Claire grew up after her mom left. I decide to save it for last.

I glance back at the barn. Lightning silhouettes the silo next to the barn.

A silo.

If the barn is a car workshop, then what need is there for a silo? Frank Lockhart is a collector, not a farmer.

The rain is cold against my cheeks. I feel a chill down my spine despite the wet suit doing its job. The door has the same entry-door keypad as the barn. I try the door handle, hoping Shense is right this time, but it doesn't budge.

I step back to inspect the silo. The structure is about twelve feet in diameter and twenty-five feet high with a roof shaped like a cone. Decorative square windows, smaller versions of the ones along the upper level of the barn, wrap around the top of the silo. The overhang of the conical roof protects the windows. There isn't a way to reach them except to rappel from the roof. I did not bring the equipment necessary and am not sure I'd attempt it even under optimal conditions. But in a heavy rain? With lightning?

The sky lights for a long moment. The accompanying boom of thunder reverberates throughout my body. The lightning reveals a fixed ladder on the side of the silo, in the crook between the barn and silo. The ladder doesn't reach the full height of the structure. Instead it stops halfway, where a square door is built into the structure.

Am I going to climb a steel ladder during a lightning storm?

I can't explain the feeling of something drawing me to the silo. It pulls me as if by a magnetic force.

My gloved hands grip the wet rung. My water shoes, with rubber soles thick enough to protect my feet from rough rocks, were a good choice, especially if I get struck by lightning.

Am I actually trying to convince myself that rubber-soled shoes will save my life?

Don't look down. Just take it one rung at a time.

The square metal door is two feet by two feet. There is a padlock on a hasp latch.

Could I even attempt Shense's magic trick in the rain?

I reach the square door and touch the padlock. My heart leaps. It's not locked.

After unlatching the clasp, I swing the square door open. I take a deep breath, heart pounding, before peeking my head inside.

Lightning illuminates the interior of the silo for an instant.

My scream fills the cylinder. I shake all over. One foot slips and I scramble to regain my footing. I press my head to the cold, wet steel.

I look again, this time at a metal ladder on the inside of the silo. Where the ladder on the outside is bolted to the silo, the one inside is attached to a rail around the perimeter. It's like a rolling library ladder extending from floor to ceiling, gliding on wheels to reach any part of the silo interior. I climb inside the silo and make my way down the ladder. I need to see.

I wait for the lightning to reveal exactly what that bastard has done. It is an agonizing wait that feels like an eternity. Then it's as if multiple thunderbirds blink their eyes like a drumroll, sending bolts of lightning across the sky.

My howl of anger mixes with the thunder.

Frank Lockhart has lined the interior of the silo with at least forty shadow boxes. Stacked—no, *hanging*—all along the walls. Each one contains an ancestor. Each box is deep enough for a skeleton, like a shallow casket but with a window of glass so the contents may be viewed. In the bottom right corner of each frame, he's written notes on an index card. It must be the provenance of each ancestor.

In the center of the floor is a comfortable chair. It swivels when I touch it. This is the collector's setup, so he can see his "treasures."

I don't want to leave them, but I need to go home.

I need to plan.

I need help.

I speak to them, introducing myself.

"Aaniin. Perry Firekeeper-Birch indizhnikaaz. Waabizhish indoodem. Ziisabaaka Minising indonjiba." I try not to cry, but the effort requires energy I cannot spare. *Amii izhi nibaan. Gego gotaajiken. Gizaagi'in.*

CHAPTER 27

FRIDAY, AUGUST 1ST

I wake up still cradled in Pauline's arms. Vague memories burn off like fog during sunrise. After returning home last night—wet, exhausted, and inconsolable—I crawled into my sister's bed.

"You're safe now," she consoled.

I couldn't manage any words.

She held me, and I cried myself into something beyond sleep.

Once, I told my twin about a time when we were the same egg. Pauline wanted Auntie to explain how it wasn't scientifically possible to remember that far back. But Auntie believed me.

My sister tries not to jostle me in the morning. As she inches her way off the bed, every tiny movement hurts my body. Elvis Junior takes Pauline's place, snuggling in the still-warm indent next to me. We cuddle until he unleashes an atomic fart that burns my nose.

"Holaay, chi boogid monster!" I scramble off the bed. A second later, I yelp from the pain of moving. Everything hurts.

Pauline comes in, wrapped in a towel and with her hair piled on top of her head.

"Why are you—" Her question halts as soon as Junior's toxic cloud of boogid reaches her. We flap our hands to wave away the stench while laughing without opening our mouths.

It isn't until I'm in the shower that I see remnants of last night on my body. The undersides of my arms resemble mashed raspberries where I clung to the metal ladder. Random bruises appear on my legs, hips, stomach, and chest. Even the soles of my feet are red and swollen. I wipe the steam from the bathroom mirror and blink my surprise at the image staring back. My eyes are bloodshot and puffy from crying so hard. There is a horizontal bruise along my forehead, but I don't remember hitting my head on anything.

Pauline comes into my bedroom while I dress myself in slow motion. Her hair is still in a messy topknot. I realize it's been a while since she's pulled it up like that. She's worn her hair down lately. My sister crowds me in front of my full-length mirror.

I zero in on the bare patch of scalp behind her ear. It's the size of a half-dollar coin.

She catches me staring and immediately tugs at her hair tie. Her hands quickly smooth her long hair into a braid over one shoulder.

"You're actually coming to seminar today?" she says nonchalantly. "Mom and Pops are gonna ask about your forehead."

"What if I keep my hair sideways across it?" I run my fingers through my hair, trying to create a side part.

"Why are you asking me?" Pauline says, instantly on edge.

I say the thing that we both know but never mention.

"Because you're good at hiding secrets with your hair."

She recoils as if I've slapped her.

Before she lashes out, I calmly say, "It's okay, Egg."

Her shoulders slump. I don't like how defeated she suddenly seems.

"It brings you comfort when you're stressed." My voice is soft.

"My hair pulling." She takes a deep breath. "It's called trichotillomania."

I hadn't planned on talking to her about it this morning, but here we are. Besides, after the shock and horror of what I experienced last night, my sister's big secret doesn't feel monumental anymore.

"It's kind of amazing, if you think about it," I say, arranging my hair. "That patch behind your left ear is like your own Zen garden."

"It's anything but amazing," she replies. I might be imagining it, but Pauline's face seems slightly relaxed. Maybe the idea needs time to fertilize before it can sprout.

I think about the other things my sister does to alleviate stress: eat weed gummies, play Flappy Bird for hours, and the other thing.

"Are you sneaky-snagging Lucas?" I say quietly.

"So what if I am?" Her defiance is a knee-jerk reaction. We've had a lot of revelations over the past six hours.

I want to say something about how it's Lucas. Our Lucas. Our buddy. But my head hurts with everything swirling around.

Using a wide-tooth comb, Pauline makes my side part look intentional instead of haphazard. She dashes to her room and returns with sparkly bobby pins to create a sideswept bang that hides my forehead.

I pretend to pick a piece of lint from her shirt, just so I can touch her. It feels like our heartbeats sync when we are next to each other.

"Your hair is super dry." She squints above my forehead before sighing, "I'll let you try my hair truffles."

Pauline is hella stingy with her hair products. This is her *I love you* gesture.

I couldn't list any of the presentations or activities from the morning session. Other than taking frequent bathroom breaks to reapply Visine to my eyes, all I've done is think about the ancestors in the silo. Lockhart has been gone a full week already. I picture him meeting with private museums in countries where they still display Indigenous skulls and skeletons. I have at least two weeks, possibly more, to come up with a plan for retrieving the ancestors.

Cooper's voice asks, *And then what?*

I'll need help preparing them for reburial. My parents and other community volunteers are learning what other tribes do, in order to come up with our own ceremony. But this repatriation won't be a negotiated process. It's a heist. An illegal action that I am justifying in the big picture of righting wrongs.

I remain subdued all day until Claire releases us to our team meeting rooms to work on our final projects.

Before Pauline starts talking about Project Bigiiwen Enji Zaagigoo-yin, I clear my throat.

"I need help."

The other Misfits look at me. I make eye contact with Erik.

"You should leave the room," I say solemnly. "I'm sharing information that you would be better off not knowing."

He rises and takes the long way around the table. When Erik walks behind me, he pauses, and I feel his fingertips stroke across my back. He leaves.

I tell Shense the same thing.

"I'm good," she says, crossing her arms across her chest. She stays put.

"Shense," I say. "You need to think about Washkeh."

"I am. She will know that some battles are worth fighting. I want her to be proud of me." Shense gives her best side-eye. "Besides, you aren't the boss of me."

I sigh. "Frank Lockhart has at least forty ancestors stored on his property. I found them. He can sell to private collectors and foreign museums. I'm going to reclaim them before he can."

My attempted heist last night of the ceremonial pipe from Teepees-n-Trinkets was overshadowed by the discovery of the ancestors in Lockhart's silo. But it has stayed on my mind. I didn't plan well, and then I deviated from my half-assed plan. It was a close call.

"I can't do it on my own. I need help coming up with a plan." I look to my sister. "If it's a group of kids reclaiming the ancestors, we wouldn't face the same consequences an adult would for theft."

Pauline asks the logical question. "Why don't you tip off the police? Or the media?"

"The FBI is in Indiana right now," I begin. "There's a private collector who sounds a lot like Frank Lockhart. He has thousands of items." Cooper had included a *Time* magazine article on the reading list he prepared for me. I fell into an internet rabbit hole looking for additional information. "There are skeletons from burial grounds. Elders. Babies. Entire families. The items they were buried with. Sacred items from ceremonies." My voice catches. "The FBI estimates it will take decades for them to inventory everything. Decades."

Lucas reaches across the table for my hands. Grasping them, he squeezes.

"You jump, Pear-Bear, and I'll catch you. Every time."

"I'm your ride or die, niijiikwe," Shense says.

"I'm always with you," my twin says. "We're the same egg, remember?"

And, just like that, the heist is on.

Shense adds one more thing. "You should make every Misfit Toy swear a blood oath to go through with the heist no matter what. It's that important."

We take a break when Shense has to pump. Pauline and Lucas head to the bathrooms. I grab a book from my backpack and read for a few minutes.

Erik returns to the Misfits meeting room and sits across from me. I look up from my book. He's staring at his hands. His Adam's apple moves as he swallows.

"Perry, I'm sorry I can't be involved."

I reach for his hand. "I understand."

"No, you don't understand everything . . ." Erik leaves me hanging.

"Spill it, Erik Pulls-No-Punches."

His smile is too brief. He also has to take a deep breath before he continues.

"After I found the auction listing for the turtle shaker—"

"That was you? I thought it was Pauline," I say.

"It was me. I wanted to help you. But then I started digging around the dark web for other auctions, and I'm not supposed to be on that part of the cyber universe."

"What did you find?" *No, wait,* I think. "Why would you do that?"

"It was so easy. I was curious." He looks down again. "I wanted you to like me. Even if we weren't speaking to each other."

"You didn't need to go on the dark web for that." I smile, but he's still not looking at me.

His bright blue eyes meet my gaze.

"It scares me how easily tempted I was," he confesses. "That's why I can't be part of whatever you're planning. It's not because I don't want to do it." He grips my hand a bit tighter. "It's because I'd want to help you do anything you asked."

I'm on my way out of Chi Mukwa at the end of the day with Pauline and Lucas when Web enters with his gym duffel.

"Hey, Perry," he says. "Any good fishing lately?"

I grin. "Yeah. I found a great spot. Lots of fish."

"You don't say." Web sounds impressed but continues toward the stairs.

I tell Lucas and Pauline to hold up. Dashing upstairs to the mezzanine, I find Web in the same corner where we spoke previously about Lockhart's donation.

"Where?" he asks.

"The silo on his property." My voice quivers. "He has a shrine to them."

"You got inside?" Web stares, wide-eyed with something like awe.

"There's a metal ladder leading to a small square door near the top of the silo. I was prepared to pick the lock, but the stem of the padlock wasn't inserted."

"That's fantastic." His eyes sparkle.

"It's horrible. How he has them . . . displayed." I cough to disguise the catch in my voice.

Web's tone is instantly somber. "What size of a vehicle would we need to transport them to a safe place?"

I imagine Pauline, Lucas, and Shense helping me carry the shadow boxes from the silo to a moving van. Forty shadow boxes, stored upright, packed tightly.

"A medium-sized moving van, to be safe. I worry that a small van or trailer wouldn't fit all the shadow boxes." I look up at Web. "No one gets left behind."

He nods in agreement.

"I will have two or three helpers," I say.

"Team Misfit Toys?" He grins.

"Can you rent a U-Haul?" I ask. "They probably won't rent to a teen paying in cash."

Web shakes his head. "Lockhart could have private investigators check with local businesses. We need something off the books." He pauses before smiling. "Let's think this through together. You don't have to figure everything out on your own, Ogichidaakwezans."

I breathe a sigh of relief. Between Web and Team Misfit Toys, I don't feel alone. There are times, not just when I'm dreaming, when it's as if the Warrior Girl is with me as well. Maybe I'm imagining it—the idea that she is part of everything that is happening. It's going to be difficult, reclaiming our ancestors . . . but Web's right: I don't have to do it on my own.

CHAPTER 28
SUNDAY, AUGUST 3RD

Shense texts, asking if I want to come along to pick up Washkeh in St. Ignace. We plan to meet at the ferry launch on the mainland side. Pops drives me to get the ferry.

"Call when you need me to pick you up," he says.

I lean over to kiss his whiskers. "Gizaagi'in, Imbaabaa."

He musses my hair. "Gizaagi'in, Indaanis."

I walk onto the ferry and plant myself in the front left corner so Shense will see me. Just to be silly, I wave like a maniac when the ferry captain blasts the horn at our departure. I wait until the middle of the river to say a prayer and toss a few flakes of semaa from my jeans pocket onto the water. I imagine the tobacco floating downriver to Neebish Island. My thoughts go to the Warrior Girl, restless in a box at the museum archives in St. Ignace.

"Aandi wenjiiyan? Ziisiibaaka Minising? Neebish Minising?" I call out over the engine roar. "Bigiiwen enji zaagigooyin."

When the ferry docks on the mainland, I jog over to Shense's car.

"Get in, niijiikwe," she says.

Once we reach the highway, she floors it.

"Holaay, Speed Racer. Cops work Sundays, ya know." I help myself to a Twizzler.

Shense's foot lifts off the gas and settles at a comfortable level.

"Hey, I had a cultural dream," she says. "You were kicking some guy's ass, like really pounding his face, and then I had to stitch him up."

"What was cultural about that?" I ask, taking a bite of the red licorice straw.

"I stitched him up with a number-thirteen beading needle," she says. "That's cultural."

I laugh so hard that a half-chewed red blob dribbles onto my T-shirt. She joins in, revealing her crooked tooth that I think looks perfect on her.

We eat Twizzlers for a few more miles.

"Oh, hey," Shense says, like an afterthought. "I solved your electricity problem."

"My what?"

"You need to have the security system shut off when we take the ancestors, right?" She doesn't wait for my response. "My uncle Jimmy works for the electric company. I asked him a hypothetical and he got super interested. Like a squirrel with a nut," she laughs. "Okay, so you need to add another team member by the name of Mother Nature."

"What the—" I start, but Shense raises her hand. As in *talk to the hand*.

"Next big lightning storm, he cuts down a big-ass tree and kills the main power line. He puts the work order to the back of the queue. The bigger the storm, the longer the queue." She gives me a cheesy big grin like she's the one taking down the main line. "Uncle Jimmy says he can push it to four days tops."

We pass the Kinross exit, and there's a state trooper lurking in the median.

"Cop," I say. "Just act natural."

She laughs.

I continue, "So, that's four days for . . . what?" I need details.

"'Member the fenced-in generator area I showed ya?"

"Yeah."

"Well, I borrowed my dad's drone and went back to the property yesterday. I used the drone to drop a bird nest over the security camera. Before the wind blew it down, I got video over the fence." I recognize her proud tone from having heard it so often from Pauline. "I know the make and size of the generator." Shense gives a sideways glance. "And, before you say anything, I kept my phone on airplane mode all afternoon so it wouldn't connect with the cell signal on the property or anywhere else along the way." She looks positively smug.

"You're a little smarty-pants," I tell her.

"Here's how it works," she says. "The power goes out and the generator kicks on. Based on size, it has enough fuel for twenty-four to forty-eight hours. Plan on forty-eight hours to be safe. Then he's probably got a battery backup for his surveillance and security system, which means waiting another eight hours before that goes out. Now, Uncle Jimmy says he can push it to four days max in the queue, but, to be safe, plan on three. So, sixty hours after the power is cut, you have a twelve-hour window to do what you need to do."

I'm speechless. Shense Jackson figured out a way for me to bypass the security cameras. Pauline, Lucas, Web, and I will have twelve hours to get a truck onto the property, transfer the ancestors from the silo to the truck, and transport them somewhere safe.

When we pick up the binoojii, I decide to sit next to her in the back seat. I lean over to inhale the top of her head, burying my nose in the thick tufts of soft, sweet-smelling dark hair.

"Your mama is a genius," I tell Washkeh, who scowls as if to say, *I know.*

Shense insists on taking me all the way home, even though Pops would meet me at the ferry and save her the trip. She refuses the ten-dollar bill I offer for the ferry, so I tuck it under the binoojii in the car seat. Washkeh responds with a grumpy little kick.

Walking through the mudroom entrance, I catch a whiff of smudge and familiar voices speaking Ojibwemowin. I catch the word for "ancestors": aanikoobijiganag. Every muscle in my body tenses at the sight of Stormy sitting at the kitchen island, drinking coffee with my parents.

Do they know about Frank Lockhart's secret collection?

Mom's smile calms me. If I were in trouble, she wouldn't look happy.

I listen to their conversation. Mom does most of the talking, explaining what she and Pops learned from a tribal community they recently visited in Minnesota. Stormy tells them the spirits of those who came before us are uneasy in the next world, as their physical gift back to Mother Earth has been desecrated. Thankfully, we aren't the only ones trying to help the ancestors.

Each community is different, even among other Ojibwe bands. One tribe prefers to return ancestors to an undisclosed location through a private ceremony with the repatriation specialist and a pipe carrier. Another holds a community gathering to celebrate the homecoming—even inviting non-Native museum folks to participate. And yet another community conducts a ceremony in which they ask the ancestors for forgiveness.

Pops asks Stormy, "Aan enendaman?"

"Perhaps an answer will come from the ancestors?"

What does Stormy mean, *Perhaps an answer will come from the ancestors?* Does he mean that we won't know what to do until we have the ancestors back? Will he pray with the ancestors after we reclaim them from the silo and listen to what they tell him?

I take my time getting a glass of biish, standing at the sink and taking in the rest of their conversation. Cooper has invited my parents, Stormy, and several other community members to a MACPRA meeting next week in Battle Creek. I would've been included in the Sugar Island delegation if I still was Cooper's intern.

I invite Lucas to Sunday dinner. Stormy is staying, and Mom takes a dozen salmon fillets from the freezer. I volunteer to pick vegetables from the garden. At the last minute, I invite Stormy to join me.

I want to ask Stormy about preparing ancestors but wonder if he would alert my parents or Cooper. Would he tell Auntie . . . who would tell my parents or her friend who happens to be the police captain? Or is it like during ceremonies—something sacred and not shared with anyone outside of the ceremony?

I hand a small tobacco tie to Stormy as we walk to the garden. He puts the semaa in the pocket of his black jeans.

"Gikaadendam," I begin, although it is obvious that I have something serious on my mind. Looking up at him, I get right to it: whether my secret will be safe with him.

"Eya," he says to my great relief.

As we pick tomatoes, broccoli, and cauliflower for a salad, I choose my words carefully. I tell Stormy there are stolen ancestors nearby. My voice quivers as images from the silo flash before me. I can bring them home, but it would be in secret. I accept the risk for my actions. I want to return the ancestors to the earth in a good way, but I don't know how to prepare them.

His gaze is so intense. I avert my eyes because it's like staring into the sun.

Stormy says that, as a life-giving kwe, I shouldn't do the preparations for any babies. Only women who are beyond that part of their life cycle can prepare those bundles for their recommitment.

If I can't do it, then neither can Pauline or Shense. We will need to recruit some Elders.

"Aaniin gaa-dashiwaad?" he asks.

My best guess is forty. "Niimidana?"

"Aanapii?" Of course he needs to know when.

I catch myself shrugging. "Aazha gegaa." *Soon.*

Stormy repeats the question. He wants specifics.

"Niisho-dwaate. Ango-giizis." Two to four weeks is as precise as I can be.

He looks away, staring into the woods. I've asked for too much. Stormy spent two years in jail because he wouldn't utter a word when Uncle Levi, his best friend, was in trouble. What if involving Stormy is risking his freedom?

He says nothing. I have to respect his silence as his answer.

I check the sweet corn, shucking a husk to see if it's ready for harvest. Stormy joins me in selecting the plumpest ears of corn. My stomach growls in anticipation of our feast.

Stormy carries the full basket as we walk back to the house. I hold the door open for him.

As he passes by me, he says, "Wiidookodaadimin."

I grin. Stormy Nodin is my ally. I don't know how he will help, but I trust him. After all, he knows the risk.

At dinner, Pauline treats Lucas the same as always. Just like our child-hood days when it was the three of us. I can almost forget that they've been sneaky-snagging all summer long.

Then I catch Lucas looking at my twin when she leaves the dining table to clear her plate. His gaze is a momentary slip that nobody else sees. He smiles. Not his usual crooked grin, but something soft and delicate.

Lucas Chippeway is in love with my sister. It's not a casual thing for him like it is for her. When it ends, he will be hurt. Pauline will break his heart.

I'm suddenly angry at my sister for playing Friends With Benefits with Lucas. Or maybe I'm angry at him for not abiding by the FWB ground rules.

Perry Pulls-No-Punches would tease Lucas with a cutting remark just deep enough to sting. And before Pauline could react, I'd detonate a few truth bombs her way. The words are there, in the back of my throat, burning to be released.

I don't know why I keep them inside me.

The burning sensation fills my nose instead. I want to be the version of me from the beginning of the summer. The girl who fishes and strolls through life with no worries.

That would be nice.

Stormy leaves after dinner. Mom and Pops watch a romantic movie. And I lead Pauline and Lucas to the tree house. We sit in a triangle, each one of us believing we are the apex.

"We'll have a twelve-hour window to get the ancestors away from Lockhart's property," I say, diving right into it. "I'll give a heads-up, like a countdown."

"How?" Lucas sounds agitated.

"I'll figure it out." I mentally add the task to my list.

"No, I got it." Pauline looks hella smug. "I started buying burner phones—one at a time, different stores, and always with cash." She twirls a section of hair. "I've got five, and I already programmed them with a group text."

"Whoa," Lucas voices for both of us.

Pauline basks in our admiration until her need for more details overtakes her pride.

"And den what?" She looks to me for an answer.

I've been thinking about this. I'm prepared to take the responsibility for our actions. The only way to minimize risks for everyone else is if I'm the only one who knows the entire plan.

Shense will know about the security system and won't help retrieve the ancestors.

Pauline and Lucas will help retrieve the ancestors, but not be involved in anything else.

Web will arrange for the transportation, and I will drive the moving van.

Stormy will know what to do for the ancestors after we bring them to a safe place.

I tell my sister and our buddy their part of the plan.

"Yous will help me retrieve boxes of ancestors from Lockhart's property and transfer them to a truck." My throat tightens. "They're in shadow boxes with glass fronts for display."

Pauline gasps.

I deepen my voice to keep the overwhelming emotions at bay.

"You must prepare yourself to face them. They need us to comfort them. Not the other way around."

My sister sits a bit taller, her spine straightening with resolve. Lucas follows suit.

"We are going to need two or three Elders to help." I turn to Lucas. "I'm hoping you can ask Granny June, but only if you think she can handle it."

"Handle what, exactly?" His brow furrows with concern for his great-grandmother.

"Helping prepare the ancestors who are babies for their reburial. She will be helped in how to do it. Only people who are past their child-bearing years can do the preparations on those little ones." I catch the look between Pauline and Lucas at the mention of procreating. Focusing on Lucas, I add, "She can't tell anyone, not even Auntie Daunis."

"If we need another Elder, Granny will want Minnie with her," Lucas offers.

"Yeah, but can Minnie keep a secret like this? From her son, the tribal chief? And her grandson? You know . . . the tribal cop?"

Lucas shrugs. "We got a better chance of them staying quiet if they're keeping an eye on each other."

Pauline asks him if Granny June and Minnie are good with texting.

"I shouldn't know this," Lucas says. His wince turns into a grin. "But Minnie showed Granny some texts from the guy she's hooking up with."

"Sexting?" my sister and I say at the same time.

"Yeah." He grimaces before adding, "And visuals."

"Dick pics?" Pauline sounds horrified.

"Go, Minnie Mustang," I say. "Okay, Lucas is in charge of Elder recruitment." His next task will be even trickier. I lean toward him.

"Lucas, can you borrow one of the Fisheries boats? A really old boat? Or something you could remove the GPS tracker from?" He nods, so I continue. "That's how you and Pauline will get to and from the property. It will be safer and less suspicious than having all of us traveling together."

I task Pauline with securing five sets of black ski masks and leather gloves, utilizing the same protocols as she used with purchasing the burner phones. Since she is still the Tribal Police Department's intern, Pauline will know who is working at any given time.

As for transportation logistics, I'll need to figure out everything with Web.

"One last thing," I say to wrap up our heist team meeting. "Everyone's gotta leave their electronics at home. I'm talking cell phones, Fitbits, and anything else that can track us." Again I look to Lucas. "Granny and Minnie will need to use a car or truck that doesn't have GPS. I'll make sure they can access one."

Giving Pauline and Lucas privacy, I lag behind after we climb down the tree-fort ladder. They walk ahead so I won't overhear their sneaky-snag plans. There is a rustling in the woods behind the tree fort. Before I can attribute the noise to a small animal, the snap of a branch makes my body tingle with gooseflesh.

I freeze, listening intently. The screen door swings shut. Lucas starts his car. Tires crunch gravel the length of the driveway.

A movement catches my eye. The tall, slender figure skirts the edge of our yard. He pauses beneath the carved wood sign spanning the entrance to our property. The traditional healer, who only speaks Ojibwemowin, looks back and acknowledges me with a nod.

Stormy Nodin heard everything we said.

WEEK NINE

It is most unpleasant work to steal bones from a grave,
but what is the use, someone has to do it.

—Franz Boas, the "father" of American anthropology, 1888

The crania were "harvested" from massacre sites, battlefields,
prisons, schools, burial grounds . . . and even from hours-old graves.
One officer reported waiting "until cover of darkness" and departure
of "the grieving family" before "[he] exhumed the body and
decapitated the skull."

—Suzan Shown Harjo, (Cheyenne & Hodulgee Muscogee),
introduction to *Mending the Circle: A Native American
Repatriation Guide*, 1995

CHAPTER 29
MONDAY, AUGUST 4TH

I fetch Uncle Bucky's maple latte, muffin, and newspaper at the casino deli. His routine is like clockwork. Literally. The coffee and roughage kicks in at 9:40 a.m. His twenty-minute bathroom break provides a window of opportunity for me to check out the casino's fleet of moving vans. I want to provide Web with any information that might help with his task.

The smallest is a plain white *Hey, kid, you want some candy or a free puppy?* van. From there, each vehicle is bigger, with a truck cab separate from the enclosed trailer. The largest one looks like it could move our entire household.

I imagine the shadow boxes stacked vertically, packed tightly to avoid toppling over. The framing around the boxes looked to be ten or twelve inches deep. Shuddering, I recall the ancestors contained inside the frames. Their bones had to have been wired together to be displayed as they were.

The smallest moving truck looks like someone attached an eight- or ten-foot-long flat-roof shed to an ordinary pickup. I could drive it, no problem, but it's not much more capacity than the stranger-danger van. I keep going.

The next has a cab like TJ's diesel pickup truck. He attaches a snowplow to the front after the first snowfall each season. This moving van is bigger and wider than the small one. It's longer by half. My best guesstimate is fifteen feet in length. Is it big enough?

What terrifies me is the thought of leaving any relative behind because we can't fit them in the moving van. We cannot take a chance on multiple trips back and forth.

I inspect the largest moving truck, which is at least double the first one. It has a cab that looks like the front of a semitruck. I step on the running board to peer in the window. My stomach sinks at the complicated gearshift. I can drive stick, but not this heavy-duty truck.

I feel like Goldilocks and the Three Bears. One truck is too small. One is too big. Is the medium one just right?

"What's going on?" Bucky interrupts my thoughts.

Crap. I fake nonchalance by adding a side kick when I jump off the running board.

"Just wondering when I get to run errands with one of these pretty girls," I say.

"You drive?" He seems genuinely surprised. "I figured you didn't have your license, seeing as your ma drops you off and picks you up."

Before I unleash a snarky response, I dial it back. I need to keep Bucky on my side. The last thing I need is a supervisor who wants to get rid of me.

"I'm a fantastic driver," I say. The truth makes me stand an inch taller. "Happy to drive anything." I point to the fleet. "Any one of them."

Uncle Bucky grunts an unenthusiastic, "Hmph."

I pretend not to hear him.

"Yes, indeed, Uncle Bucky. I am ready for some driving assignments. Just like you had Erik doing." That last bit came to me in a flash.

"You got your CDL?" One of his bushy eyebrows rises higher than the other. It looks like one gray caterpillar about to jump on its resting twin.

What the hell is a CDL?

Bucky correctly interprets my silence. "Commercial driver's license."

I have an older cousin's license so I can buy booze, but I'm not sure how to get a fake CDL. Attempting to bluff my way past Bucky seems like a dumb move.

Do I even need a CDL to drive the smaller vehicles, or just the biggest one?

Wait a minute . . .

"Erik had a CDL? For real?" My voice practically squeaks. "Is that something I can test for? Maybe start with the stranger-danger van?"

"You turnin' eighteen anytime soon?" Bucky asks, already knowing that I'm not.

"That's ageism." I attempt to sound indignant, even though I'm just mildly annoyed.

"That ain't ageism," he scoffs.

Web shows up during my lunch break. He doesn't come over to my table in the employee cafeteria. Instead he talks with other employees. There's a lot of Nish handshakes and chuckling over jokes I can't quite hear. Maybe he isn't here to talk to me, and this is just him politicking with tribal citizens who work at the casino. Except . . . he glances in my direction and tilts his head toward the stairwell next to the elevator.

I shove the last of my bologna-and-cheese sandwich into my mouth. Saving my banana for later, I dump my trash and walk to the stairwell. As I pass Web, he ignores me and laughs with one of the older Nodin guys. The Nodin family is one large voting bloc; they have their own meeting before election season to decide who in the family will run.

It isn't until I've gone down one flight of stairs that I hear footsteps behind me.

"Let's strategize this moving-van situation," Web says, catching up.

"About that. Shipping and receiving has a medium-sized truck that I think would be the right size. I'm gonna find out where the keys are kept and where the surveillance cameras are."

"Great work. Keep it up." He beams at me.

Instead of the pride I normally feel at Web's praise, I'm suddenly uneasy. This heist must work. So much is riding on it.

"Now we need someone to drive it," he says. "The deckhands on the ferry all know me. What about the intern who worked with Bucky before you?"

"Erik Miller?" I look at Web, unsure of what he intends.

"Yeah. He's driven the trucks before, right? And he's new to the area, so the guys on the ferry won't recognize him." Web's making good points, except for . . .

"Erik can't be involved."

"Really?" Web sounds surprised. "I thought all the Misfit Toys were on board."

It's not my place to reveal anything about Erik's probation situation. All I can do is to repeat myself for emphasis.

"No Erik," I declare.

Web looks irritated for a moment before his face smooths over.

"Ogichidaakwezans has spoken," he says. "Guess I'll have to figure out a solution."

CHAPTER 30

FRIDAY, AUGUST 8TH

laire's mission for today is to make repeated use of the word *penultimate*. As in this is our penultimate Friday session. It's also her penultimate week of work, because she's taking a new job as soon as the Kinomaage program wraps up. And when Claire announces the schedule for next week's final challenge presentations to Tribal Council, Team Misfit Toys receives the penultimate spot.

Lucas whispers, "Why doesn't she just say the next to the last spot?"

"Because she wants to get on my penultimate nerve," I say.

Everyone nearby snickers. Nudging me, Pauline delivers her usual scowl. I sneak a peek at Erik and am rewarded with a smile.

Maybe after the heist, he and I can have a fresh start. Again.

During the guest presentations, I run through my heist plan. I visualize it like one of Pauline's vision boards, with itemized lists and corresponding images downloaded from Pinterest. She wastes all the toner in the color printer on these pictures.

Before Go Time

1. Each person receives their burner phone and their individual assignments.

2. Pauline has already programmed the burner phones with a group text chain that is labeled *G* for *Group*. No sense complicating things. My burner number is programmed into each phone as *R* for *Ringleader*. Team Heist Misfits either send texts to *G* or *R*. No other activity on the burners.

3. Wait for gichi noodin to hit.

4. We don't worry about hurricanes, volcanos, earthquakes, or tsunamis on Sugar Island, but we do get hella big storms. Last September, a huge storm washed out a bunch of roads on the island. The detour to reach our section of Northshore Drive was a major pain in the diiyash.

There probably are a few ROAD CLOSED AHEAD signs that I should track down and repurpose during the heist.

5. Shense lets me know when her uncle is headed to Lockhart's property.

6. Her first call is similar to a tornado watch: Conditions are optimal; stay ready.

7. Shense lets me know when the main power line is cut.

8. Her second call is the tornado warning. It starts the sixty-hour countdown to Go Time. It's also Shense's last task on the Misfits' heist team.

9. I text the group and notify Stormy in person with the date and time of Go Time.

10. This is also the alert for the Misfits heist team to complete their preparation assignments.

Assignments:

    a. Pauline—find out which officers are on duty during the heist window.

    b. Lucas—make sure boat is ready.

    c. Web—make sure truck is available.

    d. Stormy—prepare temporary place to house ancestors before reburial.

    e. Me—do a practice stakeout with Granny June and Minnie Mustang.

In addition to the practice stakeout with Granny and Minnie, I will help pack a Go Time bag for their vehicle—Auntie's old truck. They will need food and water, and any prescription medications. They won't be able to take phones or anything else with a digital footprint that can be traced back to them. We will drive to the stakeout location and run through different scenarios, so they are prepared to handle anything.

Sixty hours later, it will be . . .

Go Time

1. Wearing all black (just in case cameras are still on), we arrive at the property.

    a. Lucas and Pauline arrive by boat and walk to silo.

    b. I arrive by truck and back up to main silo door.

    c. Stormy arrives . . . somehow.

    d. Granny and Minnie swap the Mustang for Auntie's old truck and go to their stakeout location.

2. I climb the outside ladder to enter silo through mini door and unlock main door from inside.
3. (I assume) Stormy will smudge inside the silo and moving van, as well as all of us. I'll need to get some cedar oil for our temples.
4. Lucas and I take turns retrieving the shadow boxes and handing to Stormy and Pauline.
5. Stormy and Pauline carry the shadow boxes containing our ancestors to the moving van.
6. Lucas and Pauline return the boat and go home.
7. Stormy rides in back with the ancestors. I drive the van.
8. We stop at the stakeout so I can collect Granny and Minnie's burners before I return Auntie's truck and they go home.
9. Stormy and I move the ancestors from the van to Stormy's temporary holding place.
10. I drop off the van wherever Web has arranged.
11. I dispose of the burner phones.
12. Stormy stays with the ancestors and prays for guidance about their return.
13. After Granny and Minnie rest, they join Stormy in preparing the ancestors for ceremony.

At the end of the day, Claire comes by to check on us. We show our progress on our final project, and she praises our efforts.

Claire asks to speak privately with me in her office.

Uh-oh. This cannot be good. I follow behind her and sit in the same place as before.

"Perry, I hate to do this to you, but we need to change your assignment one more time."

"For my last week?" My voice squeaks with disbelief.

"Yes. We're moving you over to the Tribal Police Department."

"With my sister and Erik Miller?" I don't understand. Has another Nish kwe gone missing?

"Shipping and receiving requested Erik back for the last week. They need another driver with a CDL for a project."

"Seriously, Claire? This really sucks." I am indignant for real this time.

"Yes, well, the internship is supposed to provide a learning experience," she says.

"I'm learning that I'm disposable."

"I'm so sorry, Perry. I agree this is . . . excessive. And you've been such a trouper. I will make sure your evaluation notes your ability to adapt to chaotic situations."

"Can I get a bonus for adapting well?"

Claire giggles. "Oh, Perry. I shouldn't have favorites, but I so enjoy your joie de vivre!"

"My what the what?"

"Your zest for life! I admire your irrepressible spirit."

"Oh, that," I say, which makes Claire laugh again.

Since she's in a good mood, I seize the opportunity to fish for information.

"Hey, Claire?" I drawl. "I meant to tell you . . . I liked the presentation about studying abroad. I mean . . . for when I'm in college. I've never been to any of the places you showed us."

"Which would be your top choice?"

Crap. Now I've gotta come up with a location. I make a safe bet.

"Paris. Absolutely," I gush.

"But . . . you don't speak the language," Claire points out.

"Still got two years of high school to learn French." I vaguely remember a group photo in front of the Eiffel Tower. I add, "Plus, you and everyone looked so . . . joie de vivre."

"Paris is always wonderful."

"Speaking of Paris," I say smoothly, "how is your stepfather's trip going?" Her smile falters, so I try to salvage my fishing expedition. "You mentioned his trip the other week? I guess I'm jealous of people who can travel like that. Europe. Wow! And for weeks at a time. Will your new job let you travel like the study-abroad program?"

Claire gets an odd, pained expression. I've said something wrong. Spoken without thinking about the consequences.

"I don't know if you're aware, Perry, but my mother moved away when I was little." She pauses. Her eyes look watery. "It was after an argument she had with my stepfather, about why he wasn't taking her to Europe like he'd promised. She was angry and said something about going by herself. I overheard and said something horrible to her." Claire wipes at her nose, which has begun to run. She sniffles.

I don't know what to do. Claire went from laughing about my joie de vivre to crying about her mother's abandonment. Telling her that I said plenty of stupid shit when I was eight doesn't seem like the right thing to say.

I startle when Claire speaks.

"I'm sorry, Perry. It's not very professional of me to crumble like this."

I hand her a tissue. She takes it, waves it around like a surrender flag. Tries to laugh.

"I'm sorry for what happened to you." It's all I can think to say that won't make it worse.

"Miigwech." She dabs her eyes. "I wish I could take back what I said to her: how she was a bad mom and that my aunt was a better mom because of everything she did for Hugo. My mom always thought my cousin was a spoiled brat. I knew the worst thing I could say was that she should go away so my aunt could be my mom instead."

Instead of gaining info about Lockhart's current trip, I've learned more about Claire. It isn't what I need. I feel the same way as when Auntie told me about being raped and I wished I could unhear her story.

CHAPTER 31

SATURDAY, AUGUST 9TH

After I help Pops weed the garden, he drops me off so I can go fly-fishing with the old-timers at Baie de Wasai. I'm quiet, as usual, but this time it's because I continuously recite the Gichi Heist Plan, which I've condensed into thirteen steps. Thirteen is a good number. We have thirteen moons in a lunar year. And Cooper is working hard to bring thirteen ancestors back home.

Gichi Heist Plan

1. Shense calls twice—first to alert and second to confirm power outage.
2. I text the date and time for Go Time.
3. We complete our final preparations.
4. We arrive at Go Time and surveil the property.
5. Enter silo and smudge.
6. Retrieve shadow boxes containing our stolen relatives and load into moving van.

7. Leave by boat (Lucas and Pauline) and van (Stormy, Web, and me).

8. Collect burners from Granny and Minnie.

9. Transfer our stolen relatives to Stormy's holding place.

10. Web drops me off and returns van to parking spot on island.

11. I get rid of burners, leather gloves, ski masks, and our shoes.

12. Stormy, Granny, and Minnie prepare ancestors for ceremony.

13. We return our reclaimed relatives to the earth so their final journey may continue. Aho.

The old-timers ask me for a story. Since there is a full moon tonight, one old guy requests a scary story about haunted places on the island, instead of the usual fish story. I want to beg off but can't behave out of the ordinary. After all, I always have a story to tell them.

"Here ya go," I say. "One time my cousins told me about an old shack near the cliffs over by Eastshore Drive. They said it was haunted by a wiindigoo. Now, wiindigoos feed on your fears and greed. They're never satisfied; they just keep getting bigger and more terrifying, hey?" The old-timers stare wide-eyed at me. "But this one also knew your worst character trait just by touching ya. And it didn't care if its victims were Nish or Zhaaganaash." I make eye contact with each non-Native guy when I stretch that last word. "If you were wasteful with money or just the opposite, stingy as hell. Or if you were a malicious son-of-a-bitch, the type who laughs inside a little bit when a kid trips over something or their ma smacks 'em in the store. Or maybe . . ." I raise an eyebrow. "You made a promise you never kept. Maybe you knew it was a false vow even as you swore it." One guy shifts uncomfortably in his waders. "Well, if you crossed paths with this wiindigoo, it took the darkest part of your soul and breathed the foulest, most hateful breath into you. Its evilness took root there and grew inside of ya. On the outside you looked just as you always had. But on the inside? If you looked in a mirror during the full moon, you'd see the truth of the wiindigoo's damage to your body and soul."

I pause and look around in case other fishers down the shore are listening. Ominous clouds gather in the distance. Since the old-timers are facing me, I'm the one who sees the approaching storm. My heart races at the possibility of tonight being *the* night.

When I speak again, my voice is low and trembles slightly.

"Netamop's thirteen daughters each married into a different family on Sugar Island. They knew of that wiindigoo and the secret to defeating it. When one of the thirteen died, the other twelve sisters selected a new secret-keeper from their dead sister's family. At the next full moon, they brought the new woman to the wiindigoo's location. They told her about the wiindigoo and, most importantly, how to defeat it. They waited with her for the wiindigoo to appear, so she could prove they had made the right selection. If they had chosen poorly, she would be left with the wiindigoo to feast on her flesh and bones; they would try again at the next full moon."

A single drop of rain hits my cheek, sending a cold shiver through my body. A low rumbling comes from the northwest, where the dark clouds have either gotten much closer or have grown exponentially. Maybe both.

Time to wrap up my story.

"The thirteen secret-keepers still meet when needed. They protect their families from the wiindigoo." My voice is nearly a whisper. "Sometimes, if a guy hurts a woman in the family, the secret-keepers will take him to the shack. He might make it home; he might not. But . . ." I pause for dramatic effect just as silver thread flashes against the dark half of the sky. "He will never be the same after the wiindigoo touches him."

The crack of lightning comes three heartbeats later. The old guys nearly jump right out of their waders. Usually, my stories are silly fish stories, or funny little observations about them. They always laugh.

Not today.

I'm the only person smiling. Inside, I'm laughing my ass off.

The truth is that my cousin did tell me a version of that story. He ended it by revealing that Auntie Eva was the secret-keeper in the Firekeeper family, and I should ask her to tell me a scary story. He made it into a dare. *I dare you to ask Auntie Eva for a scary story.*

Of course, I marched right up to Auntie Eva.

"Auntie Eva," I said loudly and, hopefully, bravely. "Tell me a scary story, hey?"

Auntie Eva paused smoking her cigarette and narrowed her eyes at me. She remained silent long enough for me to think it had been a fool's quest.

"I'll tell ya the shortest scary story ever, hey?" She flicked the ashes into her pop can. "There once was a haunted house. A nosy little girl asked her auntie about it. The auntie told her to stay the hell away from the haunted house. The girl listened to her auntie. Aho. The end."

I can still hear the echo of Auntie Eva's cackling laugh as I turned to go. Auntie Eva was also the one who warned us that the wiindigoo looked for naughty kids sneaking out past bedtime. Classic Old Indian Trick: scare the shit out of the kids and they'll be easier to babysit.

The old-timers asked for a scary story. Nish kwewag and kwezanswag know too many scary stories that are real. Today they got a warning to share with their grandsons or whoever.

The rain begins before dinner. I watch the color-coded radar map on my phone's weather app. The storm front is light green, and behind that is a stretch of darker green indicating heavier rainfall. What holds my attention is the center part of the storm. Scheduled to hit sometime tonight, the blob seems alive—a dark red heartbeat surrounded by an orange mass with yellow skin at its perimeter. The blob morphs as the storm moves closer to Bwaating.

I flash the radar screen at Pauline and give a thumbs-up. She flashes her phone at me. Her screen shows different colored dots on a map. I squeeze next to her on the big chair for a closer look.

"A lightning app?" I whisper.

She nods.

I feel stupid for not knowing about specific apps for tracking lightning. I thought I had everything covered by checking the weather app.

"Which colors mean what?" I ask, feeling even more like an idiot.

"Red means within the past fifteen minutes. Yellow means fifteen to thirty minutes," Pauline says. Thankfully she isn't being smug about having better information than me.

"Lots of red dots headed this way," I say excitedly.

Auntie Daunis calls Mom after dinner. They're canceling the full-moon ceremony we were supposed to host later tonight. Auntie has a group chat on Facebook and a group text on her phone to let the women who usually attend know when a ceremony is canceled. If the storm had been a gentle one without lightning, we would've met still.

"Completely understand," Mom tells Auntie. "Lightning is a game changer."

Indeed it is.

My burner phone vibrates in my sports bra around midnight. I flip it open while dashing downstairs so I can talk with Shense in private.

"He's headed there," she says.

"Got it," I tell her. "Talk again soon."

"Absolutely, niijiikwe."

When it's time for bed, I plug the burner into the charger on my nightstand. The lightning strikes are like the finale of a fireworks show, one right after another.

Our power goes out. We have a backup generator, but my parents don't run it unless it's an emergency. I check my burner, which is at 97 percent charged. Pauline and I have portable power banks to recharge our electronic devices. It's good for at least four complete recharges on my phone, which should be plenty for the burner also.

I feel like a kid on Christmas Eve. Not wanting to go to sleep but knowing that I will have to, eventually. I pray for Shense's cousin—to keep him safe during the lightning strikes, and that he cuts the power line without any issues.

I wait for Shense's second call.

It never comes.

CHAPTER 32

SUNDAY, AUGUST 10TH

I wake up holding the burner phone. For an instant, I wonder why.

It hits me like a sucker punch: Shense was supposed to call.

I check for missed calls. The call log doesn't show any, just the date and time:

Sun 8/10/14 6:20 AM

At what point did I fall asleep? And *how* could I fall asleep while waiting for such an important call? Her second call is supposed to let me know when her uncle is finished cutting the main power line to Lockhart's property.

I call Shense's burner phone. It rings until an automated voice states the caller hasn't set up voice mail. An uneasy feeling turns sour in my stomach. Willing it to subside, I think of any reason why Shense would not have made the second phone call.

Her burner phone broke? It's not exactly a high-quality device.

Perhaps her uncle couldn't get it done? She'll explain everything today.

Oh my God, did something happen to Washkeh? My stomach drops.

The plan calls for Shense to get ahold of me. If I blow up her smartphone trying to reach her, that will be super sketchy. Although I hate it, I gotta wait for her to contact me.

The family room is darker than usual. It takes a beat to realize the power is still out. Must've been a hella fierce storm—exactly what we needed for the heist. Anticipation begins as a prickly sensation at the base of my skull. I dress quickly and don't bother running a pick through my hair.

Not wanting to leave a digital footprint leading to Frank Lockhart's property, I leave my phone home. I bring my burner phone in case Shense calls or texts.

I run to Lucas's driveway, hoping he left his truck key above the visor. When the key drops into my hands, I thank Creator for my best buddy.

I take the back roads to the south end of the island. The storm took down a few trees but didn't wash out any roads. I don't encounter any vehicles. I park the truck just off the seasonal road closest to the power line. Checking for tire marks, I don't find any evidence that other vehicles have been down this road. I walk the same approximate route that I took with Shense and Washkeh.

Just when I wonder if Shense's uncle even made it this far last night, I see a huge tree lying sideways, and a dangling wire. I don't go any closer. From where I halt, I can make out that the bottom half of the tree looks burnt.

He did it. Shense's uncle came through.

So why hasn't Shense called with the second update?

As soon as I'm back home, I calculate Go Time. Since I don't know exactly when the uncle took down the power line, I count sixty hours ahead. It puts Go Time at seven p.m. on Tuesday. The sun won't go down until two hours later. Is it worth losing two or three hours out of the twelve-hour window if it means we can have the cover of darkness? And what if Shense's uncle cut the power right away? Maybe the Go Time countdown started at one a.m.?

How long does it take to retrieve forty shadow boxes?

I wait to send a text to the heist team. I set an alarm for 9:59 a.m.

Time slows. It doesn't help that I check my phone every other minute.

I make the mistake of opening a news app. Another Black man was shot and killed by a police officer. This time it was a much younger man, barely an adult. Witness accounts vary so much, it's as if each person saw something different.

It's overwhelming. Black and brown people killed. Men, women, children. Attacked. Accused. Quick assumptions and even quicker knee-jerk reactions. Both my Native and Black ancestors were treated unjustly. Denied justice.

The young man's family is preparing to bury their loved one.

I don't know of any burial traditions from Grandma Cake's side of the family. I only know about Ojibwe funerals. Pops helps with the fire when someone we know dies. Sometimes he strikes the fire and serves as the lead firekeeper. Other times he brings firewood and offers to relieve anyone who needs a break. I'm not supposed to know that one time someone asked him not to show up because the family had certain views about Black people; they saw Pops and reduced him to nothing but the color of his skin. Pops came home and told Mom just as I was waking up from a nap on the sofa. Maybe it's happened more than once, but that was the only time I overheard.

Everything weighs on my heart. The loss of a young Black man. Native women going missing. People hunted down like prey. Researchers wanting our bones. No respect for Black and brown bodies when we're breathing. No justice for the living or the dead.

I suddenly want to check on my pumpkins. Maybe I need to be outside and smell the earth after the rain. Or I want to touch green vines that bend but don't break.

My rubber boots squish and sink in the soggy soil.

What if, after everything I've done to get these seeds, I lose them to rot?

I breathe a sigh of relief at the sight of each heirloom pumpkin resting atop a leftover flagstone paver. They resemble squat green balls on life rafts.

My phone chimes as if cheering my good fortune. It's the alarm I set for 9:59 a.m. I retrieve my burner phone from the other pocket and compose the brief text, making sure Pops doesn't see. Still no word from Shense. Again, the hair on my neck stands alert, as if each strand senses the importance of this moment.

I press send.

R: go time tues 10pm

After Mom and Pops leave for the repatriation meeting in Battle Creek, Pauline agrees to drive me in our Jeep to the mainland. From there, we will drop by Granny June's place where Lucas—who is housesitting—will be waiting to sneaky-snag with my sister all Sunday afternoon. I will then have full use of the Jeep to check on Shense and find out why she hasn't been in touch since last night.

"Take your time running errands and call before you come get me." Pauline reaches for the door handle.

I remember the way Lucas looked at her last Sunday. The glimpse of something soft and hopeful.

"Don't hurt him," I blurt. This halts her halfway out the truck.

"What do you mean by that?" She scowls.

Dang. I'm trying not to say every thought that comes into my head.

"With wild sex," I improvise. "Don't hurt the dude with acrobatic moves and whatnot."

Sliding over to the driver's seat, I push my sister the rest of the way out of the truck.

"Maybe he likes it like that," she says.

I cannot drive away fast enough.

Shense's car is not in her driveway, but her dad's is. I knock on the door. Mr. Jackson opens it quickly. He looks like he's operating on very little sleep.

"Aaniin, Mr. Jackson. I'm looking for Shense."

Something in his expression deflates.

"I'm Perry Firekeeper-Birch, Shense's friend from the Kinomaage internship."

He steps aside, motioning for me to come inside. I do. The living room is tidy. A large portrait of Shense holding her binoojii is above the fireplace. Other framed photographs are placed on bookshelves and walls: Shense as a little girl with an enormous smile, her defiant tooth making an early appearance; Shense with her thick reddish-brown hair pulled into a bun and wearing a black leotard with pink ballerina slippers; Shense at her baby shower, looking as if she might deliver Washkeh any minute. Everywhere I look, I see her life before she became my friend.

"She wasn't home when I got in from work last night," Mr. Jackson says. "I figured she was out with friends since the baby is at her dad's this weekend. She talks about you a lot." He runs a beefy hand through his graying hair. "I was about to call your house."

"I didn't see her last night," I say.

This is the tricky part. Shense called me last night around nine p.m. on the burner phone. If I disclose the call, it means revealing the burner phone and her involvement in the heist. But if she is in trouble, I may have been the last person to talk with her. Her safety is more important than the heist.

"I had to work late," her dad says. "I texted her around nine thirty last night to tell her."

My heart leaps. "Did she reply?"

"Yeah. She texted back emojis for a salad and a pizza slice." He looks sheepish. "It meant to bring home a veggie pizza for her to eat either when I got home or in the morning for breakfast." Pointing to the fireplace portrait, he adds, "She can't eat pepperoni anymore."

I nod, remembering her devouring pizza during our first Friday workshop.

"I thought she decided to go out later. I should've waited up for her, but I pulled a double," Mr. Jackson says apologetically.

"That's understandable," I offer.

"She's been stressed out, you know—if the baby's dad and his mom go forward with the custody fight." Shense's dad is doing his own version of stressing out. "Do you think she might've, you know, looked for somebody to . . . ah . . . hang out with? Maybe to take her mind off her worries?"

He thinks she went out snagging?

"You mean a hookup?"

Mr. Jackson's cheeks flush as he stammers and looks at his moccasin-style slippers.

"Shense doesn't talk about hooking up with anyone," I reassure him. "She talks about the baby and finishing school. Electrical engineering. And about working with you," I add.

This makes him smile.

"Mr. Jackson, I'm happy to go with you to the police station if you want to alert them. Maybe they can keep an eye out for her car?"

"Would you?" His eyes get watery.

"Of course."

The city police are the opposite of helpful. First they point out she's only been gone twelve or thirteen hours. Second, once they learn she is seventeen and has a baby, they suggest she's out with a friend.

"Maybe her baby's dad or another guy?" the old cop says. "Sometimes young moms want their freedom again."

"My daughter's focused on her baby and finishing school," Mr. Jackson says indignantly.

The cop looks at me and raises an eyebrow.

"You sure about that?" he asks.

Wait. Is he implying that I know about some sneaky snag?

"Seems to me there's a lot of Indigenous women going missing lately." I hold the cop's gaze. "I'd think yous would want to take any missing-persons case seriously right from the start."

"Maybe you should talk with Tribal Police." His eyes narrow. "Seems to me they should be looking after their own."

"We don't live on the reservation," Mr. Jackson points out. "We live in the city."

"Well, it's a Sunday morning and I don't have the manpower to look for a teenage girl who hasn't come home yet." He raises his hands as if to halt our protest before we can speak out. "Give her till tonight, twenty-four hours at least. Keep calling her cell phone—"

"She left it at home," Mr. Jackson interrupts.

My stomach thuds.

If Shense went somewhere and didn't take her smartphone, there won't be a digital footprint to help find her. And if she didn't want to be tracked, then she was most likely doing something connected to the heist.

Goddamn it, Shense. You were supposed to stay out of it.

The cop is looking at me as if reading my guilty mind.

"Mr. Jackson, did you check if Shense took her breast pump? Or does she normally keep it in her car?" My questions tumble out quickly.

Shense's dad looks startled for a moment. Then he matches my urgency.

"She sanitizes it after each use. I remember seeing it in the dish rack when I took my medicine and put my glass away."

"Sir." I address the cop. "Shense Jackson breastfeeds her baby. When the baby is at her dad's in St. Ignace, she pumps all weekend to keep her milk going." The cop blanches like I said something nasty. "She wouldn't leave her breast pump if she planned on staying out all night."

Mr. Jackson voices his agreement, adding, "I'm telling you my daughter is missing."

The cop hands Mr. Jackson a business card.

"Call me tonight when it's been a full twenty-four hours," he says with a disheartening finality.

Suddenly eager to search every road on Sugar Island for Shense's car, I pull Mr. Jackson away before pushing him toward the exit.

"Sir." I turn back to the cop. "If your daughter was the missing girl, what resources would you use to find her? Why should his daughter get treated any differently?"

My sister is not happy when I bang on Granny June's front door before barging into the house.

"Pauline! C'mon. We gotta go!" I shout down the hallway.

They both swear at me from Lucas's bedroom.

"No, I won't get the fuck out. C'mon. It's important."

The mumbling is too low for me to decipher. I hear a bed creaking from movement. Gross. Then a zipper and a few more choice words. When Pauline emerges from the bedroom, her hair is loose around her shoulders instead of braided or in a bun. Bedroom hair. Gaaah. Lucas follows behind.

"You're killing me, Smalls," he says.

"What is so important?" Pauline doesn't step around me in the hallway, choosing instead to make a petty point by checking me with her shoulder.

"Shense is missing."

They're instantly alert.

I continue, "She texted last night on the burner phone according to the heist plan. Her and her dad texted after that, around nine thirty p.m. She was supposed to text me again last night on the burner, but she never did. Her dad worked late, and her car was gone. She's still not home. She didn't take her breast pump, so she didn't plan on staying out all night. And she left her smartphone at home, so she was probably on Sugar Island checking on a task someone else was doing during the storm."

"You're still not telling us the entire heist plan?" Pauline is incredulous.

"I need to protect everyone," I say, less sure of my often-repeated answer. "Let's focus on finding Shense. Maybe she got stuck on a washed-out road on the island?" The quiver in my voice is no act. "Lucas, will you help us look for her?"

He beats my twin and me to the front door.

I hate that Pauline has to drive me around Sugar Island just in case Auntie or one of her spies sees the Jeep. Lucas follows us to the southern tip of the island. We use Homestead Road as a dividing line. Pauline and I search every road to the right; Lucas goes left.

Finding a map of the island in the glove box, I mark Xs through the roads we take. There are more than a few two-tracks not on the map that I add. I call Lucas to share my search method.

"Great minds think alike, Pear-Bear," he says before ending the call.

I love Lucas. Not *in love* love. But I love him as a genuinely good person and for always being there for me. To my six-year-old mind, it seemed as if Uncle Levi went away and Lucas Chippeway took his place as the most fun person in my life.

Now he's in love with my twin sister, and I don't see how their sneaky-snag relationship runs its course without Lucas getting dumped. Then I'll be the sister of the girl who broke his heart instead of his best buddy, Pear-Bear.

Two hours later, we follow yet another seasonal road on the east side of Sugar Island. It ends at an open field overlooking Lake George and, beyond that, Canada. Just as Pauline puts the Jeep in reverse gear to turn around, I notice a set of tire tracks cutting through the wildflowers.

"Hold up," I say quickly. "See the way the flowers are pressed down?"

"No . . . where?" Pauline's eyes search in vain.

I get out of the Jeep. My sneakers sink into the soft ground, which is still wet from last night's storm. If my sister drives over the tire tracks, she might get stuck in a mushy part.

"Where are you going?" she yells from her window.

"Let me follow these tire tracks. I just wanna see how far they go across the field." When I hear her door open, I shout, "Stay there. No sense you getting your shoes soaked too."

I continue across the field. The flowers and tall grass crushed beneath the tires are fresh. If a car had come through here before the storm, the trail of damage would look different.

The way the field seems to continue forever reminds me of an infinity pool. One year we visited Auntie at school in Hawaii, and the resort pool had one of those infinity edges. Only when we swam to the edge and peered over the side could we see the steep hill below.

I don't realize I'm running until I slide on a particularly muddy track and have to slow down to steady myself. There is no reason for a vehicle to cut through this field. The hair on my neck feels prickly. I've been misreading what my body is trying to signal. It's not anticipation.

It's alarm.

The field ends abruptly. The tire tracks, however, continue down the muddy embankment to where Shense's car rests on the shore. It's upside down, like a turtle on its shell.

I reach for my phone.

Pauline answers on the first ring.

"Her car!" I shout into the phone. "Down on the shore. It's Shense's car."

My sister does all the actions I instruct her to do. She calls 911, then Tribal Police Captain Kewadin, and Shense's dad.

I make my way down the embankment, trying not to lose my footing in the mud or twist an ankle on a random rock. A slippery patch of clay has me practically skiing the last ten feet, which is at a much steeper angle. By the time I reach the shore, my legs are wobbly from the odd angles I've had to navigate. I stumble the final steps to Shense's car.

Broken glass is scattered along the shore. Her car didn't flip until the final bit. I use the side of my shoe to brush away a clearing so I can lie down and peer into the car.

I'm shaking all over with fear and dread as I collapse into push-up position alongside the car and look for Shense.

She isn't there.

I scan the interior again. There isn't anyone in the car.

On my third inspection of the car, I see a familiar flip phone. Shense's heist phone. I reach into the vehicle. It still has power. I check the call log and see one outgoing call to R. She called me on my burner phone last night. There is one missed call from R this morning—when I tried to reach her. No other activity.

A faint siren reaches my ears. It's most likely TJ Kewadin or another tribal cop who might have been on the island already.

I have a moment when everything slows. An odd sense of calm wraps around me.

You should make every Misfit Toy swear a blood oath to go through with the heist no matter what. It's that important.

"I don't know, Shense," I say aloud to the echo of her words.

Web's voice chimes in. *Warriors do for their people what others can't or won't.*

Shense's burner phone has no useful information.

It cannot track where she's been or who she encountered.

All it can do is tie her to the heist. If she is tied to the heist, it might complicate her custody fight with Washkeh's dad.

I slide it into my back pocket as the siren grows louder.

WEEK TEN

I am an anthropologist and a museum curator, trained to balance a curiosity about religion with science's cold view that human remains are only devices for decoding history. For me, bones are no different from shards of pottery to be pieced back into beautiful vases. But I know for these Native American traditionalists, the bones in the boxes are pulsating with power. For them, the dead are not really dead at all. The museum's collection has interrupted the natural order of the world, threatening the health of the living and the spiritual journeys of the ancestors. My museum has unleashed a chaos that only might be contained if the remains are returned to the earth. For them, repatriation is a religious duty, not a political victory. Although these Native Americans did not ask for their ancestors to be excavated, they have accepted the burden of reburial, to become my museum's reluctant undertakers.

—Chip Colwell, *Plundered Skulls and Stolen Spirits: Inside the Fight to Reclaim Native America's Culture*

CHAPTER 33

MONDAY, AUGUST 11TH

My first task as an intern for the Tribal Police Department is to complete the missing-person flyer that Officer What-The started last night. I overhear someone say that What-The was too upset to finish his shift because it was the first missing person who had been one of the kids he knew from his school resource officer assignment.

I get Shense's dad to text a recent photo to me. He provides the information I need to complete the flyer: date of birth, height, weight, and distinguishing marks.

I've seen so many of these flyers. Have I ever passed one without reading it? Or without noticing the name of the Nish kwe or kwezans?

Each MMIW flyer is a plea to find a real person. Someone who is loved and missed.

This time, it's my friend.

When I finish the flyer, I ask Pauline what I should work on next.

"God, Perry, how should I know," she says without looking up from the computer screen. "Ask someone. Figure it out."

All around me, everyone is busy in a way that feels frantic. I don't know if the Tribal Police Department is always chaotic or if it's this way because another Nish kwe is missing.

I decide to make copies. A ton of color copies of Shense's flyer. Then I load up on pushpins, clear tape, duct tape, and three staplers. I take the Jeep keys from Pauline's backpack and leave a sticky note that I'm driving around town to post all the flyers. TJ isn't in his office, so I leave another sticky note with the same information and add my cell phone number. Just to be thorough, I add: *P.S. This is Perry.*

I blanket the town in flyers. Every community bulletin board in grocery stores, local businesses, and apartment complexes. At the Soo Locks Visitor Center, I tape a flyer in every bathroom stall—both in the women's restrooms and the men's. Same thing at the Michigan Welcome Center, Walmart, and Chi Mukwa Arena. I even hit the fish-cleaning station at the campground and the outhouses at Rotary Park.

After I post flyers at the Tribal Administration building, I stop by the tribal library and museum.

"Cooper Turtle is gone all week," Miss Manitou says by way of a greeting.

"I know. My parents are with him at the repatriation conference in Milwaukee." I show her the flyer. "I'm here to post this in the break room."

Her face flashes with recognition.

"I knew her mom," she says as softly as I've ever heard her speak.

We share a quiet moment before Miss Manitou motions toward the break room. I continue down the hallway, halting when I pass by the little office that used to be mine. The mechanical hum provides a familiar comfort. It was a great spot for reading.

Was I wrong to take the pumpkin seeds from Dr. Fenton's office?

If I hadn't stolen them, I'd still be Cooper's Repatriation Jedi Padawan. I'd be in Milwaukee learning all sorts of interesting things. Maybe I wouldn't have gone on to steal the baskets. Maybe everything about the summer could have been different.

Maybe Shense wouldn't be missing.

I staple the flyer to the bulletin board in the break room. Shense's flyer is next to Razz's flyer. They went missing a month apart. Will there be another flyer to add next month? Or even sooner?

When I walk past the receptionist's desk, I hold my phone to my ear and fake a call with Pauline. At the library entrance, I wave a hasty goodbye and pretend not to see Miss Manitou dabbing at her eyes with a tissue.

The only reason I stop for lunch is so my stomach will quit growling. I grab a sandwich at a restaurant near the Soo Locks. Eating quickly, I decide that my next stop will be the Superior Shores Casino and Resort. Lots of bathroom stalls there. I'd stop by to say hi to Uncle Bucky, but I don't want to run into Erik. Not right now. After we find Shense. And after the heist. Then I'll tell Erik that I want us to have another chance.

Walking back to the truck after lunch, I pass a motel and realize I haven't posted flyers at any motels or hotels yet. I greet the man behind the front desk and ask if I can post a flyer near their coffee station.

"What kind of flyer?" he asks warily.

"Shense Jackson is missing. She's a local girl." I hold up the flyer.

"I don't want none of that bad stuff in my business," he says.

I'm speechless. No one has said no to my wanting to post Shense's flyer.

"B-b-but I'm posting these for Tribal Police," I manage to say.

"Not here you're not."

As much as I'm tempted to tell him off, I remember that I'm on the clock and representing the Tribal Police Department. I leave without a word and slap a flyer on the newspaper dispenser on the sidewalk next to his business.

I go to every hotel and motel in the Sault except for the one owned by Erik's parents. It's not that I'm scared to meet them. It's more like I'd rather meet them during better circumstances.

The rest of my workday is spent at the Superior Shores. When I finish posting the flyers in the restrooms in the hotel lobby and conference center, I make my way to the casino. It isn't long before a security guy who used to date Auntie Eva stops me.

"Perry Firekeeper-Birch, you turn nineteen that quickly?" The minimum age allowed on the casino floor is nineteen years old.

"I'm not here to gamble." I pull one of the flyers from my back-pack. "I just want to put these in each of the bathroom stalls."

He stares at the picture of Shense.

"Isn't she Dan Jackson's daughter?"

My throat closes and pinpricks stab the inside of my nose. All I can do is nod.

"C'mon," he says gruffly. He motions for me to follow him.

My eyes start leaking when we near an exit. It isn't until I blink that I realize he's holding out his hand for the flyers. We are in front of a set of restrooms.

"You do the ladies' room and I'll do the men's room," he says.

"Minwaadizi-nini," I manage to say. When he doesn't react, I translate for him. "You are a good person, a man of good character."

He clears his throat before saying, "Miigwech."

We finish with the bathrooms in half the time.

I return to the Tribal Police Department a few minutes before five p.m. TJ Kewadin looms over the front desk. For an instant I wonder if he's mad about me being gone all day.

"Heard you did an extremely thorough job with Shense Jackson's flyers," he says. "Good work."

"Miigwech, TJ . . . I mean, Captain Kewadin."

"I appreciate your professionalism, Perry," he says with a grin. "You can call me TJ at work."

I follow TJ to his office. His stride requires twice the steps from me.

"TJ?" I approach his desk. "Any update on Shense?"

"Nothing yet," he says solemnly before sitting down and glancing at a framed picture on his desk that I can't see.

I notice another framed picture on a dusty bookshelf—it's TJ and his ex-wife Olivia with baby Toivo Jon Kewadin, IV, known as Teevo. Even as a baby, Teevo was a beefy little bruiser. Is it odd to be divorced and keep photos of your ex-wife around? Maybe TJ put the framed picture there a long time ago and forgot about it? Or maybe they're one of those couples that can't stay together but can't let go either. And here Pauline was thinking something was going on between Auntie and TJ.

"Um, TJ?" He looks up. "Miigwech for letting me do my last week as an intern here. Even though I'm not, um, a database geek or anything. I appreciate you letting me finish out the Kinomaage program.

I owe my aunt some money for Jeep repairs and, well, anyways. Miig-wech."

"It wasn't a mercy placement," TJ says. "Perry, you were my first choice when we went through the initial applications in May. You never showed up for your interview, so I figured you made other plans. Then I, uh, heard about what happened with the Jeep and the placement with Cooper."

I was his first choice?

"I was your first choice?"

"You're Marten Clan, like me. We protect and provide for our community. You notice things that others don't. You fight for people who can't fight for themselves. If you need to be fierce, you can get there in a heartbeat. But at heart, you are a gentle soul who wants tranquility. It's why we make the best protectors. It's not about showing force. It's about strategizing, negotiating, and making difficult decisions quickly. It's recognizing that knowing when not to fight is more important than knowing you are capable of fighting."

It's like TJ Kewadin knows me to my core.

"We're going to find Shense Jackson alive, right, TJ?"

"Perry, we are doing everything possible for that outcome."

That evening, I leave Pauline to hang out with Auntie and Waabun at our house while I have Lucas drive me to the rendezvous spot where Minnie's Mustang is parked.

"Ya showed up," Granny June says as if she's scolding me.

I check my phone while getting out of Lucas's car. I'm on time.

"Well, let's get to practicing our stake-in," Minnie says.

"It's a stakeout," Lucas says with a laugh.

Minnie doubles down. "But we're sitting *in* the car, not *out* of the car."

"You want me to hang out and help?" Lucas offers.

"Maybe?" I concede. I have a feeling this won't be a simple run-through. I open the door and slide into the back seat of the Mustang. It is a sweet ride.

"Let's go, den." Granny snaps her fingers to hurry things along.

"Why? What else you got going on?" Minnie eyes Granny suspiciously.

"A helluva lot more than you got going for ya," Granny mutters loudly.

"Hey, ozagakim," I say. They both settle down, and I make a mental note that they might follow instructions better in Ojibwemowin than English. I make a strategic decision to save the Ojibwe words for the urgent stuff. "Okay. So, this is where you're going to do the stakeout."

"Stake-in," Minnie corrects.

"Stake-in." I humor her. "You'll sit in the truck we borrow, and watch for traffic on the road leading to Frank Lockhart's place. We don't want anyone to stumble upon what we'll be doing. So, your mission"—I pause for dramatic effect—"is to detour, delay, and divert."

Now that I have their attention, and Lucas's . . .

"First, detour. We'll put a road sign at the north end of the road, telling drivers that the road ahead is washed out."

Minnie looks confused.

"It's not washed out, obviously," I state. "But yous are the second line of defense. Drivers who don't pay attention to the road sign need it to be reinforced by you two. So, what can you tell them to reinforce what the sign says?"

Granny looks to Minnie and then to me.

"I tell them to get the hell off this washed-out road!" Granny says.

I consider telling her to try being nicer at first . . . but, what the hell. Granny's method is probably the most effective.

"Yes. Exactly, Granny," I say.

"High five for Granny," Lucas high-fives his great-grandmother through the open window.

"Now." I lower my voice for seriousness. "If they want to keep driving past yous, we want you to delay them." I give each my most solemn look. "What could you do to delay them?"

"We could offer them a drink," Minnie says enthusiastically. Lucas laughs.

"Gaawiin. No." I didn't think I'd be raising my voice quite so soon. "Yous can't be drinking on the stakeout."

"Stake-in." Now Granny's on board with stake-in.

"No drinking on the stake-in," I say emphatically. "Yous have to be clear-eyed."

Something tells me I need their verbal agreement.

"Granny June, repeat after me. No alcohol."

"No giishkwebii."

"Minnie, I need you to repeat it too."

"No giishkwebii," she sounds a bit defiant.

"Our ancestors are counting on us to help them get home," I say.

They both look properly chastened, so I continue.

"What can yous do to delay them from getting past you?"

Minnie looks upward as if the answer is somewhere in her sunroof. Granny follows her bestie's gaze. I even look upward. Lucas swans his head into the window next to Granny and looks at what we are all looking at.

This is my heist team.

"We could tell them that we're having engine problems?" Minnie says.

Holaay. That actually makes sense.

"Yes," I say. "You can tell them your battery is dead. They can give you a jump—"

Granny snickers like a ten-year-old boy.

"It won't hurt the truck, Minnie, if they hook up jumper cables and give you a charge," I say. "But it will buy some time. And meanwhile, Granny can send a group text to let us know someone might be headed down the road." I look to Granny. "Can you do that?"

She scoffs. "In my sleep, little girl."

"Okay," I continue. "You've tried to detour them and delay them. So, step three, divert. What can you do to divert their focus from continuing down the road?"

"We could offer to show them a good time," Granny offers too quickly.

Lucas stammers, "Sh-show them? Uh . . . no."

"I could fake a heart attack," Minnie offers.

Everyone goes silent. It's dark . . . but would actually be a good diversion.

Minnie expands on her idea. "I grab at my chest and say it's tightening. I ask them to help me get to the hospital because it will take an ambulance too long to reach me."

"Tell them you see a white light," Granny suggests.

"Ooh, that's good," Minnie agrees. The two friends grin at each other, and I'm reminded they haven't always been Elders. They must've schemed plenty in their time.

"I do not condone using a health emergency," I say, because I feel as if I should state this. "But if you think it would be the best way to divert attention, then you should do what you feel is necessary." Everything I just said sounds like something a lawyer would say to protect themselves.

"What do they do if it's a cop?" Lucas asks.

Fuck. That's a good question. *C'mon, Pear-Bear, where is that strategic decisiveness that lurks within your Marten Clan?*

"If it's a cop, you go straight to the fake heart attack," I say.

We end the practice run by having each repeat the following:

1. No digital footprint: This means no phones other than the burners. No Fitbits or iPads or other tablets. No laptops.
2. Pack medicines, water, and snacks.
3. Text any questions or concerns to the group.

Granny waves, shouting, "Detour, delay, divert."

I look to Lucas.

"Did that practice go well? I always heard that if it's a bad rehearsal it means the actual performance will go smoothly."

"Pear-Bear, I haven't got a fucking clue."

CHAPTER 34

TUESDAY, AUGUST 12TH

I wake up in a panic, gasping for air. An alert Elvis Junior has his front paws on my bed. His cold nose nudges my cheek. I pat the sheet for him and he's next to me in an instant.

It was a bad dream. I can feel it still trying to pull me back down.

Pauline's face is on a missing-persons flyer. The mean guy from the motel won't let me post it.

"It's them bad girls who go missing," he says.

I try to tell him it isn't true. But when I look at the flyer a second time, it's my face instead of my sister's. Everything closes in on me and goes dark. I'm inside an earthquake that sounds like crinkling paper. Then I'm falling. I land with a thud. One of my eyes has a clear view beyond the paper wrapped around me.

No. Wait.

I am the paper. I'm my image on the flyer. Smushed into a ball and tossed into a wastebasket that is tall, round, and lined with shadow boxes. I'm not alone. Shense is the crumpled paper ball next to me. That other missing girl, Razz, is there also. I glimpse another flyer folded like origami; the only part showing is a beautiful aquamarine eye. Darby O'Malley's distinctive eye color.

More crumpled and folded papers land on top of me. More flyers of missing girls who no one can find. Each one is substantial, not feather-light. The weight of the flyers grows heavier until I sink into the earth.

I hold on to Elvis Junior. I inhale his scent. As long as I feel his heart beating and stinky breath on my face, I know that I'm in my bedroom and not inside the bad dream.

The panicky feeling is still inside me. I consider running to Pauline's bedroom and curling up next to her like the night I found the ancestors in the silo.

Junior whimpers sympathetically.

I have a bad feeling about the heist. Maybe I've forgotten something. Omitted a crucial step in my planning.

I check my phone for texts or private messages. Nothing.

I check the burner phone. Nothing.

I go back to the phone and check Snapchat, Instagram, and Facebook. If there were news about Shense, someone would have posted it on one of the local gossip pages on social media.

Junior uses his teeth to tug at my T-shirt. It's his *I gotta pee* message. I get out of bed and consider opening the sliding glass door in the family room to let him outside. He's acting strange, though, sniffing and whining. This convinces me to make the extra effort to go upstairs to the mudroom. After stepping into my rubber boots, I grab the leash hanging on the hook in his cubby. Sometimes Elvis Junior catches a scent and wants to bolt into the woods. I don't want to chase after him. I can't miss work today. Everything has to be normal.

Sure enough, my dog tugs at the leash wrapped around my wrist and half drags me toward the road. I snap at him.

"Damn it, dude. I don't need this today."

I run through a list of everything that's bad this morning:

Shense is still missing.

That was one fucked-up nightmare, and it's still lurking in the dark places in my mind.

Elvis Junior nearly dislocated my wrist.

I can't shake the feeling that I am forgetting something important.

Auntie comes outside while I'm waiting for my dog to do his business. She nods hello. Then she offers semaa to a tree and prays silently. When she finishes, I expect her to head out for her morning run. Instead she sits on the front steps and waits for us to go back inside.

"No morning run?" I ask.

"I'll run later at the indoor track after I take Waab to my mom's."

"No one's gone missing in the morning, hey?" I point out.

"I'm not taking any chances," she says.

Junior sniffs at the air and barks once. Waabun comes around the side of the house. He's pulled on his tiny rubber boots over his dinosaur pajamas. He hugs Elvis Junior before sitting on his mom's sturdy lap.

Pauline joins us a few minutes later.

"Holaay," she says. "What's everyone doing outside?"

I shrug. "Elvis Junior's acting weird, so don't let him outside without his leash on."

Auntie offers to make pancakes for breakfast, just like usual. It feels so normal that I push away the lingering wisps of my nightmare and the uneasy qualms about tonight's heist.

Once I decide to focus solely on Shense and not on the heist, my workday flies by. TJ asks me to put up flyers in St. Ignace. He gives me a purchase order to get color copies made at the printing shop in town because the toner is running low on the department's copier. This time I ask Pauline for the Jeep keys instead of swiping them and leaving a note.

It's pretty much a repeat of yesterday. I post flyers in businesses and in every public restroom stall. I park at one end of Mackinac State College and hit every building. When I stop by Teepees-n-Trinkets, I notice a large moving van next door at the storage units. Curiosity gets the better of me and I check it out.

I'm surprised to find Dr. Fenton. She seems just as surprised to see me.

"Perry!" The initial pleasantness leaves her face as we both remember the last time we were in the same place. It was the night Grant Edwards was killed. The evening when Cooper, Web, and I were blindsided by Lockhart's decision to donate his collection to the college instead of the Tribe. My angry outburst in Ojibwemowin directed at Dr. Fenton.

"Hello, Dr. Fenton." I've never thought about what I'd say if our paths ever crossed again. I take a deep breath and make a strategic decision. "I want to apologize for my outburst at the Lockhart donation event."

Dr. Fenton's face shows no reaction. I continue anyway.

"I was stunned by the announcement and what his change of heart meant for my tribe. All I could think about was the years it will take to repatriate our ancestors, when Mr. Lockhart could've kept his word and returned our relatives and their belongings to Sugar Island."

Dr. Fenton's silence hangs in the air like humidity, uncomfortable and stifling. I decide to cut bait and get the hell out of here. I am less than twenty feet away from Lockhart's official collection, and there is nothing I can do to return what belongs to Sugar Island.

I conclude with, "Cooper Turtle tried to teach me that repatriations are a long process and how important it is to build relationships. I should have been a better apprentice to Cooper and followed his example."

My step backward is like a coordinated dance move to her step forward.

"Thank you, Perry," she says. "I've thought a lot about that night and how I might have felt had the situation been reversed." She pauses and smiles as if remembering something funny. "I daresay I've had many an angry outburst in my day."

Dr. Fenton tips her head to the side as if appraising me. I get a weird feeling about being watched. For an instant I feel like a specimen in a glass case. My arms cross my chest protectively. I look back toward the Jeep.

"I think you should consider studying in my field. We need fresh ideas and passionate energy in anthropology."

Wait. What?

She continues. "Will you be a senior this year?"

"No, ma'am," I say. "I graduate in two years, unless I fast-track and squeeze my credits into one year." I remember Mrs. Turtle's presentation about accelerated classes at Malcolm.

"I would be happy to write a letter of recommendation," Dr. Fenton offers. "And if I may plug my own school, we have an excellent anthropology program at the college. There might even be a way for you to complete an independent-study project as a research assistant cataloging this collection." She motions to the storage unit behind her.

My heart swells with a feeling that takes me back to that day when Cooper drove me in his canary El Camino he named Miss Sunshine Days. When he asked for either my resignation or my word that I would help him bring the Warrior Girl home.

It's a seed of something that I want to nourish and protect.

It is hope.

On the drive back to the Sault, I think about the heist tonight. Specifically, I think about calling it off. We can focus our efforts on finding

Shense. I can talk to Web and Cooper. Maybe we can have Tribal Council make a formal request for the return of the ancestors in the silo.

I could come clean about my trespassing on Lockhart's property and breaking into the silo. No one else has done anything illegal yet. Just me. I could keep it that way.

Mom and Pops would be disappointed in me.

I can guarantee that I'd never get my driving privileges reinstated. The Jeep would be Pauline's.

I'd probably face charges and would end up with a juvenile record. I would most likely be on probation with Chippewa County until I turned eighteen.

Erik might have advice about being on probation.

I suddenly have the urge to find Erik and tell him what I am going to do.

He is back to working at shipping and receiving, I remember. Because they needed Erik and his CDL.

I stop at the casino coffee shop for a bran muffin and a maple latte.

Uncle Bucky's face lights up when I walk into his office with my gifts.

"Perry! My best intern!" he says, reaching for the coffee first.

"You're just saying that because it's true," I reply.

He laughs.

"Hey, Uncle Bucky, can I talk with your second-best intern?" I look around but don't see Erik anywhere.

"He's full of piss and vinegar, but have at him." Coffee cup in hand, Uncle Bucky motions toward the loading dock.

I see Erik before he notices me. Standing next to the stranger-danger van, he seems taller. Maybe his body is catching up with his voice.

Whether he grows or not, I like him. I like everything about him. His oddly deep voice that makes me feel tingly in a good way. I like that he got in trouble for trying to embarrass his old school into changing their racist mascot. Even my dog likes him, and Elvis Junior is an excellent judge of character.

"Hey," I call out before cartwheeling off the loading dock. I land with perfect catlike reflexes. Continuing the momentum, I jog over to where he is . . .

Glaring. At me.

"What's going on, Erik? Why are you glaring at me?"

"Don't play dumb." There's a crispness that makes his voice sound even deeper than usual.

"Holaay," I say automatically. "I seriously have no idea what the hell's going on."

Erik puts his hands into the pockets of his jeans, flexing his muscles as he moves. The short sleeves of his polo shirt reveal biceps that seem to have grown overnight.

Maybe he's on steroids? It would explain the rage and sudden growth. Before I can ask, Erik practically snarls in my face.

"Subchief Webster switched my assignment back and said I'd be driving the truck for you tonight or else he'd be in touch with my probation officer."

"He *what*?"

"You heard me," he says.

"I told him to keep you out of it."

That day in the stairwell, Web accepted it. He said he'd come up with a solution.

"Perry." Erik's voice falters. "I can't believe you told him about my probation."

"I didn't."

"He said you did."

"I never told anyone. Not even Pauline." Why would Web lie?

Erik blinks, and his Adam's apple gulps. Maybe he believes me. I hope so.

"What can he possibly tell your probation officer?" I point out. "You haven't done anything wrong. Your work on the missing-persons database was assigned to you by TJ Kewadin."

"Your buddy the subchief said he'd make sure I ended up with a record." He looks scared. "You know I went on the dark web."

Erik has no reason to make this up.

Web was momentarily irritated when I said Erik couldn't be involved. He said he'd have to find a solution.

"I've gotta go," I say quickly.

"Wait." Erik reaches for my arm as I turn away. His touch is soft and warm.

Our eyes meet. I know he's telling the truth, and he knows I am as well.

"What did you come to tell me?" he asks.

"I wanted you to know I'm calling off the heist. I'm gonna confess to trespassing and B and E. I accept all the consequences. At least it will call attention to Lockhart being an obsessed grave robber." I mumble the final bit. "I wanted to ask you for tips about being on probation."

He smiles. My heart lifts. Erik leans in and kisses me.

"My probation got transferred to Chippewa County," he says. "We'll probably end up with the same probation officer."

"Mine will be from juvie." I kiss him back. "But we could schedule our check-ins at the same time and go on dates afterward. Compare notes and whatnot."

"Sounds like a plan, Perry Pulls-No-Punches." My heart sings. I pull him in for one more kiss, perfect like all the others.

Web's car is in the parking lot behind the Tribal Administration building. I pull into a nearby spot and run to the front entrance. After taking the stairs two at a time, I burst into Web's office and slide the door shut with a thud.

My former boss looks up and his smile falters. He rises to greet me.

"Ogichidaakwezans!" It's his trolling-for-votes voice.

"Cut the crap," I say, hands on my hips. "I told you Erik was out."

"And I said I'd fix it." Web's grin doesn't reach his eyes.

"By threatening him?"

"I told you: Warriors are willing to do what others can't or won't."

"By threatening him," I repeat.

"He's on board now." Web continues his verbal dance. "We need to bring our relatives back home."

"I'm calling it off. We're not doing it."

"That would not be smart." There is a glint of something hard in his expression.

"I'm the only one who did anything illegal," I say, trying for a calmness I do not feel. "Since everything was my idea, I'll take all the blame. After I confess to breaking into the silo, Tribal Council can negotiate with Lockhart. He's got illegal items. He can donate to us in exchange for no charges."

"There's an incorrect assumption on your part. You aren't the only one who did something illegal."

I say nothing. I just wait for him to reveal his trump card.

"I had a conversation with your sister. We were concerned about you taking on the lion's share of responsibility. We shared the parts of the plan that we knew. I went first. When it was her turn to talk, I recorded her."

No, Pauline. I shout inside my head. *Tell me you didn't take the bait.*

"If you confess, Perry, your sister is an accomplice. I heard Dartmouth is her first choice, but that might not pan out if she's facing charges."

"You are twisted, Web."

He shrugs. "We do what it takes to ensure the outcome we need. You're upset now, but once we're successful, I'll give you the recorder. You'll see that the end justified the means."

It's only now that I get what my Repatriation Jedi Master modeled for his Padawan. Why Cooper followed the law and committed to a long process. Why he invested his time and effort into building relationships with academics and museum folks who dragged their heels.

Cooper wanted me to understand that the means justify the end. Doing the right thing for the right reason, with a good heart and clear intentions, matters. Bringing home our ancestors with blackmail and manipulation . . .

I don't see any way out of this mess except to go forward. Pauline and Erik will pay the price if I don't do what he wants.

"Go Time is ten p.m., right?" He needs to hear me say it.

"Yes," I say through gritted teeth.

His smile reaches his eyes this time.

"You'll see, Ogichidaakwezans. It will be worth it in the end."

With my hand on the door latch, I look back at Tom Webster.

"Don't ever call me that again."

I return to shipping and receiving. One look at my face tells Erik the heist is back on.

"Tom Webster has Pauline on record sharing every detail she knows." I kick at a piece of gravel. "He'll give me the recording after tonight. Otherwise he gives her up as an accomplice, and she faces the same charges as me."

Erik reaches out his hand. I hold on to it like a lifeline.

"It will be okay, Perry. We'll do this."

I don't realize I'm crying until Erik wipes a tear away.

Auntie thinks we are at the candlelight vigil for Shense Jackson. Waab doesn't feel well, and Auntie is super tired, so they go to bed early in the guest room.

Pauline drives me in the Jeep to the mainland so I can borrow Auntie's old pickup truck. Then she returns to Sugar Island, picks up Lucas, and they head over to the old Fisheries dock where a boat is ready for them.

I swing by to get Granny June and Minnie before returning to the island. Since it's dark now, I turn down a side road to hop out of the truck and change into my black wet suit, black sneakers, ski mask, and gloves. My burner phone fits inside the sleeve of the skintight wet suit. Everything I take off goes underneath the driver's seat. All that's left in my backpack are bottled waters and protein bars.

"Hubba-hubba," Minnie comments when I get back behind the wheel.

I lean forward to ask, "What's that mean?"

"If I had your body, I'd be trying out every guy in town," she says.

"Ew, Minnie." I decide to serve some smack to her. "If I had your sweet Mustang, I wouldn't waste it by going five miles under the speed limit."

Granny cackles.

I drive the back road to Lockhart's property. Before I exit the old truck, I have them recite everything from yesterday's trial run.

"Okay, ladies, let's do this."

"Stoodis," Granny echoes.

I watch Minnie drive the truck to the stake-in location down the road.

Stormy is already on-site. Tall, lean, and dressed all in black, as usual. The only difference is the bandanna he wears like a mask. I am afraid that if I make eye contact, he'll know something is wrong. He cannot find out that Erik and I are being blackmailed by the subchief. We need the heist to go exactly as planned. I remember Stormy's face when he rolled with my uncle, young and cocky. I remember how that face changed after two years behind bars.

Everyone's future is on the line, including his.

Erik is behind the wheel of the moving truck. Tom Webster sits in the passenger seat. They're both wearing ski masks. The subchief says something to Erik, who remains looking at me and never acknowledges his passenger.

Pauline and Lucas emerge from the trees at the east edge of the property. They're masked and dressed identically in black sweatpants and long-sleeved T-shirts. They approach the rest of us and look at me expectantly.

"We know why we're doing this," I say. I rummage in my backpack for the cedar oil I thought to include. I apply a dab to each temple before handing the vial to my sister. "So let's repatriate our relatives and get them away from this property."

With that, I stride over to the silo. I quickly scale the ladder and remove the unlatched lock. I turn on the flashlight on my headband and enter the square opening. Once I'm inside, I climb down the rolling library ladder. I slide the swivel recliner to the edge of the area, freeing up the center, before I unlock the main door.

Stormy smudges the entrance before stepping inside the silo.

Pauline gasps when her headlight lands on a shadow box with the skeletal remains of a person inside.

I begin singing.

"Gego gotaajiken." *Do not be afraid.*

"Bigiiwen enji zaagigooyin." *Come home where you are loved.*

Climbing the movable ladder, I reach a shadow box. I hold it to my chest with my left arm while I carefully descend the ladder. I'm thankful for the leather glove, which, in addition to leaving no finger-prints, helps my right hand to grip each rung.

Pauline focuses on the shadow boxes nearest to the floor. Lucas and I take turns with the ladder. They sing along with me.

We quickly pair up. I work in tandem with Erik, handing each box to him. He continues singing. At first he seems to mimic the sounds I make. But it doesn't take long for him to sing with meaning like he's known these words since birth.

Lucas pairs with Tom Webster, leaving Pauline and Stormy to work together.

We work steadily. I fear slipping on the ladder or losing my grip if I try to go faster.

"Perry." Pauline catches my attention. "That one has a pipe." Her headlight shines upon the shadow box Lucas has in hand.

My flashlight catches an assembled pipe and stem. It is affixed inside the shadow box at an angle. I see markings along the stem. It's the ceremonial pipe from Teepees-n-Trinkets.

I motion for Lucas and Pauline to huddle with me.

"Switch with her," I whisper. "You need to make sure Stormy holds this one."

My sister cries as she holds a shadow box containing a baby's remains. I take it from her and coo to the binoojii like I would with Washkeh. This happens four more times. I ache all over.

It takes nearly three hours to empty the silo.

I lock the main door from inside. All alone in the empty silo, I return the swivel chair to the middle of the floor. Inspecting the floor for footprints in the dust, I scuff the side of my water shoes around like a broom. The walls are bare except for forty-two random picture hooks where forty-two shadow boxes had covered the interior of the silo.

My arms quiver from exhaustion as I ascend the library ladder to the square exit door. Once I climb through the escape door, I replace the padlock and make my way down the metal ladder. When my foot slips on the penultimate step, I land with a thud. The impact loosens the burner phone from my sleeve. It too falls to the ground.

It buzzes, which I initially assume to be from the fall. But everyone's burner phone buzzes at the same time.

I flip my phone open.

Cop. Heart attack.

"We need to go," I announce.

Pauline and Lucas run toward the woods leading to the east shore and the Fisheries boat.

Erik prepares to close the back of the moving truck with Stormy inside when Tom Webster pauses next to me. His arm brushes against mine. I recoil and take a step away. I keep walking until I reach the cab of the moving van.

I climb inside and position myself off-center, so as to sit closer to Erik. I wait for him to join me.

"Perry." Erik's voice is urgent. "We got a problem."

When my foot hits the running board, I roll my ankle and fall the rest of the way. Wincing, I jump up. I test my ankle with light steps favoring my other foot.

At the back of the moving van, Erik still hasn't closed the doors. He isn't even looking at the doors. Instead he's staring in the direction that Pauline and Lucas went.

"What?" I say, following his gaze.

Tom Webster answers. "Stormy went that way."

I spin toward the trailer. No Stormy. I look to Erik for an explanation.

"He just took off at the last minute and ran that way," Erik says. The ski mask reveals eyes wide with surprise.

Not trusting Tom Webster to investigate whatever is going on with Stormy, I run with lopsided strides toward the woods.

"I'll be right back," I shout over my shoulder.

My headlight provides a jarring beacon. The night I found the ancestors, I checked out the boathouse between the water and the woods. I push forward, glad that I had that experience to guide me now.

I am breathing so rapidly that I get a stitch in my side just as I emerge from the woods.

The Fisheries boat isn't anywhere along the shore. I look north, and my headlight catches the silhouette of a boat too far for shouting.

Did Stormy decide to ride back with Pauline and Lucas?

I yank the headband and hold the headlight to shine north. With my gloved hand, I cover the spotlight and remove it quickly. I repeat the hasty action two times before doing another set of three, this time leaving the headlight uncovered for a count of three each time. Finally, I do three more quick reveals.

Dot. Dot. Dot. Dash. Dash. Dash. Dot. Dot. Dot.

It's how to signal *SOS* in Morse code.

I repeat the sequence twice more, listening in between for the engine. Hoping to hear any indication that someone in the boat has seen my distress signal.

What I hear instead is the rumble of a truck. Which makes no sense.

Erik wouldn't leave without me.

Maybe they want me to hurry back.

I hobble back through the woods.

When I near the silo, I halt in disbelief.

The moving truck is gone.

I reach for the burner phone, but it isn't tucked inside my sleeve.

"Fuck!"

I scan the ground for it.

"Fuck!"

What if it fell out in the woods?

"Fuck!"

I do the only thing I can think of—I chase after the moving van.

The route between Frank Lockhart's property and Stormy's place was chosen because it was a back road without traffic, houses, or streetlights.

I keep running without any thought of the dangers lurking along a dark road in the middle of the night. The light from the moon is enough to keep me from stumbling into a ditch.

There is a lump ahead in the road. For an instant, I think it's a small bear. I turn on the headlight and shout. My hope is for it to run away. The lump is not round enough to be a bear. It also doesn't move.

Dread slows my steps. I'm already crying when I approach the body on the gravel road. Its dark clothing reveals no clues about the wearer's identity until I touch the pants. They're not sweatpants.

Erik and Stormy both wore black jeans.

I turn the figure over and remove the ski mask.

"Erik!" I scream.

His eyes are closed. My fingers stroke his cheek. I teased Erik about having cheeks like ripe crab apples. His cheek is warm and soft. I bend down to kiss it.

Shallow breath brushes my ear.

I feel for a pulse at his neck. It's faint. He is alive.

I notice the smell next. The familiar coppery tang of blood. I've been lost in blood before.

My fingers start at the top of Erik's head. I work my way down, feeling for dry surface or sticky wetness. It doesn't take long. The side of his head is oozing blood.

I'm too frightened to scream. I check his pockets for the burner phone. It isn't anywhere on him. I hear singing.

Amii izhi nibaan. *Go to sleep now.*

Gego gotaajiken. *Do not be afraid.*

Bigiiwen enji zaagigooyin. *Come home where you are loved.*

I'm lost in blood again. This time I sing. It keeps me from sinking into a dark hole.

I need to find help for Erik.

I rise and continue singing. My ankle is stiff now. I hobble until I reach a trailer with a car parked in front. My fist pounds on the front door.

What if this is where the wiindigoo lives?

I continue knocking. Once I hear movement, I step back.

"No valuables except for the gun I'm aiming at the door. Go on now. Git!"

"I'm not trying to get inside. Please call for help," I plead. "Call 911 and ask them to reach TJ Kewadin. Someone's hurt bad about a half mile down the road."

"I'll call," the voice on the other side of the door says tentatively. "Might not do any good. The police scanner been blowing up last hour or so. Ambulance on the ferry. Someone died, by the sound of it."

"Did they say who? Please, sir. It's important." I could have him call Pauline, but . . . I don't know any of the burner phone numbers.

That's what I forgot to prepare for. What if I needed to reach someone but couldn't send a group text? I should've memorized Pauline's burner number. I was adamant about not leaving a paper trail or a digital footprint.

"Sir, can you take down my parents' phone numbers?" I recite the numbers. "And my aunt, Daunis Fontaine." I give her number as well. "And the Freighters Motel. Tell the owners their son Erik is hurt." I take another step backward. "I've gotta get back to him."

I hear the person talking on the phone.

"Some kid is banging on my door, telling me their friend is hurt. Wanting me to call their parents and aunt and that Tribal Police officer TJ Kewadin. He used to play football with my son."

My lopsided run takes me back to Erik. He's still warm.

The stranger called me "some kid." He's right.

I'm just a kid.

The headlights grow bigger until I'm blinded by them. I wave frantically for TJ. He must have been nearby to get here this quickly. Or maybe Officer What-The was called; he lives here on the island.

But they would've turned on their police lights.

The wiindigoo grows taller with each step.

I'm supposed to put dirt in my mouth to ground me.

Pauline is supposed to hold my hand so we can face him together.

CHAPTER 35
WEDNESDAY, AUGUST 13TH

I thought yesterday was the worst day of my life.

Turns out today is even worse.

I taste sour dirt and remember the wiindigoo. When he got me, I was on a gravel road. I crawled as fast as I could but didn't reach the dirt beyond the gravel.

If the Thirteen Grandmothers selected me as a secret-keeper, they chose unwisely. Pauline would've gotten everything right. She's always the top choice.

I was eight when a teacher's comment changed me.

Pauline and I were in Mrs. Noble's class. I forgot my mittens at recess and got permission to go back to my classroom for them.

Mrs. Noble was talking to Miss Buttersfield. I wished I had been assigned to Miss Buttersfield's class. She was pretty and kept snacks in her classroom if you got hungry. Not just any snacks, but the good kind: string cheese, Go-Gurts, and single-serve containers of mandarin oranges. Mom said single-use plastics were bad for the environment. Mrs. Noble kept a bowl of apples on her desk. The bad apples that were mushy when you bit into them, and really bland—the sort of apple that wasn't sweet or sour. Just blah.

"I've got a student reading chapter books," Mrs. Noble bragged.

"Who?" Miss Buttersfield sounded like an owl.

I stood still like a statue, begging for Mrs. Noble to say my name and Miss Buttersfield to add a comment like, *Oh, I wish she were in my classroom.*

"Pauline Firekeeper-Birch," was the name provided.

"Which one is she? I have a hard time telling them apart."

"The smart one," my teacher said.

Wait. If my twin was the smart one, what did that make me?

I went back outside, where my fingers turned white and stung like tiny piranha bites when recess was over. I had just read about piranhas.

I'm actually inside my nightmare.

There is a hole where it is dark and cold. It smells like something Elvis Junior rolled in. Oh, and I'm with other missing Nish kwewag.

Shense swears from time to time. I thought she was furious. Then I wondered if she was delirious. I decided she was both. Furiously delirious or deliriously furious.

It must be daylight, because I can see a shape that has Shense's voice.

"I had a bad dream," I tell her.

"Ooh, me too," she says, like we're in a game of Who Had the Shittiest Dream?

"My bad dream came true," I say. "I think I'm in it right now."

"Ooh, yeah. That is bad." She's a good friend. Full of sympathy.

"What was your bad dream?" I ask her.

"It was a bad *cultural* dream . . ." She emphasizes *cultural* but trails off like she decided to take a nap.

"Mine was about MMIW!" I shout. What good is it to be stuck somewhere with someone if they're not conscious with you?

"What?" Shense perks up as if a thirty-second nap was all she needed.

I repeat my bad dream.

"Ooh, yeah. You're inside that one, Perry."

We are quiet for, well, I don't know for how long. Then we start crying at the same time.

Shense cries for her binoojii.

I cry at the thought of Pauline leaving Sugar Island someday without me.

CHAPTER 36

*T*he Warrior Girl makes no effort to help me out of the hidey-hole. She isn't evil about it; I think she's keeping me company. She sits when I sit—our backs rest against the dirt wall and our knees are pulled up to our chests. She rises with me.

Shense remains sleeping, curled around a pumpkin she guards even now. The orange-and-green-striped orb pulses and glows, a living entity, safe for now. I tiptoe past, following tendrils of vines that grow underfoot just in time for my next step.

I continue toward the opposite end of the root cellar. Razz is a broken bird lying in a nest of collected bones. She hadn't played hockey and was the first to go missing after Grant Edwards was murdered. Whatever happened to her, it was quick—an unfortunate landing.

The hidey-hole extends farther back than I thought. The Warrior Girl moves next to me, neither leading nor following. Just by my side as we walk through an exhibit of black ash baskets. I point out which ones are my great-grandmother's creations. Each movement is painful. Muscles cramp and tighten. I cleaned every glass case here, I tell her.

The leafy green walkway becomes unruly. Elvis Junior runs ahead, gently nudging stray vines back on the path. My sneaker activates a hidden laser beam, which triggers the next exhibit room. It's the Tribal Council conference room. Ellen two-steps past with her partner, someone blond in a matching ribbon vest. Their movements are joyful. We pass the chief's office, where Rocky Manitou performs a hoop dance exhibit from behind the sliding glass doors.

Another step forward and the room fades into a small dining room with hardwood floors. I stay on the vine pathway. The rest of the space is slick with something red and sticky. My steps quicken. The only way out . . . is through. I reach for the door, but it only just closed. The click reverberates. Someone just left the room. The person who killed Grant. They're just ahead. One more room to go.

It's the room where our creation story plays on curved screens. The otter is the one who became a ceremonial medicine bag, paddling to reach the bottom of the cylinder. Unable to do so, it floats to the surface to gasp for air. A Flappy Bird flies in a pixelated, bouncy pattern around the perimeter inside the display. Now it's Cooper Turtle, posing as a cigar-store old-timey Indian wearing a white T-shirt with lettering spelling: THIS IS A REAL INDIAN WHO KNOWS THE WAY HOME.

I tap on the glass. Cooper admonishes me with a wagging finger. His voice comes through speakers I cannot see in the dark.

"Everything is connected, Little Sister. The past. The future. The beginning and ending. Answers are there even before the questions. You're supposed to go back to where you started. And if you step off the path, you better keep your eyes wide open."

I expect the Warrior Girl and I will end up in the lobby of the Tribal Museum that connects its beginning and ending. Instead, it's the room where Cooper brought me to my first NAGPRA meeting at Mackinac State College. The Warrior Girl looks at the vase of white lilacs next to the place card with my name. I recognize most of the attendees now, whereas during that first meeting I knew only Cooper. That day,

I'd met Dr. Fenton, somehow missing that her first name was Raquel until Cooper brought me to her office. I'd also met Grant Edwards, not knowing who he was and what he'd done to Auntie. And Dr. Leer-wah, the fussy hipster version of the Monopoly guy, with the ordinary name made posh by its pronunciation. Hugo LeRoy had introduced me to the Warrior Girl.

Now I was dreaming about her. She was by my side for these strange glimpses of memories and scenes with a heavy dose of creative license for processing whatever my brain wanted to upload into long-term storage.

These goofy images aren't my real life, I say. Suddenly, I feel her inside me, remembering my life with me.

The smell of molasses biscuits that made my dad remember Grandma Cake's laughter going right through him.

My stinky dog wrapping my ankles in his leash so I'd fall in the mud and play with him.

The way it feels to kiss Erik and know that he is a good person.

Laughing with Lucas, and how he would drop everything if I said I needed his help.

Getting my dad to hold my hand and run through the sprinkler with me on a hot July afternoon.

The moment when I feel a tug on my line, and I know it's a big fish.

A long time ago when Auntie Daunis wore a red gown to a fancy hockey dinner with a boyfriend who looked at her in a way that made me want to have a boyfriend too.

When Waab kissed a piece of spaghetti.

Driving the Jeep with the windows down.

When Cooper Turtle trusted me.

Eating blueberries with Uncle Levi.

The way Mom smells before she takes a shower or brushes her teeth.

My sister, when we were the same egg. And when she closed her eyes and listened to the chimes at Dartmouth. She looked serene. Not anxious at all.

Then, I hear a scratching noise.

We must sleep for a few hours because there is a ray of sunlight shining straight down like a spotlight. I take advantage of the light to check out this hole. I need to stand up to get an accurate view.

It reminds me of someplace. Maybe from a book?

It's at least ten feet tall. If it was round, I'd swear I was in an underground silo. It's trapezoid shaped, as if it started out like a rectangle but parts of the dirt walls collapsed. There isn't a ladder or even exposed tree roots to grip.

I look at Shense. Her nails are packed with dirt. There are vertical scratch marks about two-thirds of the way up.

I take a step to the corner nearest Shense. I start to count out my paces.

"Don't go over there," she says. "It's Razz. I don't think she suffered. She must've hit her head or broken her neck when he tossed her in."

"Tell me anything you know about him," I plead.

"My car got a flat in the rain. I went to get help. He had his brights on so I couldn't see him. I thought he was coming to help me, but he pushed me backward. I was in shock, I think. He zip-tied my legs. Then he was able to zip-tie my hands."

"How'd you get out of those?"

"I did like a reverse jump rope to get the zip tie from behind me to in front of me. Then I found an old arrowhead in a corner to cut through the plastic. I got my legs free next."

"I wonder how he got me," I say. "It's kinda fuzzy."

"He did the same thing to you. Lowered you down instead of pushing you over. I cut through your zip ties," she says.

I wondered why both wrists were sore.

"He comes by at night and just sits by the edge, looking down here with a really bright flashlight so you can't see what he looks like."

"Why would he do this, Shense? What's his reason?"

"He likes Native women, obviously, but he doesn't interact with us. Just observes."

"Okay, we got a fetishy creeper," I state the fact.

"Speaking of fetishy, what are you wearing, Perry?" I can't believe she can still crack a smile through all this.

"A black wet suit. It was my ninja outfit for the heist."

"Did you do the heist?" she asks urgently.

"Yes. We loaded up the moving van. Then something happened and the plan went to shit. Stormy ran off with a ceremonial pipe and stem. I went after him. The subchief turned out to be a blackmailing asshole. He took off with the truck and left Erik unconscious in the road, bleeding from a head injury. I got help from someone who lived nearby, and when I went back to check on Erik, that's when the creeper got me."

My next sentence rocks me to my core.

"I don't know if Erik is alive. I don't know if the ancestors were delivered to the old firekeeper lodge by Stormy's place."

We are silent, and I think she might be napping again. I should keep track of how often she fades out. If it's Wednesday and she went missing on Saturday night, it's her fourth day without food or water.

She seems pretty lucid for four days without water. Maybe she collects water in a piece of clothing whenever it rains and is able to stay hydrated.

The sunlight is fading. It's probably not nighttime yet, but the angle of the late afternoon sun can't reach us.

I state all the facts I know. Everything I've observed firsthand or have knowledge from Shense.

The creeper is at least moderately familiar with the roads on Sugar Island.

He uses force to surprise and then subdue his victim.

His method for delivering his victims into this hidey-hole is inconsistent. He was gentle with me but not with Razz.

There are three women here. Razz went missing last month. Shense last week. And me last night. That's an inconsistent pattern.

I need to ask Shense if she was dumped in here or lowered.

My stomach growls, and I can't remember the last time I ate.

Despite the constant gurgling, I manage to fall asleep.

It's dark when I wake up.

Shense is talking to her binojii.

"You are the best thing that ever happened to me. I got so lucky being your mama. Grandpa likes doing puzzles. Maybe you will too. That would be a fun activity for you to do together, but only if you want. Your grandma loves you, but she tries to get you to smile for the camera or kiss people you don't know. You don't have to smile unless you feel like it. Same with hugging or kissing. You never gotta do it to be polite or make someone else happy. That's a big lesson right there."

I don't want to interrupt, so I stay quiet. When her pause lingers, I hear a tiny click.

"Shense, what are you doing?"

"I'm recording voice messages for Washkeh. Maybe someone will find it and get it to her someday."

"You have one of those voice recorders?"

"Yeah. I forgot it was in my jacket pocket."

I sit up quickly and feel light-headed.

"Was it in record mode when the creeper took you?"

"No, because I had to turn it on," she says.

"Do you know how much battery life you have left?"

"Twenty-two percent."

"That's good, Shense. Let's shut it off until he comes by. I'll try to get him to talk."

We sit in silence for a while. I hear evening sounds. The nighttime critters waking up. Fewer bird calls.

"I gotta tell you something, Perry."

"Sure," I say easily.

"I've been drinking my own breast milk. I express it into my T-shirt and suck it from the fabric."

"That's really resourceful," I say. "Your body is a bona fide miracle."

Her voice is lighter now. "I thought so too. It's like Washkeh is helping me survive so I can get home to her." Her pause is followed by a question I can only describe as shy. "Do you want some? My supply is getting less and less each day. But I want to share."

"Let's see if it rains tonight. I'll borrow a shirt from you or Razz as a hydration cloth. And let me just say the weird thing now. You have my blessing to use any part of my body to survive, if it comes to that."

Her voice is less light now. "That's hella dark."

"I'd rather have you or some animal gnaw on my leg than have some creeper watch me decompose," I say. "That only benefits him. Why should he benefit but no one else?"

"I agree with you in theory. But damn, Perry."

A tingly feeling at the back of my neck makes me hyperalert. I listen for sounds.

Something feels familiar about being in this hole. It's not something I've read. It's a story I've heard. I close my eyes. Pops has me do that when we're hunting. I can listen to the layers of sounds with my eyes shut, even the direction they're coming from.

I flash back to the feeling of my rifle in my hands. Except it's resting on my lap. The decaying wood has a particularly mossy scent. And I'm not hunting.

I'm the hunted.

When we were six, Mom told me and Pauline about boarding schools. I remember talking to Auntie about it. My sister was scared that bad things would happen to Auntie when she went away to college in Hawaii. We learned about our grandma having a hidey-hole for when the Zhaaganaash men came around collecting children. Auntie told us about Grandma Pearl's forgetfulness. She lost track of what year it was and kept calling Auntie Daunis "Theodora." One time, she made Auntie hide beneath a trapdoor under the bed. Auntie was there for so long she wondered if Grandma Pearl forgot about her. So Auntie pushed the trapdoor enough to peek at Grandma sitting in the rocking chair, with a rifle on her lap. Grandma dozed off, but Auntie could hear her saying in Ojibwemowin that no one was taking any of her children away. Auntie told Mom about what happened, and after that Daunis wasn't able to visit Grandma Pearl unless Mom was with her.

There were other Nishnaab families with hidey-holes. I run through the names of the larger families with a longtime presence on Sugar Island: the Manitous, O'Malleys, Chippeways, and Nodins.

Shense and I are in one of the old hidey-holes in the rubble of a fallen-down house.

I think we're on Lockhart's property, beneath one of the collapsed houses.

"Shense, I need the recorder now."

She reacts to the urgency in my voice.

I sit next to her. My hands follow her arms to where she holds the voice recorder.

"This is Perry Firekeeper-Birch. It's Wednesday, August thirteenth, 2014. I've been missing for nearly a full night and day. Shense Jackson is here too. We think we are on Frank Lockhart's property, where the Nodins had their enclave. She's been here since she went missing last Saturday during the full moon. She's alive." I nudge her. "Say something."

"Dad it's me, Shense. I'm trying to stay strong and get home to you and Washkeh."

"The same man took both of us. He took Razz Williams last month." My voice catches. "She didn't make it." I speak quickly. "Shense and Razz were both taken during a full moon, but I don't fit that pattern."

"Tell how creepy he is," Shense says.

"He comes around to the hidey-hole at night and watches his victims but doesn't interact."

"I never heard his voice," she adds.

"We're gonna save the battery until he shows up. We'll try everything we can to get him to say something. I love you, Mom and Pops and Pauline. And Auntie and Waab." My throat closes up, so I nudge Shense to click the power toggle to off.

We hold each other. I can't imagine Shense being here three days all alone.

Shense sniffles in her sleep. I wrap my arm around her so she can lie against me instead of having her back against the cold earthen walls and floor.

I sing to her. The same way I sang to Erik and the ancestors.

It's as much for my comfort as hers.

Amii izhi nibaan.

Gego gotaajiken.

Bigiiwen enji zaagigooyin.

I hear a scratching noise, a critter foraging for food. It doesn't sound like a bear unless it's a cub. But by this point in the summer, cubs are too big to sound like that.

A bad thought comes to me. What if it falls into the hole with us and has rabies or ticks? It gets closer.

I close my eyes, focusing on the sounds and scents that might be boosted in the dark.

The stench hits my sinuses an instant before the sound of whining.

"Elvis Junior," I say, standing quickly. "You're the best dog ever." I tell him over and over in Ojibwemowin how much I love him. Before I go silent and my blood runs cold.

I hear a distant car. If this is someone coming to rescue us, we need to yell. But if it's the creeper, we need to start recording. Junior needs to be far away. He needs to go for help.

I call for Junior to jump into my raised arms. I can't see him, but I assume he can see me. We've done this before, just never with my eyes essentially shut. I count in the language: "Bezhig, niizh, niswi."

He knocks me to the ground; his back legs dig into my stomach. The handle end of his leash hits my face.

"Good boy," I whisper. "Shense, give me the recorder."

Junior licks my face, and I love his stinky breath.

"Are you sure, Perry? What if he doesn't make it? We're on the south end of the island. There's twenty miles between us and your house."

"I think people are looking for us. He will lead them to us."

She pushes the device into my leg. I reach down for it.

I place the recorder between his shoulder blades and wrap the leash around his underbelly, front legs, and shoulders. I treat the leash as if it is duct tape, securing the device like a bulletproof vest. I tie the ends together in a water knot. Pops taught me it's the best one for tying a flat weave like a leash.

Junior sniffs the air and whines.

I hear it too. Footsteps getting closer.

"Perry . . ." Shense's voice is pure terror.

"Gizaagi'in." I tell my beloved dog once more that I love him. "Giiwenaazha. Naadamaw." My voice is a stern command to go home and get help. I repeat it. With a deep breath, I throw Elvis Junior out of the hole. He lands with a thud.

By the time I count to ten, a bright light crosses above the hole.

We need him to talk—no longer to record his voice, but to gain information.

"Hey, creeper," I begin. "You get off on Native women?"

The flashlight would have blinded me if I hadn't shielded my eyes.

Shense's voice trembles. "You're gonna make him mad."

"Good. He thinks he can control me down here?" I shout at the light. "What happen, some Nish kwe reject your beta ass and now you want to make us all pay? You're a sicko," I goad him, deepening my voice. "Ooh, element of surprise. Grab a woman alone on a road. Let me blind you with my flashlight."

He shifts, and with the movement, the flashlight goes haywire.

"Better hang on to that. After all, who are you without your big light stick?" I scoff. "Yeah, I got your number. Let me guess, she rejected your whiny Zhaaganaash ass and started you on this path. Now the only way you can get off is to throw us down this hole so we gotta deal with you on your terms." I feel as if I'm delivering a Shakespearean monologue under one blinding stage light. "Collect and observe. Is that how you want us? Helpless specimens to fuel your God complex?"

Something clicks in my mind.

Collect and observe.

This wiindigoo's ego grows bigger with each Nish kwe he collects and observes. We fascinate him. Whether we're alive or dead, he thinks of us as his treasures.

He knows this land; he grew up here.

One of the repatriation books I read described something called "helicopter research." Researchers would come into a tribal community, collect Indigenous knowledge, and fly away to write up the results. The researcher—with their degrees, prestigious grants and publications, perhaps even a tenured faculty position—ended up as the biggest beneficiary. Tribes wanted an end to this helicopter-research mentality and asserted control over studies involving their citizens.

Cooper said this was also when tribes used activism and political pressure to get NAGPRA passed. To have our voices matter when decisions are made about our ancestors and cultural materials. But the intent of NAGPRA is at odds with how it is implemented by museums. Too many loopholes for people like Dr. Fenton to drag their heels. Too many researchers wanting to hold on to human remains that they regard as "theirs."

Back to see my girl?

"We aren't yours, Dr. Leer-wah."

"I'm so proud of you, Perry," says the rock star of Mackinac State College's archaeology program.

"Fuck you," I retort.

He shines the spotlight toward Razz. It casts shadows in the corner of the hidey-hole. Shadows that move with the light.

My eyes might be playing tricks on me. It looks as if there is a skeleton beneath Razz's twisted body.

"What did Razz Williams ever do to you?" I continue without letting him answer. "She was a girl who was named for the full moon she was born under. Miskomini Giizis. The Raspberry Moon."

"She was perfect," he says dreamily. Dr. Leer-wah lets the flashlight linger in the corner. "Born and died on the Raspberry Moon. A perfect way to start my collection. The Thirteen Grandmothers. One woman for each moon." The flashlight is back in my face. "You gave me the idea. Thirteen women, each from a different family on Sugar Island, to replace the thirteen to be repatriated next summer. Such perfect balance."

"Why Shense?"

"She was a lucky break. A girl with car trouble on a full moon. It's early in my collection. I took a chance that she wasn't from the same family as Razz."

"And me?" I say.

"Another chance encounter. I had planned on your sister being my last tribute next summer. I've heard so much about her. People say your sister is the best of Sugar Island."

I've heard the same thing. But . . . hearing something over and over doesn't make it true. Hearing and listening are different, I once told Waabun. I listen to my heart.

"She's not the best of Sugar Island," I say. "I am."

"My, my—who has the God complex now?"

"I am every good thing about Ziisiibaaka Minising. I grew up drinking her spring water. I took my first steps on her back. I run and play and hunt and fish with her. I live in a home filled with love and Anishinaabe minobimaadiziwin. I speak the same language as my grandmother's grandmother. I am blessed. I am brave. I am intelligent. I am my ancestors' greatest wish." My voice is triumphant. "And I am the Warrior Girl who figured you out."

From the corner of my eye, I notice Shense's movements halt as the spotlight shifts to her. It's enough to catch the arrowheads and balls of hard dirt gathering next to her lap.

"The first woman, underneath Razz. She was the seed for all of this." I step toward the corner. "She was important to you. A great inspiration."

"You know nothing about her," he snaps.

It's the first time I've rattled him.

"I probably can figure it out. Like I say, I've got your number."

My mind races to connect the dots. Shense slowly rises. The front pocket of her hoodie is bulging as if she has more than one joey in her kangaroo pouch.

"An Ojibwe woman went missing when you were young, Dr. Leer-wah. Or should I pronounce it the less fancy way? Dr. LeRoy." I chuckle just to mess with him.

"Claire Barbeau's mother isn't in Europe, Hugo LeRoy. Your aunt Caron has been on Sugar Island this entire time. C'mon, Dr. LeRoy. Why not give me the abstract of the story? The last piece to the puzzle is why your mom went along with the European postcards. I know I could imitate my sister's signature. Your mom was protecting you."

"It was an accident," he says. "They were always arguing. Aunt Caron and Frank Lockhart. He adored her, but she wanted him to keep his promises about the life he would provide for her. Trips to Europe. Private schools for Claire. Nice jewelry and clothes."

He shines the spotlight on the skeletal remains.

"She was more than he could handle. So beautiful." The flashlight is back on me. "You had it all wrong. Your angry Indigenous feminist rant was basic, as my students would say. She didn't reject me. My aunt loved me. She ran across the property one night after an argument. Aunt Caron would do that from time to time. She liked wandering around the cabins. Her mom was a Nodin. It made her feel good to think about being Mrs. Frank Lockhart. Caron Barbeau-Lockhart owning the Nodin property that had been in her family just a generation or two prior.

"She went missing, and Frank Lockhart was beside himself. I knew about her wandering habit. I looked for her and there she was. The floor had collapsed beneath her. She broke her neck. She was still so beautiful. I'd watch over her. My mom followed me one day. I told her what happened. My mother asked if I had pushed Aunt Caron. As if I would ever harm her." His voice becomes wistful. It's hella creepy.

He continues. "My mother decided to help me. She took a postcard that had been her sister's. It had her fingerprints. She wrote a message, signed her sister's name. And arranged for someone to mail it from Barcelona."

"So why add more women *here*?" I ask.

"A thousand years from now," Dr. LeRoy says, as if giving a lecture to a class of adoring students, "archaeologists will find this burial place. They'll research and write papers." He is envisioning it. "I will be the only person who knows the real story," he says triumphantly.

"Your cousin Claire deserves to know the real story, Hugo."

"You're wrong, Perry. Instead of a tragedy, she still has hope that her mother is out there. It drives her to explore exciting places and have great adventures."

"Your mom is Ojibwe, right? She and Caron are sisters? You're Ojibwe."

"My dad wouldn't let her enroll me," he says.

"You're still Ojibwe," I say. "The ancestors are yours. Not to own or control, but to help them get home." If there is any decency to him, this is the only way I can think to reach him. "Shense has a daughter named Washkeh. Don't let that little girl grow up without her mom the way Claire had to. You can give her back her mother."

Hugo LeRoy is quiet and unmoving. I hold my breath while he contemplates my plea.

"You will be revered," he says triumphantly.

Something inside me breaks. "Revered?" I echo.

"Yes. I don't take these matters lightly. I'm not like that monster." He sounds indignant.

"Which monster?" The hair raises at the back of my neck.

"Grant Edwards," Hugo LeRoy says. "I was at the back entrance, just about to enter the room, when that old man rambled about Grant killing his daughter. Grant laughed and said Robin was a lot of fun. He must not have thought the old man was a threat. I heard a yelp and when I looked in the room, Grant was staring at the knife in his gut. The old man left through the main door. I went to Grant. He seemed to be coming out of his shock and reached for the knife. I pushed his hand. Pushed the knife deeper."

I remember tripping over Grant Edwards. Hearing the click of the door leading to the service hallway. It had been Hugo LeRoy.

"Grant treated that man's daughter with such casual disregard, Perry. He didn't respect her life." Hugo's voice becomes dreamy. "You are to be revered."

"Revere this, pajog!" Shense shouts. She aims a projectile at the man behind the flashlight. Then another. She has a hell of a pitching arm.

Hugo LeRoy must trip backward. The flashlight tumbles into the hole and lands at my feet. He scrambles to run away.

I shout as loudly as I can.

"Aunt Caron thought you were a spoiled brat!"

I grasp the flashlight and find the on-off switch.

I aim the beam of light through the jagged opening and start the *SOS* sequence in Morse code.

The battery is nearly exhausted about the time the sky lightens on another day.

"Today's the day we're getting out of here, Shense," I announce.

She doesn't answer.

I shine the flashlight in her face. She looks peaceful. I feel for a pulse at her neck.

It's there, shallow and rapid like a hummingbird's wings.

"Shense!" I scream at her. "Wake up!"

My raw throat is on fire. I'm so dehydrated that I can't spare any tears.

She doesn't wake up.

I don't know how much time I sit next to Shense. The silence becomes a cocoon. Shense is my cocoon sister. Coming into this world or leaving it, I'm glad to not be alone.

Junior's faint barking penetrates the cocoon. It gets louder until he peers down at me. All I can do is smile.

Pops calls for me, "Indaanis. We're coming for you." More deep voices reach us.

Someone is yelling for Shense.

My heart races at the deepest baritone calling for me.

It isn't Erik; it's TJ.

He makes a rope ladder for me, but I won't leave Shense behind. Not even for a minute.

"Does she have any neck or back injuries?" TJ asks me.

I shake my head no.

For as gigantic as TJ is, he is surprisingly nimble. I'm surprised the rope holds him as he rappels into the hidey-hole. TJ gently lifts Shense in a fireman hold, one arm grasping behind her knees. The other bicep bulges as he walks himself back up to the surface, where her dad reaches for her limp form.

"She's in shock," TJ tells her dad. "Let's have the EMT look at her."

Pops ties a loop at the end of the rope and throws it to me.

"Brace one foot in the loop and hold on." My parents pull me up like reeling in a fish. They hold me so tightly that Elvis Junior has to nudge his way into the group hug.

The sunshine stings my eyes. TJ gives me his mirrored sunglasses. The frames are too big for my head, so I hold them up.

"Hugo LeRoy was the person stealing us. He grew up here. His aunt Caron's remains are in the hidey-hole," I manage to say.

"Shhh, shhh," Mom coos to me. Beneath her denim button-down, she is wearing a tank top. I nuzzle her chest, inhaling her scent. I peep an eye at the EMTs carrying a body board with Shense getting oxygen from a manual pump. One first responder holds a raised bag of fluids as he keeps up with the transport.

I turn back to my mom and tune out everything around me. I listen to her heartbeat.

They wait until I'm rehydrated and resting quietly at War Memorial to give me the updates.

Erik regained consciousness last night.

He said that not even a mile down the road, Tom Webster pulled the moving van over. He claimed I could be seen in the side mirror, running to the van. When Erik got out to look for me, he heard a sharp crack before everything went dark.

Tom Webster was found unconscious, also with a skull wound, in the back of the empty moving van on a dead-end road on the opposite end of the island.

No one knows where the ancestors are. After everything we did to get them back, someone took them from under our noses.

Pauline and Lucas told TJ everything they knew. As they were fleeing for the boat, my sister had glimpsed Stormy taking one of the shadow boxes from the back of the moving van and then running away. No one has seen him since.

Minnie-ba's heart attack wasn't fake. She passed away on the Sugar Island ferry headed to the mainland. Granny June cried for her friend. There were many times over the years that Lucas and I thought they irritated the hell out of each other. Some friendships can endure anything.

CHAPTER 37

FRIDAY, AUGUST 15TH

Mom and Pops won't let me leave the hospital for the last Kinomaage seminar. Pauline, Lucas, and Granny will do the final presentation for Team Misfit Toys.

Shense was treated for shock and dehydration. She was revived after getting fluids and is being monitored for a few more days.

Erik is stuck at the hospital too. I visit his room briefly. The blinds are drawn, and the lights remain off. He has a headache that feels slightly better in darkness.

We hold hands. I stay until he falls asleep.

It's lunchtime, but all I do is pick at the food on my tray. Then Auntie comes in with Waab, holding a bag from the drive-in. One cheeseburger with bacon, ketchup, and mustard. He climbs onto the hospital bed and snuggles next to me. I pull a strip of bacon from my burger and dangle it between us.

"Kiss the earthworm," he says.

I do, taking a bite from the end and adding *nom-nom* sound effects while I chew.

"Your turn," I say.

Waab bites and mimics my sound effects.

Cuddling him makes me feel like he's made of sunshine. He helps me eat the cheeseburger. I don't want him to leave but my eyes get heavy, and when I blink, he and Auntie have left.

"Daunis needed to get Waab to his figure skating lessons," Mom explains.

A text buzzes on my phone.

PAULINE: All burners accounted for except Shense and Web.

Since I made a statement to the lead detective from Tribal Police, with my parents and Cooper Turtle present, I don't worry about cloaking details about the heist.

ME: I have Shenses.

More unanswered questions. Where is Stormy Nodin? Where are the ancestors? Who attacked Erik? Was it the same person who attacked Tom Webster? Will Hugo LeRoy admit to killing Grant Edwards? And where is Web's burner phone?

I nap again, for longer this time. When I wake up, Mom is sleeping in the big chair. Pops must have gone for food or to run an errand. I slip from the bed like a ninja and make my way back toward Erik's room. I bypass his door and continue until I find Web's room.

He's awake.

Now that I'm next to his bed, I don't know what to say to him. He is still a blackmailing ass who wouldn't let me cancel the heist when I wanted to. Maybe he's the one who hurt Erik? If so, it would be a strange justice that someone else did the same thing to him.

Web's eyelids flutter. He looks at me but doesn't say anything.

"I hope you get better, Web," I say. After a pause, I add, "So TJ Kewadin can nail your ass for what you did."

His eyes widen with fear. It's not fear like, *Oh no, I'm going down for this shady shit*. It's more of a fear-for-my-life expression.

I get a prickly sensation at the back of my neck as he opens his mouth to speak.

"You're one of Teddie's twins, right?" His voice is raspy.

What the fuck?

I am yanked away from his bed by my angry mother.

After dinner, Claire Barbeau stops by. My parents talk quietly to each other; it's their way of giving me privacy. After Mom woke up from her nap and I wasn't in my bed, she looked for me in Erik's room before finding me at Web's bedside. Now I can't go anywhere without Mom or Pops. No privacy is definitely worse than no wheels.

"I'll be leaving for Paris soon," Claire says. "Your mother told me what happened when Hugo had you and Shense in that place." She looks over at Mom. "It will be an odd experience to be there and not spend any time looking for my mother. Miigwech, for finding out the truth about what happened to her." Her eyes quickly fill with tears.

"I'm glad you know the truth," I say. My curiosity gets the better of me. "What will your stepdad do about the missing ancestors and funerary items?"

"His insurance company will do a financial settlement for the loss," she says with a shrug.

"But the ancestors are still out there somewhere," I whisper.

"I am so sorry, Perry. I only know a little about what you went through. I wish it had turned out differently." Claire brightens. "I heard Shense Jackson is doing much better now."

"They're supposed to let me visit her tomorrow if she keeps being stable, or whatever," I say, unsure of the hospital jargon.

Just then Officer What-The walks in. He seems different. Usually there is a goofy friendliness to him. He's always glad to see former students from his days as the school safety officer.

Today he is an impersonal robot. I don't like it. He walks over to my parents.

If there is any breaking news, they'd better not keep it from me.

Claire stands to leave.

"Well, I'd best be on my way," she says.

An incoming text chimes on my phone.

> PAULINE: The person with subchief burner phone is the one who assaulted him and took truck. Sending group text now.

Holaay.

I scan my room. Mom and Pops are here, Claire Barbeau, and Officer What-The Sam Hill. Cooper Turtle walks past my room and pauses in the hallway.

The text settings Pauline programmed in all the burner phones included a low chime for texts, and straight-to-vibrate for calls.

I startle when the low chime dings from somewhere in my room.

TJ Kewadin and another uniformed officer step into the room.

If Pauline is sending the text, she must have copied and pasted a large document, because the chimes are nonstop.

TJ walks up to What-The. It sounds as if the texts are coming from behind him.

Officer Sam Hill steps aside, revealing a cross-body bag hanging from the chair.

"Are you going to answer the phone, Claire?" TJ asks.

She looks around the room, suddenly flustered.

"I have no idea whose phone that is or how it got into my bag," Claire says.

"Frank Lockhart is on a flight from Paris to Detroit," TJ says. "I informed him this morning that the stolen items were recovered from the old cultural camp. He wants to press charges against everyone involved. I gather that would include you now."

That means me and the other Misfits. And Stormy. And Web, whenever he regains his memory or gets caught faking it.

"Press charges?" Claire's high-pitched disbelief echoes in the room. "It was his idea."

Pops is at my side in three steps. He puts himself between my bed and Claire, who takes a step backward toward the door.

"Frank Lockhart *recruited* Tom Webster and me," Claire says. "He said he'd split the insurance money with us and keep the money from what he is selling overseas to private collectors." She looks at me. "Using the interns to steal everything was Tom's idea. I was just supposed to come up with team challenges to identify the best people."

The monkey-bars challenge suddenly makes sense. Lucas and I aced our heist audition without even realizing it. Erik had access to moving vans. Pauline was supposed to be a mole in the chief's office but later became even more valuable working in the Tribal Police Department. And Shense, the daughter of the surveillance director, would know the most about getting around security systems. Picking locks was her secret bonus talent.

The Misfit Toys were pawns.

But how did she know we had decided to reclaim the ancestors? How did Web know about Erik's probation? Erik told me during our road trip to St. Ignace. Had Web bugged the car? But Erik didn't tell me about it in the car. We were eating ice cream on a picnic table away from the car. There was another time he mentioned it. When he told me in the Misfits' meeting room about being tempted by the dark web.

It comes to me in a flash. The day I ran back into the meeting room to grab my backpack. I tripped over Claire, who was halfway under the table.

"TJ, she's got voice recorders," I say quickly. "She's been recording conversations that we had in our meeting room. She and Tom Webster used them to blackmail us so we'd have to follow through with the heist."

Claire Barbeau looks at me as if seeing me for the first time. Not as a smart-ass kid or a teen with plenty of joie de vivre . . . but as a young Nish kwe she underestimated.

If Web is trying to fake-memory-lapse his way out of this, I sure hope Claire used the voice recorders with her partners.

Wait . . . did *I* ever record him? I remember Pauline distributing recorders to us in our meeting room. It would have been a Friday. Maybe one of the days when Web came by with his gym duffel and we had a conversation in the corner of the mezzanine. I was always forgetting to switch the recorder off and running down the battery. I'll have Pauline look for my recorder at home and bring it to TJ.

My mind is racing through possibilities, but I see Officer What-The lead Claire away. I tell TJ about the possibility of having Web on my recorder. He seems impressed.

"You have a job ready for you anytime you want it," TJ says. "Team Marten." He laughs. "Do you know what a gathering of martens is called? Like a school of fish, a gaggle of geese, a murder of crows?" He smiles as if he has been waiting years for the opportunity to share this knowledge with someone. "A richness of martens."

I thank him for the standing offer, but it's not where I want to be.

"TJ, could you put in a good word for me with Cooper Turtle?

I'm hoping once everything settles down, he will give me a second chance."

"I'll make my strongest argument," he promises.

Pops gets ready to go to the store for a treat for me. Mom and Pops offer to get me anything I want.

"Anything?" I ask.

Pops agrees while Mom purses her lips and tries to figure out the catch.

"I want Elvis Junior to stay overnight with me."

That's the thing about negotiations: when you see an opening, it's the perfect time for bold moves.

EPILOGUE
SATURDAY, OCTOBER 25TH

I stand at the corner of the ferry as it approaches Sugar Island. After introducing myself in the language, I give thanks for a safe crossing, for a river that gives so much to us, and for Ziisabaaka Minising. I've added the island to my prayers, always posing with my hand at my forehead to block the glare. I'm being "forward thinking," just like Cooper Turtle.

As the reverse thrusters signal our imminent arrival, I dash back into my car. Once I race down the causeway, I glance from the road to the dashboard clock. Despite my temptation to let the tomato-red Mustang gallop even faster, I ease up.

I'll get there when I get there.

The gravel road curves sharply. I follow the switchback uphill to a clearing, where several cars are parked haphazardly. When I shut off the ignition, I leave the key in place. Wet brown leaves cling to my Doc Martens as I walk briskly to the overlook.

I stand next to Auntie, who squeezes my hand. She nods her approval at my new ribbon skirt. Satin strips in the four traditional colors circle the bottom half of the skirt. The ribbons are kept long, flowing from the seams on each side. Granny June sewed an appliqué cutout in the shape of Sugar Island on the front of the skirt. Auntie's expression ends with an eye roll and a smile as she notices my new MERCILESS INDIAN SAVAGE sweatshirt.

"How's she running?" Auntie asks, glancing back toward the car. A gift from the estate of Minnie Manitou to Auntie, with a message: *This good pony came to your rescue once before. Maybe you will know who she might help next.*

"Great! I got Minnie up to one-sixty the other day."

I delight in my aunt's reaction, steam practically coming out of her ears in a high-pitched kettle shriek. A beat later she notices the twinkle in my eyes and just shakes her head. Of course, I'm just messing with Auntie.

Besides, I only got Minnie up to 120.

"Mama!" Waabun races toward us from TJ's truck. Teevo tries to catch up, but Waab is too quick. TJ follows behind both boys.

"Oooh . . . pretty," Waab says, reaching to stroke the ribbons. Teevo does the same.

"Boys," TJ says in a familiar drawn-out way.

"I know, Uncle TJ, I know. Touch with your eyes, not your hands." Waab mimics the low-key warning tone.

When Waab looks up at me, I wink. We grin.

A crisp drumbeat draws our attention to the gathering below. A circle of drummers sit around the ceremonial drum. Among them, Stormy's dad sings the opening notes alone. A second beat calls for his fellow drummers to join him in singing a welcome song. Lucas's mouth opens, and I swear I can hear my buddy among everyone else. Standing behind Lucas is his mom, one of the songbirds adding their voices.

After the heist, Lucas hoped Pauline would want to be boyfriend and girlfriend, like Erik and me. He didn't share all the details, but my sister didn't respond the way he'd hoped. When she wanted to continue with the FWB, Lucas decided the only way the friendship would work was to discontinue the benefits. It was more difficult for him to move on, but only he and I know about his heartbreak.

Pops and Erik tend the fire in the nearby lodge built for today's recommitment ceremony. My boyfriend is one of the young men Pops has been teaching how to construct the lodge and strike ceremonial fires.

I think back to Erik's honored yet anxious reaction to Pops's invitation last week.

At least you know that anytime you're with Pops around a ceremonial fire, he can't say anything negative to you. Only good things to feed the fire, I told Erik before kissing his crab-apple cheeks.

Pauline is one of the Jingle Dress dancers surrounding the drummers and songbirds. The *tink-tink* of the tin cones reaches us on the bluff. I can't see her wrist from here, but I know Pauline is wearing a bracelet she wove from colorful pipe cleaners. It matches the bracelet she made me. Even Elvis Junior has a woven pipe-cleaner collar. Her therapist suggested trying different activities as self-soothing alternatives to her compulsive hair pulling. It also means she always has pipe cleaners on hand, literally, whenever she feels anxious. Her trich isn't an illness to be cured, but a condition to be managed. Pauline keeps a trich journal, practices yoga and breathwork, and keeps her fingers busy with pipe cleaners, fidget spinners, beading projects. In fact, Pauline spent her entire Kinomaage bonus on beading supplies. Everyone received eight hundred dollars. Tribal Council—minus Tom Webster, who resigned from office—voted to divide the bonus equally among all interns. They're also retooling the Kinomaage program and rethinking the team-competition aspect.

Shense is among the young women preparing spring water and traditional foods at the tent off to the side. Washkeh is in St. Ignace with her daddy this weekend. Her favorite food is the heirloom pumpkin

I shared with Shense, who cooks and purees enough to pack in the binoojii's weekend bag. I dried the seeds and gifted some to Washkeh's daddy yesterday when I accompanied Shense for the weekend drop-off. His eyes lit up when he talked about starting a pumpkin patch with his little girl next summer at his new place.

Washkeh still scowls at me, but giggles whenever Elvis Junior fetches toys for her.

Mom and Granny June are among the women who have prepared the ancestors for their return to the earth. Since Mom cannot have more children, she volunteered to prepare the littlest ones. Today the women wear their regalia and hold the bundles of our relatives. The note cards from the shadow boxes included information about the funerary belongings that had been unearthed with the ancestors. Not every object made it home; in those situations, the women in my community prepared replacement items for the bundle.

Frank Lockhart reversed his decision yet again, gifting everything back to the Tribe. I wish he had donated his collection to us because it was the right thing to do. It's obvious he is looking for any actions that might bode well for him when his case goes to court. His detailed notes on the shadow boxes revealed which remains were taken after 1990 when NAGPRA became law. Lockhart also tried to strike a deal to testify against Claire Barbeau and Tom Webster in exchange for immunity. But he was too late. The early bird gets the worm, and Tom Webster suddenly remembered everything about his involvement in time to cut a deal first.

Cooper and Stormy lead the recommitment. It is not a funerary rite; it is a healing ceremony. My community has chosen to sing, dance, and feast as we return our relatives to the earth. We ask the ancestors to forgive what was done to their physical bodies, and we pray their spirits are at peace.

The clearing is near enough that I can see Cooper present Stormy with something. The pipe carrier holds it up, and someone on the drum responds with four high beats. From this angle, the item is as long as Stormy's arm. It looks like a brown oval on a stem . . .

He's holding the snapping-turtle shaker.

"How?" I turn to Auntie. She smiles knowingly.

"You have no idea how hard it was to say no to your loan request," she says. "There's a group of us who finance Cooper's bids."

Before I start asking the fifty questions I have for my aunt, Waabun tugs her skirt.

"Mama, can we go down there?" He points at the people below us. His mom kneels in front of him.

"No, my boy. Sometimes a lady can't be around ceremonies."

Waabun's face scrunches, deep in thought.

"When they're on the moon," he offers.

I giggle into my sleeve.

"When it's their Moontime," she corrects. "And other times, too." Auntie shares a look with TJ. "We're helping our ancestors today. But I can't be too close to them, because your sister is on her way here. They're on different journeys." She flashes a wide smile at me.

Auntie is pregnant? With a girl? One glance at a beaming TJ answers my next question.

"My sister? Like Snowball?"

"Waabun," Auntie says softly. She kisses the back of his hand before pretending to lick it and clean his face like a mama cat. He smiles. "Not a cat sister. A baby sister named Lily Grace. She'll be here after Christmas."

"Daunis is havin' a baby?" Teevo looks at his dad.

"The baby is all of ours." TJ reaches his hand for Auntie to take.

Just before they touch, a strange expression crosses Auntie's face. It's like she's remembering a dream. Her eyes fill with tears as she rises. TJ wraps his arms around her.

I can't believe I didn't see it before. Auntie and TJ are a family.

"Auntie Perry, are you having a baby too?" Waabun asks.

I sputter. "Holaay, Waab. No way."

"Then why aren't you dancing with Auntie Pauline?"

I could have been next to her, with the other dancers. Or with Shense in the refreshments tent. Or helping Cooper behind the scenes. Anyplace, I suppose, except for preparing the baby ancestors.

"I'm waiting for one more ancestor to be brought home," I say. "I need to prove she's ours. But first I gotta finish high school."

"You're doing the accelerated program at Malcolm?" Auntie hugs me.

I pull back from the unearned praise.

"No. I'm staying in the regular program." I meet her eyes. "Auntie, I want time for fishing, and Erik . . . and working part-time with Cooper. I'm gonna get the Warrior Girl home. Cooper told me about the Institute of American Indian Arts in Santa Fe. They're adding a new major in museum studies." I motion toward our community members working together to help our relatives along their journey. "I could race through everything, but . . ."

"But you want to enjoy your life," she finishes for me. "The Warrior Girl was willing to sacrifice herself for her community. So that others could live full lives."

When Auntie hugs me again, I feel the hard bump of her belly, followed by a kick. A tiny foot with a lot of power.

"That's one mighty warrior," I declare.

"She comes from a long line of them." Auntie rubs her belly. "Sugar Island is always ready to welcome our warrior girls home, where they are loved."

I take in my view—everyone I love, my community, and Ziisii-bakwe Minising. When I speak, it sounds like a prayer.

"Bigiiwen enji zaagigooyin, Ogichidaakwezans."

AUTHOR'S NOTE

I love a great origin story. What was the one particular idea that took root in the writer's mind and survived in some iteration through harvest?

The story behind *Warrior Girl Unearthed* began in 2018 on Twitter. Someone tweeted an idea for a Lara Croft movie, "but she's native and returning artifacts that museums stole."[1] It was a great movie idea, but that's all it was to me. My focus was on completing *Firekeeper's Daughter* and getting a literary agent for the Indigenous Nancy Drew story that had been on my mind since I was eighteen years old.

Flash forward a year. I now had an agent and spent the summer of 2019 revising *FKD* based on Faye Bender's astute feedback. Our plan was to submit the manuscript to editors that fall. After thirty-six years of working on this story of my heart, I could see the light at the end of the tunnel.

But what next? Writing a sequel with Daunis's next adventure felt more exhausting than exciting. Perhaps all I had in me was this one story; I could be satisfied with that. Then one Sunday while on a long walk, a voice popped into my head: *I stole everything they think I did. And even some stuff they don't know about yet.* I stopped in my tracks.

Who was this defiant girl? And what else was she going to reveal?

I ran into the nearest business and hurriedly asked for a pen, paper, and a Chardonnay. For the next few hours, I wrote the inner monologue of a teen girl sitting in a police station, waiting for her

---

1. Sarah C. Montoya (@sarahcmontoya), "movie idea: laura croft but she's native and returning artifacts that museums stole," Twitter, March 18, 2018, 12:28 P.M., https://twitter.com/sarahcmontoya/status/975408620400730112.

parents and wondering how she got herself into this mess. Oh, and she is covered in blood (not hers). The door bursts open. It's not her parents, but one furious auntie. Auntie Daunis pauses her scolding to pull Perry into a hug and whisper, "Don't tell them anything."

I had my next story. Perry Firekeeper-Birch as the reluctant intern at the tribal museum, supervised by a kooky guy. When she learns about stolen ancestral remains in other museums and private collections, Perry decides to return the ancestors to Sugar Island, like a reverse Indiana Jones . . . or an Indigenous Lara Croft.

The tweet from a year earlier had taken root in my mind, germinating at the optimal moment. Through a mystery/thriller pitched as Indigenous Lara Croft, I could increase awareness about ancestral remains and cultural items still held by museums despite a law requiring their return.

Perry's outrage mirrors my own. It's been over thirty years since the Native American Graves Protection and Repatriation Act (NAGPRA) was signed into law.[2] Of the approximately 208,000 human remains that have been reported by institutions since 1990, more than 108,000 ancestors have yet to be repatriated.[3] This means that, as of September 2022, more ancestors remain in collections (52 percent) than have been returned (48 percent).[4] And there are thousands (and some estimate millions) more ancestors in boxes and in basements all over the world, held by institutions and private collectors, that we do not know about.

---

2. "Native American Graves Protection and Repatriation Act," National Park Service, updated November 3, 2021, https://www.nps.gov/subjects/nagpra/the-law .htm.

3. Jenna Kunze, "AAIA Conference Opens in Michigan to Explore Repatriation Through the Lens of Compliance, Advocacy and Activism," Native News Online, October 12, 2022, https://nativenewsonline.net/sovereignty/aaia-repatriation -conference-opens-in-michigan.

4. National Park Service, U.S. Department of the Interior, "Fiscal Year 2022 Report, National NAGPRA Program," for the period October 1, 2021 to September 20, 2022, https://irma.nps.gov/DataStore/DownloadFile/677814.

Institutions continue to delay the return of our ancestors. The vast majority (94 percent) still held in collections have been designated as *culturally unidentifiable* by the institutions.[5] The category was intended for use when there weren't records about the ancestral remains. In practice, however, *culturally unidentifiable* became a convenient catch-all for institutions struggling to complete their inventories and summaries within the required time frame.[6] Further, many institutions failed, and continue to fail, to properly consult with Tribes and Native Hawaiian organizations to identify cultural affiliation.

Under the federal regulations, as currently written, institutions "do not have to repatriate associated funerary objects for remains that are categorized as 'culturally unidentifiable.'"[7] This is a powerful incentive for institutions to default to the designation. In addition, some Tribes would choose not to repatriate their ancestors without their funerary belongings, thus giving the institutions undue control over the repatriation process. In effect, the current regulations do not stop institutions from retaining the spoils of grave robbers and looters.

As I write this note, the U.S. Department of the Interior has proposed crucial revisions to the NAGPRA regulations to clarify and improve the repatriation process. The proposed changes "emphasize consultation in every step and defer to the customs, traditions, and Native American traditional knowledge of lineal descendants, Indian Tribes, and Native Hawaiian organizations."[8] More informa-

---

5. National Park Service, "Fiscal Year 2022 Report, National NAGPRA Program."

6. Sonya Atalay, Jennifer A. Shannon, and John G. Swogger, *Journeys to Complete the Work: Stories About Repatriations and Changing the Way We Bring Native American Ancestors Home* (NAGPRA Comics, 2017), 8.

7. Atalay et al., *Journeys to Complete the* Work, 19.

8. U.S. Department of the Interior, Office of the Secretary, "Native American Graves Protection and Repatriation Act Systematic Process for Disposition and Repatriation of Native American Human Remains, Funerary Objects, Sacred Objects,

tion about NAGPRA is available at https://www.nps.gov/subjects /nagpra.

Ultimately, *Warrior Girl Unearthed* is about the need to control Indigenous bodies—both in the past and today. Perry encounters the dehumanization of Native peoples in the treatment of ancestral remains. She is aghast upon seeing bones written on with permanent marker and a collection of teeth stored inside a cereal box. (FYI: These are but a few of the real-life experiences shared with me by Native folks doing repatriation work.) Meanwhile, Native women are going missing in Perry's community (and elsewhere). I wanted to show different examples of how Indigenous bodies are disregarded and devalued even today. Grant Edwards sexually assaults Native women with impunity, taking advantage of the jurisdictional loopholes that deny justice to victims of crime on reservations. Dr. LeRoy (Leer-wah) represents an extreme of those who fetishize Native women and rationalize dehumanizing treatment under the guise of "honoring" the stereotype. And Chief Manitou's grooming of Pauline is an example of how supervisors and leaders (even in our tribal communities) take advantage of their positions to manipulate, abuse, and control others.

In closing, what began as an Indigenous Lara Croft story turned into Perry Firekeeper-Birch navigating injustice and indifference and claiming her inherent value. I wanted to show a young woman who cares about her community and finds her calling. Most importantly, she chooses to live a full life that honors the sacrifices of her ancestors.

Miigwech for reading.

Angeline Boulley

---

and Objects of Cultural Patrimony," Proposed Rules, Federal Register 87, no. 200 (October 18, 2022): 63202–63260, https://www.govinfo.gov/content/pkg/FR -2022–10–18/pdf/2022–22376.pdf.

COOPER'S LIST OF
REPATRIATION RESOURCES

*indicates a free resource

FOR "PADAWANS"

*Atalay, Sonya, Jen Shannon, and John G. Swogger. *Journeys to Complete the Work: Stories about Repatriations and Changing the Way We Bring Native American Ancestors Home.* (NAGPRA COMICS 1) https://blogs.umass.edu/satalay/repatriation-comic/.

Benton-Banai, Edward. *The Mishomis Book: the Voice of the Ojibway.* Minneapolis: University of Minnesota Press, 2010.

Black Ash Basketry: A Story of Cultural Resilience. Documentary produced by Kevin Finney, 2010. https://www.youtube.com/watch?v=sBM5BcUxeXM.

*Kunze, Jenna, "Slow Repatriation Efforts Plague UC Berkeley," *Native News Online*, November 17, 2022, https://nativenewsonline.net/sovereignty/slow-repatriation-efforts-plague-uc-berkeley.

*O'Loughlin, Shannon, "Episode 63: From Repatriation to Rematriation: Honoring the Ancestors and Their Seeds (from the 2020 6th Annual Repatriation Conference)," July 2, 2021, in *Red Hoop Talk*, podcast, https://www.youtube.com/watch?v=t4E5pQj-iro.

*Riskin-Kutz, Oliver L., "Native American Nonprofit Accuses Harvard of Violating Federal Graves Protection and Repatriation Act," *The Harvard Crimson*, March 12, 2021, https://www.thecrimson.com/article/2021/3/12/nagpra-peabody-letter/.

*Sanburn, Josh, "How the FBI Discovered a Real-Life Indiana Jones in, of All Places, Rural Indiana," *Vanity Fair*, October 19, 2021, https:// www.vanityfair.com/style/2021/10/how-the-fbi-discovered-a-real -life-indiana-jones-in-indiana.

*Small, Zachary. "Push to Return 116,000 Native American Remains is Long-Awaited," *New York Times*, August 6, 2021, https://www .nytimes.com/2021/08/06/arts/design/native-american-remains -museums-nagpra.html.

*Regan, Sheila, "The Story of an Ojibwe Drum Shows How Auction Houses Can Help—or Hurt—Efforts to Repatriate Indigenous Objects," *MinnPost*, November 22, 2022, https://www.minnpost .com/artscape/2022/11/the-story-of-an-ojibwe-drum-shows-how -auction-houses-can-help-or-hurt-efforts-to-repatriate-indigenous -objects/.

*U.S. Department of the Interior, National Park Service, Native American Graves Protection and Repatriation Act. https://www.nps.gov /subjects/nagpra/index.htm.

FOR "JEDI" (INCLUDING ALL OF THE ABOVE)

Aanikoobijigan   [Ancestor/Great-Grandparent/Great-Grandchild]. Documentary directed by Adam Khalil and Zack Khalil, (Date of Release TBD).

Accomplishing NAGPRA: Perspectives on the Intent, Impact, and Future of the Native American Graves Protection and Repatriation Act. Edited by Sangita Chari and Jaime M. N. Lavallee. Corvallis: Oregon State University Press, 2013.

Atalay, Sonya. *Community-Based Archaeology: Research with, by, and for Indigenous and Local Communities.* Berkeley: University of California Press, 2012.

Claiming the Stones/Naming the Bones: Cultural Property and the Negotiation of National and Ethnic Identity. Edited by Elazar Barkan and Ronald Bush. Los Angeles: Getty Research Institute, 2002.

Colwell, Chip. Plundered Skulls and Stolen Spirits: Inside the Fight to Reclaim Native America's Culture. Chicago: University of Chicago Press, 2017.

Cooper, Karen Coody. Spirited Encounters: American Indians Protest Museum Policies and Practices. Lanham: AltaMira Press, 2008.

Fine-Dare, Kathleen S. Grave Injustice: The American Indian Repatriation Movement and NAGPRA. Lincoln: University of Nebraska Press, 2002.

Lonetree, Amy. Decolonizing Museums: Representing Native America in National and Tribal Museums. Chapel Hill: University of North Carolina Press, 2012.

*O'Loughlin, Shannon, "Episode 61: Suzan Shown Harjo, Cheyenne & Hodulgee Muscogee," June 18, 2021, in Red Hoop Talk, podcast, https://www.youtube.com/watch?v=MzSy4NDceGE.

Repatriation Reader: Who Owns American Indian Remains? Edited by Devon Mihesuah. Lincoln: University of Nebraska Press, 2000.

*Stolen Spirits of Haida Gwaii. Directed by Kevin McMahon, 2004. http://www.isuma.tv/DID/community/Haida/stolen-spirits-of -haida-gwaii.

Thomas, David Hurst. Skull Wars: Kennewick Man, Archaeology, and the Battle for Native American Identity. New York: Basic Books, 2000.

MIIGWECH

Everything I've heard about the dreaded second novel is painfully true. *Firekeeper's Daughter* took ten years to write. My sophomore effort took just over one year. Have I mentioned that I am *not* a speedy writer? Fortunately, I have an incredible team that supported me and made *Warrior Girl Unearthed* a reality (and on deadline).

My deepest gratitude to the following:

Jess Harold, my editor at Henry Holt Books for Young Readers, for the incredible guidance every step of the way. For your willingness to accompany me along snowy (unplowed) roads, make a ferry run to Hill-top, and envision Perry's world through my eyes. Feisty teens rule!

Faye Bender, agent extraordinaire, for always being the calm to my storm.

Everyone at Macmillan Children's Publishing Group: Jean Feiwel, Molly Ellis, Ann Marie Wong, Kristen Luby, Morgan Rath, Mary Van Akin, and Leigh Ann Higgins. A special shout-out to the production team who kept *WGU* on schedule: Allene Cassagnol, Ilana Worrell, Alexei Esikoff, and David Briggs.

Sarah C. Montoya (Navajo) for tweeting a great idea in 2018 about a Native Lara Croft movie.

Friends and family who shared teachings and laughter: Jada-Marie Hall-Pine (Baaweting Anishinaabe), Lexi Hall-Pine (Baaweting Anishinaabe), Bella Smith (Baaweting Anishinaabe), Laura Fisher (Sault Chippewa), Dani Fegan (Ojibwe-Anishinaabe), and Bianca Williams (Lummi Nation).

Ogichiidaawag naadin eshpendaagwak: All the warriors working to bring home what is sacred, especially Shannon O'Loughlin (Choctaw), Colleen Medicine (Ojibwe, Anishinaabe), Sonya Atalay (Anishinaabe-Ojibwe), Marie Richards (Baaweting Anishinaabe), and everyone in the Michigan Anishinaabek Cultural Preservation and Repatriation Alliance (MACPRA).

Bonnie Kequom Ekdahl (Saginaw Chippewa) for being my first Repatriation Jedi.

Shannon Martin (Match-E-Be-Nash-She-Wish Pottawatomi), for sharing your expertise and your parents—Sydney Martin (Match-E-Be-Nash-She-Wish Pottawatomi) and George Martin (Odaawaa-zaaga'iganiing Ojibwe)—with me.

My sister, Sarah-ba, for everything you gave.

My children—Chris, Ethan, and Sarah—for being the loves of my life. Writing is what I do. Loving you is who I am.